I Now Pronounce You MAN AND WIFE

by Barbara Grace English

PublishAmerica
Baltimore

At the specific preference of the author, PublishAmerica allowed this work to remain exactly as the author intended, verbatim, without editorial input.

First printing

ISBN: 1-4137-8976-5
PUBLISHED BY PUBLISHAMERICA, LLLP
www.publishamerica.com
Baltimore

Printed in the United States of America

Chapter 1

The chill of the old courtroom disappeared as warm air flowed through the clanking heating ducts, warming the string of wooden pews constructed seventy years earlier. The heat provided a toasty platform, and the scent of the old wood consoled Shelley's overwhelming anxiety.

Shelley's day in court arrived, certainly unhurried. But after all was said and done, she was confident she would leave the courthouse, never to cry again. Tribulation had been a relentless teacher, forcing her to evolve a much more clever person.

Jacqueline, and Jason, her two children, woefully, were educated with her and for the rest of her life, Shelley would mourn the childhood denied them.

"All rise!" the court clerk shouted to the overcrowded courtroom, announcing the entrance of the Honorable Judge Netty.

Shelley knew from experience, to arrive early, noticing that the inadequate seating, left quite a few people standing.

Sitting beside Shelley, Nathan whispered, "We're fifth on the roster, so we have a bit of a wait." He gave her hand an encouraging pat, then, returned his attention to the file he'd been reviewing.

Gazing at him, Shelley had to smile. He was a bizarre man, always dressed in black suits much too large for his small frame, causing him to look frightening. However, unexpectedly, Nathan had proven himself an excellent attorney.

"How long is a bit?" Shelley asked, eager to have the unpleasant matter behind her.

"Enough time to get a cup of coffee," Nathan responded with full understanding.

The man respected Shelley and her tenacious will. Although he had known her just a short period of time, he easily recognized the woman of steel, created from what he guessed was once a more gentle female. Nathan often said, he wished he had known that woman.

"I'll let you know if we're going to be called sooner," he added, smiling, knowing she was reluctant to leave the courtroom.

"Oh, Nathan…coffee sounds great. I think I'll do that." Shelley anxiously grabbed her coat in case the heat had not reached the other floors of the old building.

Moving sideways through the crowded courtroom, Shelley felt relief when she heard the big, wooden doors close behind her. Though the delay would be short, the escape would be wonderful, and she had learned the value of patience. Waiting had become an important part of her life.

Shelley paid for her coffee and sat at an empty corner table, facing the crowd. A habit she'd developed over the years to stay safe. Sipping her coffee, she studied a circle of businessmen talking amongst themselves. Each man was dressed in a different suit, manufactured in different fabrics and colors, yet they all looked the same. She remembered the way Neal had mockingly referred to the suits as 'company issue', knowing they were important tools for success. He purposely bought his in dark colors to accentuate his unusual green eyes and sandy colored hair. After years of working towards perfection, Neal Jordon generated curiosity when he entered a room, emanating elegance like a fine tuxedo.

Shelley thought back to the moment it began, every detail remaining vividly distinct over the years. Back to the day she'd met Neal Jordon.

Chapter 2

It was July 10, 1977, Shelley's first day as Executive Secretary for P.L.K. Bearing Corporation. The company had arrived four months earlier in the United States from France. What the initials stood for was a mystery to everyone, except that they meant something French.

Shelley endured three intense interviews to secure her new position, but didn't mind since being an upstart company, P.L.K., offered better opportunity, along with a higher salary than most companies.

When Shelley walked through the double glass doors, the air conditioning delivered a welcome relief. New Jersey summers could be considerably unpleasant. Particularly in Carlstadt, where an overabundance of manufacturing facilities nurtured high pollution levels.

P.L.K.'s center office was a large, open space, presenting four symmetrical rows of empty desks, assembled with apparent expectations of future success. Shelley noticed that the handful of employees roaming about, were close to her age of twenty-nine, granting her a certain sense of acceptance. An extended hand, flashing a recent manicure, abruptly greeted Shelley.

"Hi! I'm Connie Stern, Tom Lowe's assistant, can I help you?" the young, blonde woman asked.

"I hope so, I'm Shelley Hemlo," she answered.

"Oh! Fantastic! You don't know how glad I am to see you!" Connie proclaimed cheerfully. "Mr. Jordon, our Marketing Director, freaked when his secretary wasn't here, full of energy, ready to type. No one here, and I repeat, no one, beside you, knows how to type."

Shelley was surprised by Connie's statement. She was anxious to succeed and being the only typist in the company added a certain amount of job security.

"Isn't it unusual for a company to hire only one typist?" she asked.

"Definitely! However, right now we can barely afford you. Later, we hope to fill more of these empty desks," Connie said, taking hold of Shelley's elbow. "Come with me. Mr. Jordon is waiting for you, and our President, Mr. Frank, has been absolutely intolerable waiting for a secretary," Connie admitted, rolling her amber eyes as she ushered Shelley between the rows of desks.

She walked so fast, Shelley had a hard time keeping up with her without bumping into things. Boxes of unpacked office supplies were stacked in piles along the way, and Shelley felt sure she would be the one to send them hurling to the floor.

Connie led Shelley to one of the four private offices lining the back of the enormous office space, and tapped lightly on the door.

"Come in," a masculine voice shouted from the other side.

Shelley smoothed the bottom of her black dress, nervous about making a good impression.

"Good morning, Neal," Connie bellowed, leading Shelley through the wooden door. "I'd like you to meet Shelley Hemlo, your new secretary," she announced with a smile. "Shelley, this is Neal Jordon, our Marketing Director and one of your new bosses." Connie looked pleased with herself for delivering such a beautiful treasure.

Jake Cavello, P.L.K.'s Office Supervisor and Manager of Inventory Control hired Shelley from a long line of applicants. Her references were excellent and her typing skills impeccable, offering a perfect package.

Neal Jordon, sitting behind the huge, mahogany desk stared at Shelley for several moments before he stood, as if he were suddenly reminded of his manners.

"Hello. It's nice to meet you," he blushed, extending his hand.

Shelley timidly took his hand. The warmth of the man's smile relaxed her, and despite the fact that he was dressed rather casually for the Marketing Director of a 'soon to be big' corporation, Shelley thought he was handsome.

"I hope you're ready to work with lunatics," Neal teased, dazzling her with his enamoring grin.

"I think I can handle it," she answered, smiling.

"Actually, this is only my second week in the office," he whispered. "Hopefully, we won't make too much of a mess of things."

"I hope not," Shelley laughed.

She liked him and began to feel more comfortable and fairly confident that joining P.L.K's staff would be a positive influence in her life.

"Sorry, Neal, but I have to steal Shelley away from you. Mr. Frank is anxious to meet her too," Connie interrupted.

"I'll bet he is," Neal said, still smiling.

"I promise to bring her back as soon as he's finished speaking with her," Connie continued.

"I'll look forward to that," he responded, winking at Shelley, causing her to blush.

Connie quickly ushered the new secretary out of Neal Jordon's office.

Shelley looked back over her shoulder and sensed something pleasantly unusual about Neal Jordon. As a matter of fact, the entire atmosphere at P.L.K. was new and exciting. Complacently, Shelley was sure her life somehow, was about to change.

Chapter 3

By the end of August, Neal Jordon and P.L.K.'s Sales Engineer, Rick Banta, sent into motion, a swift and successful beginning for the company.

Neal had astonished P.L.K.'s Corporate Executives when he negotiated three million dollars in sales during their first month on the American market. He surpassed P.L.K.'s expectations, making Neal Jordon a strong name in the company.

Meanwhile, Shelley adjusted to her new position and was doing exceedingly well.

Neal Jordon's feelings toward his new secretary quickly advanced to infatuation. However, his strong work ethic prohibited his mixing business with pleasure.

Since most of the staff at P.L.K. was young and single, Neal did not expect to find the same agonizing control among his staff. Consequently, it was not astounding when Rick and Connie became intimately involved outside of the office. However, Connie's very obvious, steamy feelings for Tom Lowe made her affair with Rick less significant than it might have been otherwise.

Tom's wife and four children tormented the available Connie, and she would have given anything to make them disappear, but was smart enough to realize that was not going to happen, at least not in the near future.

Rick was single, but shared an apartment with his girlfriend, Gloria, who was easily charmed into leaving Pennsylvania when he'd accepted the position with P.L.K. Due to that relationship, Rick was not always available when Connie demanded his attention.

Connie was nothing more than a fling to Rick, however, his lack of commitment was advantageous to Connie, whose overwhelming infatuation for Tom Lowe consumed her. Her romantic feelings toward Tom were mostly founded on his position with P.L.K. Shelley knew power meant more to Connie than decency, but in spite of the woman's character, she befriended her, maintaining a healthy respect for the opportunist manifested within her new friend.

Shelley also knew Rick shared Connie's lack of integrity. Whatever relationship Connie had managed to stir up with Tom Lowe, he hoped would somehow benefit him, making it difficult for Shelley to decipher who was being taken advantage of more.

Meanwhile, Neal became P.L.K.'s man of the hour, putting in long hours and a lot of traveling. He stayed in a hotel close to the office during the week, driving two hours to his home in South Jersey on weekends.

P.L.K.'s corporate office was determined to have Neal fully groomed to relieve John Frank, as Executive President within five years. That was the maximum time John agreed to stay in the United States, adamant about returning to France.

Shelley shared a two-bedroom apartment in Hasbrouck Heights with Elkie Loughton, her friend since childhood. The low rent apartment was built over a pizzeria on the main street known as 'The Boulevard'. Although it lacked ambiance, it was comfortable and she was happy living there with her friend.

Elkie managed 'Kaboodles', a nightclub in Manhattan and because of the enormous responsibility of that job, she spent quite a few nights in the city.

Connie was not overly fond of Elkie, so she preferred to visit Shelley on those nights.

During one of those visits, Shelley tried to discourage the back street relationship Connie had cleverly started with Tom, but her defense was teasing Shelley about her obvious crush on Neal Jordon. Shelley knew her school girl feelings were futile.

Then, one afternoon as she was leaving Neal's office, he surprisingly asked her if she would have dinner with him the following Wednesday night.

Flabbergasted, Shelley quickly accepted, afraid he might change his mind if he had to wait too long for a response.

"I'd like that very much," Shelley answered, wanting to scream with joy after waiting so long for that moment. She believed it would never happen, and made haste walking towards the door before he had a chance to reconsider his invitation.

He stopped her as she reached the door, and she thought he had.

"Oh, I hope you don't mind, but I've invited Rick and Connie to join us," he added sheepishly.

"That's fine," Shelley answered quickly.

Neal was different from the other men she'd dated. The date would mean something much more substantial to her because she had feelings for him, no matter who went with them.

"Shelley, since my divorce, I haven't dated very much, and I'll be less likely to make a fool of myself with other people around. It's me, not you. I'm sorry. I'm insecure, what can I say?" Neal asked, embarrassed.

"It's okay, You don't have to say anything, really. Connie and I are friends and Rick is a lot of fun. I'm sure it will be a great evening."

Wednesday night was slow to arrive. Connie offered to pick Shelley up at her apartment by six thirty so they could meet Neal and Rick at the office by seven, eliminating Shelley's car.

The extra time would allow Neal to finish some neglected paperwork and help maintain discretion, since the rest of P.L.K.'s staff would be gone for the evening.

Shelley slipped into the lavender pants suit she'd bought on impulse six months earlier. She'd kept it stored for a special occasion, and Neal Jordon was that special occasion. Viewing herself in the mirror, she was glad she'd made the investment. Otherwise, she would have spent the entire two days before her date, scanning the stores for the 'perfect outfit'.

Her platinum hair looked delicate against the lavender color of the satin, and her blue eyes became more luminous with the contrast.

As usual, Connie was prompt. When she knocked on the old wooden door, Shelley shouted for her to let herself in while she wriggled her feet inside the black, suede pumps, still tight from lack of use. They'd shared a place in her closet with the pants suit.

"Don't you lock your door?" Connie yelled when Shelley joined her in the living room.

"It doesn't lock," she answered, grabbing her purse off the couch.

"Are you nuts?" Connie screamed with horror. "You don't know what kind of maniac could walk in here, and guaranteed it would be someone who lives in this building!" she added.

Her pretty face looked lovely against the beige sweater that Shelley had never seen before. Connie was never without a perfect tan, enhancing the light color of her clothes.

"Connie, you're so dramatic. I like this building, it has character," Shelley responded in defense.

Connie lived in a new apartment complex that was nice, but certainly lacked the charm of Shelley's Boulevard apartment.

"Seriously, Shelley, that door should be fixed. Someone will find you dead one day. Do you have your keys?" she asked, as Shelley closed the door behind them.

They both had to laugh at the satire of Connie's question.

All the parking spaces in front of Shelley's apartment were metered, and Connie angrily pulled a ticket off the windshield of her old, yellow Chevy.

"I don't believe it! I was in your apartment for a total of what…ten minutes?" she screamed, completely furious as she unlocked the car and took her seat on the driver's side. She unlocked the passenger door and Shelley mildly sat beside her as Connie tore the ticket to shreds.

"Aren't you afraid to do that?" Shelley asked, questioning Connie's lack of respect for the power of City Hall.

"Hell no! Those perverts have a lot of nerve giving tickets out like that! What did the creep do, hide until I went inside?" she asked, disgusted. "Oh, who cares? Don't you know cops are the people you didn't talk to in high school? Let's just go and have a good time tonight," she said, throwing the torn pieces onto the back seat.

Shelley shook her head as Connie started the car. "I agree. I'm looking forward to a wonderful evening," Shelley responded, as Connie left skid marks pulling out from the parking space.

She drove twenty miles over the speed limit, and fifteen minutes later, she'd turned into P.L.K.'s parking lot. Shelley sighed with relief when the car came to a full stop. She decided driving with Connie would definitely go on her list of things to avoid.

It was obvious that Neal and Rick were waiting for them when Rick was out of the office by the time Connie turned off her headlights, and Neal had already locked the doors to the office.

They used Neal's Thunderbird since it was much larger than Rick's Buick.

Rick and Connie, long past the first date jitters, sank into comfort in the back seat. Shelley envied their ease with each other. She could hardly look at Neal her feelings were so intense, and Neal kept his eyes on the road, apparently to avoid looking at Shelley. The powerful chemistry between them, caused by months of suppressed feelings, visibly made them both feel awkward.

The inside of the new Japanese restaurant where Neal had made reservations was everything it boasted to be from the outside. The dining room was decorated in dark green and gold, and beautiful, bronze fountains flowed everywhere. Each table sat in seclusion behind walls of white rice paper, as elegant as their host was, dressed in a black tuxedo.

A grill sat in the middle of each table ready to cook any menu choice to perfection, and they thought it entertaining, watching the servers twirl their knives mid-air with one hand, while tossing steaming vegetables and meat with a spatula in the other.

Rick immediately ordered two bottles of plum wine, that he just as eagerly devoured with Connie, causing them both to become inebriated before they'd finished dinner.

Connie, was having the time of her life, and suggested they continue the evening at the 'Top of the Marriott' in Fort Lee for some dancing.

Neal and Shelley welcomed anything that would prolong their first night together, even if it meant spending more time with their not so sober dinner companions. They hoped the band would keep the pair dancing long enough for them to enjoy some less exciting time, alone.

When the waiter discreetly placed the leather folder holding the check on the table, Neal immediately slipped his American Express card inside so the man would take it back with him to avoid a delay, visibly anxious to leave the restaurant.

Rick made the most of that time by visiting the Men's Room, reappearing twenty minutes later with eight strangers that were also drunk, wobbling behind him.

"So, Rick, who are your friends?" Neal asked, clearly annoyed.

"I'm not sure what all their names are," Rick answered, slurring his words. "But, guess what? They're coming with us to dance!" he added, with delight, putting his arm around one of the four men whose head bobbed up and down as if it were on a spring.

Rick acted as though he had done a great thing by inviting the group of strangers.

Shelley knew the evening was not going as Neal had originally planned.

When they reached the hotel, Rick's new friends caused total chaos in the parking lot. They arrived in two cars and neither driver was sober enough to maneuver their car into a single space.

Neal and Shelley cringed, waiting for the sound of crunching metal, sure one of the drivers would hit another car.

"Are you embarrassed?" Shelley asked Neal. The thought of walking into the hotel with ten intoxicated people certainly embarrassed her.

"Mortified about covers it," he answered, grinning. "I'm sorry, Shelley. This whole evening has been awful."

"Neal, I'm having a great time. There's nothing to be sorry about," Shelley replied. *Every minute spent with you is special, Neal,* she thought.

After a few seconds, Neal grabbed Shelley's hand and shouted, "I know, let's run inside before anyone realizes these people are with us!"

They reached the entrance of the hotel, completely out of breath and laughing as people entered the lobby, commenting on the group of unruly people in the parking lot.

The Marriott was one of Shelley's favorite nightspots. It revolved, displaying breathtaking views of New York City through magnificent walls of glass.

Neal ordered two glasses of wine and led Shelley to a private table, away from the crowd, while in the distance, the band played rock and roll music over the gathering of noisy guests.

Sure that Rick and Connie were having fun with their new friends, Neal and Shelley spent the next three hours learning about each other, and when the waiter handed Neal the check, they were unwillingly forced to address the late hour.

"How about tomorrow night?" Neal asked, quickly.

"What about tomorrow night?" Shelley asked.

"I would like to take you to dinner again, only this time alone, if that's all right with you."

"I'd like that," Shelley answered, softly.

"Thank you," Neal whispered before he stood to take her hand. "I guess it's time we find our reckless friends," Neal suggested.

The months they had worked together stirred up feelings neither of them thought they would feel again. Shelley had a mixed set of emotions. She was magically drawn to Neal Jordon, and at the same time, felt frightened about what that magic could possibly to do to her life.

In search of Rick and Connie, they encountered a thick crowd of people surrounding the dance floor. They were clapping as the band screamed, "Johnny B' Good." Someone in the center of the dance floor was a huge source of entertainment for the lively crowd.

"I wonder what's going on," Neal said, unable to see through all the onlookers.

"I don't know, I can't see through all these people," Shelley answered, also curious.

Neal saw Connie, and taking Shelley by the hand, gently made a break through the crowd.

Rick was in the center of the dance floor. Both his hands were in the pockets of his sports jacket and he was flapping his elbows like a bird, as he slid his feet in amusing circles. Totally captivated, Connie stood with the rest of the fascinated bystanders, clapping her hands. Both Neal and Shelley had to laugh. Although he was the epitome of irresponsibility, Rick definitely knew how to have a good time.

His new friends began to sober up and agreed to drive the couple back to the office so Neal and Shelley could leave. Before he left, Neal handed one of the men in the group some money, and asked him to make sure Connie and Rick were both sober before they were brought back to their cars. The gentleman understood and agreed to take care of his new friends.

Neal and Shelley felt completely at ease with each other, making everything and anything open for discussion. Including Neal's broken marriage.

"My divorce was devastating," he confessed, following the signs leading towards Hasbrouck Heights.

"Divorce is horrible. Do you want to talk about it?" she asked, giving him the opportunity to change the subject.

"It's okay, we can. The divorce was messy. You see, we had a son."

"Oh, I didn't know that," Shelley interrupted, totally surprised.

During the months they had worked together, Neal never mentioned having a child.

"Well, I don't talk about him very often. He died when he was two years old during a tonsillectomy." His voice softened with the sadness he apparently, still felt.

"We don't have to talk about this. I'm so sorry. I'm not trying to pry," Shelley said.

"No, I'm fine," he continued. "Allen was always physically fragile. He had asthma and was sick all the time. When they put him under the anesthesia, he had a toxic reaction and stopped breathing," Neal explained. "There wasn't anything that could have been done differently."

Shelley felt tears forming in her eyes. She wished she could make all the pain he was carrying disappear, but she understood the loss of a child was a life sentence.

"After Allen's death, my wife, Arlene, felt nothing but contempt towards me. I honestly believe she blamed me in some way for his death. I don't know. It didn't matter anyway, because eight months later, I came home a few days too early from a business trip and found her in bed with my best friend. That was it…I filed for divorce. I had lost both my parents in a car accident a few months before that happened and felt so tragically alone, as if I'd lost everyone I loved at the same time. It was awful."

Shelley knew there had to be a tremendous void in his life, and she hoped in due time, she would fill at least a part of it.

"Enough about me. What about your marriage?" he asked, referring to Shelley's divorce.

"Goodness…it was nothing sensational, just two people who were too young. We got caught up with the Vietnamese war and the romance of the white dress, if you know what I mean. Those were crazy times. One night you went to a goodbye party for one of your friends, then three weeks later, he was dead, and you went to his funeral. When John made it through his year over there, we ran to the altar," Shelley explained. "Besides, most of our friends were already married. We were one of the last single couples in our group of friends, because we decided to wait until John made it home alive. A lot of our friends married beforehand to be eligible for the higher allotment checks. The extra money helped save for a home," she continued.

"I was in college then, and as unfair as it was, it made me lucky enough to avoid that whole war scene," Neal responded.

"Where did you go to school?" Shelley asked, moving to a less solemn conversation.

"Drexel. Going to Drexel had been a dream of mine since I was a child," Neal explained.

"That's great," Shelley said, pausing for a moment. "Neal, I really enjoyed tonight."

"Really? Well then, I'll bring a box of tissues tomorrow night so we can have another wonderful evening," he said, laughing.

Shelley knew when he kissed her good night at her door that Neal was special. When he was gone, she suddenly felt very much alone, delightfully anxious for their next evening together.

When she arrived at the office the next morning, Shelley saw Connie slouched over her desk wearing sunglasses, holding her head in her hands. Standing with contrasting elegance, was a vase holding a dozen pink roses on her desk. Neal was standing next to her going over some papers when he realized Shelley had arrived. He looked at her and smiled, pointing to the roses with his eyes. At that point, they both knew how Connie and Rick had finished the previous evening.

"I feel like a kid again," Neal exclaimed by Shelley's desk a few minutes later. He set down the cup of coffee he'd made her.

"Thank you," Shelley responded, flattered he'd taken the time to learn how she liked her coffee. She understood what he was feeling, because she felt the same way.

"Listen, I was thinking, why don't I pick you up at your apartment tonight? I don't like the thought of you driving home alone at night," he said.

"That would be great. Six thirty, okay?" Shelley asked.

"Wonderful! I'll see you later," he answered, giving her arm a squeeze before he returned to his office.

The hours did not move fast enough for Shelley. She felt a beginning taking place and hoped it was a good one. She knew nothing stayed the same in life, that during every moment in time, some people were happy, while others were sad. It was a question of taking turns. At that moment, Shelley was happy. It was her turn.

Chapter 4

By the end of the day, one more time, Connie outwitted Tom Lowe. It appeared innocent enough...a company trip to the 'Museum of Natural History', in the city. The trip conveniently eliminated Bonnie, Tom's wife.

She scheduled the outing a week from the following Saturday. After visiting the museum, plans were made to have dinner at one of the wonderful restaurants near the museum. Everyone at P.L.K. was excited about the excursion, including Shelley. She enjoyed spending time outside of the office with her co-workers, and had not visited the museum in quite a while. She hoped Neal would be able to join them, given his hectic work schedule.

"How do you feel about our pending office field trip?" Neal asked her that evening during a sumptuous dinner at Manero's.

"I think it sounds like a lot of fun. What about you, can you make it?" Shelley asked.

"I think it will be fun too," he answered with a smile, as if he were trying to make his answer sound convincing. He stared at Shelley for a moment. "Promise me something?" Neal asked, taking a bite of his steak.

"Mm...I don't know. It depends on what it is," Shelley replied, nonchalantly.

"Promise me you'll always keep me focused on happy things," he answered.

"I can when we're together, but you're on your own after that," Shelley answered, sipping her wine.

"Then, promise me you'll always be with me," Neal said, grinning.

Shelley looked at him. *My, God, he's serious!* she thought. 'Always' was a word she tried to avoid.

"I want to marry you," he said quickly.

Shelley was embarrassed, and astonished at the same time. Left totally speechless.

"I know today, that statement is absurd, and of course, your answer is no. I wouldn't expect anything else, but I have known for months that I want to marry you and I will do whatever it takes to make that happen," he continued. "Look, Shelley, I haven't seriously dated anyone since my divorce because I didn't feel anything towards the women I met. The minute you walked into my office that morning in July, I knew it was you. You are 'the one'."

Shelley was completely flabbergasted. Nothing she said would have been the right response. Neal not only surprised her, but Shelley was sure he'd surprised himself. He never expressed feelings, ever, and she was not sure that was the time for him to start. They finished eating dinner in silence.

When it felt as though a mere hour had passed, Shelley looked at her watch.

"Oh, my God! Neal, it's midnight!" she exclaimed, wondering where the evening had gone.

"So, what's the problem? Do you turn into a pumpkin, or something?" he asked, jokingly.

"No, but I do have to work tomorrow, and so do you," Shelley reminded him.

"You haven't danced with me yet," Neal said softly.

"Do you want to dance?" Shelley asked, smiling.

Neal stood, offering Shelley his hand. "Yes, I do."

Shelley took Neal's hand as the band began to play 'The Wonder of You'. She learned to love that song as Neal held her in his arms, creating a memory that would last forever. What she felt scared her, and she was almost grateful when the evening came to an end so she would not have to deal with what she knew could happen.

Neal stopped in front of Shelley's old building and double-parked. He turned off his car and quickly got out to escort Shelley upstairs.

"Neal, it's all right. I don't want you to get a ticket," Shelley said, flustered, jumping out of the car.

"No way! I'm not letting you go upstairs by yourself!" he protested.

"Neal, I'm fine…honest," she argued, walking ahead of him.

"Shelley, stop! Let's talk about this!"

"About what, Neal?" she asked, turning to look at him.

"About what we're feeling right now," he answered.

"Neal, look...I won't be just another secretary sleeping with her boss," Shelley snapped.

"What?" he asked. "Shelley, where did that come from? I understand your feelings and I truly respect them. I promise you will never be that to me!"

After a brief pause, Neal smiled and said, "Well...I'm glad we have that out of the way."

They walked hand in hand up the lobby stairs. When they reached the top floor, the sound of loud music confirmed that Elkie was home, so, because of the late hour, and because Neal's car was double-parked, he kissed Shelley goodnight at the door, leaving her filled with so many confusing emotions.

Neal planned to drive home to South Jersey the next day. He was also preparing to leave for North Carolina on Monday, however, he promised Shelley he would call her every five minutes while they were apart.

The thought of not seeing Neal for six days depressed her. Although it happened quickly, she knew her feelings for him were unlike anything she'd known. Shelley knew the day she met Neal Jordon, that one day, she would fall in love with him.

Chapter 5

When Neal returned from North Carolina, Shelley was disappointed with his last minute decision to stop at his house in South Jersey, instead of going directly to the hotel near the office.

"Since I'll be with you all weekend, I decided to go home to get my mail and take care of a few things," he explained when he called her.

"Will you be in the office tomorrow?" Shelley asked, hoping they would have some time together before the museum trip on Saturday.

"Definitely! I'll be in after I check in at the hotel. We'll have dinner together, how's that?"

"Sounds good," Shelley responded.

Feeling enthusiastic, Shelley arrived at the office early the next morning.

"Shelley, Neal is on line five. He wants to talk to you!" Connie shouted from across the office.

"Where is he?" she asked, not waiting for a response before she picked up the phone. "Neal? What's wrong, where are you?"

"I'm stuck in South Jersey with my car!" Neal shouted. He sounded as if he were standing in a tunnel. I had to have it towed to a dealership this morning, and the Service Manager said it's going to be a while before they can look at it."

"Oh, Neal, I'm sorry. I guess you won't be in today, then," she responded, trying to hide her disappointment.

"No, I guess not. I'm sorry, but I'll be there tomorrow for the museum trip," he replied.

"Oh, Neal, I hope so. It wouldn't be any fun for me without you."

"Well...I like that. It was worth getting stranded just to hear you say that," Neal said, cheerfully. "I know, I know, you don't want to get serious. But, I'll change your mind about that, you'll see."

Saturday morning, Shelley phoned Neal bright and early, just as he'd asked her to the night before when they'd talked for three hours. The plan was for everyone who was going to the museum to meet at the office by eight o'clock. Shelley suggested that she ride to the office with Connie to save Neal time. That way he could go directly to P.L.K. instead of taking the extra forty minutes to get her in Hasbrouck Heights.

Shelley grew concerned at nine o'clock when Neal had not arrived and asked Tom to unlock the office so she could call him.

"Honey, I'm sorry. I've been trying to call the office for over an hour, but I guess everyone is waiting outside. My car won't start again," he said, sounding disgusted.

"Oh, no! What should we do? Everyone is waiting to leave."

"Just go on without me. I'm sorry. I really wanted to be with you today, but I don't want to hold everybody up," he said, sounding disheartened.

"Neal, I really don't want to go without you. Do you think the dealer will get the car fixed today?"

"I certainly hope so. But look…you go and have a good time. Staying home won't accomplish a thing and will make me feel worse than I already do," he said. "Think of me and don't pick up any strange guys. Also, listen…I'm going to worry about you going into the city, so please call me when you get home, okay?"

"Okay," Shelley answered sadly, getting ready to hang up.

"And Shelley?" he shouted.

"Yes?"

"I love you!"

Shelley heard the click and took a moment to digest what Neal had impetuously yelled into the phone. That was it. He'd said it, laying the groundwork for some kind of commitment. Half dazed, she put the conversation aside in order to deal with her coworkers.

After the museum outing came to a close, Shelley was anxious to get home so she could call Neal. She was relieved when he'd told her the car was finally repaired and that they would be able to spend the following day together. It would not come fast enough for her. He was all she'd thought about that entire day.

That Sunday, Neal eagerly arrived at Shelley's apartment sometime before noon. They'd decided to go to the movies to see 'Grease'. Afterwards they made the ten mile drive to 'Pasta Town', for the best Calzones known to man. It turned out to be a terrific day. They avidly enjoyed every moment they'd spent together.

At the end of the day, they went back to the apartment, taking advantage of the fact that Elkie was staying in the city to get some work done.

Shelley made hot chocolate and carried the steaming mugs into the living room. The atmosphere with him felt so right to her.

"Listen. What are you doing next Saturday night?" he asked, putting his arm around her.

"I don't know, why?" she asked.

"John Frank is having a small dinner party at his home and he suggested that I invite you as my guest."

"He suggested you invite me?" Shelley asked, astounded. "Neal, how did he know about us?'

"I told him," he answered, without hesitation.

"Why did you tell him? I thought we agreed to keep our relationship a secret."

"Shelley, I told him because I was sure Connie, or Tom would, if I didn't. I don't want him, or anyone else thinking this is just another sleazy office affair," he explained.

Shelley knew he was right. Chances were, John Frank already knew about their relationship before Neal told him. Connie would never be able to keep that kind of information a secret, unless it involved her relationship with Tom.

"Well? Will you go with me?" he asked, again.

"Are you sure you want to do this, Neal?"

"I'm positive," he said, smiling. "I want our relationship to be open and respected. Keeping it hidden makes it appear less than what I know it is. I'm in love with you and I don't care who knows it."

Monday morning, P.L.K.'s office staff was in a jubilant frenzy when Shelley arrived. Neal had brought in a five million-dollar deal with Melton Industries, the target of his trip to North Carolina. The excitement of his success postponed any misgivings Shelley might have about John Frank knowing about their relationship.

Neal called Shelley into his office, obviously excited and proud of his accomplishment. "Listen, I have to leave for Philadelphia tomorrow," he said. "I'll be back Friday night, but I have to go to the house so I can come here Saturday without worrying about things that should have been done there."

"I understand," Shelley said, not being totally honest. She hated his house and the distance it put between them every weekend. At the same time, she was curious about it. *What does it look like? Does it still have evidence of his cheating wife and deceased son?* she wondered.

"Now, what would you like to do about dinner tonight?" Neal asked, taking back her attention. He put his arm around her, giving her a painful look. "Please don't suggest another Calzone!" he added, smiling.

"What do you want to do about dinner tonight?" she asked

"I don't know, but let's go somewhere really nice. We should make this evening special."

"Well, then...why don't I cook?" she asked.

"You can cook?" Neal asked, laughing.

"Yes, I can cook, and quite well, I might add. How about it?"

"I'd love it!" Neal held her until they heard footsteps approaching his office. As Shelley walked out, Tom walked in, carrying P.L.K.'s latest sales reports in his hand, clearly ecstatic with the new figures.

When Shelley returned home carrying a sack of groceries, Elkie was sitting in the living room with Lenny. It was apparent they'd been arguing when he left hastily. Shelley could tell he was hurt by whatever had taken place before she'd intruded.

Elkie followed her into the kitchen and watched as Shelley set the bag on the counter, and began to pull out the large Pasta pot from under the sink. "Did I walk in at a bad time?" she asked, embarrassed.

"No, actually, I'm thankful you came home when you did. You know Lenny. He would have carried on for hours and I really have to go," she said, with a new sadness in her voice. "I'm going back to the office to catch up on some work and I'll probably stay there tonight. That's what Lenny was so mad about," Elkie added, helping Shelley unpack the groceries.

"What are you doing?" Elkie asked, watching her friend. "It looks like you're actually going to cook something," she teased.

"Neal is coming for dinner. I'm going to dazzle him with my Chicken Parmigiana."

"I'm sure your Chicken Parmigiana will be the thing to do that," she teased. "I'll be leaving in a few minutes, so you'll have the apartment to yourself. I'm just going to throw some clothes in a bag, and I'm out of here."

"Thanks, Elkie. I appreciate it. I just want everything to be really special tonight," Shelley explained.

Elkie was gone when Shelley heard Neal's knock on the door. She'd finished showering and changing her clothes while dinner progressed nicely. She answered the door quickly, afraid that Neal might discover the broken lock if she took too long.

"Good evening," he said, holding a dozen red roses, elegantly wrapped in silver paper. He kissed her, handing her the large bouquet.

"Neal, they're beautiful, thank you!" she said, with excitement. Shelley led him to the kitchen where he sat at the small table Elkie had purchased at some poor soul's divorce sale.

"Mmm. It smells really good in here." Neal closed his eyes, acknowledging the aroma of the food.

"Thank you," Shelley responded proudly, arranging the roses in the vase that usually stood empty on the windowsill.

"Don't you think it's time for you to greet me properly?" he asked, smiling, as he stood to kiss her. They kissed passionately, until the spattering sound from the oven told Shelley to do something before her dinner burned.

Neal, and everything about him, felt right to her, and for the first time, Shelley experienced peace with her new feelings. She served a perfect dinner, and they really enjoyed eating at home instead of a crowded restaurant with loud music and clanking dishes.

"Let's talk about Thanksgiving," Neal said, once they'd finished eating. He pulled the linen napkin off his lap and placed it on the table.

Shelley picked up some of the dirty dishes and began stacking them on the counter. "What about it?" Shelley asked. She felt incredibly awkward discussing the holiday with Neal because she'd already made plans to visit her family for the holiday.

"I would like us to spend thanksgiving together," Neal answered, his voice full of hope.

"Neal, I've already made plans to visit my parents in Georgia," she said feeling awful. Since Neal's parents died in the car accident, his only living relative was a brother he'd avoided because of the man's decadent lifestyle. She did not want him spending Thanksgiving alone.

"You're going to Georgia? I love Georgia. It's one of my favorite states," he said, grinning.

"Neal...would you like to come with me?" she asked, smiling. She'd considered inviting him earlier, but was afraid of putting him on the spot. Meeting parents was a big step in any relationship, especially her parents. The last thing she wanted to do was scare Neal away with her family.

"Are you sure? I'd love to. I want to meet my future in-laws," he teased.

"Neal, I guarantee you a trip to my parent's house will end any thoughts you might have of marriage," Shelley warned him.

"Oh, they couldn't be that bad. Look at you," he said, picking up the balance of the dishes.

"Yeah, look at me," Shelley responded, thinking of what she considered her dysfunctional childhood. She was the ultimate 'accident'. Her mother discovered she was pregnant with Shelley when her youngest son was only three months old. She'd been happy with her two boys and hoped that would be the end of her fertile days. Her bad attitude towards her pregnancy, carried itself through Shelley's entire childhood. She loved her mother, but could not understand why her mother appeared to dislike her at times. She watched her brothers soak up all the love Meg Hemlo had to give, leaving Shelley with whatever crumbs of affection were left. Although her childhood was not totally unhappy, thanks to her father and the love of her oldest brother, Mark, she still was always aware that something was missing.

"Neal, I'm not kidding. They are absolutely bizarre people." Shelley knew Meg would spend the entire holiday throwing Neal very blatant hints about a marriage proposal for her daughter, always calling her daughter a radical feminist for not wanting to remarry after her divorce.

"Then, why do you want to visit them, or is the problem really that you don't want your family to meet me?" he asked, dejectedly.

"I go because they're all I know. It's definitely not you, believe me. I would love to spend thanksgiving with you, and as crazy as they are, I know my family would love to have you. Especially my mother," Shelley said, smiling.

"I'm sure they're very nice people, Shelley, and yes, I'd love to go. I'll make hotel arrangements tomorrow morning."

"Oh, no! If you get a motel room, my parents will think you don't want to spend time with them. Definitely not…no hotel. You'll have to stay at their house."

"I can handle that, Shelley, if you really want me to come with you," he said, grinning. I don't want a pity invitation, you know, although, I'll take it if that's all that I can get."

"Neal, I want to share Thanksgiving with you, I'm just warning you. Be prepared."

Neal drew Shelley close to him and said, "Being with you is all any guy could want. I'll call my travel agent tomorrow and make the flight arrangements for both of us. Now…I do have some bad news," he continued.

"What is it?" Shelley asked, concerned.

"I have to go to France in December for two weeks."

"Why?" Shelley asked, upset with the thought of Neal going anywhere without her for two weeks.

"P.L.K. wants me to learn their new nomenclature and engineering techniques."

"When are you going?"

"December ninth," he answered.

"Will you be home for Christmas?" She could not imagine them spending their first Christmas apart.

"John promised I would be home for Christmas. What are your plans for the holidays?" he asked.

"I would like to go back to Georgia, since both my brothers will be there. We haven't seen each other for a long time. I would love it if you came with me on Christmas too, or would you rather decide that after Thanksgiving?"

"To do that, I would have to meet you in Atlanta on my way back from France, and it probably wouldn't be much before Christmas Eve."

"Can you fly directly into Atlanta from France?"

"No. I already checked," he said, smiling at her. "I would have to fly to England first, than take Delta's nonstop flight to Atlanta."

"You already checked?" Shelley asked, amused. "How did you know I would want to go back to Atlanta for Christmas?"

"Because I have come to know you." he whispered, as he kissed her.

Neal was right. He had come to know Shelley, along with how to make things work to his advantage.

Chapter 6

Neal phoned Shelley from the hotel in Philadelphia. He was exhausted and upset with John Frank. It seemed the two men had a dinner meeting with some clients, and John embarrassed Neal by showing up with his mistress. The clients were worth an enormous amount of money to P.L.K. and Neal had worked hard to get them to the bargaining table.

"Besides the possibility of losing this account, how am I supposed to enjoy dinner with Mrs. Frank on Saturday, after having dinner with her husband's mistress on Wednesday?" Neal asked. "All my hard work went down the tubes tonight."

"I'm sorry. Maybe it's a French thing," Shelley responded, making excuses for the man's unprofessional behavior. John Frank was so blatant about his womanizing, Shelley thought his bringing his mistress to a business meeting should not have shocked Neal. However, the rest of the week went smoothly and Neal returned safely from Philadelphia.

Meanwhile, Connie had accepted a challenge on behalf of P.L.K. to play a football game against a rival bearing company. The game was scheduled for the Sunday morning after John Frank's dinner party. The entire staff seemed to like the idea, eager to show P.L.K.'s athletic ability.

Although she knew nothing about football, Shelley agreed to play so P.L.K. would have enough players, and for the fellowship of her friends. It also meant spending the entire weekend with Neal, something they did not get to do often because of his house in South Jersey.

Saturday night arrived along with Neal and the dinner party.

The Franks lived in Normandy Estates, a large, wooded parcel of land housing fifteen homes. Each was designed to represent a different country. Ironically, the Franks leased the only French cottage available. It was very European, and the surrounding woods provided a beautiful form of privacy.

John answered the door, summoning his wife, Lorene, into the living room to greet their guests. *She's so tall!* Shelley thought. Her bright yellow blouse accentuated her long, red hair. *My, God, she's smoking a cigar!* Shelley stood in awe, as the totally feminine woman, puffed on the end of a thin, brown cigar. She was vivacious, making her guests feel comfortable.

Tom and Bonnie had already arrived and reluctantly, Tom introduced his wife. Shelley felt as though she already knew Bonnie from having so many phone conversations with her at the office. However, the woman was not at all what she'd expected. Her hair was a mousy brown color, and her teeth protruded so much, they emphasized her gums, giving her the appearance of a horse. She completely eliminated much-needed make up under her huge, black, horn-rimmed glasses. The wintry temperature had kept her hair from drying during the drive to the Franks', causing it to hang in damp little ringlets, each curling in a different direction. It was not until Jake and Loretta arrived that everyone was able to focus the attention elsewhere.

Shelley instantly liked Loretta and understood why Jake consistently boasted about his wife. She was a warm, very Italian woman, with a great deal of self-assurance.

With all the introductions behind them, John led his guests to the large, round dining room table, much too massive for the small space. The table was extraordinary, and Shelley assumed it was bought in France.

Name cards stood before each dinner plate. Shelley found hers between John and Jake. Neal was placed on the opposite side of the table, between Bonnie and Lorene, and appeared angry once he saw the strange seating arrangement. It was obvious he did not want Shelley sitting next to his over-sexed boss.

In the center of the table, sat an enormous blue flower arrangement, hiding any evidence that Neal was sitting on the other side. Jake nudged Shelley with his elbow, "This is going to be an interesting evening," he whispered.

"So tell me, Neal, who does your grocery shopping?" Bonnie asked him, once everyone was seated, insinuating a single man could not endure a trip to the super market.

"I do," he answered, quickly.

"Well, how do you know how much you're spending, you men are so awful about such things?" Bonnie asked Neal, while Jake, once again, poked Shelley with his elbow.

"Well, Bonnie, they usually tell me at the register," Neal responded with a smile. At that point, Shelley was not sure who deserved more pity, Neal, or Tom.

"You know, Neal, you should get yourself a clicker," Bonnie continued.

"Which is?" he asked, as if he had to.

"It's a little, red plastic thing that keeps track of what you're spending as you put things in your shopping cart. For instance, for two dollars, and ninety cents...you would push the two, then, nine, then, the zero. If you add two more dollars, you would click the dollar button two more times. Get it?"

"Oh, yes...I get it," he answered.

Shelley felt awful. The seating arrangement made her feel uncomfortable, and on top of everything else, when the appetizer was placed in front of her, it nauseated her. Lorene had scraped the inside of a grapefruit shell and mixed the fruit sections with some shrimp along with pieces of chopped tuna, and a lot of mayonnaise, then filled the empty shell with the mixture, the shell, taking the place of a bowl. Shelley loathed any form of seafood, and looking at it mixed with grapefruit was too much for her stomach to endure. However, for the sake of good manners, she closed her eyes, swallowing what she could of the awful food, leaving most of it in the grapefruit shell. Glancing at Shelley, Loretta, also, reluctantly swallowed a spoonful of the horrible appetizer.

Fortunately, the main course of 'Veal Condon Bleu', redeemed the horror of the appetizer, and dessert was a wonderful French version of 'Strawberry Shortcake'.

After dinner, the guests were guided to the living room for an after dinner cordial. Once again, Shelley was given a chair beside John, while Neal shared a couch with Bonnie and Tom.

"So, how was everybody's Halloween?" Bonnie asked, unaware of how ludicrous she sounded. When no one responded, Shelley sympathized with Tom, who looked totally humiliated. She quickly answered Bonnie's question.

"Good, thank you. How was yours?" Shelley asked, watching Neal roll his eyes. Loretta smiled at Shelley. There was clearly no doubt in anyone's mind why Tom was infatuated with Connie. Yet, Shelley's heart went out to Bonnie and the simple, neglected world she lived in.

"Well, it would have been super, except one of our neighbors called us accusing our Tommy Junior of soaping his car windows. I told him that was impossible since Tommy Junior was in his room already dressed in his pajamas."

"Oh, I'm sorry," Shelley responded while Tom turned a deep shade of scarlet.

"Oh, don't be sorry! It didn't spoil our fun. I enjoyed the day in spite of that mean man. I dressed little Annie like Cinderella, and took her trick, or treating with the boys until her little diaper couldn't hold anymore."

"How cute," Loretta said, scrunching her forehead with disbelief.

"Well, I learned my lesson about buying generic diapers. I was hoping to save my Tom some money, but Pampers are the only brand that keeps our little Annie dry," she explained.

Tom looked ready to cry. "Bonnie, I'm sure no one wants to hear your diaper endorsement," he said, with a shaky voice, hoping to silence his wife.

Lorene jumped up, offering Loretta and Shelley one of her slender cigars. When they both declined, she returned the wooden box to the coffee table without offering one to Bonnie.

Less than twenty minutes later, Neal offered his apologies for leaving early, alleging he was exhausted and in desperate need of rest in order to make a good showing at the football game the next morning. Within minutes, they were driving back to Shelley's apartment.

The ride home was silent. Shelley could not imagine what she had done to upset him and finally asked. "Neal, are you mad at me for some reason?"

"Shelley, I hate evenings like this one!" he answered, speeding onto the highway.

"Well, why are you taking it out on me?" she asked, irritated.

"I'm not," he said, snappily.

They spent the rest of the ride in silence, and as soon as Neal parked in front of Shelley's apartment building, she got out without waiting for him. She ran to the entrance, and angrily pulled the door handle, venting her anger until Neal grabbed her hand.

"Wait a minute, Shelley! I'm sorry!"

"Neal, I don't know why you are being so nasty!" she said, fighting back her tears.

"Shelley, you don't understand…I hate dinner parties at the boss's house. I don't trust John Frank, and, not that it says a lot about me as a human being, I'm disgusted by the Bonnies of this world!"

After a moment of silence, they both laughed. The evening had been absurd, and because of the seating arrangement, Neal did have the awful chore of entertaining Bonnie Lowe. He put his arm around Shelley as they walked into the lobby together.

"Was that our first fight?" he asked, jokingly.

"Oh, no. I can do better than that," she replied.

"I thought so," he said, grinning. "Why don't you marry me?"

"Why don't you stop trying to start trouble?" Shelley asked, trying to save what was left of the evening. "Do you want to see my clicker?" she joked.

He laughed. "If I say yes, will you admit that you love me?" he asked, leading her up the stairs.

Shelley did not know how to respond. She believed she loved him, but was afraid to express it, to commit to the words. "I think I do," she answered, trying to keep it safe.

"Then, the rest will follow," he replied.

They spent the next three hours making love. When Neal prepared to leave the apartment to return to his hotel, he gently kissed Shelley's cheek as she lay in bed, half-asleep.

"I'm a happy man," he whispered.

Chapter 7

The next morning, Neal picked Shelley up at the apartment by seven thirty. They met the rest of their co-workers at the football field Connie had efficiently reserved for the 'big game'. When they arrived, Shelley began to feel nauseous. She was sure it was due to the ingredients of the appetizers she had suffered through the night before.

Holding out as long as she could, she finally groaned, "Neal, I'm sorry, but I really feel sick."

As much as she wanted to join her friends, her queasy stomach conquered her weak determination.

"Wow! Loretta was sick this morning, too!" Jake said. "I wonder if the seafood in that appetizer was bad," he added, softly, so John wouldn't hear what he'd said.

"I don't know, but I'm taking Shelley home," Neal said, as he pulled his keys out of his pocket.

"No, Neal! You can't!" Connie objected. "P.L.K. won't have enough players for the game if you leave too!" she said, pouting.

"That's too bad, Connie. I'm taking Shelley home now!" Neal answered, obviously annoyed with her lack of concern for anyone but herself.

"Neal, listen. Why don't I just take your car and drive myself home?" Shelley asked, trying not to ruin the day for P.L.K. She was desperate to get back to the apartment. Besides, she did not want Neal to witness her vomiting, should that happen. Nothing would humiliate her more.

"Neal, I can drive you back to Shelley's apartment if you want to stay," Jake volunteered.

Neal looked at Shelley. "Are you sure?" he asked, obviously not comfortable with her driving herself home.

"I'm sure," Shelley insisted. After much persuasion, Neal finally gave in and handed Shelley the keys to his car.

She parked in front of the apartment building without concern for the bothersome meters planted along the sidewalk. In her panic to get upstairs, she accidentally dropped her open purse on the floorboard. Quickly, she scooped up her things, frantically shoving them back into her purse. When she looked to see if she had missed anything, something shiny caught her eye under the corner of the rubber floor mat. When she pulled it up, she found a big, gold hoop earring. She was stunned, it did not belong to her. She shoved it inside the pocket of her jeans as she ran upstairs.

After emptying her stomach, Shelley fell asleep on the couch until she heard Neal knocking on her door. She jumped off the couch to let him in, feeling light headed from the sudden movement.

"Hi, Sweetie! Are you feeling any better?" he asked.

Shelley knew she looked awful, but had other things on her mind. "I'm a little better," she whispered.

"Well, you look terrible! Can I get you anything?" he asked.

"No, really, I'm fine. I think it was that awful food from last night."

"I'm sorry," Neal said, kissing the top of her head. "I'm not going to stay. I want you to get some sleep."

Shelley pulled the earring out of her pocket. "Neal, who does this belong to?" she asked, watching his reaction.

Neal looked at the earring, unaffected. "I don't know. I've never seen it before," he answered, looking at it again. "It's not yours?" he asked.

"No, it's not mine. I never wear anything like this. I found it on the floor of your car."

Neal thought for a moment, when suddenly she saw that he remembered something. "I know! It must be Connie's! She borrowed my car the other day to go to the bank for Tom. Her car was low on gas."

Shelley looked at it again. *Connie does wear big earrings like this. It could be hers,* she thought.

"I'll check with her tomorrow," Shelley said, laying it on top of the coffee table.

"You will not!" Neal argued, picking up the earring. "You're staying home in bed tomorrow. Thanksgiving is this week, and I don't want anything to ruin our trip! I'll return it to her," he responded, adamantly.

It was Tuesday afternoon before Shelley felt well enough to return to work. Because of the profound events that followed, she never asked Connie about the earring.

Shortly after she arrived that morning, Eddie yelled from the reception desk, "Shelley, Neal is on line one. It sounds urgent!"

Shelley ran to her desk from the back of the enormous office, and pushed the button next to the flashing light.

"Neal? Are you okay?" Shelley yelled into the phone when she heard him sobbing. "Neal…what's wrong?"

"Shelley…it's my brother!" he answered, barely able to speak.

"Neal, what about him?" After a moment of silence, she asked again. "What about your brother, Neal?"

"He's been in a car accident. Oh, Shelley, it's just like my parent's death all over again. He's in a coma!" he cried.

"Oh, my God, Neal. What are the doctors saying? Is he going to be okay?"

"They really don't know. I'm at the hospital with his wife and daughter and I really don't think I should leave," he said, sobbing.

"No, of course not. I certainly understand. How are they doing?" she asked, longing to be with him.

"Not too good. To make matters worse," Neal paused, sounding embarrassed, "He had another woman in the car with him. She's not expected to live. The woman's husband is giving my sister-in-law an awful time."

"I'm so sorry. Tell me where you are so I can meet you. You're upset. I want to be with you."

"Shelley, absolutely not! I want you to leave for Georgia tomorrow as planned, and I'll try to join you sometime before Thursday."

"I can't leave you like this. I would do nothing but worry about you and your family," Shelley said, disappointed.

"My brother is crazy! He has a wonderful wife and daughter, and he continuously hurts them."

"I'm sorry, Neal. I just wish you would let me join you," she pleaded again.

"I'll be fine, Shelley. There is no reason for both of us to stay here. Please, go to Georgia as planned. I'll call you tonight, okay?" he asked, sounding somewhat better. "I love you."

"I love you, too. I'll talk to you later," she said, and hung up the receiver.

Shelley's co-workers heard enough bits and pieces of the conversation to know what happened.

"Wait a minute!" Tom yelled from across the office when he saw Shelley put the phone back in its cradle. "Did you find out the name of the hospital Neal's brother is in?"

"Oh, my God...no, Tom, I didn't!" Shelley yelled, smacking the top of her head. "I can't believe I was that stupid!"

"It's okay, that's understandable. I just think P.L.K. should send flowers, or something."

"Tom, you're right. I'm so sorry," she answered, feeling worse.

"Wait! Why don't we look in his personnel records to see what emergency contact numbers are listed on his paperwork?" Connie suggested. "If nothing else, someone can at least tell us what hospitals are in the area, then, we can call them and ask if someone with the last name of Jordon came through their emergency room from a car accident."

"That's a good idea," Tom agreed, as he ran to his office where the records were stored. A few minutes later, he came back looking puzzled. He walked over to Connie's desk and Shelley saw him whispering to her.

"Shelley, have you ever met Neal's friend, Matt?" he asked her, a minute later.

"No, but Neal talks about him a lot," she answered, confused. "Is something wrong, Tom?"

"He's listed as Neal's emergency contact, so I called him and explained that I was trying to get in touch with Neal Jordon. He asked me which one, Junior, or Senior?" Tom replied.

"That's weird...Neal's parents have been dead for six years," Shelley responded, a little perplexed. "If Neal were close enough with this man to use him as an emergency contact, wouldn't he know Neal's father is dead?"

Tom thought for a moment. "Well, he sounded as though he had been sleeping. Maybe that was it," Tom analyzed. "Anyway, I didn't mention the car accident because I didn't feel it was my place to do that. I just ended the phone call to avoid his asking a lot of questions."

"Maybe he thought you didn't know Neal Jordon Senior was deceased," Shelley said, trying to make sense of the strange phone conversation.

"You're probably right," Tom said pointing his finger at Shelley. He walked backwards towards his office. "Anyway, when you talk to Neal again, please ask him the name of the hospital."

Shelley finished her work and left the office at five thirty. She still had some last minute things to do before she left for Georgia and Neal's situation left her upset.

When she opened the door to the apartment, she heard the phone ringing and ran to pick it up. As she'd hoped, it was Neal.

"Thank, God! I couldn't wait until you called me!" she said, trying to catch her breath. "I never asked you the name of the hospital your brother is in."

"Why do you want that?" he asked, surprised.

"Tom wants to send flowers," Shelley explained.

"Oh," Neal responded, amused. "Well, tell him thank you very much, but my brother is in Intensive Care."

"Oh, that's right. None of us thought of that."

"However, it was a nice thought. Please tell Tom I appreciate it."

"I will. Has there been any change?"

"No, they don't know if he will ever come out of the coma."

"What about the woman that was with him?" she asked.

"It doesn't look good. I finally had to tell her husband that I would personally throw him out of the hospital if he bothered Marlene again."

"I'm sure you can understand what the man must be feeling right now," Shelley said.

"I really do. I can see that he loves his wife, and the whole thing has destroyed his life, even if his wife does make it through this," Neal answered.

"And, how are you coping?" she asked. Neal sounded exhausted.

"I'm fine, except that once again, my brother is causing everyone problems."

"I'm sure he didn't have a car accident on purpose," Shelley said, surprised.

"Shelley, Dean's a bum! He caused my parents so much trouble before they died, and God knows why Marlene continues to stay with him. Plus, he's ruined our Thanksgiving," he said, bitterly.

"Neal, I'm sorry, and I know this is a selfish question, but do you think you'll make it to Georgia at all?" This was not the picture she had of their first holiday together.

"I certainly will give it a good shot, but just in case, give me your parent's address and phone number. If not in person, I'll be there in spirit."

The next morning, Shelley packed her clothes and slipped the airline tickets Neal had purchased inside her purse. She was ready to drive to the airport, and although it would have been better if Neal were going too, she was still excited about visiting her family.

Walking off the plane in Atlanta, Shelley felt the temperature difference when she reached the exit ramp. She saw her parents waving to her from the back of the crowd, and suddenly felt like one of the many college students filling the airport that day, going home for the short Thanksgiving break.

Shelley joyfully embraced her parents, Meg and Tim Hemlo, and felt at peace during the quiet drive home. When they walked into the house, Shelley noticed the large flower arrangement on the center of the dining room table.

"Ooh, how pretty, Mother. Who sent these?" she asked, looking for the card.

"Your Neal did," she answered, smiling.

"Neal sent them to you?" Shelley asked, confused. "I wonder when he arranged this," she thought out loud.

"I don't know. They arrived this morning. Yours are in the guestroom," Meg said.

"Mine?" Shelley asked.

"Go look."

Shelley walked into the bedroom located in the back of the house. Sitting on the nightstand was a vase holding two dozen, red roses. She opened the card attached to the large, red bow hanging over the edge of the vase.

> *My Dearest Shelley, I'm so sorry we could not be together this Thanksgiving. Hopefully, next year will be better. Please know how much I love you and want to be with you. I'll call you tonight. Love, Neal.*

Shelley looked out of the bedroom window holding the card. The leaves were a dark shade of red, and a bright shade of yellow. She never noticed before how beautiful Atlanta was that time of year. Shelley was on stable ground, feeling enormously peaceful, and truly happy.

Chapter 8

After enjoying a wonderful Thanksgiving, Shelley flew back to New Jersey, the following Sunday. Neal was sitting on the stairs in the lobby of her apartment building, looking like a lost child. When she saw him, she dropped her suitcase and wrapped her arms around him.

"I have missed you so much." she whispered, while Neal kissed her neck.

"I've been so miserable without you, Shelley, I couldn't wait until you came home," he responded as he kissed her face. "Shelley, let's go upstairs and talk. I have so much I need to say."

Neal carried her suitcase upstairs. As soon as they entered the apartment, Shelley started a pot of coffee, hoping it would warm them. The weather in New Jersey had definitely chilled while she'd been gone. When the coffee had finished brewing, she brought the pot and two mugs into the living room and placed them on the coffee table.

She took her place next to Neal on the couch, where he appeared to be deep in thought.

"What's wrong, Neal? Are you worried about your brother?" she asked, pouring coffee into his mug. Dean had not come out of his coma.

"No, I just don't want to go through this again," he said, finally breaking his silence.

"I understand. Seeing your brother in a coma must be awful for you," she responded.

"As bad as that is, I don't mean that, Shelley. I mean you and I being apart," he answered, looking at her.

Somewhat offended, she replied, "Neal, you travel all the time. Outside of your brother's accident, how was my going to Georgia different from that?"

"I guess when I travel, it feels more normal to me," he responded.

"For who?" Shelley asked, becoming angry. "When you travel, I'm lonely! Why are your feelings more important than mine?"

"Shelley, they're not, but if you feel that way, then, why don't you marry me? What is your problem? Are you waiting, hoping those feelings will go away?"

"No, Neal. I don't have a problem. It's just too soon in our relationship to start picking out furniture!" she answered.

"Why? Do you love me?" he asked.

Shelley hesitated before she answered. "Yes...I believe I do."

"Either you do, or you don't. It's really not a trick question!" he said, crossly.

"All right, I do. Where is this conversation going anyway?" she asked, annoyed with his badgering.

"Shelley, I just experienced the worst five days of my life. I watched my sister-in-law go through complete hell over a man who doesn't deserve it, and I realized I want someone to love me that way," he said.

"You want me to go through hell for you?"

"No, I want that kind of devotion in my life. If you have a difficult time deciding if you love me, enough to marry me that is, then, I don't believe there's anything substantial between us," he said, returning his cup to the coffee table.

"Exactly what are you trying to say?" Neal stood, and she wondered if he was getting ready to leave.

"The way I see it, you should know how you feel about me, the way I know there will never be anyone else for me, but you. I love you, and I want to marry you, no hesitation, no doubts, no fears," Neal said, still looking at her. "I would rather nurture that love than spend my time waiting for the other shoe to drop, hoping my feelings will disappear."

"Neal, I do love you, but I need more time."

"I leave for France in two weeks. At the end of my trip I'll fly to England as planned. When I get there, I'm going to call you at your parents' house. If you agree to marry me, I'll take that flight to Atlanta."

"And...if I don't?" Shelley asked.

"If not, I'll return to South Jersey and our relationship will be strictly business," he firmly replied.

"You're kidding, right?"

"No, I'm not kidding. I won't get hurt again," he said, adamantly.

"Neal, there are no guarantees with any relationship. How do I know you won't hurt me?"

"Because, Shelley, I believe I love you a little more than you love me."

"Neal, I really do love you and I hate the thought of you leaving me at all," she said, hoping that attributed something. "All I'm asking for is a little more time!"

"You have two weeks." he answered softly.

He closed his eyes and pulled her closer to him. Shelley loved what she felt when Neal held her. *Why is he in such a rush? Why can't things just happen?* she thought.

Chapter 9

The following two weeks were like being immersed within a fairy tale. Neal took Shelley to the finest restaurants. They danced all night, and enjoyed several Broadway shows, spending every available moment together, and making each one count.

Then, the day they both dreaded arrived, the last night before Neal's trip to France. They walked along the cold beach in Atlantic City, and talked until dawn, heartbroken about the inevitable separation, and when morning arrived, Neal and Shelley solemnly sat over a delicious breakfast that at any other time, would have been enjoyed.

Neal's flight was scheduled to leave at three-thirty from J.F.K. Airport. The pouring rain seemed appropriate to the sadness of the day. Every thump of the windshield wipers bringing them closer to the airport.

After they found the right departing gate, they sat in silence until Neal's flight was called for boarding. With tears in their eyes, they kissed each other goodbye, and when Shelley watched him leave the gate, she felt as though her entire life was leaving on that flight.

The plane disappeared into the dreary sky and quickly Neal was gone. Shelley searched for the sign that would lead her to the Baggage Claim area through tear-filled eyes. J.F.K. Airport felt overwhelming to her through her intense sorrow.

Opening her purse to search for a tissue, she felt an envelope clumsily jammed in the middle of it. She recognized Neal's handwriting scribbled on the front of it, when fumbling with shaky hands, she managed to pull it out.

Inside was a letter wrapped around ten one hundred dollar bills. She passionately held onto the letter as she searched for an empty seat. Anticipating bad news, she wanted to be seated. Perhaps he had changed his mind about giving her two weeks to answer his proposal. Maybe he thought it would be easier to just end it. Those were just a few of the many fears gripping her as she unfolded the badly creased piece of paper.

Dear Shelley,
Please don't be mad about this money. I don't want to worry about you while I'm in Europe. Use this money to do some Christmas shopping. If you have already finished that, then, buy yourself something wonderful from me. I love you, and I'll call you from France next Saturday night. Please, know how much I will miss you, and I will pray for a happy ending for us.
Again, I love you.
Neal.

"Oh, Neal, I love you, too," Shelley whispered, as if he could hear her words. The flow of her tears seemed relentless, and it seemed like a long time before she felt composed enough to leave the airport.

The first week Neal was away, passed quickly. Shelley, shopped, having a dreadful time finding the right gift for Neal and finally settled on a red, cashmere bathrobe that she had monogrammed. Her desperation to find the perfect gift seemed futile when she wasn't even sure he would be with her Christmas morning.

Saturday, Shelley was grateful that Elkie decided to stay in the city. She wanted total privacy when Neal called from France.

Eight fifteen, the phone rang. Shelley heard nothing but the forceful static blaring into her ear. Behind it, she heard Neal's faint voice trying to overcome the scratchy noise. "Shelley! Shelley?" he cried.

"Neal, can you hear me?" she yelled, frustrated with the awful interference.

"Yes, but not very well. Are you all right?" Neal shouted.

"I'm fine. What about you?"

"Other than missing you, I'm alive and well," he answered.

"I miss you too, Neal. How are things in France?"

"It's awful. The French hate Americans and they're very rude!"

"Well, you only have one more week there. Do you think you can make it? I'm anxious for you to come home."

"I don't know, that depends. Can you help me get through it with some good news?" he asked, obviously hoping she'd reached her decision.

"I have until you arrive in England to give you my decision, right?" Shelley asked.

"I'm sorry, I guess I'm too anxious."

"How's the food?" Shelley asked, trying to change the subject.

"Leave it to you to think of the food," he said, laughing. "Shelley, even you would starve here. P.L.K. pre-ordered my meals, and the other night, I was served a cow's head."

"No way!" Shelley screeched.

"I'm telling you, I hate it here!" he answered, with disgust.

The static took over their conversation. "Neal, I think we'd better go. I can't hear you very well and I don't want to lose our connection without us saying goodbye," Shelley yelled sadly.

"Well, I guess this is it," Neal said, hesitantly. "I'll call you when my plane lands in England. I love you."

"I love you, too!" Shelley shouted.

She heard the click as the phone line disconnected, and was incredibly conscious of the lonely silence that followed. She would not talk to Neal again until she was in Georgia, instigating her inability to fall asleep. Her relentless crying finally exhausted her enough to send her into rest.

Chapter 10

During the next few days, Shelley busied herself with preparation for her trip to Georgia. Before leaving the office on Wednesday, everybody wished her a 'Merry Christmas', and asked her to offer the same greeting to Neal when he arrived back in the States. Shelley told them she would, not giving away the circumstances of his return. *If I see him,* she thought, sadly.

As planned, she drove Neal's car to the airport, totally under-estimating the horror of New Jersey's holiday traffic. People in cars were running each other off the highway, speeding to their destinations, while inside the airport, crowds of people pushed anything in their way of getting where they had to go. Because of all the confusion, Shelley arrived at her gate just in time to board, and was more than relieved when the plane had been cleared for take off. She couldn't relax until she saw its wings soar into the clouds, leaving New Jersey behind.

She still had no idea how she would answer Neal's ultimatum. The more she'd thought about marriage, the more it frightened her. Marrying Neal was not the issue, she knew she loved him. It was the total commitment, the loss of self she feared most, knowing how subtly the death of a woman's spirit could occur in the wrong marriage.

Once again, Shelley's parents were cheerfully waiting for her when she got off the plane in Atlanta. Christmas carols played throughout the terminal, filling Shelley with a certain amount of Christmas spirit that had been lost through her indecisiveness.

"When is Neal coming?" Meg asked, not wasting any time, while Tim quietly drove towards home.

"He's going to call me from England with his flight information," Shelley answered, thinking it wiser to keep Meg uninformed, at least for the moment, so she could reach her decision without the extra pressure telling her would generate. Meg Hemlo remained hurried to see her daughter walk down the aisle a second time. In her unenlightened world, a woman's life held no validation outside of marriage.

"Your father and I are anxious to meet him. He must be important to P.L.K. if they sent him all the way to France," she said.

"I guess so, Mother," Shelley answered, already feeling uneasy.

Shelley dragged her suitcase into the smaller bedroom that Meg had converted into an art studio. Meg loved to paint, and was quite a talented artist. She'd sold several of her paintings in the little country store they owned in the old town of Milton. The shop gave her parent's purpose, and added some old country charm to the community.

Shelley's brother, Drew, and his wife, Mindy, were due to arrive on Saturday. Drew was blatantly Meg's favorite child, the one given all opportunity. Mark, the oldest, harbored a certain amount of resentment towards Drew because of that, and the fact that he so desperately craved their parent's approval. Shelley ignored Meg's favoritism even though at times that was difficult to do.

Once settled, Shelley joined her mother in the kitchen where Meg had a pot of coffee ready, and a plate of fresh doughnuts waiting on the kitchen table. Apprehensive of Meg's reaction, Shelley used that time to tell her the situation.

"Mom, I have something to tell you."

"What is it? I hope it's not bad news. You know your father and I can't take too much bad news," she said, quickly.

"No, Mother, it's not bad news. As a matter of fact, it has nothing to do with you."

"Then, what is it?" she asked.

"Neal has asked me to marry him."

"Oh, my goodness! That's wonderful!" she exclaimed, clearly elated.

"He told me he would call me when he reached England, and if I refuse his proposal, he's going home to New Jersey instead of taking his flight to Atlanta. Actually, he said that if I say "no," our relationship will be over, and that we won't see each other anymore, outside of the office."

"Why wouldn't you marry him, Shelley? You obviously care about the man."

Meg used the intimidating tone she'd hated throughout her childhood, the one that suggested her thinking was abnormal, as was anything that interfered with Meg's wishes for her daughter.

"Mother, this is a big decision for me, and I don't want to make another mistake."

"Well, I know what I'd do," her mother snapped.

To avoid any further confrontation, Shelley dropped the subject and did her best to avoid discussing it again until she absolutely had to.

Saturday morning, Drew and Mindy arrived from Virginia, after driving most of the night. Shelley spent the rest of the day talking with them, bringing each other up to date on the events of their lives.

When the grandfather clock Tim Hemlo had made years earlier bonged six times, Shelley began to feel nervous, expecting Neal's call. The phone rang at seven.

Everyone looked at Shelley, while her mother ran to the kitchen to answer it. Within seconds, Meg shouted, "It's an overseas operator!"

Shelley ran to the back bedroom for the seclusion she needed for her conversation.

"Neal, can you hear me?" she shouted, once again through dreadful static.

"Yes, I can...but not very well!" he replied. He sounded nervous, obviously anxious for Shelley's answer.

"Are you okay?" she asked, hoping he'd arrived in England without problems.

"I'm fine, really, except I'm going nuts worrying about us!"

"Neal, I'm sorry if I ruined your trip, but this was a big decision for me," she yelled.

"Honey, listen, I'm standing outside in a foreign country, enduring the worst rainstorm I've ever encountered, carrying a bag with five cans of some stupid coffee John insisted I bring back for him...please, if you don't mind, just give me the bad news so I can cry my way back to the States!"

Shelley started to laugh. "Neal, if you still want me...I would love to marry you," she yelled.

"Yes! Yes! Yes!" he shouted, happily. "I can't believe it! Shelley, I promise you will never be sorry!" he exclaimed.

Sorry? How could I be sorry about marrying someone as wonderful as you? she thought. They were so excited, it took three attempts by

Shelley to write down the correct flight information. Neal would arrive at eight o'clock, Christmas Eve, and they made plans to meet outside the baggage claim area of the airport to avoid the aggravation of trying to park.

Shelley placed the phone back where it belonged, truly content with her decision, then, returned to the family room. Everyone stared at her, waiting to hear the results of the phone call.

"I said yes," Shelley said, softly.

There was an assembly of congratulations, while Shelley's mother ran to the phone to call her sister, Joan. It was an exciting moment, and Shelley, honestly never felt happier. She knew Neal was different, and that he would keep his promise about never giving her any reason to be sorry.

Chapter 11

Meg ran through the house on a cleaning frenzy, creating chaos in the process. Shelley wanted to find a corner and hide until it was time to go to the airport. Tim suggested they go alone, and Shelley thought it was a great plan. When seven o'clock arrived, Shelley and Tim walked out the door. Opening the car door, she looked at her father and smiled. They were the lucky ones. They were going somewhere else. Aunt Joan would be there in less than two hours, and that alone would create turmoil.

Neal was leaning against one of the columns under a granite awning with luggage piled in front of him.

"Stop the car!" Shelley yelled, causing Tim to slam on the brakes.

Neal saw Shelley the moment she jumped out of the car. They looked like lovers in an old romance movie, running towards each other in slow motion while some amorous love song played in the background. They grabbed each other, oblivious to the world around them.

"I've missed you so much," Neal whispered, kissing Shelley.

"I'm so glad you're home," Shelley murmured in his ear, almost breathless, until they looked up, realizing Shelley's father at some point had joined them on the sidewalk.

Regaining her composure, Shelley introduced Neal to her father. After they'd stuffed Neal's bags in the trunk, the couple climbed in the back seat, and they were on their way home.

When Neal took Shelley's hand, she felt at peace with the world. Meanwhile, Tim used the ride home to get acquainted with his future son-in-law. Shelley could tell right away that they liked each other, however, Meg Hemlo would be the real test.

The number of cars in the driveway alerted Tim and Shelley that the other guests had arrived. When they walked in, everyone stood with anticipation, as Shelley introduced Neal.

Drew, politely hung Neal's coat on the wooden rack standing by the door, then took his bags, leading Neal to the studio so he could get settled before dealing with the house full of people.

While Neal became situated, Meg grabbed her daughter's arm, guiding her into the kitchen.

"He's exactly as I pictured him," Meg whispered, with excitement.

"Isn't he amazing?" Shelley asked, smiling, happy when her mother approved of anything.

"He's wonderful, and your father likes him too!"

"Great! What about Aunt Joan?" Shelley asked, snatching a cookie off the tray her mother had decoratively arranged. They both laughed, knowing Joan was expected to hate him. She hated anyone more successful than her son-in-law, a produce manager for a local grocery store. Even though he worked hard to support his family and did that very well, he was not what she had in mind for her daughter.

The last guests left at one o'clock, and not too soon for the men as they literally ran to their beds. Neal was exhausted and everyone understood when he excused himself. The different time zones and the anticipation of Shelley's decision had drained his reserve of energy.

Shelley walked Neal to his room to say goodnight privately. He'd been nervous about meeting Shelley's family and with that out of the way, he said he could finally catch up on his lost sleep.

"Well…have you changed your mind about marrying me, now that you've met my family?" Shelley asked, smiling.

"Shelley, I'll never change my mind. All of this feels right. Your family, Georgia, even Aunt Joan," he said, grinning, as he held her.

"Oh, definitely Aunt Joan!" Shelley agreed, smiling back. Neal kissed her and she became absorbed in the comfort of his arms. It was good to be alone with him.

"I wish I could hold you all night," Neal whispered in Shelley's ear.

"I know. This has been a dreadful three weeks," Shelley replied.

"Well, they're over now, and I don't ever want to leave you again," he said.

Once all the gifts under the Christmas tree were given out the next morning, Christmas morning, their first Christmas together, Neal stood and pulled a little box out of his pocket. Slowly, he handed it to Shelley.

"Merry Christmas," Neal said, softly, staring into her eyes.

The room remained silent as Shelley opened the little parcel. Neal watched, clearly anxious for her reaction to his choice.

Once she'd managed to open it with her shaky hands, Neal pulled the beautiful diamond ring out of the box and placed it on Shelley's finger. It was magnificent. He'd purchased the ring in France, hoping Shelley would accept it. Suddenly, the bathrobe she'd bought Neal seemed extremely insignificant.

"Oh, Neal...it's so beautiful," she whispered. "I don't know what to say," she added, tilting her left hand, overwhelmed with the sparkle emanating from the two carat diamond.

"Just say 'I do'," he whispered. "I love you."

"I love you, too, Neal," Shelley whispered before she kissed him.

The beautiful ring and Neal's strong hand holding hers represented her future. Neal promised her a life filled with love and splendor, an opportunity for complete happiness. He was a wonderful man, what most would consider a 'perfect catch', and he was in love with her.

Chapter 12

Neal and Shelley flew back to New Jersey the day before New Year's Eve. During the flight home, Neal began to feel sick, and by the time they'd reached Shelley's apartment, he was burning with fever. Shelley insisted that he stay at the apartment, rather than return to the hotel alone. The couch in the living room was a sleeper, accommodating Shelley, so Neal would have full use of her bedroom to recover.

They used the time to discuss their wedding plans. They both agreed to get married in Georgia, which pleased Meg and Tim.

Neal had a pilot's license and owned a Piper Cub that would enable him to fly six people to the wedding. That meant Elkie, and Neal's friend Matt, could be included. Working around Neal's busy traveling schedule, they set the wedding date for February seventeenth.

Fully recovered by January fourth, Neal returned to his hotel and the office. His first order of business was to call a meeting, asking the entire staff to be present.

Everybody asked Shelley what the meeting was about, but she honestly did not know and grabbed a chair along with everyone else, waiting to find out. It was not unusual for Neal to call last minute meetings to educate the staff on price changes, or the latest company news, or product. So, Shelley had no reason to feel uncomfortable about the meeting.

Neal began by wishing everyone a belated Happy New Year. He briefed them on the results of his trip to France, then, proceeded to explain the most important reason for the meeting.

"I'd like to make an announcement," Neal said, keeping an eye on Shelley's reaction.

Shelley stiffened in her seat. *Surely not...surely, Neal would not do this without discussing it with me first!* she thought. They'd decided not to tell anyone just yet.

"Shelley and I became engaged over the Christmas holiday, and we plan to be married on February seventeenth." He watched as Shelley blushed with embarrassment. Everyone at the table expressed the usual oohs and ahs, taking hold of her left hand to examine the ring that Shelley had managed to keep hidden. She was furious with Neal.

"Therefore, much to everyone's dismay, I'm sure...Shelley's last day at P.L.K. will be January twenty ninth," he concluded.

What is he doing? Shelley asked herself, completely enraged with Neal's announcement. She behaved diplomatically, pretending they'd planned Neal's speech together. After the meeting, each staff member offered best wishes and expressed their sadness about Shelley's resignation. When the last person was gone, Shelley slammed the door to the conference room and confronted Neal.

"What the hell was that about?" Shelley asked him, consumed with anger.

Neal shrugged. "I didn't think you would mind if I told everyone we're getting married," he said, in defense.

"I'm not talking about that, although that wasn't what we agreed to do!"

"Well, then, what is it?" he asked, acting as though he truly had no idea why she was upset.

"Neal, you told everyone I was quitting my job. How dare you make that decision for me!"

"Shelley, company policy states, spouses cannot work together at P.L.K., so I saved P.L.K. the trouble of asking you to resign," he said, sharply.

"Well, whatever your reason, it should have been discussed with me first. It's my job!"

"Honey, I know, and I'm sorry if this disturbs you, but John Frank told me this morning to take care of it, or he would."

Neal pulled Shelley closer and hugged her. She knew he was right, but she enjoyed her job and had worked hard to gain the respect she had for her performance.

Understanding how Shelley felt, he said, "Honey, look at it this way. You'll have a full time job."

"And what might that be?" she asked, knowing what he was referring to.

"Me! And I'm enough work for one person, don't you think? Why don't you forget about working for a while? Maybe take some classes, or you could learn to play the piano. Whatever you want to do."

Before Shelley had a chance to respond, Neal kissed her and the argument became history. She decided to stay home for a while to make Neal happy. Perhaps that was when it started, the beginning of her losing her autonomy. *Love entails a certain amount of sacrifice, does it not?* Shelley reasoned.

Chapter 13

Making plans for the wedding kept Shelley busy. They both agreed on a small church ceremony with a dinner party afterward of twenty guests. Shelley made reservations at 'The Sandy Nest' in Atlanta, then, called to schedule an appointment with the minister of the church during their next visit to Georgia, the last week in January. All details were taken care of, and eventually, the inevitable had to be addressed. Shelley brought up the touchy issue one evening after dinner.

"Neal, have you thought about where we're going to live yet?" she asked.

"No. I thought we would deal with that when we returned from Atlanta," he answered, unconcerned. He was busy reading the paperwork John Frank had asked him to review.

"Well, what about your house in South Jersey?"

"I've already signed a contract with a Realtor to sell it," he answered.

"Why don't we live in it until it sells?" Shelley asked. "It doesn't make sense to have two homes, does it?"

"Look, Shelley! I have a lot of bad memories in that house, and I refuse to carry them into our marriage!"

Shelley hesitated, somewhat confused by Neal's anger. "Neal, it wouldn't be permanent. After it sells, we can find another house."

"Honey, let's get done what we need to first. When we get back from Atlanta, we'll decide where we should live," Neal said, agitated. he kissed Shelley's nose, which marked the end of the discussion, then went back to his paperwork.

On the evening of Shelley's last day at P.L.K., Shelley and Neal flew to Georgia in the rain. Shelley was grateful for the first class seats Neal had purchased, since it turned out to be an extremely bumpy flight.

They rented a car so they would not have to inconvenience Shelley's parents. During the drive to the Hemlos, Neal grabbed Shelley's hand and said, "Honey, listen. I have something I want to discuss with you."

Sensing something was about to happen, she hesitated before she asked, "Is everything okay, Neal?"

"Yes, Sweetheart, everything is fine, but we have an important decision to make."

"Okay, just tell me before I die from curiosity," Shelley urged.

"I've been offered a position in Atlanta with Mountain Industries. As a matter of fact, part of the reason for this trip is because their corporate people asked to meet with me."

"What kind of position? What could be better than what you have with P.L.K.? Neal, people work years to earn your position."

"Regional Manager for the entire Southeast!" he boasted.

"Is that good?"

"Yes, it's good! Plus, if we move to Atlanta, you would be closer to your family," he said, actually thinking that would entice Shelley.

"Neal, think about this. If I'd wanted to live closer to my family, I would have moved to Georgia when they did, years ago. Long map lines have proved to be very healthy for my relationship with them," she responded.

"Honey, Atlanta is a wonderful place to live, and this is a good opportunity for me," he said, defending the move.

"This is important to you?" Shelley asked, after a few minutes.

"It's a major career move for me," he answered.

Shelley thought about it for a moment, then half-heartedly agreed. "All right. If it means that much to you, I guess we have to do it," she answered, reluctantly.

Shelley knew from the beginning that one of the drawbacks of being married to an executive meant there was no such thing as a permanent address. There would always be the threat of a transfer.

That evening, they told Shelley's parents about the move. Tim was pleased he would get to spend time with Neal. He missed Mark and Drew, and a son-in-law offered a good substitute.

Neal had an appointment with Mountain Industries the next morning and he thought it would be a good idea if when he returned, they began house hunting. It was obvious to Shelley that Neal was determined to move to Atlanta as soon as possible.

Shelley called and made appointments with the minister and the restaurant to finalize the last details of the wedding, while Neal was at his meeting. When he returned, he was extremely excited about a home he'd seen while driving back to the Hemlo's house.

"Shelley, I saw a 'for sale' sign on the corner of this fantastic looking sub-division in Stone Mountain," Neal exclaimed. "So, I drove down the street, and Honey…it was magnificent! I wrote down the name of the realtor and his phone number. I'm going to call him right now to see when he can show it to us."

Shelley felt rushed. Once again, everything was happening too quickly. Neal ran to the phone, returning a few minutes later wearing a big smile.

"He can meet us there now. Is this a good time?" he asked.

Shelley felt as though a tornado had entered the house, yet part of her was amused watching Neal act so enthusiastically.

"Yes, it's fine. We don't have to meet with the minister until three o'clock," Shelley responded, hoping to make Neal happy.

"Would you like to join us?" Neal asked Meg and Tim, who had entered the room in time hear about the house.

"Yes, we'd love to, if you don't mind," Meg immediately responded. She grabbed her coat before Shelley was able to throw out some of the many reasons why her mother should stay home.

"Great! Then, let's go," Neal said, cheerfully, holding the door open for everyone to leave.

It took four minutes to get there from the Hemlo's house, which was a serious concern to Shelley, but Neal was right. Steeple Drive was magnificent, and when he pulled into the driveway of the beautiful, two story colonial, Shelley knew the inside just had to be nothing less than wonderful.

Within minutes, a brown Cadillac joined them in the driveway and a very well dressed, distinguished man stepped out.

"Good morning! I'm George Lipton," the man said, extending his hand to Neal, automatically assuming Neal was the man he'd spoken with on the phone.

Neal introduced everyone, while the man opened the door. When he did, the new smell of the cream-colored carpet assured any potential buyer that the house had never been occupied. As they followed the Realtor's tour, each room was more perfect than the one before.

"What do you think, Honey?" Neal asked when he managed to get Shelley alone. He seemed entranced with the house.

"I think it's wonderful, but don't you think we should see other homes? This is the first house we've seen!" Shelley argued.

"Why, if we love this one?" he asked. "Let's buy it!"

The back windows revealed a brook, making its way through an endless view of trees. Standing outside, all they could hear was the sound of the water running against long settled rocks.

The house was built on a beautiful piece of land and was everything they'd said they wanted in a house. Since Neal was so elated, Shelley decided to go along with his decision, and he made arrangements to meet the Realtor at his office so he could sign the proper papers.

"I'll drive you and your parents home before I meet with Mr. Lipton," Neal said.

Meg looked confused. "Don't you think Shelley should go with you?" she asked.

"Mr. Lipton said it wasn't necessary since the mortgage would be based solely on my income," Neal answered, unconcerned.

"Well, I think she should be there anyway," Meg whispered to Tim.

"This is their business, Mother," Tim whispered. "Stay out of it."

"What's the mystery? They're going to be married. His business should be her business," Meg persisted.

"Keep your thoughts to yourself!" Tim told his wife. "Maybe this is the way it's done now," he added.

Neal returned two hours later, completely satisfied. "Well, Honey, it looks as though we bought ourselves a house!" he said, happily. "The builder accepted our offer, and the closing is scheduled for the twelfth of April."

That's great!" Shelley said. The house truly was beautiful, and she never imagined living in a home that elegant. She felt as though she were living in the middle of a fairy tale and could only see the happy ending.

Chapter 14

Shelley's first day of official retirement was spent packing. Elkie and Shelley had shared many wonderful times in the apartment and she was going to miss them both. She was beginning to feel melancholy when Neal called from the office, somewhat upset.

"What's wrong?" she asked.

"I'm so mad. I just called the FAA and they said I don't have enough flying time to fly my plane to Atlanta. I swear, Shelley, I might as well sell the plane!"

"What are we going to do?" Shelley asked, dismayed. *What about Elkie?* she thought. Elkie was going to be Shelley's Maid of Honor. *And what about Neal's Best man?* she wondered.

"Don't worry, I've thought of a solution." The calmness in his voice soothed her.

"Okay, what?" she asked. *Why don't we just go to a Justice of the Peace to get married? That's what I wanted. Why did you insist on this formal wedding?* she thought.

"I'll fly everybody to Atlanta on a commercial airline," he said. "That will end the problem."

"Do you have any idea how much that would cost?" Shelley asked, horrified.

"It's okay, we can afford it," he answered, laughing. "Just tell me how many people you want to come and I'll get the tickets," he responded.

"If Matt is coming, that makes four. Neal…you know, we really don't need this wedding. We could just get married somewhere without all this hassle and expense."

"Oh, yes, we do. The day we get married will be the happiest day of my life and I intend to celebrate. And yes, Matt will be going."

"What about your sister-in-law and niece?"

"Marlene can't leave my brother, but Matt is really the only person I'm adamant about having there," he answered.

Shelley understood. It was just as important to her that Elkie attend. They decided four reservations would be enough.

Neal took care of mailing Matt his flight tickets, and by phone, they made plans to meet at Newark Airport, two hours before take off. Shelley was eager to meet Matt, since he was the only person Neal had left in his life besides his brother.

Shelley was confident that his parents must have been special people to have a man as terrific as Neal for a son. When Neal talked about them, tears formed in his eyes, and so many times he said he wished they were still alive to share his joy. Shelley tried to imagine how painful life must have been for him, to be so alone in the world.

Now, he has me, she thought. *He will never be alone again.*

Chapter 15

Neal, Shelley, and Elkie, drove through a heavy snowstorm to Newark Airport. When they reached the departing gate, they took seats to wait for Matt's arrival, hoping he would find the gate easily since he had never been there before. The weather was treacherous.

Take-off time was nearing and Neal grew concerned. Matt had not yet arrived, and the airline was preparing to board its passengers.

"Neal, I'm sure he's delayed because of the bad weather," Shelley said.

"I don't know, maybe I should call his home."

As Neal walked away to locate a phone, Shelley thought about his close relationship with Matt. They probably shared the important events of Neal's life together, like marriage, divorce, and the death of his parents and child.

"Has Neal spoken to this guy?" Elkie asked, interrupting Shelley's thoughts.

"I don't know, but I think he would have called Neal if he had anticipated any problems, don't you agree?"

"I hope so, because it's really going to hurt Neal if he doesn't show up," Elkie said.

A few minutes later, Neal returned with tears in his eyes.

"Neal, what's wrong? Isn't he coming?" Shelley asked, beginning to panic.

"Matt's mother died this afternoon," he answered, burying his face in his hands.

"Oh, my God! I'm so sorry." Astounded, Shelley put her arms around his shoulders. "We'll have to postpone the wedding."

"Postpone the wedding? Definitely not!" he gasped. "I'll just have to find another Best Man."

"But, Neal, what about the funeral? He's your best friend!" Shelley said, amazed that was not a concern to him.

Neal put his arm around her and spoke softly. "Shelley, Matt sent his love and insisted we get on the plane to get married, and that is what we're going to do."

Chapter 16

Reverend Reid scheduled the church rehearsal the evening before the wedding. Fortunately, Drew and Mindy managed to come, and Drew felt honored when Neal asked him to be his Best Man.

Neal seemed nervous during the rehearsal. His behavior made it more apparent when Reverend Reid's nine-year-old son jumped in front of the altar and Neal yelled, "Get down Jeffrey!"

Silence took over the church. "Neal, who is Jeffrey?" Shelley whispered, looking around to find everyone staring.

"Oh, I don't know...isn't that the boy's name?" Neal asked, embarrassed.

"No, his name is John, and why did you yell at him?" Shelley whispered, mortified.

"He was jumping on the altar. It was instinct."

Well, why don't you leave John's discipline to his father?" Shelley gently suggested.

Reverend Reid, staring at Neal, summoned his son to stand next to him, then, continued the rehearsal.

"I think you two better find another church. The Reverend doesn't look too pleased," Elkie said.

Shelley laughed, but Neal's behavior was not forgotten.

Even though an ice storm brought the reception to an early end, it truly was a beautiful wedding. Neal and Shelley had written their own vows, saying things to each other that were important for them to say, giving the ceremony special meaning. The restaurant did a lovely job with the dinner, and everybody had a good time.

Neal and Shelley began their life together in the Bridal Suite of the Stone Mountain Inn. It looked like a bedroom inside of the White

House, and even though they would be leaving for Florida after everyone left Atlanta, in Shelley's mind, that evening would always be their honeymoon.

The world was a wonderland of white outside the large, colonial window of the Bridal Suite. Shelley noticed the icicles holding onto the trees outside, and felt grateful for the warmth inside the suite and for her new husband.

Neal lit a fire in the huge fireplace, then turned off the lights. The flickering flames gave the room just enough light to make everything look more enchanting, and just when Shelley thought nothing on Earth could make that night better, she became Neal's wife.

Chapter 17

Neal and Shelley returned to her parents' house after a delightful, two-week honeymoon in Florida. They'd decided to search for an executive suite they could lease for a month until they closed on the house. However, when none were available without signing a year's lease, Meg and Tim insisted they use the guestroom.

Neal still had unfinished business in New Jersey, so he arranged for them to fly back for what would hopefully be the last time.

Two days before leaving, Neal became notably nervous. His edginess worsened, and by the time the plane landed in New Jersey, Shelley was completely annoyed with his testy attitude. He had become withdrawn, and when he did speak to her, it was with an unpleasant tone.

"Where are we going first?" Shelley asked, once he found the Thunderbird in the airport parking lot.

"P.L.K. I have to report in," he snapped, entering the highway.

"Great! It'll be good to see everyone again," she said, anxious to see her friends.

"No! I want you to wait in the car. I'll just be a minute," he said, quickly.

"Neal, are you crazy? I'm not waiting in the car! I haven't seen anybody at P.L.K. since I quit working." *What is wrong with him?* she asked herself.

"Shelley, I don't want to argue about this. Just wait in the car! I have my reasons for wanting it this way," he argued.

He pulled the car over to the side of the road and closed his eyes. When he opened them, Shelley saw tears filling them, and grew concerned.

"I'm sorry...I guess I have been treating you pretty lousy," he said, taking her hand into his. He slowly began twirling Shelley's wedding ring.

"Neal, I know something is wrong!" She loathed his secrecy.

"I don't want them to ask you questions, or put you in a situation to lie," he answered.

"What are you talking about?" she asked, confused.

"P.L.K. doesn't know I'm going to Mountain Industries yet," he answered.

"What? Why not? I don't understand why you wouldn't tell them!" Shelley said, astounded. They had completely relocated to Georgia for Mountain Industries, and P.L.K. didn't know? Thinking he had already handed in his resignation, Shelley had wondered why P.L.K. allowed Neal to keep the Thunderbird as long as they had.

"Shelley, if I told them I was signing with Mountain, they would burn me in the industry, and I would have been ordered to clean out my desk immediately. Then, I would have to fight for the bonus money they owe me," he explained. "And I worked too hard for it to let them steal it from me."

"Why would they do that, Neal?" Shelley asked. She found P.L.K. to be an honest company, and she was sure neither, John, or Tom would act so underhanded.

"I could steal price lists, even prints to special designs, or customer lists. Worse yet, copies of special contracts," Neal answered, trying to make her understand the mentality of P.L.K. "This is the general philosophy of most corporations, Shelley. Welcome to the real world.".

"Well, did you get your bonus money yet?" she asked.

"That's what I'm going to do now. I won't hand in my resignation until I get it!"

Neal pulled the car back onto the highway, and several minutes later, they arrived at P.L.K. As planned, Neal went inside alone, and an hour later, he came back to the car carrying a cardboard box that he threw onto the back seat.

"I'm glad that's over," he said, relieved. "Nobody suspected anything when I left with a box. They probably thought it was catalogues."

"What's really in there?" Shelley asked, trying to see over the seat.

"My personal papers and the things from my desk," he answered, proud that his plan had worked.

"Won't they notice your desk is empty?" she asked, confused.

"No, because several months ago, I began replacing my good things for some old junk I had at home. From a distance, my desk looks the same. Before P.L.K. realizes what I've done, they will have my resignation and my bonus check will have cleared the bank!"

Neal had all the answers, and Shelley never doubted his integrity. He had to protect himself from bad business, she reasoned.

Remaining behind to take care of a few things in South Jersey, Neal asked Shelley to fly back to Atlanta, alone. Once again, he refused to take her to his house, causing them to argue, and, as usual, in the end, Neal won and Shelley agreed to return to Georgia, unsure of what the purpose had been of her going to New Jersey at all.

Neal made arrangements to dispose of Shelley's car since he was giving her a new one, and took care of shipping Shelley's personal belongings from the apartment to Atlanta. He decided to give Shelley the Renault he'd bought a few months before starting work at P.L.K. It was new, and he thought it would be a good car for her. Besides, it was a good way to bring his personal things to Georgia. He did not plan to move any of his household belongings until his house sold.

Neal spent his first three days in Atlanta attending meetings with Mountain Industries. On the third day, Meg and Shelley had the house to themselves, since Tim went to the shop. The two women were preparing lunch when the phone rang.

"Hello," Meg answered. "No, he's not here, but his wife is. Hold on," she said, offering Shelley the phone. "It's for you," she whispered.

"Who is it?" Shelley asked.

"I don't know. Some woman. Do you want to take it in the back room?"

"Yes, thank you," Shelley answered, walking down the hall. She picked up the phone and heard her mother hang up the receiver.

"Hello," Shelley said.

"Hi, Shelley. It's Connie," the familiar voice responded.

"Connie! How are you?" Shelley asked, surprised to hear from her.

"I'm okay, and you?" she asked. Connie's tone suggested it was not a friendly call.

"I'm fine. Connie, is there something wrong?"

"Well, quite frankly, yes, but I'm not sure I should discuss this situation with you," Connie said.

"Does it involve Neal?" Shelley asked, irritated with Connie's attitude.

"Yes, it does."

"Connie, if there is some kind of problem that involves my husband, then you'd better tell me!" she insisted.

"So...you two are married?" she asked, somewhat surprised.

"Yes, we are. Didn't you know that?"

"No, actually, I didn't." Connie paused for a moment. "Shelley, Neal has been getting some weird phone calls here."

"From who?" Shelley asked, confused.

"I think you should ask Neal that question," she suggested.

"Connie, Neal doesn't keep secrets from me," Shelley said, defending her husband.

"I hope not, Shelley, but speaking of secrets, has Neal ever mentioned some special orders he'd received from Mountain Industries?"

"Only that there were some. Why?"

"Because we just tried to deliver five million dollars worth of specially manufactured bearings to Mountain Industries, and they were refused. Mountain claimed they never ordered them," she explained.

"So, what does this mean to Neal?"

"It means that Neal turned in those orders and was paid big bonus money on them," Connie answered. "And on top of everything else, they were special order designs, made just for them, with special applications. They are of no use to anyone else."

"What are you saying?" Shelley asked, realizing that Connie was making some kind of accusation.

"I'm saying, they were bogus orders. Mountain Industries never ordered the bearings, and Neal received big bucks from P.L.K. on fictitious orders!" she exclaimed.

Shelley grew angry at Connie's attack on her husband. "I think you're right, it would be best if you spoke to Neal about this," she said.

"That's fine. As a matter of fact, why don't you have Neal call Tom, or John?" she suggested. "They're more than anxious to hear from him, and you might ask yourself, Shelley, why Neal was so determined to get you out of P.L.K. and New Jersey?" Connie added.

"Goodbye, Connie." Shelley slammed down the receiver. She was furious with Connie. She knew Neal would never do what Connie was accusing him of, and she could not wait to tell him about the phone call.

"That's just great!" Neal yelled in anger.

"Why would P.L.K. do that, Neal?" Shelley asked. The phone call haunted her that entire day.

"Don't you see?" he asked. "They must have discovered that I signed with Mountain Industries!"

"How? And what does that have to do with this situation? People do change jobs, Neal!"

"If I go with Mountain Industries, it will cost them a ton of money. They know the only reason Mountain Industries was doing business with them to begin with was because of my relationship with them! The orders they gave me were not due for delivery until June, and that's the only reason they had for refusing them now," he explained. "But, I can guarantee you, P.L.K. told Mountain Industries it was Neal Jordon who ordered an early release."

"Connie said you were already paid bonus money on those orders. Is that true?"

"Well, she lied, and she had a lot of nerve involving you in this. I just hope P.L.K. didn't ruin things for me with Mountain Industries."

"How could they do that, Neal, when you already have the job?" Shelley asked.

"If they convince Mountain Industries that I put orders in early just to get bonus money…trust me, they won't want me."

"Connie also said there has been a lot of weird phone calls at P.L.K. that somehow involve you. Do you know what that is about?"

"What kind of weird phone calls?" Neal asked, looking baffled.

"I don't know, but I got the distinct feeling she didn't mean business calls. It was as if she knew something about you that I don't."

"She was being antagonistic, Shelley. She's so jealous that we got married, she's trying to start trouble."

"But, why? I've never done anything to her."

Neal pulled her close. "Sure you did. You were her only friend and you moved, leaving her behind. On top of being friendless, she's in love with a married man. Think about it."

"But, I don't understand how P.L.K. could get away with hurting your career?"

"A libel suit could take seven years of unending litigation and attorney fees. They know they're safe. It's done everyday, Shelley."

Neal knew it was time to terminate all unfinished business with P.L.K., which meant turning in his company car and written resignation. He would have to return to Newark Airport where he parked the car in the long-term parking lot. Neal said he knew that before Connie's call.

On top of everything else, Shelley was awake most of the previous night, complaining about an upset stomach. When she refused to eat breakfast, Neal grew concerned and called for a transport van so she would not have to make the trip to the airport. She was unquestionably still disturbed about Connie's phone call.

Upon his arrival, Neal called Shelley from Newark Airport and told her that P.L.K. had already taken the Thunderbird from the airport parking lot. By doing so, P.L.K. had basically informed him that he'd been fired. There was no need for a letter of resignation.

"How are you feeling?" Neal asked. "I was so worried about leaving you while you were upset."

Shelley groaned. "Not much better. I must have the Flu, or something."

"Well, make an appointment with a doctor, and I'll go with you when I get home," he insisted.

"When will that be?" Shelley asked, hoping he had already changed his return flight for that afternoon.

"In a few days," he answered.

"Why? Where are you going? You went to New Jersey to return the car and it doesn't appear that you have to do that anymore."

"I'm going to the house to check on things there. Maybe I can get some more things packed and put in storage while I'm here."

Shelley hid her anger. She was beginning to feel sick again. "Neal, how long are you planning to stay in New Jersey?"

"Probably four days so the airfare won't be wasted. I start at Mountain Industries next week, and after that, I won't have a chance to get anything done because I'll be back on the road."

"I understand," Shelley answered, annoyed that once more, that house was an issue. "When will I hear from you again?"

"I will have to call you in the morning since the phone is off in the house."

"Okay. I'll wait to hear from you. I love you."

"I love you, too, Honey. Get some rest and I'll talk to you tomorrow morning. and don't forget to make an appointment with a doctor."

Shelley hung up the phone and ran to the bathroom in the guestroom. *Four days…I'm sure I'll feel better by then. My, God, it's just the Flu, or something,* she'd decided.

Meanwhile, Neal left the phone area of the airport to rent a car so he could drive to South Jersey. He had four days to take care of 'things'.

Chapter 18

When Neal returned to Georgia and called Mountain Industries, they withdrew their employment offer. Fortunately, Neal received a more lucrative offer with Skiff, a much larger bearing company in Atlanta. He eagerly accepted and was scheduled to start his new position on the nineteenth of April. He would spend the first two weeks in New York, learning the company's nomenclature and engineering techniques.

One afternoon, before starting at Skiff, Neal called his neighbor and friend in South Jersey to check on his house. He was told it had been vandalized. Everything was completely destroyed. Huge holes gaped in the walls, and most of the windows had been smashed. Ink had been poured on a good portion of the white carpet Neal had installed a few months before he met Shelley. The expensive furniture he'd bought one piece at a time was gashed beyond saving.

Neal's neighbor had called the Police when it happened. Neither the neighbor, nor the Police, knew how to get in touch with him once he'd left P.L.K. All the neighbor could do was wait for Neal to call.

Disheartened, Neal phoned the insurance company handling his homeowner's insurance. When a claims inspector examined the house, he advised Neal to accept any offer made on the house, selling it 'as is' if necessary. So, he called a home purchasing service and was offered just enough to pay off the mortgage balance.

I never got to see it, Shelley thought when he'd told her the house sold at a loss. Just one of those nagging details that would bother her for years to come; and although Neal no longer owned the house, seeing it, became one of her goals in life.

Meanwhile, Shelley's illness refused to disappear and finally Neal insisted she do something about it.

"Honey, I don't want to leave for New York without knowing you're okay," he pleaded.

"Neal, I'm fine. I'm sure I just caught a bug, or something silly."

Finally, after much coaxing, she gave in, and together they searched the Yellow Pages for a doctor, making an appointment for that same afternoon.

After an extensive examination, Dr. Bentley decided to run a few simple tests. Neal and Shelley were asked to sit in the waiting room while he reviewed the results. A few minutes later, Dr. Bentley invited them into his private office.

"Have a seat," he said. He got right to the point. "Congratulations, Mr. and Mrs. Jordon. You're about four weeks pregnant."

Shelley's body went numb. She looked at Neal. *My, God, he's smiling!* Neal obviously was happy, while she controlled her overwhelming need to cry.

"My nurse will give you some prenatal instructions, and you can make an appointment for next month," Dr. Bentley said. "Do you have any questions?"

Neal offered the doctor his hand as he stood to leave. "I don't think so, Doctor. We appreciate your time."

Neal seemed ecstatic. So much so, that on the way home, he was picking out names for a boy.

"My life is perfect now," Neal said, as he turned into Meg and Tim's driveway. "You're my wife, and we're going to have a baby. I can't wait to tell your parents!"

Neal will make such a wonderful father, Shelley thought. *He deserves to have children. He's so caring, and look how excited he is to tell the world that he's going to be a father!*

They joined Meg and Tim out back, on the sun deck. They were sitting on a pair of comfortable lounge chairs, enjoying the beautiful spring day.

"Hi. How did you make out with the doctor?" Meg asked. "Tell me it was nothing serious, just like I thought."

"We made out fine, Mother. I'm pregnant," Shelley said, waiting for a look of horror to appear on her Mother's face. Shelley remembered how unhappy Meg had been when Mark and his estranged wife informed her she was going to be a grandmother. She made sure they understood her baby-sitting days were over.

"Isn't it wonderful?" Neal asked, his words screaming with excitement.

"My, goodness! Why, yes, Neal that's wonderful!" Meg shouted.

Tim smacked Neal on the back, as if he had demonstrated a great stroke of genius by impregnating his daughter.

Having felt desperate to be alone since the doctor hit her with the news of her condition, Shelley said, "Neal, Listen, I'm going to take my prescriptions to the Pharmacy. I'll be right back."

"Wait, Honey! I'll drive you," Neal responded quickly.

"No, really, I would rather go myself. Besides, I think a few minutes alone will help me get my thoughts together."

Neal walked Shelley to the car. He seemed filled with apprehension.

"Are you unhappy about the baby, Shelley?" he asked, opening the car door for her. "Because if you are, I would like to talk about it. I don't want any walls between us...ever."

"I'm happy," she answered, getting into the car. "I was just taken by surprise today. I have to get used to the idea, that's all. I promise."

She hoped that was the truth, and was thankful for the time alone. She was also thankful when she backed the car out of the winding driveway without hitting her parents' mailbox. It was hard to back out of the driveway on a good day.

Inside the drugstore, Shelley gave the clerk her prescriptions, and after a brief wait, the Pharmacist handed Shelley a large container filled with unusually large pink pills. The label told her that those were her prenatal vitamins. He also gave her a smaller container of little white ones meant to stop her nausea.

She did not want to go back to her parents' house. At least not for a while, so she decided to go to their house to sit on the bridge in the backyard for a few minutes. She wanted to gather her thoughts. *Whoever you are, I'm going to show you where you're going to live,* Shelley thought, patting her stomach. She began to smile. *How could I be anything but happy about this little life growing inside of me? Isn't that part of getting married and starting a life together? Little person, I'm sorry for the way I've been acting. It's just that you showed up so soon. But, I promise I will love you with all my heart for the rest of my life!*

Shelley drove the Renault over the small incline on Steeple Drive. As the road began to decline, she saw a moving van in the driveway of the house. *Oh, good, the builder is finally moving out his furniture.*

Getting closer to the house, she saw a tricycle standing next to the large truck, and when she stopped in front of the driveway, two men were carrying a couch into the house, instead of taking it to the truck. Her body began to shake when she saw a small child climb onto the little tricycle. Someone was moving into her house.

Trembling, she knew she could not deal with whatever was going on there, and decided the best thing to do would be to go home and tell Neal what was happening. She turned the car around in the cul-de-sac at the end of Steeple Drive, and drove back to her parents' house.

This is crazy! Shelley thought. *Why would someone move into our house two weeks before our closing? There must be a logical explanation. I'm probably overreacting.*

Neal was inside the house, looking for something he could take outside to read when Shelley burst through the door.

"Shelley, what's wrong?" he asked, setting the magazine down the moment he saw her.

"Neal, someone is moving into our house!" she shouted, beginning to cry.

"What? What are you talking about?"

"I drove there after I left the Pharmacy to see if the builder had moved his things out yet. When I got there, I saw a truck in the driveway and some men carrying things into the house!"

Neal grabbed his keys off the coffee table where he'd dropped them after they'd returned from the clinic.

"I'll be back as soon as I find out what's going on!" he shouted, as he left.

"What's wrong, Shelley?" Meg asked, looking concerned. Clearly, she'd heard part of the brief conversation between Neal and her.

After Shelley explained, Tim joined them and they waited in the family room for Neal to come home with an answer. Two hours later, he returned looking totally disheartened, and Shelley knew, somehow, they'd lost their dream house.

"Shelley, sit down...please," he said with a sad tone. "The builder told me he was going to call us tonight about the house, and he was very sorry you had to find out the way you did, but he can't sell us the house."

"Why?" Shelley asked, tears once again, forming in her eyes.

"He said his sister had an emergency and needed it. He offered to build us another one at a discounted price, or sell us one of his empty homes, but I really don't want to deal with that man again after this fiasco. Can you blame me?"

Shelley's main concern was her husband. She knew what that house meant to him.

"Neal, why couldn't his sister take the empty house he offered us? We have a contract on that house. Doesn't that mean anything?"

Neal remained silent for a moment, his face grim. Finally he said, "Shelley, sometimes you just have to let things go. Yes…we could sue him, but that wouldn't get us the house, would it? Let's just go out tomorrow and find another one."

With that, Neal stormed into the guest bedroom, slamming the door behind him.

"What are you going to do now, Shelley?" Meg asked, looking confused.

"I guess Neal and I will go out tomorrow and find another house," she said.

Eventually, the truth behind the circumstances of the house lost its importance to Shelley through the excitement of building a new one.

Chapter 19

Meg and Tim insisted that Neal and Shelley continue to use the guestroom while their house was being built. Shelley knew bad feelings could develop if she lived with Meg too long. But so far, things had gone well.

Neal was happy working for Skiff. The company treated him well, and within one month, he was named Regional Manager for the entire Southeast. As the months passed, Shelley and he watched the construction of their home and the growth of their baby, near completion.

Towards the end of August, Neal's friend, Ernest Sacks, visited Atlanta on business. The two men made arrangements to have dinner together, along with their wives. Neal and Ernest met at Corpus Bearings during the start of their careers. Seven years later, Neal had left the company, while Ernest stayed.

Neal always spoke well of Ernest's wife, Donna, and after meeting her, Shelley agreed with him completely. The two women clicked instantly, feeling sure they had become friends for life. Shelley and Neal promised to spend the weekend, two weeks later, at the Sack's home in South Carolina, but plans were changed when Shelley went into premature labor. After eighteen hours of labor, Dr. Thomas, the associate on duty for Dr. Bentley, performed an emergency cesarean.

Jason had his father's blonde hair, and Shelley's blue eyes. He was beautiful, and Shelley fell instantly in love with him.

The Jordon family left the hospital and went to their new home, anxious to start their life together. Neal and Shelley felt as if they, too, were starting out their new life after living with her parents for so long. They loved spending their time entertaining Jason, and decorating their home. On the evenings that Neal was home, they would eat dinner, then take Jason for a walk in his stroller. They walked through their sub-division and enjoyed watching it grow into a beautiful neighborhood. All was well with their lives and they were both truly happy.

Eventually, Leah and Paul Renko, moved into the house across the street. Paul was a Civil Engineer for the government, and traveled just as often as Neal had to travel for Skiff. Leah and Shelley kept each other from feeling lonely, and in the process, became best friends.

When February arrived, the same sick feeling Shelley had experienced a year earlier, returned. Neal once again took a day off from work to accompany her to Dr. Bentley's office where her suspicions were confirmed. She was pregnant again. This time, both Neal and Shelley were excited, hoping desperately for a girl.

One month later, Leah informed Shelley that she too was pregnant. Shelley's due date was in September, while Leah's was in October. However, in Leah's third month, she developed complications and her doctor confirmed that she was carrying a set of twin boys, and it was doubtful that she would carry them full term.

Jacqueline Jordon was born on September twenty sixth, via cesarean. Neal arranged time off to care for Shelley, and his beautiful new daughter.

Shelley was deliriously happy with her new family. She'd agreed to a tubaligation, since age and energy, would be against her enduring another pregnancy. However, Shelley felt complete. Their lives were the closest one could imagine to living in the 'happily every after'.

The completed sub-division boasted beautifully landscaped homes in newly designed rows.

Shelley and Leah formed new friendships with three other women in the neighborhood. They attended brunches once a month alternating homes, and 'coffees' ever second Thursday night. The women were close with each other and their families, all sharing the same interests.

The following November, Leah gave birth to identical male twins, but sadly, due to the incompetence of her doctor, one was stillborn. It took Leah months to heal from the unnecessary death of her child. She was so devastated, she withdrew from the small group that had become her friends, and for six months, she spent every afternoon at the baby's grave. When Leah finally did recover, Shelley was delighted to have her friend back.

Those were the happiest years of Shelley's life. The whole world was hers with a fence around it and she thought the gate would stay closed forever. However, nothing stays the same.

Chapter 20

Fall was Shelley's favorite time of the year. She came to life in the Fall, and that particular October morning, was no exception. Shelley and Leah planned a trip to a local fabric store to buy material to make Halloween costumes for their children.

By eleven, Shelley was dressed and ready to go. From the window of her bedroom, Shelley watched as the red, white, and blue truck stopped in front of her house, for the driver to place the usual bundle of mail in her box, as he did the same time every day.

Shelley went downstairs, poured fresh coffee in her cup, then, took it with her to get the mail. She grabbed the stack of envelopes and brought them inside, throwing the pile on the kitchen table.

By the time Shelley finished dressing the children, Leah arrived at the front door, holding an excited Martin in her arms. The three children scattered towards the toy box Shelley kept in the family room.

"Would you like some coffee? I just made it." Shelley led Leah into the kitchen.

"I'd love some," she answered, reaching for a mug to help herself.

"When is Paul coming home?" Shelley asked.

"Friday night. How about Neal?"

"Friday night," she answered.

Leah saw the mail on the table and became excited. "Hey! Did you see the coupon in today's mail for the fabric store?"

"No...do we have a coupon?" Shelley glanced at the pile.

"We sure do. Look for it. I have mine, it's worth forty percent off," Leah said, always proud of her thriftiness.

Shelley began to thumb through the stack of letters leading to the junk mail. She noticed a plain, manila postcard with Neal's name written on the front, and turned it over to see who'd sent it. Shelley's eyes locked. It took her a few seconds to consume the message written on the back.

"Shelley, what is it?" Leah asked, seeing her friend's reaction to the card.

"Leah, look at this," Shelley said, handing her the postcard.

Dear Son,
It was good to see you again. Please call us at the following number...
Love, Mom and Dad.

Leah slowly placed the card on the table, shocked as Shelley by the message.

"What do you make of this? Is someone playing a joke on Neal? Who would do such a thing?" Shelley asked. "Who would play such a cruel joke on Neal?"

"I don't know. Why don't you call the phone number written on the card? That's what I would do!"

"I'm afraid to. I don't know what kind of nut wrote this!" Shelley answered.

"Shelley, I'd call right now. I wouldn't be able to stand the suspense of not knowing who sent it," Leah persisted.

"I don't know, Leah. I don't have a good feeling about this at all. I'll have to think about how to handle it."

"Are you at least going to tell Neal about it when he calls you tonight?" Leah asked.

"I don't know what to do. He won't be home for three days, and I don't want him worrying about the children and me. Also, I think it would hurt him. The death of his parents left him devastated," she answered.

"Well, I would call that number now, but that's me."

Shelley just stared at the card. Its sender had to know Neal's parents were dead. She placed the stack of mail on the kitchen counter and grabbed the children's jackets.

"Are you ready?" she called, knowing for the moment, she had to think of something else. The kids came running.

"Shelley, do you still want to go?" Leah asked, as Martin tried to free himself from his mother's grip.

"Of course, I'm fine…let's go." Shelley grabbed her purse and keys.

Throughout the day, Shelley's mind stayed focused on the postcard and what it could mean. There was another possibility, one that had not previously occurred to Shelley. What if the postcard really was from Neal's parents? *That's ridiculous,* she thought. *He would never lie to me. And what would be the reason for that? No, he's the victim of someone with a very sick sense of humor.*

Shelley was emotionally drained by the time Leah and Martin got out of her car in Leah's driveway. She went home and put the children in bed for their afternoon nap, a convenient answer to her overwhelming need to be alone and to think.

For three days, the postcard sat on Shelley's kitchen counter, tormenting her. Leah continuously urged her to call the phone number written on the card apparently to tempt her, but still, Shelley hesitated.

Besides Shelley, Leah was the only person who knew about the puzzling piece of mail. Shelley decided against telling her parents, knowing they would worry while Neal was out of town.

Finally, on Friday, Shelley decided something had to be done before Neal returned home that evening. She picked up the phone and reluctantly, with shaky hands, dialed the number.

"Hello," an older woman answered.

"Hello," Shelley replied, nervously. "May I ask who I have called?" she asked, knowing her question sounded ridiculous.

"Who are you?" the woman snapped, frightening Shelley.

"My name is Shelley Jordon," she responded, instantly regretting giving the woman her name.

"Well, my last name is Jordon too. Are we related somehow?" she asked.

"I don't know. I'm married to Neal Jordon."

Silence captured both ends of the phone.

"He's my son," the woman finally responded.

My, God! Shelley cried out inside her throbbing head. The woman's words repeated themselves in the middle of her scattered thoughts, over and over again, while they both remained silent. *He's my son…he's my son. This can't be true…why would Neal lie to me about something so horrible? My, God, there are some things even the worst of liars, wouldn't lie about. I've got such a terrible headache…I have to find out the truth!*

Something dreadful inside, assured her that the woman on the phone was not misrepresenting herself. She was, who she claimed to be, Neal's mother.

With a quivering voice, Shelley broke the silence. "Mrs. Jordon, I don't know what is going on here, but before we go any further with our conversation, can you give me any reason why your son would not want you to be a part of his life?"

Shelley wasn't sure any parent would answer that question, but she had to ask it. The woman hesitated.

"I don't know. I don't think so anyway. We've always tried to be good parents to Neal," she said.

"Mrs. Jordon, can you tell me how you got our address?" She hoped to catch the woman in some false statement that would prove her husband was not a liar.

"It wasn't easy, but we managed. We wanted to find our son," she answered, also with a quivering voice.

"Wait a minute, Mrs. Jordon. Who is, we?"

"Why, my husband, or course," she answered.

My, God, he's alive too! Shelley thought. *There never was a car accident! Why Neal? Why did you lie to me?*

Slowly, Shelley said, "Mrs. Jordon, I'm sorry, but receiving your card in the mail was a total shock to me. Neal and I have been married four years, and for some reason, you and your husband have been left out of our lives. I want to understand the reason for that. If you know why, Mrs. Jordon, please, be honest and tell me."

Bitterly, Mrs. Jordon said, "I don't know why. That's something you'll have to ask Neal. As a matter of fact, it has been just over four years since he called that Christmas morning to wish us a Merry Christmas. That was the last we heard from him. He disappeared without a trace. He'd left his job and New Jersey," she explained.

Shelley tried to remember that Christmas morning she was talking about, going back four years. It was the morning they'd become engaged. Neal had just returned from France. She remembered Neal's decision to walk to a convenience store about a mile from her parents' house, to buy some cigarettes. Tim had offered to drive him, but he'd insisted on walking, claiming he enjoyed walking when he had the time. That was the only chance Neal would have had, to call his parents. He must have used the pay phone at the store. *No wonder he didn't want a ride,* she thought.

"So, how did you find him after four years?" Shelley asked.

"We own a beach house in Atlantic City where we spend our summers. One day, my husband and I were walking on the boardwalk. We'd just sat down on a bench for a few minutes to watch the ocean, when a young man sat next to us wearing a jacket monogrammed with the name of a bearing company on its back. When we told him our son also worked for a bearing company, but that we couldn't remember which one. He asked what his name was, because he said everybody knew everybody else in the bearing industry. After we told him Neal's name, he said he knew him and told us that he worked out of Atlanta for a company named Skiff. It was a miracle," she said.

"So…then what? Did you contact him?" Shelley asked.

"Yes. It was last April. We arrived in Atlanta, found Skiff's address and walked in on him unannounced. Frankly, he looked as if he had seen a ghost!"

Shelley felt sick. *How many other secrets do you have, Neal? How could you lie about such an awful thing like the death of your parents?*

"What happened during your visit?" Shelley asked.

"Well, after a while, I noticed that Neal was keeping his left hand under his desk, and finally, I asked him if he'd gotten married. He admitted that he had."

So, the purpose of the postcard was to reach me, so I would do exactly this, Shelley thought, angry with herself for being so easily manipulated.

"Then what?" Shelley asked, trying not to show her anger so she could get as much information as she could. She knew there had to be more to the story than Mrs. Jordon's explanation.

"He told us he didn't want anything to destroy the life he'd made in Atlanta. That he was happy and he wanted to keep it that way," she answered, sounding injured.

"Why would he say that to you?" Shelley asked, again hoping for a reason. *Is this woman a problem in Neal's life?* Shelley wondered. *Are they both lying?*

"I don't know. I think he always thought that we expected too much of him, that we wanted him to be more like his grandfather," she answered.

"In what way? What was his grandfather like?"

"Well, he held a doctorate in Math and taught in the high school Neal attended. Neal always thought his grandfather hung the moon."

"What about Neal's father?" Shelley asked, remembering when Jason was born how Neal had cried and said he wished his father were still alive to see his new grandson.

"His father is retired now, but he was President of a bank in Pennsylvania," she answered, proudly.

"Why would Neal feel bad about himself? He's not that kind of person," Shelley asked in her husband's defense.

"Who knows? Neal has always been a hard nut to crack. Perhaps it was the accident."

"What accident?" Shelley asked, innocently.

"Why, the fire accident," she replied.

"What fire accident, Mrs. Jordon?"

"Goodness, I thought Neal would have told you about that. It happened when Neal was a child. Eight years old to be exact. We went to our town's fourth of July celebration held in the local park. We were expected to go, being so heavily involved with the Chamber of Commerce and all. A little boy and girl, started a ground fire to roast some marshmallows on a path leading to the woods that surrounded the park. Neal innocently, walked past them when the little girl, somehow, fell into the fire. She was severely burned. but, the ordeal began when before she died, she claimed Neal had pushed her into the fire. Thank God, everyone knew she was hallucinating from the enormous amount of drugs she'd been given. Nothing came of it. The little boy that was there, refused to say anything about it, they said he was too traumatized. However, some of the kids in school harassed Neal for many years, calling him a murderer, and he took it very hard."

"Oh, my God! How terrible for Neal! I didn't know anything about that. It still must be upsetting to him."

"Oh, my, I hope I haven't told tales out of school," Mrs. Jordon said, unable to hide the pleasure in her voice, knowing that was exactly what she'd done.

Shelley did not want to hear any more details about the death of the little girl.

"Did Neal tell you we have two children?" Shelley asked, wondering how much of their life Neal had shared with them during their surprise visit.

"No! He didn't!" the woman shouted with excitement. "Oh, my goodness, boys, or girls?"

"Actually, both. We have a son, who is three, and a daughter that's two."

"What are their names?"

"Jason and Jacqueline," Shelley answered.

"Oh, that's wonderful! Hold on for a second so I can tell my husband."

Shelley fought back tears as she heard Neal's mother share the happy news with her husband. She'd been offered no explanation for what was happening, and none for Neal's horrendous deceit. She felt confused and sick with grief.

A few minutes later, Mrs. Jordon returned to the phone. "He's so happy! We desperately wanted more grandchildren."

"Yes, of course, Mrs. Jordon, I'm sorry. I'm sure Allen's death hurt you as much as it has Neal," Shelley said, softly.

"Allen? Whose Allen?"

Suddenly, Shelley felt cold. So cold, her legs went numb. She quickly stretched the phone cord so she could sit in one of the kitchen chairs.

"Neal's son," Shelley answered, her voice quivering.

"Allen? Neal doesn't have a son named Allen. His son's name is Jeffrey, and he's not dead. My, God, where did you get such an awful idea?" she asked, horrified.

Jeffrey. Jeffrey? Oh, my God...the wedding rehearsal! When the minister's son jumped on the altar, Neal yelled out the name Jeffrey! she remembered.

"Mrs. Jordon, is there any possibility that you and your husband could visit Atlanta again?" Shelley asked. She had to meet these people. One thing Shelley was sure of, was that she was definitely speaking with Neal's mother.

"Yes, of course. We'd love to. When would you like us to come?" she asked, sounding excited.

"As soon as possible," Shelley answered. She wanted the truth, and sitting face to face with them, apparently, would be her only hope of getting it.

"Wait just a minute. Let me ask my husband."

Shelley listened as the woman lowered the receiver and whispered, "When can we visit Neal and his family?"

Mrs. Jordon returned to the phone. "Would two weeks from today be okay?" she asked. "We could get there on Friday and leave Sunday. How's that?"

"That's great. I'll certainly look forward to meeting you, and if you give me your address, I'll send directions from Interstate 85, once you reach the Georgia border."

Shelley made sure she got their address before she ended the conversation. She wanted an explanation for her husband's dishonesty. Mrs. Jordon sounded genuinely enthusiastic about seeing her son again, and meeting her new grandchildren.

Why all the lies, Neal? How could you lie about your son being dead? She felt as though she no longer knew the man she was living with, and began to cry for the loss. She wanted to return to the place she'd lived before the postcard arrived, but in her heart, she knew things would never be the same again in her marriage. Something major had been destroyed...trust.

Chapter 21

Neal was waiting outside the Baggage Claim, as usual, when Shelley picked him up at the airport. After he put his bags into the trunk of the car, he opened the door for Shelley and she walked around to the passenger seat, enabling him to drive.

"Hi, Honey," Neal said, as he kissed her. "Hi, guys," he said to the children strapped in their car seats in the back. They smiled to greet him. Neal always seemed so excited to be home on Friday nights, and after all, everything was still normal for him.

"Ready?" he asked, grinning, patting his wife's hand

"I'm ready," Shelley answered somberly, hating him for being so happy. *It's a lie, Neal. This day, and all our other days…have all been lies.*

"Are you okay?" Neal asked. Shelley could sense he was wondering why she'd answered him with such indifference. He edged his way into the Friday night traffic.

"I'm fine," Shelley answered, trying to keep what little composure she had left.

"No, you're not…come on, what's bothering you?" Watching as cars raced in and out of traffic, Neal complained. "Look at this! Nobody lets anyone in! They'll total out their cars just to get one car length ahead of another driver!"

Shelley's voice trembled with the urge to cry. It took all her determination, not to burst into tears. "Neal, something came up while you were out of town."

"What is it?" he asked, impatiently.

"We'll discuss it when we get home," she said, avoiding his eyes. The duration of the ride home was quiet. A feeling of ruin possessed the moment.

When everything was settled at home and the children were asleep for the night, Shelley retrieved the postcard from the kitchen drawer where she'd placed it earlier that morning.

Neal unpacked, then took his usual place on the couch, turning on the television with the remote he managed to control every weekend.

Shelley slowly walked over and handed him the piece of mail. He read it, then looked at her. The look on his face said it all. Plainly, he was mentally questioning how much she already knew.

"I see," he said, turning off the television. He closed his eyes as they filled with tears. "She had to do it," he moaned in a barely audible whisper. "I told her I didn't want anything to destroy my life with you and she couldn't resist it!"

"Neal, I want to know why. No, I need to know why, you lied to me and the rest of the world about your parents being dead!"

Shelley felt a release of the anguish that had filled her heart since the card arrived five days earlier.

"Did you call them, Shelley?" he asked.

"Yes, I did. I had to. You see, I was stupid enough to think some horrible person was playing a cruel joke on my wonderful husband!" Shelley yelled.

"Shelley, leave it alone!" he said, tears running down his face.

"How can I leave it alone?" she asked, collapsing to the floor in front of him.

"I'm happy, Shelley. Can you understand that? I don't want anything to come between us...ever," he responded.

"Please, explain this to me. How would your parents being involved in our lives do that, Neal? What made you think dishonesty wouldn't come between us?"

"My mother can start trouble in an empty room. We don't need her in our lives. Trust me."

"Well, I'm sorry. I can't trust you anymore. Besides that, it's too late. I've invited them to visit us in two weeks, and they've accepted."

Neal stood up, his face red with anger. "You'd better be lying, Shelley!"

"Sorry, Neal. I'm not lying." Shelley also stood. "They're coming because I want them to come. That will be the only way I can find out the truth about my husband!"

Neal grabbed Shelley's arms and shook her. "How dare you! Are you crazy? You can just call them again, and tell them to stay the hell home!"

He stood in front of her, staring at her for a moment before he was able to speak again.

"Well, get ready. Because now you're going to find out what trouble really is. I won't be here when they come," he said, pushing her out of his way, causing her to bump into the wall behind her.

Neal stormed out the front door as Shelley continued to cry. She heard him drive away in a fury, as if he were the one betrayed.

An hour later, Neal returned. Shelley had gone to bed, emotionally drained from the events of the week and the argument she had with Neal, but was unable to sleep.

He knelt beside the bed, taking her hand into his. When she opened her eyes, Neal whispered gently. "Shelley, I'm sorry. I treated you dreadfully. I know that. But, Honey, this visit can't happen."

"I'm your wife, Neal," Shelley answered, propping her head up with her arm. "I deserve an explanation, don't you think? Your children have not had the opportunity to meet their other grandparents. Good, or bad we need to meet them."

"Honey, there's just too much to explain. You don't know her! My mother has ruined every good thing that has ever taken place in my life." He turned away from her.

"How Neal? Will you at least answer me that?"

"When I was married to Arlene, she drove me crazy! My mother habitually called me at work to complain about Arlene, trying to start arguments between Arlene and me."

"That's ridiculous. You're a grown man. You could have controlled that." Shelley wasn't buying Neal's story.

"I did, by keeping her out of my life, because that's the only thing that works with her," he answered, pausing for a moment. He closed his eyes, trying to hide the tears forming in them.

"Okay, Shelley, you win. You're not going to change your mind. Let them come, but be prepared for trouble, because I can guarantee you there will be plenty."

Somehow Shelley knew it wasn't over yet. That somehow, Neal would try to stop his parent's visit, and make it look as though it were their idea.

Later, Shelley had to wonder what would have happened if Neal had won that argument. If she had listened to him and canceled the Jordon's visit to Atlanta.

Chapter 22

Shelley grew apprehensive when the white Thunderbird, pulled into the driveway. She glimpsed through the lace curtains on the living room windows as the elderly couple climbed out of the car. She waited until they rang the doorbell, then, opened the door.

Mrs. Jordon, brushed past Shelley without saying a word. She was not what Shelley had anticipated. Perhaps because of her slightly husky voice on the phone, she'd imagined a much larger woman. However, she was no taller than Shelley, and her frame was just as small.

Neal showed no resemblance to his mother. She had steel-gray hair, perfectly arranged with a coating of hair spray meant to last. Her hazel eyes cut through Shelley, making her feel uncomfortable. When she saw Jason and Jackie playing on the living room floor, she shouted with delight.

"Oh, my goodness! Neal, look at our grandchildren! Aren't they beautiful?"

"Yes, they're wonderful! You must be Shelley," the man said, extending his hand to her with a smile.

My, God, Neal is a clone of his father, Shelley thought. "And I can tell by looking at you that you're Neal's father," Shelley said, returning his smile.

"I'm Mattie Jordon, Neal's mother," the woman interrupted.

"Yes, it's so nice to meet you. I prepared lunch for us," Shelley responded.

Shelley knew it would take time to learn about Neal's family, but she was haunted with determination to get some answers before they returned to Pennsylvania. They spent that afternoon exchanging guarded information and Shelley gave a sigh of relief when Neal finally arrived home.

He walked in the door with a look of panic. Unbeknownst to Shelley, he had called his mother from his office when he'd returned to work the Monday after she'd told him of the pending visit. He chastised his mother for sending the card and told her not to come to Atlanta. True to the woman's nature, she came anyway.

Neal put on a great act. He seemed ecstatically happy to see his parents. Shelley noticed there was no exchange of affection. No kisses, no hugs, or tears of joy. As a matter of fact, they never touched one another, and Shelley found that peculiar since they had not seen each other for quite some time.

She served dinner, and by eight thirty, the children were exhausted from the active day. When Shelley tucked them into their beds, they seemed truly thankful to be there.

She joined Neal and his parents in the family room. They were whispering in a very obvious deep conversation that stopped when she walked in. Not long after that, the Jordons excused themselves to go to bed.

"I was hoping to get some answers tonight," Shelley told Neal as they prepared for bed.

"Just what kind of answers do you need to get, Shelley?" he asked, frightening her.

"Why did you lie to me? Why did you tell me your parents were dead? This is serious! For four years we have been living a lie…I have to know the truth if we are ever going to move on."

Totally unprepared for Neal's reaction, Shelley gasped as Neal pushed her onto the bed.

"You won't ask them, or me anything again, do you understand? It's none of your business what took place before I met you!"

Shelley slowly sat up, bewildered by what had just taken place. "Neal, I don't understand what has happened to us. I feel you have some kind of evil past that you don't want to me to know about. I don't know who you are anymore. The man I married is gone, and I'm afraid I may never get him back!"

Neal covered his face with his hands. "Shelley, please…I'm begging you, let's just get through this lousy visit with as little trouble as possible so we can get back to where we were."

Shelley was scared, she felt as though the most precious thing in her life, her family, was in danger, and for some reason, she knew the source of that danger came from Pennsylvania.

"I don't know if we can, Neal. I honestly don't know," she answered softly.

The next morning after breakfast, Neal took his father for a walk through the neighborhood. Shelley realized any chance of gaining information, stood with Neal's mother. Surprisingly, Mattie Jordon seemed just as anxious to talk with her.

"Well, now that we're finally alone, woman to woman, tell me about your relationship with my son."

Her smile had a devious edge to it. and Shelley felt justified in not trusting her.

"Like what? What would you like to know?" Shelley asked, not sure just what her relationship with this woman should be. But she wanted answers.

"Well, such as...how did you two meet each other?" she asked.

Shelley spent fifteen minutes giving her mother-in-law the details of their meeting.

Hesitantly, she asked her mother-in-law, "Mrs. Jordon, why do you think Neal avoided contact with you when he returned from France?" She thought that was a good place to start.

The woman hesitated before answering. Apparently, she also felt the need to be careful. "You'll have to ask Neal that question, Shelley. Surely, I wouldn't know."

Shelley shook her head. "I don't understand all this secrecy," she said.

"Well, Neal's father and I don't understand a lot of things, but I guess we have to accept that, don't we? And...so will you," she answered, smugly.

Shelley was stunned by her mother-in-law's response. She was being treated like a stranger. The people in her home frightened her. She knew somehow, the cruel woman sitting in front of her had the power to end the happiness she had with Neal, and because of that, she prudently watched her husband for the remainder of the grueling weekend. She watched him interact with the parents he claimed were evil, in a way only they could understand, while she remained excluded from any of their significant conversations. She apparently posed some kind of odd threat to the Jordon's obscure secrets. They did not want intruders, and Shelley knew she was definitely one.

Without consulting Shelley, the Jordons decided to leave Monday morning instead of Sunday night, as planned.

That morning, Shelley came downstairs to make breakfast for everyone, and overheard an argument taking place between Neal and his mother. Quietly, without being noticed, she slipped into the laundry room in the hall, hoping to hear what was being said.

"What am I supposed to tell the others?" Mrs. Jordon asked Neal, apparently annoyed with her son.

"I don't expect you to tell them anything. It's none of your business!" he snapped.

"Well, it's hard watching every word, or constantly trying to remember who I'm talking to. I'm warning you, Neal, you'd better fix this mess!" she demanded.

With that, Shelley's arm slipped, slamming against the door, ruining any chance of their discussion continuing. She had no choice but to join them.

At seven o'clock, Neal, briefcase in hand, tearfully said goodbye to his long lost parents before leaving for work.

Why are they staying? Why don't they leave with him? Shelley asked herself.

Mrs. Jordon returned to the dining room table and asked Shelley for another cup of coffee, while Mr. Jordon carried their suitcases to the car. Shelley wished the children would wake up so she could busy herself with them instead of Neal's mother.

"I do have one question for you, Shelley," the woman said with the planned precision of an attacking tiger.

"What's that?" Shelley asked, suspiciously.

"With Neal traveling all the time, don't you worry about other women?"

What a witch! Shelley thought. *What is wrong with this family?*

"No, Mrs. Jordon, I don't worry about that at all. Why would you ask me something like that?" she asked, upset and insulted for her husband.

"Because, Neal has always liked women, and traveling gives him plenty of opportunity to meet new ones," she answered, with a twinkle in her eye, definitely in her element. "Neal requires a lot of love and attention, ever since his grandmother's unusual death."

"His grandmother's death?" Shelley asked, completely puzzled. "What did her grandmother's death have to do with Neal?"

"Why, he was there both times," she answered, once again, as if Shelley already knew what she was talking about. "The first time when the oven blew up, and the second time when she'd hung herself in the basement."

"Neal's grandmother hung herself?" Shelley asked horrified.

"Yes, poor thing, but you must understand why. She was lighting her brand new gas oven, and it exploded in her face. She was never the same after that. The doctor said she had a lot of brain damage, and poor Neal, just ten years old, saw the explosion. Then, as if that wasn't bad enough, two years later; while Neal was visiting her again, she went downstairs to get a jar of Neal's favorite preserves, when an hour later she had not returned. Neal went to look for her, and there she was, swinging from the rafters in the basement."

"Swinging from the rafters? And Neal was there both times?" Shelley gasped, feeling dizzy. "What went wrong with the oven?"

Neal never told her how his grandmother died, only that he had loved her more than his own mother.

"Apparently, she turned on the gas and forgot about it. When she tried to light the pilot, it blew up. The sad part was Neal's grandfather, Doc, had just finished building the house. It was the house they'd always wanted. Of course, Neal was upset that his grandparents no longer lived within walking distance for him to visit every day, but his father and I made sure he got to see them as much as possible. Fortunately, Neal was sitting in another room when he heard the explosion. He ran to the kitchen and found his grandmother holding her face, screaming. Third degree burns from the neck up. He called the operator for help, since nobody had 911 yet. The operator, then, called the Police, who sent an ambulance."

"What did they say happened?" Shelley asked. *How could so many awful things happen to one child?* Shelley asked herself. There was so much horror and death surrounding Neal's life. Beginning with the death of the little girl in the park, and then his grandmother. Perhaps by eliminating his parents from his life, he was able to eliminate the past.

"They said what I already told you, that she had turned on the gas, and forgot about it. She was lucky it didn't turn out worse than it did.

The whole house could have burned down and both she and Neal could have been killed. Thank God, Neal had enough sense to turn off the gas."

"My, God, that's so awful!" Shelley exclaimed. Suddenly, she felt the chill of evil Neal had warned her about, but she couldn't explain why. Something didn't feel right.

When her in-laws finally stood to leave, she was relieved the visit had come to an end. Escorting them to their car, she watched her father-in-law start the engine. Mrs. Jordon rolled down her window and said, We'll see you in two weeks!"

Taken by surprise, Shelley panicked. "What do you mean?"

"Well, as you know, Neal competes in the Senior Track competitions. He's won several awards, you know, even some Olympic medals. Well, he has a race in Atlanta in two weeks, and Neal Junior insisted we stay with you that weekend. Of course, we accepted," she answered, smiling.

Mr. Jordon waved, pulled his car out of the driveway, and sped away.

Chapter 23

The three days following the Jordon's visit were extraordinarily unusual. Neal's attitude completely changed, introducing a person Shelley didn't like. He was short tempered, and always felt either angry or depressed.

Shelley also could not shake the uneasiness she felt about the death of Neal's grandmother. It astonished her that a seventy year old woman, supposedly suffering from severe brain damage, could make a noose, climb up on top of a chair, then hang herself. It bothered her, but she kept her thoughts to herself, knowing how much her death affected Neal.

The next morning, Neal told Shelley he was driving her car to work to have it serviced while he was at the office. He left Shelley his company car, which was not unusual. Therefore, no antennas went up in Shelley's mind suggesting that something might be wrong.

Nine o'clock that evening, Neal still had not arrived home, troubling Shelley as she put the children to bed. She was going to call his office, when suddenly, he burst through the front door, out of breath.

"Close your eyes!" he said, with excitement.

"Why?" Shelley asked, glad to see her husband smile again for whatever reason.

Taking Shelley's hand, he began to lead her outside. "I have a surprise for you."

"What is it?" she asked, closing her eyes.

"Just keep your eyes closed. Let me lead you," he said.

Shelley did as he asked. When they reached the driveway, he yelled, "Surprise!"

Shelley opened her eyes, and hoped they were deceiving her.

Parked in the driveway was an aqua blue truck with gold flames and eagles painted on its front and sides. A huge, gold eagle covered the hood, and the beige, velvet interior included curtains on the cabin window, where pieces of large chain performed as tiebacks.

"Where is my car, Neal?" Shelley asked, hoping her instincts were mistaken.

"Where do you think it is? I traded it in for this truck!" he answered, as if she should have automatically known that.

"You traded my car for this redneck wagon?" Shelley asked, raging with anger.

"This truck is one of a kind! It was designed for shows and exhibits!"

"Neal, I won't drive this. I hate it!" she yelled as she went back into the house. She ran upstairs, sobbing, as he followed her, shouting.

"You're an ungrateful bitch, Shelley! You don't appreciate a damn thing I do for you!"

Shelley slammed their bedroom door. Right behind her, Neal kicked it open. Standing in the doorway with his hands on his hips, he glared at her. She was spread across the bed, crying. Everything sad that Shelley had been holding inside her heart released itself in her sobbing. The postcard, the lies, the visit from Neal's parents, his horrible behavior…all of these things, carried heavy tears.

After a few moments, Shelley spoke, her voice shivering with unhappiness.

"Neal, you never asked me you just did it. The same way you invited your parents to visit us again. We haven't had a meaningful discussion since they left."

"Look, I saw the truck and fell in love with it. I honestly thought you would too!"

"Why? What would make you think any woman would love that truck?" Shelley asked, knowing he really had not given her feelings any thought.

"Because I love it, and if it was something that would make you happy, I would want you to have it," he responded.

"No, you wouldn't, Neal, because if you worried about making me happy, you would never have bought it to begin with! You would sit down and discuss the deterioration of our marriage, and you would tell me the truth about the things I have a right to know!"

Neal's expression hardened with anger. "Well, that's just too bad,

Shelley, because that's not going to happen. You'll have to drive the truck and be thankful you have it!"

The visit from Neal's parents had changed many things. Shelley wished she had never called them that Friday morning that seemed so long ago. If one visit caused so much damage, Shelley had to wonder what a second visit would do.

The next morning, Neal tried to act as though everything were normal. He got ready for work, then ventured downstairs for his morning coffee. He used the same coffee mug he'd used every morning since the beginning of their marriage. It had 'number one husband' printed on it.

"Can you take my shirts to the cleaners today?"

"In what, Neal?" she asked, sarcastically.

"In your new truck."

"It's not my new truck. It's your new truck. I'm not driving it," Shelley informed him.

Neal paused, deep in thought, sipping his coffee as he leaned against the kitchen counter.

"All right, I'll take the truck to work today, and you can have my car. I want to show it off anyway."

He picked up the truck keys sitting on the counter, replacing them with the keys to his company car. "I'll be home around seven," he said, walking out.

From the window in their living room, Shelley watched Neal leave. The big, gold eagle painted on the back of the truck grew smaller as he reached the end of the street. It took Shelley ten minutes to place an ad in the newspaper, advertising the sale of the truck. Until it sold, she decided she would avoid driving.

When the Jordons arrived for their second visit a week later, Shelley felt sick. She had hoped a miracle would cancel their visit. As she was making lunch an hour after their arrival, the phone rang. It was an inquiry about the truck. The caller was woman, looking for something unique to use for her maid service business. Shelley assured her the truck was definitely different, and within an hour, the woman arrived with a cashier's check in her hand to buy it. The Jordons watched, visibly confused as to why Neal would buy a brand new truck, then sell it at a depreciated price a week later.

Shelley watched the woman drive the truck away and immediately went to the phone to call Neal at his office, hoping to avoid a scene in front of his parents.

Neal picked up his private line.

"Neal, I have something to tell you about the truck," she said, quickly. Shelley's courage began to fade with the sound of his voice. Also, to her dismay, Neal's mother had stopped playing with the children in order to hear her phone conversation. No doubt, she'd hoped the sale of the truck would cause trouble between them.

"What about it? You didn't have an accident, did you?"

"No, I sold it," she said, waiting for his response.

"You'd better be kidding, Shelley," he said, as if she were joking.

"No, Neal, I'm not...I sold it," she said again.

Neal suddenly realized Shelley was telling the truth. She could almost visualize his body stiffening with the anger he was forced to control.

"Shelley, I promise...we will do more than talk about this when I get home," he said, tightly.

"Good! That sounds great. We can argue in front of your dead parents," Shelley retaliated. "Because, in case you forgot, they're here again," she added caustically.

Later that afternoon while he was still at the office, a Real Estate agent called to set up an appointment to do a market analysis on their home. Shelley was stunned by the call as the Realtor explained how Neal had phoned her earlier, requesting she call his wife to arrange a convenient time for it to be done. Once gain, Neal had a surprise for her.

Chapter 24

The weekend with Neal's parents was terrible. Slowly, Neal was becoming a stranger to Shelley. If she could have turned back time to the morning she'd picked up the phone to call the Jordons, she would have burned the postcard, no questions asked.

When Shelley confronted Neal with her feelings, his answer was always the same.

"Look, you knew how I felt about bringing those people into our lives, but you insisted on doing it anyway, so now, you'll have to live with the consequences of that. It's not like I didn't warn you."

He spent the first night of his parents' visit, pretending everything was perfect, refusing any discussion about the sale of the truck until they were alone in their bedroom. They were getting ready for bed when she addressed it.

"We have things to talk about, Neal."

"Like what, Shelley? The sneaky way you sold my truck?"

Shelley retaliated. "It was no more sneaky then the way you bought it, Neal!"

Neal grabbed Shelley's arm, and with hatred in his eyes, told her, "Look, I'm not going to argue with you while my parents are here. After they leave, we'll discuss whatever you want to discuss. Until then, keep your mouth shut!"

Shelley pulled her arm out of Neal's grasp, staring at the stranger in her bedroom. Neal's behavior frightened her, causing her to cry as he crawled into bed beside her.

She believed Neal's bad treatment towards her, pleased his mother, and that Neal knew it. She was aware of her mother-in-law's contempt for her, no matter how unjustified the woman's feelings were. Shelley also knew that Mrs. Jordon had some mysterious, privileged information about her son that generated unfailing loyalty from him in exchange for her silence.

That was the first night Neal and Shelley had slept with their backs towards each other. Neal kept his unspoken promise to his mother and breached the one he'd made to her at the altar four years earlier.

Monday morning, Shelley stayed upstairs until she was sure her in-laws were gone, quietly playing with her children, so everyone would think they were still sleeping.

She heard Mrs. Jordon ask Neal at the bottom of the stairs as she was leaving, if he thought it was unhealthy for Shelley and the children to sleep so much. After that, the Jordons walked out, and not a moment too soon for Shelley.

"Well, that was a nice display of rudeness," Neal said when Shelley finally brought the children downstairs.

Jackie ran to her father, and Shelley watched as he pushed her away from his newly pressed suit.

"I wasn't rude to your parents, Neal, but I won't tolerate anyone trying to cause trouble in my home. Quite frankly, I don't understand why you do," Shelley said, putting the children in their seats at the table. She gave them a piece of apple to nibble on while she prepared their breakfast.

"I haven't tolerated anything, Shelley. I'm just not letting my parents affect me anymore. Those days are over. And, I might add, I told you so."

Shelley winced. "The purpose for inviting them was for me to find out why you lied to me. But, all I got was a very distinct feeling that there's some wicked, morbid secrets in your family that I'll never know."

"Shelley, you don't have to know about my family. You should have accepted things the way they were, but you didn't. Now, we both have to deal with the results of that," he said.

Neal picked up his briefcase to leave, and Shelley stopped him. "Neal, please, don't leave until we've talked," she begged.

Neal placed his suit jacket on a chair to keep it from creasing and looked at his wife for a moment. He took her in his arms, and she was relieved when she still felt the overwhelming love between them that was there before the Jordons entered their lives.

"I'm sorry, Honey. My mother brings out the worst in me," Neal whispered, slowly kissing her forehead.

"Well, Obviously, you were right. Maybe we should stay away from them. Keep things the way they were. Let's just end our relationship with them now, before it's too late," she pleaded.

"I'll go along with that," he said, smiling. "I love you, Shelley. I can't imagine my life without you."

"I love you, too, Neal," she responded. Then, she remembered the phone call from the Realtor. "Oh! Our next issue. What's this about selling the house?" she asked, leaning back to see his expression.

"I think it's a good idea, Honey. This long ride back and forth to the office when I'm in town is really getting to me, and I think it's time for a step up," he answered, quite seriously.

"Step up? But, Neal, I love this house, and what about my friendship with Leah? She helps me get through the days you're gone. We brought our children home from the hospital to this house and finally after four years, I have it decorated the way I want it."

Shelley, I've worked hard to get us where we are financially, and we deserve a nice home," he argued. "You'll make new friends, you always do."

"But, we have a nice home," Shelley responded, feeling a little insulted. Just as he had worked hard, so had she at making the house a nice place to come home to.

"I want a better one. There's a community called 'Peach Haven', on the South side of the airport. It's supposed to be beautiful. I would like it if you would at least check it out. Just on speculation, how's that? Okay?"

"And, how do you expect me to get there when I don't have a car?" she asked.

"You had a car, you just chose to sell it," Neal answered, curtly.

"And when are you going to shop for another one?" she asked, getting exasperated.

"When I have the time. Meanwhile, you can drive me to work tomorrow, and use the company car since I'll be in town this week," Neal replied. He picked up his suit jacket one more time.

"Neal, I really don't want to move. I don't want to look for a new house," Shelley said.

"And I don't want to shop for a new car," he responded, leaving the house.

They'd both meant what they said.

Chapter 25

Three weeks had passed since the sale of the truck, and true to his word, Neal made no effort to buy Shelley another car.

I'm sick of Neal controlling whether I get a car, or not! Shelley thought, as she lifted the yellow pages out of the hall closet. She started to call local dealerships. All the salesmen she spoke with, said the same thing.

"Come in and we'll give you a good deal."

Only one was willing to discuss selling her a car over the phone.

The man mentioned a yellow station wagon with brown, leather interior, fully loaded and naturally, it was ready to leave the lot with the right buyer.

"Would you deliver it?" Shelley asked. There was a moment of silence before the salesman started to laugh.

"Let me guess, Tom put you up to this, right?"

"Whose Tom? No, Sir, I'm serious," she said. "If you would be kind enough to drive the car to my house, we can go to the bank, and I'll get a cashier's check to pay for the car. Then, I'll take you back to your dealership."

The man listened to Shelley's offer. "Hold on a minute, I'll have to talk to my manager about this one," he said, sounding amused.

Two hours later, Shelley returned the salesman to his dealership in her new car, a Dodge Aspen.

When the clock in the living room chimed seven times, it was already dark outside. Shelley panicked when she saw the headlights of Neal's car pull into the driveway. She was sure they would have an awful battle once he found out she'd bought a car without him. She'd planned to break the news about the car gently, perhaps over dinner.

Neal walked into the house, slamming the door behind him. He looked at Shelley and walked directly towards the door leading to the garage from the kitchen.

Oh, my God! He saw the reflection of the car through the curtains on the garage window! I forgot about that!

When Neal saw the station wagon, he looked at Shelley. His face flushed deep red. She knew he was getting ready to explode.

"How dare you do this!" Neal said, his voice shaking with anger.

Shelley tried to hide her fear, "Neal, I tried calling you all afternoon at your office and nobody knew where you were."

"No, stupid, because I was out, buying you a car!" he shouted, furiously.

"What? Why, were you buying another car without taking me?" she shouted back. "Does my opinion, or feelings, mean anything to you at all?"

"Look," Neal said. "I bring home the money in this house, therefore, I make the decisions! Whatever I decide to buy you to drive is what you'll drive. Do you understand that?"

"No, I don't understand that. Or, you. And I'm done trying to!" Shelley shouted. Angrily, she walked out of the kitchen.

Neal came after her. Grabbing her arm, he quickly spun her around. When Shelley yanked her arm free, he grabbed it back, pulling her into the family room against her will. She could not believe what was happening. Frightened, she struggled to get away from him.

She screamed at Neal to let go of her arm. He didn't. She felt Neal's fist strike her chin instead, the blow and the physical pain, knocked her to the floor. She blinked at him in total shock as Neal stood over her with a look of disbelief on his face. Obviously, he could not believe what he'd done either.

Managing to get back to her feet, Shelley ran to the hall bathroom and locked the door. Wiping the blood from her mouth, all she could do was cry. Within moments, she heard the front door slam, and a few minutes later she heard Neal's car leave. Slowly, she came out of the bathroom. Her entire life, she had never been hit by anyone, and overwhelmed, she knew she had to leave Neal immediately. Their marriage was over.

Quickly, she gathered some of the children's things, shoving them into an overnight bag, hoping to be finished and out of the house, before Neal came home. *Why do we have to leave? Why can't he go?* she thought bitterly.

"Mama...what are we doing?" Jason asked, sleepily rubbing his eyes as Shelley woke him.

"Baby, I'm so sorry...but we're going to take a little trip. Would you like that?" she asked, her voice trembling.

"Where will we go?" Jason asked, sweetly.

"Well, how would you like to see Aunt Donna and Uncle Ernest?"

Shelley knew South Carolina would be the last place Neal would look for them.

"Why are you crying, Mommy?" Jason asked, wiping her tears away with his little hand. "Mommy, where did you get that boo boo?" he asked.

"Mommy fell, Honey...it's all right." She smiled, trying not to frighten him.

When she finished dressing Jason, she quickly ran into Jackie's room to get her dressed. She had no idea where Neal had gone and could not predict when he would return. She only knew she had to be out of the house before he did. The last thing she wanted was to have another physical confrontation in front of the children.

Shelley lifted Jackie from her crib, her mind in turmoil. She knew they wouldn't arrive in South Carolina before midnight. Urgently, she dressed Jackie, and with a child in each arm, carried both children and the bag downstairs, keeping the garage door closed until she'd strapped the children into their car seats. She felt the urgent need to keep running and didn't slow down until she'd reached the highway. By that time, the children, once again, had fallen asleep.

Shelley sobbed during the four hour ride to South Carolina. As soon as she got off the highway in Kingston, she searched for a public phone to call Donna. She realized it was twelve thirty and felt awful about waking her, but she didn't know what else to do.

"Donna, I'm sorry to wake you. This is Shelley."

"Well, hey! What's wrong? Are the babies okay?" she asked, half asleep.

"They're okay, but we need to stay with you for a few days, if that's okay."

"Sure, Honey. You come on!" Donna said, beginning to wake up.

"Donna, I'm already here."

"What do you mean, you're already here? What's happened?" Donna asked fully awake then.

"I mean, I just got off the highway in Kingston," Shelley answered.

"Are the kids with you?"

Shelley started to cry again. "Yes, they're asleep in the car."

"Shelley, what's wrong? Are you okay?"

"No...not really," she said, sobbing. "I'll explain everything to you when I get there. Just, please, don't call Neal."

"I won't, Honey. Come on. I'll put some coffee on. Do you remember how to get to the house?"

"I think so. I'll call if I get lost."

"I can meet you where you are if you want. I don't want you riding around with those babies in the car, lost somewhere at midnight."

"No, really, I'm fine...see you in a little bit." Shelley hung up.

Donna helped Shelley put the children to bed in the spare bedroom, then put her arm around Shelley's shoulder. "Let's talk," she said as she led Shelley into the kitchen where the coffee was waiting.

"What's happened to your face, Shelley?" Donna asked, as soon as the coffee was poured.

"Neal and I had an argument," she answered, hiding her mouth with her hands as she spoke. "I don't think he meant to do it."

"Who cares if he meant to do it, or not. He did it. It wasn't necessary, was it?" She looked away in disgust. "I'm so disappointed in Neal. I've known him for years and didn't think he was capable of doing such a thing."

Embarrassed, Shelley spilled out the whole story about Neal's parents being alive, the awful visits, and the argument about the car.

"My, God! What's going on with him?" Donna asked, clearly appalled by Shelley's story.

"Maybe I provoked him, buying the car the way I did. I guess it was wrong," Shelley answered, sadly. "I just don't know."

Irritated, Donna said, "Shelley, no woman provokes that kind of treatment, under any circumstances. Neal could have left the house before he hit you."

"Well, I don't know what to do. I have to get my head clear." She looked at Donna and tried to smile. "Are you up to a visit from us?"

Donna smiled and patted her friend's hand. "Of course, silly. You're welcome here anytime you want to come, and I agree, you need to get your head together before you go home. Neal also needs to think a little bit about what he's done."

"If he calls, what are you going to say?" Shelley asked. "I don't want him to know where we are right now."

"You don't think he'll figure it out?" Donna asked.

"Maybe, but by that time, I hope to be ready to talk to him. I'm not now," Shelley answered.

"And that's just what I'll tell him when he calls. I think that's understandable under the circumstances. We have plenty of room and this will give me time with those precious babies of yours," Donna said, affectionately.

Shelley awakened the next morning to find her children missing. Throwing on the bathrobe she'd stuffed into the bag the night before, she found everyone in the kitchen. Trilla, Donna's thirteen year old daughter, was already feeding Jackie and Jason breakfast.

"Did you think someone came in during the night and stole your kids?" Donna asked laughing when she saw Shelley standing in the doorway looking relieved.

"I'm sorry I slept so late. Thanks for taking care of my little angels," she said, kissing the tops of her children's heads as she passed them to sit on an empty chair at the table.

"Believe me, this is my pleasure, Shelley. These kids are so cute! Your face looks much better this morning," she commented, looking at Shelley.

"I'm so embarrassed about all of this," Shelley said.

"Why? You have no reason to be embarrassed."

"I just wish I knew how to handle all of this, but I don't."

"Shelley, you know there has always been a lot of mystery and confusion regarding Neal."

"Such as?" Shelley asked.

"Such as, during the seven years Ernest and Neal worked together at Corpus Bearings, Neal took a full week off, three times, using the excuse that his grandmother died, which I guess is kind of an employee's 'I have no sick days left' excuse. However, Ernest and I both remember the sadness that was in his voice as he described his grandmother's funeral...all three times. We have laughed about it for years. It was unreal. Definitely Oscar stuff. Before he used her as an excuse, he would tell us how he was taking his grandmother here, or there, and he would buy her little things. Then, in your conversation last night, you said his grandmother died when he was twelve."

"Maybe his other grandmother died later," Shelley suggested.

"Three times?" Donna asked, laughing.

"No, definitely not three times," Shelley, answered, also laughing. "Tell me something," she said, more seriously.

"Sure. What would you like to know?" Donna filled two cups with fresh coffee.

"You and Ernest knew Neal years before I met him. What was he like?"

"What do you mean?"

"I mean his parents, his marriage. How did he describe his life to you? Was he nice? Did you think he was honest?"

"We knew him as the same person he presented to you. He basically gave us the same facts. However, we were shocked when Neal got married again, because he always seemed so against it."

"There is something very bizarre about Neal's life, and I don't have a clue what it is," Shelley said. "But, I do know it frightens me. I have this awful feeling of doom."

"Well, the best advice I can give you is to spend more time thinking about everything that's happened. Some of it's pretty weird. You can stay with us as long as you need to, just be sure if you go home, it's what you really want to do."

"Thanks, Donna. I really appreciate your understanding. I just don't know what has happened to Neal. I love him so much and I thought he loved me too, but I'm beginning to think that was also a lie."

"No," Donna responded. "We saw Neal come to life when he married you and don't get me wrong, what he did was terrible, and you definitely deserve the truth, but Ernest and I, honestly, have never seen Neal happier."

The phone rang and Neal ran to it. It was Meg. Tim was on the other line, a habit they'd developed from talking long distance with their sons. Neal had called them when he'd gotten home the night before and found his family gone.

"Has she called?" Meg asked. Meg and Tim were frantic with worry. Neal had told them of the argument, but of course left out the fact that he'd hit her.

"No, I haven't heard from her yet," Neal answered. "I hoped she would have contacted you by now to let you know she was safe." There was a long pause.

"Where could she be, Neal?"

"I don't know. But, I promise Meg, I'll call you as soon as I find out anything."

Two days later, Neal figured out where Shelley was. He called her, urging her to come home. "Shelley, I swear that will never happen again, Honey. I love you and I'm begging you, please…come home."

Shelley's heart would have instantly put her on the road back to Georgia, but her head kept her in South Carolina. Neal kept calling, several times a day, promising the same thing, until she weakened, and finally agreed to return home that Friday.

Chapter 26

Shelley pulled her car into the garage, thankful to be home. She called Neal at his office to tell him they were home, just as she said she would.

When Neal arrived home that evening, he prowled behind Shelley as she put Jackie into her bed. He kissed the back of Shelley's neck before he bent down to kiss his daughter's cheek. After that, he went into Jason's room to do the same, looking relieved that his family was home.

"You're not going to talk to me, Shelley?" Neal asked, after the kids had been tucked into bed and they'd returned to the kitchen. Silently, Shelley continued to clean the counter from the dinner mess.

"Hey," he said. "Talk to me."

"Neal, you're going to have to do the talking this time," she answered.

"What do I have to do to make things right between us?"

Shelley put her sponge down and took a seat at the kitchen table. Neal took the seat across from her.

"I don't want your parents here again…ever," Shelley said, adamantly.

"Fine," he answered. "I never wanted them here to begin with."

"I mean it, Neal. Are you sure you can agree to this?" she asked, surprised by his easy response.

"Shelley, look, I haven't been myself, but I'm telling you, it's having my mother in my life that's put me over the edge. So, why wouldn't I agree? I know that's no excuse for everything I've done, but she definitely needs to stay out of our lives."

"And, what about all the crazy things you've done lately?" she asked. "Like buying the truck and wanting to sell our home?"

"I saw the truck on my way home one night and fell in love with it," he answered, smiling. "I'm sorry. I know it was a totally irresponsible move."

"Why didn't you just buy it without trading in my car?"

"Because I didn't want the higher payment," Neal explained.

"Then, why didn't you pay cash for it? We have enough money," she said.

"Honey, I know it will take time to gain your trust again, and believe me, I'm sorry for that, but I love you. I don't want to lose you because of some stupid truck that I don't even own anymore."

"It's not just about the truck, Neal. I have a million questions flying through my mind, and I'm not getting any honest answers."

He settled back in his chair. "Okay, like what?"

She gave him an example. "For instance, why did you call your parents from Georgia that Christmas morning before we got married if you didn't want to talk to them?"

"Because I didn't want her to look for me," he answered. "I decided when I fell in love with you that I would protect that. I lied to P.L.K. because I didn't want my mother knowing where I was working, and I didn't want them ever to call her for any reason. Only because I knew she would call me at P.L.K. and torment me."

Shelley had known all along that she would forgive Neal. She'd accepted the fact that she would never understand the Jordon family, nor did she want to. She decided, for the time being anyway, to leave Neal's past alone. She hoped, eventually, the secrets of her husband's life would surface and not affect their marriage in a negative way.

A week later, Neal handed Shelley a brochure titled, *"Peach Haven, A Community Within Itself."*

"Honey, just look at it and try to give it some thought. It looks like a beautiful place, and living there would cut two hours off my driving time from the office."

Shelley looked at the brochure, then at Neal, to weigh his expression. For some reason, moving was important to him. She'd decided she would at least consider the idea.

The following Monday, Shelley drove Neal to the airport. He would be in Houston for the week. When she returned, she pulled into Leah's driveway instead of her own, leaving the car running so the silence wouldn't wake the children asleep in their car seats. Shelley had not seen Leah for almost two weeks and she knew her friend would be worried. Beside that, she missed her.

"Can you come over for coffee?" Shelley asked when Leah answered the door in her bathrobe and slippers.

"Sure, if you give me a minute…I'm working kind of slow this morning. We can have it here, if you'd like," Leah offered.

"If you don't mind, I would rather you come to my house. We had to take Neal to the airport, so the kids had to get up at the crack of dawn. I think they're ready for some serious sleep. Is that okay?"

"That's fine. I'll see you in a few minutes."

Shelley went across the street and put the children in bed, then went downstairs to prepare a large pot of coffee. Leah arrived with Martin, who was also asleep. After laying him on his favorite blanket on the couch, she joined Shelley at the kitchen table.

"Look at this," Shelley said, handing her the brochure about Peach Haven.

Leah took it, and after reading part of it, said, "I've heard about this place. It's about an hour from here on the South side of the airport. It's supposed to be beautiful."

"Neal wants to move there," Shelley said, waiting for her friends reaction.

Leah paused for a moment before she responded. "Shelley, Paul wants to move too," she said sadly. "He told me last night."

"Why?" Shelley asked, surprised with her news.

"Paul has a chance for a really good promotion, but we would have to move to West Virginia, if he accepts it."

"Are you going? Do you want to?"

"What matters is, Paul wants to. It would mean a lot more money for us. You know, I had the same reaction you're having. I told him I didn't want to move because of you, but I know I'll have no choice except to go," she said. "I think moving is something we have to give them," she added.

"I know, Leah. I know you're right. so, I guess, it's time to move," Shelley said sadly, looking around her kitchen. She loved her kitchen.

"I guess so, but friends never get too far away, do they?" Leah asked. "We'll still see each other, and we'll always be friends."

"I'm sure you're right," Shelley agreed. Distance would mean nothing to their friendship. Leah would always be her dear friend, even in West Virginia.

The next day, Shelley made an appointment with a Realtor in Peach Haven. As she was getting ready to leave, Shelley received a phone call from Donna. She wanted to check up on Shelley and share some good news.

"Donna, you're so excited, what's up?"

"Ernest was offered a promotion with Corpus. Regional Manager of Sales," she answered, "I'm so proud of Ernest and his accomplishments. He's worked so hard to make something of himself."

"That's great, Donna! Give Ernest our congratulations. Did he tell Neal yet?" Shelley asked, sure Neal would have said something to her, if he had.

"No. Ernest said he was going to call him sometime this week at his office."

"Neal's in Houston this week, but when he calls tonight, I'll tell him to phone Ernest."

"Great! Now, here is the best part. Guess where Corpus is transferring us to?"

"Okay, I give up. Where?"

"South Jersey! The same office where Ernest and Neal met each other."

Shelley's mind raced with a thousand thoughts and possibilities. *South Jersey! Donna is moving to South Jersey, the place where Neal lived before we got married. The place where Neal's house was, the one I never got to see!*

"Of course, we'll probably never see you once we move there," Donna added, playfully.

"Oh, no, Donna. On the contrary. As soon as you get settled, I promise I'll be one of your first guests."

Chapter 27

The agent from City Realty, gave Shelley wonderful directions from Norcross, and even though her heart was not completely in it, she'd decided she would at least look at some homes in Peach Haven to make Neal happy. Leah volunteered to watch the children so she could do that more easily.

Evidence of Winter approaching became more obvious once Shelley passed the airport. The South side was new to her, and she was pleasantly surprised by its rural beauty.

She felt a definite sense of accomplishment when she saw the sign for Peach Haven. She turned left into the entrance of the community. The town was incredibly beautiful. Every elaborate home sat on a huge parcel of land. The long road leading towards the center of town was artistically landscaped with a perfect choice of flowers and shrubbery. Shelley thought it was wonderful.

She easily found the Real Estate office, where Ruth Bernard was waiting by the door to greet Shelley, car keys in hand. She obviously did not want to waste any time.

First Ruth gave her a tour of the town, showing her the amenities of living in the private community. Each street was more elegant than the last one. The residents never had to leave the town. The community had its own private food market, drug store, two banks, and gas stations, plus several clothing and shoe stores. It also had a country club with an eighteen hole golf course, and eight tennis courts. Ruth told her 'the club' was the nucleus of the town, and that a thick membrane was formed to protect the people living inside from what they considered, 'outsiders'.

After seeing twelve beautiful homes, Ruth turned her car onto a fairly new street. At the end of a large cul-de-sac, she entered a long winding driveway, leading to a gorgeous, rustic ranch home. Shelley grew more alert. The house was wonderful and immediately, she knew it was 'the one'. She also knew Neal would love it.

"This house sits on two acres, and if you notice through the large windows, it backs up to a wooded cart path. The woods behind the house will, of course, never be removed," Ruth explained, pointing out the property lines from the double sliding doors off the family room. The view from the house was breathtaking and Shelley spent several minutes studying it.

When they returned to the office, Shelley told Ruth she would like to make arrangements for Neal to see the ranch house when he returned from Houston. That evening, Neal called as she was preparing dinner and she told him about the house. He sounded excited that Shelley actually went to look at homes, much less that she allowed herself to like one.

Back in town that Monday night, Neal phoned Shelley to tell her he was leaving the office to look at the house. He wanted to go over the directions with her one more time. "I'll leave here exactly at five, so I can time the drive during business traffic," Neal said.

He arrived home that evening at nine thirty. "I love it!" he exclaimed. "Shelley, its everything we wanted. Please, Honey, let's make an offer on it." He turned around and looked at his wife. "What's wrong? Don't you like the house as much as I do?"

"Yes, I'd be nuts not to like that house, but it saddens me to think of leaving this one. Isn't that normal?" Shelley asked, trying not to be difficult.

"Yes, I guess it is. That's what makes you, you," he answered, affectionately. "But, it's time, Shelley, Do you understand?" he asked, lovingly.

"I understand. I'm okay, honest."

"Good, because if all goes well, I think we can be settled in our new home by Thanksgiving since the builder wants to do a lease purchase. He wants to close after the first of the year."

Fortunately, the Norcross house sold within two weeks. Shelley began to pack and slowly grew more enthusiastic about the move.

Paul was given his promotion which meant Leah would be moving to West Virginia. It appeared the time had come for everyone to move on. Shelley and Leah were grateful they were both leaving at the same time, and friends to the end, they helped each other pack

Meg offered to keep the children so Shelley could organize the movers when they arrived. Neal was in Alabama that week and was not expected home until Friday night, after everything was already moved. It bothered Shelley that Neal always managed to be out of town when there was a tough job to be done, or when a problem popped up that he did not want to deal with. He conveniently appeared after the solution was completed. The move to Peach Haven was no exception.

The following morning, her first in the new house, Shelley woke up trying to remember which pile of boxes would lead her to the dishes. She needed to make breakfast.

Once she'd found some of the dishes, she continued to search for the coffeepot. Looking up, she became captivated with the view staring at her from the huge kitchen window. She hoped the new house wouldchange things. She looked at that morning as a new beginning for her marriage. *God, please don't let me be disappointed. I love Neal so much. I want our marriage to work.*

She looked out the window again and smiled. For the first time in a long time, she felt happy.

Chapter 28

The day after Thanksgiving, Atlanta plunged into the Christmas season, and Shelley thoroughly enjoyed decorating the house. It was so rustic, it looked like an old fashioned Christmas card by the time Shelley finished putting up the last set of lights.

Neal asked Shelley if she would mind calling Janet, his secretary, to help organize Skiff's Christmas party. He wanted to reserve a banquet room at 'The French Quarters', in Atlanta.

The first Monday in December, Shelley phoned Janet after she had taken Neal to the airport to catch a flight to Florida. As usual, they talked for over an hour, mostly about their homes and children. When Shelley shared something Jackie had said that she thought was absolutely adorable, Janet's response was peculiar.

"Shelley, I was looking at Jackie's picture on Neal's desk the other day and I just could not get over how much that little girl looks like you," Janet declared.

"Oh, thank you. I think so, but I definitely can see some of Neal in her also," Shelley said, proudly.

"I wonder if they make a special effort to place children with parents who actually look like them."

"What do you mean…they? Who?" Shelley asked, bewildered by her statement.

"The adoption people…I'm sorry, I mean the agency that handled Jackie's adoption for you."

Shelley was stunned. "Janet, who told you Jackie was adopted?"

"Neal told us. Oops! Shelley, was he not supposed to?" she asked, clearly afraid she had said too much.

"No, that's okay," she answered, beginning to shake from head to toe. "Listen, I hear Jason calling me. Would you ask Neal to call me when he phones in for his messages?" Shelley tried to sound as normal as possible.

"Sure, I can do that. And I'll take care of the arrangements we talked about for the party."

"Thanks," Shelley said, "I'll talk to you again, soon."

Shelley felt sick. The feeling stayed with her all that afternoon. She went through the day feeling hurt for Jackie. *Why Neal? Why are you lying about being Jackie's father? What are you up to now?* She felt as if she would go crazy waiting for him to call.

"Neal, I spoke to Janet today," Shelley said calmly, when Neal finally called home.

"Great! Did you get the plans in motion for the Christmas party?"

Her voice shook with hidden anger. "Yes, we did, but I have a more important issue."

"What is it, Honey? Is something wrong?"

"Why, in the name of God, would you tell people Jackie was adopted?"

"Oh I see," Neal said, caught one more time in a lie.

"Look. You almost died giving birth to Jason, and everybody at Skiff was really concerned. I would have looked like a murderer if I'd told them you were pregnant again. I lied so I wouldn't look irresponsible," he explained.

"Neal, that's sick! You'd better tell them the truth, because I refuse to lie for you! Do you understand?"

"Honey, I can't tell them the truth now. I'll look like a fool."

"Well, Neal, you'd better. I guess now I know why I didn't see anyone from your office the last five months of my pregnancy," Shelley said, livid.

"Shelley, do you know how bad it would have looked for me to tell them you were pregnant again?"

"What are you saying, Neal, that I'm an embarrassment to you?"

"No, but I would have looked totally inhuman to Corporate Headquarters, because of your health situation at that time," he answered, defensively.

"Well, you'd better make things right for Jackie," she demanded. "She is your biological daughter, and I won't let anyone think differently about her!"

"Okay, I'm sorry. You know I love her, too! I promise I'll tell them. Now can we drop it please?" After a moment of silence he added,

"Shelley, I told them that a long time ago. Things have changed between us since then. There are no more secrets between us anymore."

"What other lies are going to surface with you, Neal?" Shelley whispered, ending the phone conversation.

When Neal came home from Florida on Friday, he assured Shelley he had taken care of it. Once again, Shelley blindly trusted her husband and had no reason not to believe Neal's explanation for lying about his daughter's birth. After all, she was very ill after Jason's birth, and things had changed in their marriage.

Neal was right. That was then, this is now, and now, there are no secrets, Shelley thought.

Right after New Years, Neal approached Shelley with a request.

"Oh, Honey, I forgot to tell you," he said. "There's a Skiff employee from our office in England coming into town next week, and we've been asked to entertain him...dinner, drinks, you know the drill. Is that okay?"

"That's fine. What night?"

"Probably Wednesday. Is that good for you?"

"What time, do you know?"

"Why? What's up?" Neal asked, suspiciously.

"There's something I want to do, but I don't want to say anything about it, yet," Shelley answered with a smile.

"Like what? Is Macy's having a white Sale?"

"Very funny, Neal. Actually, it's a surprise."

"Okay, fine. Next time see if I tell you anything," he said, joking. When she didn't respond, he remained thinking for a moment, then asked, "You're not thinking about getting a job, are you?"

"I told you, it's a surprise. Why can't you just accept that?" Shelley asked, irritated.

"You're right. I'm sorry," Neal replied.

Wednesday arrived, and before Shelley left the house, she phoned 'Anthony's Restaurant' to confirm the dinner reservations she'd made for that evening.

She finished doing what she'd planned to do, then dropped the children off at her parents' house, arriving home with just enough time to get ready for Neal, who was picking her up at six thirty.

During the ride to Atlanta, Neal briefed Shelley on their English guest. He'd spent two grueling days with the man at the office, and Neal loathed him.

"You'll be quite impressed with him, I'm sure," he said, mocking his guest with his interpretation of an English accent. "He's very charming. The girls in the office drooled over him all week. Maybe it's the James Bond accent, I don't know, but I found him to be very crude."

"Oh, no," she groaned. "He's not disgusting is he?"

"I think so," he said, laughing. "He loves pretty woman, too. I'd better watch you," he added, rubbing Shelley's knee with his free hand.

"I hope he's not going to embarrass us at the restaurant. You know how much I love Anthony's."

"I'll handle it if he does...trust me," he said.

When they arrived at the man's hotel, he was waiting outside on the sidewalk with a plastic Martini glass in his hand.

Apparently, he'd visited the bar in the hotel before they'd arrived. Shelley thought he was okay looking, in a British sort of way. She understood why the ladies were taken with him, and his accent certainly didn't hurt his charisma.

"Thomas, I'd like you to meet my wife, Shelley," Neal said. "Shelley...Thomas Barnes."

"How do you do?" he asked, grabbing Shelley's hand over the front seat of the car. "My, Neal, she is a lovely bird," Thomas said, giving Shelley a wink.

She immediately understood what Neal had said about the man.

"Yes, she is," Neal responded, smiling at Shelley.

Anthony's was an old, historic mansion converted into a restaurant. It had twelve dining rooms representing an old English manor, furnished with eighteenth century furniture. Each room was enhanced with a large stone fireplace, all of which were lit, adding warmth to the rooms.

Once seated, Thomas picked up the wine list and raised his arm, snapping his fingers at the Maitre'd. Mortified, Shelley kicked Neal's leg under the table as the gentleman approached.

"May I help you, Sir?" the man asked, pulling at the bottom of his tuxedo jacket, obviously insulted.

"Yes, I would like a bottle of your finest Bordelaise wine," Thomas answered, flippantly.

"Yes, Sir," he answered, leaving the side of their table. A few minutes later he returned, carrying a silver terrain containing a wrapped bottle of wine. Popping the cork, the server handed it to Thomas so he could sniff its wet end. He then, poured a splash of wine into a glass. Thomas swirled the glass around, then held it up to the light before sipping it. The scene was definitely meant to impress.

"Superb!" Thomas exclaimed. The Maitre'd responded to Thomas' approval by filling the remaining glasses.

While reading the menu, Shelley felt a leg rubbing against hers under the table. She looked at their dinner guest who smiled as she moved her leg. She nudged Neal under the table, and he looked at her, confused. He'd missed Thomas' move.

After the waiter took their orders, Neal noticed that Thomas was staring at his wife, and tried to divert the man's attention to a discussion about the weather in England.

"Shelley, do you have a sister?" Thomas asked, ignoring Neal's attempt at conversation.

"No, I don't," she answered, feeling uncomfortable.

"Pity. I would have loved to meet her," he said, winking at her again. He consumed the entire bottle of wine during dinner, and before dessert was served, he'd decided to share his repertoire of jokes with them. His voice grew louder with every punch line, and eventually, he made it to his list of dirty jokes, while other people in the dining room began to whisper and look towards their table. Neal reached the end of his patience when Thomas shouted the infamous, internationally vulgar, four letter word.

Neal grabbed his wrist, and through gritted teeth, made his anger known to him.

"This is my wife, Moron, not some slut we picked up on the way over here. Apologize to her now!" he demanded.

Time stood still during the long minute that the two men stared at each other. Finally, Thomas pulled his arm away from Neal's grip and conceded.

"Well, excuse me, Sir. I most certainly do apologize if I have offended the lady in any way," he said, grinning at Shelley.

"Neal, I think we should leave," Shelley said, revolted by Thomas' behavior, and embarrassed by the scene.

They ended the evening by dropping Thomas off where they found him, in front of his hotel. Neal was furious, and his mood escalated during the drive home.

"Why did you have to lead him on that way, Shelley?" he asked.

Shelley couldn't believe what Neal asked. "What? Are you crazy?

That man is a complete jerk, and certainly I had nothing to do with that!"

While Neal locked up the house, Shelley went into their bedroom. He stormed in the room after her, a few minutes later, pushing his closet door so hard it bounced off the wall.

"Are you going to tell me why you're so angry with me?" Shelley asked, furious with his unreasonable treatment. It was she who'd been the target of Thomas' disrespect.

"Are you going to tell me you didn't enjoy the attention that pig gave you tonight?" Neal shouted.

"You're nuts!"

Neal rushed across the room and grabbed Shelley's throat, pushing her down on their bed. The scene happened so fast, there was no time for her to defend herself. She began to scream after he let go of her throat, and he slapped the side of her face to make her stop.

"Damn you, Shelley! Why do you make me do things like this? You make me crazy when you argue with me this way!"

He left the bedroom, as Shelley lay sprawled on the bed, crying. The door to the garage slammed, and a moment later, she heard the sound of screeching tires as Neal raced his car down the driveway.

Several hours later, Shelley felt Neal's arm slide around her waist as she pretended to be asleep.

"Honey, I'm so sorry…please…forgive me. I swear this will never happen again," he whispered.

She felt a chill as her cold tears fell against her swollen cheeks. The pain she felt went much deeper than bruises. Those would heal.

Chapter 29

Shelley opened her eyes the next morning and slowly focused them on an envelope with her name on it, propped against the telephone on the night table. As she unfolded the letter inside, five one hundred dollar bills dropped onto her pillow.

> *Dear Shelley,*
> *I'm sorry about last night, and I beg you to forgive me. Please do not leave me without giving me a chance to speak with you. Call me when you get up. I love you. P.S. The money is for you to buy yourself something special from me.*

Shelley stepped out of bed and slipped her feet into her slippers. She dropped the letter and the money onto the floor, finding no value in either.

When she walked in front of the bathroom mirror and saw the bruises on her face, she began to cry again. *What has happened Neal? I can't believe you did this to me! What can I do? I can't go to my parents for help. They wouldn't understand. But, I can't stay with him either, hurting me this way. What about Jackie and Jason? Why should they have to leave their home again? I can't take care of them financially, I'm not prepared for that. And what about Neal? I can't believe I still love him. Something is making him act this way, and I don't know what it is! I'm so scared!*

The phone rang, intruding on Shelley's thoughts.

"Honey, please…don't hang up!" Neal pleaded, after he knew she picked up the receiver. "I'm so sorry about last night. Shelley, you have to believe that!"

"Neal, I'm finished with your crazy behavior. I did nothing to make Thomas act that way last night, and you know it. Now, you deal with it, and while you're at it, figure out when you're going to pick the kids up from my parents' house, because I'm not going there looking as though I've been hit by a train!"

"Shelley, wait! Please!" she heard Neal beg, on the other end as she started to slam down the receiver.

"Why, Neal?" she asked. "There isn't anything you can say, or buy me to make this right. Five hundred dollars sure won't fix it!"

"Listen, please. I'll pick the kids up around twelve o'clock, then I'll come home so we can talk about this. Please, Shelley, I'm sorry."

She swept the hair away from her wet face and held the phone in silence. There was nothing she could say to assure Neal she would not leave him, because she was not sure herself how she was going to react.

"Neal, we'll talk when you get home. Right now, I don't want to think."

She didn't want to hear his voice anymore.

"Honey...I love you so much," Neal said, sadly.

Shelley hung up the phone. At two o'clock, she saw Neal's car pull into the driveway, and the thought of being near him, made her sick. She went into their bedroom and closed the door behind her, having no idea what to tell the children if they asked about her face. Neal had also left some vivid, red finger marks on her throat.

"Mommy!" Shelley heard Jason yell as he ran down the hall to her bedroom. Jackie was right behind him. He pushed the door open and ran in and hugged her legs. Jackie joined him, forcing Shelley to smile as she felt the love emanating from her children. They were all that mattered to her, and she knew she would endure anything necessary to guarantee their security and happiness.

Shelley spent the rest of the afternoon playing with them, ignoring all of Neal's shallow attempts to talk.

Once she put the children to bed for the evening, she quietly slipped back into her bedroom, where Neal joined her a few minutes later.

Are you going to stay in here all night?" he asked crossly, when he saw she was dressed for bed.

"Yes, I am, Neal."

"Can we talk?"

"What is there to talk about? I'm done with all this craziness."

"Honey, you know how much I love you."

"Well, you have a strange way of showing your love, Neal. It's kind of dangerous for me, don't you think? I'm sick of your temper, and all the mystery surrounding you and your insane lies!"

"Shelley, I can't stand it when another man looks at you that way. Is that so wrong? I'll admit it. It makes me feel nervous," he said, pathetically.

"Your jealousy is not flattering to me, Neal. I haven't looked at another man since I met you, and if I was going to, it definitely would not be Thomas Barnes!" she stated. "Maybe you should have hit him, instead of me."

"Look, Shelley, I know I don't deserve your forgiveness, but I'm going to beg for it anyway. Please forgive me."

"Neal, I can't go on with this anymore. Also, I talked to my mother today. I love the little story you concocted for her when you showed up to get the children. So, I was too tired from our late evening out last night to pick them up myself, was I? You're getting quite good at what you do. Lying I mean. Don't you agree?"

Neal looked at her as if he finally realized it was going to take some time for his wife to get over his terrible behavior. He closed the bedroom door and went into the great room, leaving her alone.

Shelley wanted the horrible feelings she'd developed towards her husband to vanish. When she thought about the Neal she'd married, she drew lonesome for that man to return. In trying to determine what, exactly, had changed their marriage, the answer was always the same, the postcard from his parents, and the years of unresolved mystery that was delivered to their home along with it. Whatever horrible secrets the Jordons had, those secrets controlled Neal.

After a week of silence, Shelley put her bitterness aside in order to have a civil discussion with Neal. She prepared a nice dinner, having it ready when he arrived home that evening. Although the air remained thick between them, she knew he would be open to anything she had to say, if it meant her speaking to him again.

"Neal, I'm going to bathe the kids, then, I'd like to speak to you about something," she said.

"What about?" he asked, cautiously.

Shelley gave him a look. "I'm sure you forgot there was something I was going to do last Wednesday before we had dinner with Thomas."

He'd never asked her what she had to do that day, and it insulted her the way anything in her life that did not revolve around him was unimportant.

"I'll tell you about it after I get the kids to bed."

Neal never helped Shelley with anything, but that night, he bathed Jason while she bathed Jackie. Once the children were settled in bed for the night, Shelley started to clean the kitchen from dinner. Neal joined her.

"So…what's up? Are you divorcing me?" he asked, looking at her as if he expected her to say she was.

She continued to wipe off the kitchen table. "Before I took the children to my parents on Wednesday, I registered for school at 'Community College'."

Neal gave her a look of disbelief. "Is that what this is about? You signed up for school?" He seemed relieved, but remained guarded.

"It's something I want to do," she answered, adamantly, ready for an argument.

"Honey, I think that's wonderful. What did you take, arts and crafts, poetry…what?"

"No, I signed up for a Real Estate course," she answered.

Neal began to laugh. "Real Estate! What the hell are you going to do with Real Estate?"

"I'm going to sell it," she answered, feeling her anger stir.

"To whom, Darling?" he asked, in a condescending tone.

"To the general public, Darling," she shot back furious with his mockery.

"Shelley, I thought we agreed that you would not return to work until the children were older," he said, sounding annoyed. He never wanted her to work…ever.

"No, that was just another decision you made for me. I'm going to school, end of discussion."

"Wait a minute," Neal retracted. "I didn't mean anything negative. I just wonder where the children fall into your plans?"

It galled Shelley the way he cared about the children's welfare only when it might help him win an argument.

"I've already thought that through. I would only be gone when you would be home with them. Besides, Real Estate is something that I could do a lot of the work from home."

"Well," Neal said. "I guess your going to school beats having you divorce me. I think you should do it," Neal said, kissing the top of her head.

Neal left the following Monday to spend the week in Florida. Shelley's class began Tuesday evening, so she asked their neighbor's teenage son if he would like the job of caring for the children on the nights Neal was out of town that she had class. He seemed very responsible and his parents would be next door, if an emergency came up.

She found room three hundred without too much trouble, and took an empty seat. She fought to settle her nerves. The class could provide her with a possible escape from her marriage, if things did not improve, therefore she wanted to do well in it.

Moments later, a good looking, dark haired man of around thirty five entered the room and laid his belongings on the empty desk at the front of the classroom.

"Good evening," he said. "My name is Brent Barrett, and I will be your instructor for this course."

"This man is gorgeous!" the woman in the next seat whispered to Shelley. "I'm Jenny Hall," she said, initiating an introduction.

"Shelley Jordon," Shelley answered, gently, relieved to meet another classmate her age.

Mr. Barrett distributed a syllabus describing the course and what was expected of each student in order to earn a passing grade.

During the lull, the woman sitting on the other side of Shelley said, "I'm Delores."

Jenny and Shelley both introduced themselves. Suddenly, all of Shelley's apprehension about something new changed to confidence and excitement. Taking this class, she thought, was a good decision, and it was one she'd made, not Neal.

Chapter 30

During the following months, Neal pretended to be supportive, but beneath the surface, Shelley knew he didn't take her ambition seriously. He thought her 'little class', was cute and nothing more.

Meanwhile, Jenny and Delores became Shelley's friends. The three women met once a week in each other's homes to study and talk.

Neal happened to be in town one evening when the group was scheduled to meet at their house. He acted very congenial as he met her new friends, but she knew he would find something wrong with each of them after they left. Over the years, Neal had assumed the responsibility of selecting her friends. But slowly, Shelley was losing respect for his opinion about anything. She realized the control she had turned over to Neal on every aspect of her life, and decided it was time for her to take that control back.

During their study time, Jenny and Delores steered the conversation to Brent Barrett. "I think he's so sexy," Jenny said, with a giggle.

"I think so too," Delores chimed in. "What about you, Shelley?"

Shelley wished they were in the kitchen instead of the dining room. She knew Neal could hear every word they were saying.

"I haven't given it much thought, to tell you the truth," she answered. That was the truth. She hadn't.

"Well, he sure looks at you, Shelley," Delores said, laughing, unaware of the calamity her comment could cause later.

"I noticed that too. He sure does," Jenny agreed, joining in the laughter.

"You two are crazy," Shelley protested, surreptitiously pointing to Neal as an attempt to silence her friends.

Jenny didn't pick up Shelley's signal. "Come on, Shelley, Mr. Barrett will be so serious, and then you'll walk into the classroom and he'll smile, and get all blushed."

"You're nuts!" Shelley scoffed, praying the conversation would shift to something less dangerous. "Let's get back to eminent domain, shall we?"

Watch him, Shelley. You'll see we're right," Delores insisted.

When the study session ended and the women left, Neal followed Shelley as she picked up the dirty coffee cups from the dining room table.

"When does your class meet again?" he asked, watching her put the cups in the kitchen sink to be rinsed.

"Tomorrow night. Why?"

"Because I want you to drop out of that class," Neal answered with an attitude.

Shelley responded immediately, half laughing at his absurd demand. "You're crazy! I will not!"

Neal grabbed her arm and within a second, they were face to face. "Oh, yes, you will, Shelley. And you will do it tomorrow night," he demanded through those gritted teeth that had become so familiar.

"No, Neal. Not this time," Shelley said, trying to get away from him.

Neal no sooner let go of Shelley's arm, when he grabbed her textbook off the dining room table. She followed him, frightened, as he marched towards the fireplace. Horrified, she watched him toss her textbook into the fire. As she watched the flames devour her precious book, Shelley stood still, feeling sick and overwhelmed. One by one, the pages curled, and became ash before her eyes.

"Now, call the school tomorrow and quit your lousy class," Neal said, his stance daring her to argue.

Livid, Shelley's courage rose. "Drop dead!" she shouted, turning her back on him.

An hour later, Shelley crawled into bed. Her face was already beginning to swell where Neal had hit her. He crept into bed, and Shelley felt the familiar movement of his arm sliding around her waist, as once again, he attempted to make peace with her.

"Shelley, I don't know why you make me crazy like that. You know how much I hate hurting you," he whispered.

"Sure, Neal, I know how much you hate hurting me." She shrugged him off, disgusted that he was beside her, touching her.

"Now, will you please quit that ridiculous class?" he pleaded. "Can't you see what it's doing to our marriage?"

"No, Neal. I can only see what you're doing to our marriage. I won't quit my class. If you want to kill me, do it, but I won't quit my class."

She had no emotions left. The only thing she was positive about was that eventually, she would have to leave Neal. The way things were going, leaving him was inevitable. She also knew that in order to support her children., she would have to finish her Real Estate class, then, get licensed. It would take months to close on a house in order to generate any income, if she was lucky. She rolled over, more unhappy than she'd ever been.

The next day, Shelley called the Police to report the beating, but lost her nerve when a gruff sounding, male officer answered the phone.

Later that morning, Shelley drove to the campus bookstore to buy another textbook, determined to finish her class, with or without, Neal's blessing.

Getting into her car to go home, Jason said he was hungry, so she decided to take the children to the McDonald's next to the campus.

"Shelley, hello!" she heard the familiar voice call her from somewhere on the line of patrons. She turned at the sound of her name and saw Brent Barrett standing a few people behind her. She quickly lowered her head, trying to shield her face from him.

"Mr. Barrett...hello...what a surprise," she murmured.

"My goodness, what happened to you?" he asked, looking at her bruises.

"Oh, I had a slight car accident, nothing serious," Shelley answered, obviously embarrassed.

"Nothing serious? You look terrible. Are you okay?" he asked in one breath.

"I'm fine...really," she answered, her eyes pleading for him to believe her.

"Are you waiting for someone, or can I join you?" he asked. "I hate eating alone." He gave Jason and Jackie a wink, making Jackie giggle.

She glanced at her children. "No...it's just me and the kids. That would be nice...if you want to," she added, giving him a fractional smile.

"Great! Why don't you get situated at a table, and I'll get lunch?"

He glanced around. "There's a good one over there in the corner. Why don't you grab it?"

Five minutes later, he joined them with a tray full of food and drinks. He placed the children's 'Happy Meals' in front of them and watched, grinning, as they quickly tore through the boxes, searching for the toy inside.

"There. Are we all taken care of?" he asked.

"We're fine…thank you," Shelley answered, returning his smile, feeling awkward. They ate in silence for a while, and then Brent got right to the point.

"Now…do you want to tell me how you really got those bruises?" he asked her gently.

Shelley's face flushed and she looked away. "Why don't you believe I was in a car accident, Mr. Barrett?"

"First of all, please, call me Brent, or I'm going to feel very old. Second, I had a cousin whose face always looked like yours," he answered seriously. "She's dead now."

"I assure you…Brent…I was really in a car accident."

Her voice trembled with dishonesty. He stared at her for what seemed an eternity before he spoke. "Okay, I understand," he said, softly. "But, Shelley, if ever you need someone to help you, I'll be there. You know where to reach me," he said, seriously.

For two hours, they laughed and talked about everything under the sun. Shelley enjoyed herself, but, there was a sadness about her that quite obviously, haunted Brent Barrett. He looked at her, as if he were honestly envious of the man in her life.

"Oh, no! Look at the time!" Shelley exclaimed at three thirty. "I have to go."

"I've enjoyed this, Shelley. Do you think we could do it again? Maybe dinner next time?"

Shelley could see he was apprehensive about her reaction to his invitation, but had decided to ask anyway. It perceptibly felt right to him.

"Brent, I'm sorry. You know I'm married," Shelley responded, gathering her things.

He didn't let it go at that. "I know," he said. "But…from what I see, it might not last too much longer."

The troubled look on her face, assured him he was probably right. "Brent, I'm not planning to leave my husband, Shelley said. She laughed. "Bad timing, good morals I guess."

He laughed too. "I'm sorry, again, I understand but if you change your mind, let me know. I'm not married, and from the first night I saw you in class, I hoped you weren't." He paused, then said, "Let me know when it's over, will you?"

Shelley smiled. "Sure. You'll be the first person I tell."

"Fair enough. In the meantime, I'll settle on seeing you tonight in class."

"Thank you for lunch," she said. "I've enjoyed this afternoon."

She lifted Jackie from the booster seat and took Jason's hand.

"Can I at least help you with the children?' he asked.

"No, thanks, I'm used to it, believe me."

He waved at the children. "They're great kids, by the way. I'll see you later," he said.

He watched her through the tinted windows of the restaurant as she put the children into the car he had seen her get out of, in the school parking lot, the first night of class.

"Just as I thought, not a scratch on it," he whispered, looking at her car. Brent Barrett looked full of despair as he watched her drive off. He was evidently sure she was going home to a man who would hurt her again. Brent knew she was adamant about being faithful to her husband, no matter how little the man deserved that kind of loyalty.

Chapter 31

When the Real Estate class reached its end, Shelley sighed with relief. After three hours of taking an intense final exam, Brent stayed until eleven o'clock, individually giving students their final grades. Shelley had a tremendous fear of failure. She knew she had to pass that night, because Neal would never tolerate her trying a second time.

When it was Shelley's turn, Brent winked at her. "Congratulations," he said. "You passed."

She squealed with joy. Brent laughed as he filled out the certificate Shelley would need to take to the State test. As he handed her the certificate, they exchanged a sad look. They both knew it would be the last time they would see each other. Shelley felt odd, like she was leaving something behind, but was not sure what that something was. She only knew Brent's friendship brought her pleasure and she would miss it.

"This deserves a hug, don't you think?" Brent asked, holding out his arms. She understood. She wanted to hold him too, to say goodbye to what she considered a dear friend.

"Yes, it does deserve a hug," Shelley answered, letting Brent embrace her for a moment before Jenny, who was next on the list, giggled with impatience for her grade. It was just as well. "Goodbye, Brent," she whispered.

"Goodbye, Shelley," he also whispered as he watched her walk away.

As Shelley drove home, she thought of what was finished. She enjoyed her new friends and had enjoyed the class, but felt terribly sad for Jenny, who'd failed.

Jenny confessed that she had to pass the test that night because she would not be able to take the class again for a while. It seemed she had to have open heart surgery and would be recovering for a few months. Shelley admired her strength. Her own weakness made her feel inadequate compared to it.

Ralph and Mary, their next door neighbors, were standing beside Neal at the dining room table. Shelley could smell fresh coffee brewing. The results of the evening were a step forward in her life, and she felt proud about what she had accomplished.

"Congratulations!" the three yelled.

"Neal...what if I hadn't passed?" Shelley asked, slightly embarrassed.

"Honey, we knew you would," Neal answered, grinning. Shelley knew he was only pretending to be happy. Passing her class might cause some unwelcome changes in his life.

"Ralph and I crashed your celebration, I hope you don't mind," Mary said, looking truly delighted over her friend's success.

"I think it's wonderful for all of you to stay up so late to do this," Shelley replied. Outside of Jenny's bad news, the evening left her with something she'd given up on long ago...hope.

A State test was scheduled the following Saturday morning in the next county, and since the second testing date was six months later, Shelley registered immediately. If Neal was not going to change, it was imperative she pass the test on her first try.

She continued her studying as though her life depended on it, and in a way, it did.

Shelley took the State test and received notification three weeks later that she had passed and was officially licensed in the State of Georgia to sell Real Estate.

That same day, Jenny died during her open heart surgery.

Shelley placed her license with Haven Realty, anxious to start her new career. Jenny's death filled her with determination to build a new and better life as Neal continued to travel, while his behavior at home grew more bizarre after each trip.

Shelley met new people and made several friends, one of which was Clancy Greer. Clancy was a seasoned Real Estate agent, and eventually, the two women became close friends and formed an efficient Real Estate team.

When the broker of Regal Real Estate asked Shelley and Clancy to move their licenses to his office, they accepted his offer. Regal paid higher commissions and the two were given a private office, something they weren't given at Haven.

Clancy was ten years older than Shelley. She graciously took her time teaching Shelley the tricks of the trade, and things went well…for a while. Shelley was able to manage her business and still stay at home with her children.

One afternoon, while Shelley was reading to Jackie and Jason, Janet called. Neal was out of town, and it seemed a man from Texas had shown up at the office looking for him. He claimed Neal agreed to buy one of his antique cars for ten thousand dollars, if he would somehow, deliver it to Georgia. Apparently, the plans were made several months earlier, during one of Neal's visits to Texas.

"Janet, I'm sorry. Neal never mentioned anything about this to me," Shelley said. *Of course not. What else is new?* she asked herself.

"He never mentioned it to me either," Janet said. "The odd thing is this guy insists he spoke to Neal just a few days ago to confirm the arrangements."

"Maybe he misunderstood Neal's intentions?" Shelley suggested. "But, then, he did have Neal's office address."

Janet's call left Shelley feeling uneasy. Something was not right. The incident with the Renault flashed through her mind and she hoped he wasn't trying to stick her with an antique car.

Two hours later, Janet called a second time, very nervous. "He won't leave, Shelley and I haven't been able to get in touch with Neal. He even asked me for your home address. When I wouldn't give it to him, he got irate. I honestly don't know what to do about this."

"Janet, listen, tell the man he has to leave. If he doesn't do as you say, tell him you will have to call the Police."

"And what if he doesn't leave after that?" she asked.

"Then call the Police."

Shelley received several more calls from Janet, keeping her posted. It seems the man made a scene in the office, and Janet finally threatened him with the Police, phone in hand, when he finally left. He kept calling Janet from a pay phone to see if Neal had called in for his messages. The calls finally stopped towards the end of the day, but Janet was not sure what would take place the next day.

When Neal called Shelley, he was enraged about the stranger from Texas.

"What a nut! I never made plans to buy this moron's car!" he insisted.

"Did you look at the car while you were in Texas?"

"Yes, but that's all I did," Neal answered.

"Why would a man drive a car all the way from Texas to Georgia for absolutely no reason?" Shelley asked, sure he was lying.

"I don't know, but I'm going to find out."

"Well, you'd better do something to get him off Janet's back, Neal. He has harassed her all day. God knows what tomorrow will bring."

Neal's tone turned nasty. "Look, I can handle this, thank you. I don't need you to tell me what I should do."

"Great, then handle it, hot shot. I personally, find it really hard to believe there was any misunderstanding between you and this man."

She was sure Neal was not telling the truth and spent the rest of the evening waiting for the other shoe to drop. She imagined some crazy man banging on her door, demanding someone buy his car.

Later, they learned that the man went back to Texas, livid, but they never heard from him again.

The next day, Ruth phoned her to set a closing date for the house. Shelley told her she would check with Neal regarding his schedule to see when he would be available. She also told Shelley the monetary figure required for the closing.

Shelley hoped Neal had not touched the funds they'd put in a special account for the closing. The builder would only accept a lease purchase on the property when they made an offer to buy the house, because of the tax deduction he needed from it, so they'd agreed to close after the New Year. Neal knew the approximate time of year they'd agreed to when they'd signed the lease purchase, and they had the money put aside, so there would be no excuse for his not being prepared.

"Honey, I have the money, but I can't give you a date when I can definitely be there," Neal said that evening when Shelley asked about the funds.

"Well, Ruth said, because it's a loan assumption, I could go ahead and close without you if you're not in town. But that would mean the house would be in my name."

"That's fine with me, if it's all right with everybody else."

"Great! I'll find out if we can close that way and set it up for next week."

Shelley scheduled the closing for Wednesday of the following week. However, when she went to the bank the day before to get the cashier's check for the balance of the down payment, the funds were not available in the house account.

She phoned the closing attorney and asked for a delay. She also left word with Janet to have Neal call her as soon as possible, and was completely frustrated by the time he called. She hated the tight control he kept on their money, and she never understood why their account balances were always lower than what they should have been.

"Neal, why are the closing funds not available? We had sixty thousand dollars in that account specifically for the closing, yet, they just told me at the bank we're eight thousand dollars short. Why?" she asked.

"Shelley, please don't start. I'll make the funds available tomorrow."

"How, Neal? What hat are you going to pull eight thousand dollars out of?"

"I'll take it out of my personal account, okay?" he answered.

"Fine, Neal. But, I have to say, it makes me feel really financially uninvolved when you have eight thousand dollars floating around that I don't know about," Shelley replied, disgusted with his constant secrets.

Neal surprised her by having the missing funds in the house account by eleven o'clock the next morning. At closing, the deed was titled in her name only.

She thought it was odd that Neal had agreed to that, since he liked to control their financial affairs, especially their assets, but she brushed it off, just happy he came through.

Shelley and Neal had four bank accounts between them. One was Neal's personal account, that held money he used for business, gifts, etc. Another was Shelley's personal account, that was used for groceries, household items, shopping and emergency money. Neal was adamant about Shelley keeping a three thousand dollar minimum in that account, because of his traveling. He did not want her without money in the event one of his business trips kept him away from home longer than anticipated. He also had this ridiculous fear that he would die and the bank would put a freeze on their accounts until his will could be read, leaving Shelley without money for the proper funeral arrangements.

The third account held the money for the closing, and the fourth was a joint savings account. Neal kept their savings book, along with what he considered their important papers, in a 'safe place'.

Neal arrived home late the following Friday night. On Saturday afternoon, Shelley had an appointment with a prospective client. As she drove down the driveway, the postman was parked in front of their mailbox. She had to wait until he finished putting the stack of envelopes in their box, and had moved on to Ralph and Mary's house before she could back the car onto the street. She stopped and quickly grabbed the mail thumbing through it as she began to drive.

Along with the usual selection of junk mail, was an envelope addressed to Neal. *Oh, my, God! It's from Neal's parents!* It made her sick to even see their name on the envelope. *What the hell do they want now?* she wondered.

With a shaky hand, she opened the envelope while she continued to drive. She suddenly, slammed on her brakes. It was a typed, loan agreement, stating that her and Neal had borrowed eight thousand dollars from them, along with a repayment schedule. *Damn him! That's where he got the money for the house!* She could not believe Neal would actually borrow eight thousand dollars from the Jordons. He'd agreed to keep his parents out of their lives, but apparently, he'd been dishonest about that, too. *He's kept in contact with them.*

Incensed, she made a mad race up the driveway, actually leaving skid marks on the floor of the garage as the car was forced to a pounding stop. She threw the kitchen door open with such force, it smacked against the wall.

"What the hell is your problem?" Neal asked, shocked by Shelley's violent entrance.

Shaking, she handed him the paper. "What is this, Neal?"

Reading the loan agreement, Neal realized he had been caught, yet again.

"Is this what has you so nuts?" Neal asked, acting as if she were being unreasonable.

"No, Neal, actually, you are what has me nuts. I want to know what sort of garbage you're going to try to sell me now."

Neal jumped in front of her and hit her face hard enough to make her stumble. At that moment, Shelley knew she'd truly had enough of Neal, and picked up the crystal salt shaker from the table, holding it tightly in her hand, she swept it across Neal's face. Startled, he reacted like a madman. He threw her onto the floor and kicked her several times. She thought he would never stop.

Jackie and Jason came running from the great room, holding onto each other and crying, frightened by what they saw happening.

"Mommy!" Jason screamed, frightened for his mother's safety.

"Stop, Daddy…stop!" Jackie screamed with her little, scratchy voice.

At that moment, the phone rang. Neal made his usual exit, screeching the tires of his car as he left. Shelley picked herself up, and shaking, answered the phone. It was Clancy, calling from the office.

"Hey, girl, are you coming in?" she asked cheerfully. "Your two o'clock appointment is here waiting for you."

"Oh…Clancy, I forgot, Neal just left and I have the kids," Shelley said, unaware of the trembling in her voice. The children were still crying, holding onto Shelley's legs, and she was sure Clancy heard their sobs.

"Shelley, what's going on…is there something wrong?"

"Nothing, I'm fine. I just need to re-schedule that appointment, that's all," Shelley answered, unconvincingly.

"This isn't like you, Shelley. Something is not right."

"No, Clancy, really. Everything is fine," she told her again.

"No, it's not. Something is wrong, and I can only guess what it is," she hinted.

"Clancy stop. I'm fine. Please apologize to those people and ask them to reschedule, or better yet, you take them yourself. They're good prospects," Shelley said, attempting to end their conversation.

Clancy didn't sound convinced. "We'll see, I'll talk to them and call you later," she said, hanging up the phone.

Thirty minutes later, Clancy was ringing Shelley's doorbell, and Jason eagerly let her in. She took one look at Shelley and said, "We have to talk!"

"Why aren't you out with those clients?" Shelley demanded.

"I want to talk about what's going on here, Shelley," Clancy replied, clearly annoyed with her friend for trying to change the subject. "The Adamsons rescheduled. They wanted to wait until you could work with them. Now let's get back to you."

"Clancy, please. I don't want to talk about this. I'm fine," Shelley said. She wished Clancy would quietly leave so she could sort out her problems in solitude.

"Look, contrary to what you think, you're not fooling anyone," Clancy said, angrily.

"What are you talking about?"

"Mitch called me into his office about a month ago and asked me about you. He was concerned about your coming into the office sporting new bruises on a regular basis."

"Oh, Clancy, I'm so embarrassed," Shelley groaned, humiliated that her broker had noticed something was wrong. Her entire marriage had been like the proverbial boiling of a frog. She hadn't realized she was being boiled, until she was already boiled.

Tears stung her bruised cheeks. "Things have gotten so out of control, Clancy. I don't know how much more I can take."

"You're not going to take anymore. I'm going to take you to a shelter. The 'Board of Realtors' contributes heavily to the 'Shelter for Battered Women' every year. We might as well use it," she said, sternly.

"Clancy, I can't. I don't want to take my children out of their home."

"No, by all means, let's keep them in a home like this," Clancy argued. "Come on, Shelley, your thinking is irrational."

It was easy for anyone not in Shelley's situation to think when they see bruises they see the whole picture. The bruises were the easy part.

"Clancy, look. I'm thankful for your concern and friendship, but I beg you, let's just keep this between us for now at least until I decide what to do."

Clancy thought for a moment. "Okay. I know you need time to sort things out, but I'm worried about the safety of you and the children. If I bring you to my house, Neal would know in five minutes. I'll keep your secret, but it's against my better judgment. I don't want you to get hurt anymore. Understand? If he tries this again, you grab the kids and come to my house."

"Thank you," Shelley answered, smiling for the first time since Clancy arrived. She knew Clancy would be watching her. Clancy never quit on anyone, or anything she cared about.

Neal came home late that afternoon showing his usual amount of remorse. It made Shelley sick to accept his dishonest apologies, and phony promises, knowing they'd only last until the next time. She discovered that she'd been spending most of her days keeping Neal calm, and that made her weary. Neal's contentment, at some point, had stolen hers.

Chapter 32

Neal was called out of town the week of Valentines Day. A Sweetheart Dance was being held at the country club and most of Shelley's friends were attending. She wanted to go also. The thought of being stuck at home while everyone she knew was at the dance, made her feel like Cinderella.

The morning of the dance, Clancy called suggesting that Shelley go to the dance with her, and her husband, Joe. Shelley felt nervous about going to an affair like that without Neal, sure he would disapprove. Things had been calm for quite a while, and she wanted to keep it that way. However, with some coaxing, she finally agreed to go.

She wore her black dress with a swirl of rhinestones sewn onto each shoulder. Neal loved the dress, and she almost felt as though she were betraying him when she slipped it on. She was ready to spend some time with normal people. To have a little fun, maybe even laugh, and enjoyed knowing that she did not have to deal with Neal's bad attitude. It was something she usually endured every time they went somewhere that did not revolve around him, or the people from Skiff. Neal was reliable for casting a pall on any occasion that involved anyone in Shelley's life.

That night, Shelley put Jason and Jackie to bed early so they would be asleep when Carl came to baby-sit. For once, she was going out smiling, feeling free to enjoy her evening. It was wonderful knowing Neal would not be home when she returned.

When the three of them walked into the banquet room of the club, they saw people waving their arms at them from one of the center tables. Most of Regal's agents and their spouses, were there.

Glenda Skinner, one of their fellow agents, introduced Shelley to her husband, Jerry. She'd heard numerous stories of Jerry's blatant infidelity, and most people wondered why Glenda stayed married to him. Everyone felt Glenda deserved so much better. Shelley imagined that was what Clancy wondered about her because she continued to stay with Neal.

Somehow, Jerry managed to sit next to Shelley, while Clancy sat on the other side. Shelley was surprised at Glenda's tolerance when Jerry kept asking her to dance. Out of respect for Glenda, and total disgust for Jerry, Shelley refused his invitations. Jerry was a handsome man, but his charm ended with his reputation. Love of self, definitely, was his first priority.

Out of courtesy, Shelley danced with several of the husbands at their table. Jerry noticed he was the only man she'd refused to dance with and mentioned it to his wife.

"Shelley, why do you keep refusing to dance with my husband?" Glenda asked smiling, totally innocent and trusting.

"I'm not. I just don't want anyone to feel they're responsible to entertain me. I'm having a wonderful time by myself...really," Shelley explained, trying to be tactful.

"You would have a much better time if you would dance with me," Jerry said, grinning.

Against her better judgment, Shelley agreed to dance with Jerry when the band returned from their break. Clancy heard the conversation and grabbed Shelley's arm.

"Come to the Ladies Room with me...now!" she said, pushing Shelley towards the restroom. Once they were inside, she looked under the stalls to make sure they were all empty.

"Clancy, what the hell are you doing?" Shelley asked, amused with her friend's dramatic performance.

"I'm making sure nobody else is in here," she answered, laughing at herself. "I know I look ridiculous, but I also know the people in this town and what they're capable of doing with a little information."

"Why the dramatics?" Shelley asked.

"Because, I want to talk to you in private," Clancy said. "Look...watch out for Jerry Skinner."

"Clancy, I know. I've heard all about him."

"Well, you'd better be careful. I know you think I'm melodramatic, but I know for a fact that he loves blondes and a good challenge," Clancy warned.

Shelley scoffed. "Okay, I promise. I'll beware of Jerry Skinner...because you know how much I need another crazy man in my life."

They left the Ladies Room and rejoined their friends at the table. The band returned from its break, and like a serpent, Jerry, leaped in front of Shelley. "Are you ready?" he asked, holding out his arm for Shelley to accept.

Clancy pinched her arm as Shelley followed him to the dance floor. She was sickened as Jerry pulled her closer to him, and felt uncomfortable as he stared into her eyes.

"Leave here with me, Shelley," he whispered, seriously.

"Jerry, you are such a lowlife!" Shelley responded, appalled by his audacity. "Do you ever think about your wife?"

"No more than I would think about your husband."

Shelley glanced at him. "The only reason I haven't left you standing alone out here is because Glenda would be embarrassed."

"Ouch, that hurt! Admit it, Shelley. You know you want me," he said, beginning to laugh.

"Not in this lifetime, trust me!"

"Well, someday you will," he whispered in her ear.

Back at the table, as difficult as it was, Shelley tried not to give Glenda reason to suspect how much she loathed her husband. She took the empty seat next to Clancy, who immediately tugged her arm. "Was I right, or what?"

"Oh, yeah," Shelley whispered. "He's a total jerk."

"Well, be careful. He's also a persistent jerk," Clancy warned.

The rest of the evening passed without incident. During the ride home, Shelley thanked Clancy and Joe for a wonderful time. Then Joe pulled into Shelley's driveway.

She stiffened when she saw Neal's car parked at the end of it.

Clancy picked up on the fact that Shelley was frightened, so when Joe stopped the car, she began to get out with her.

"Where are you going?" Shelley asked, reluctantly getting out of the car.

"I'm going in with you," Clancy answered, adamantly.

Shelley shook her head. "I'm okay. Really, I'm fine."

"I know you are, and you're going to stay that way because I'm going in with you. I'll be right back, Joe," she said, closing the passenger door.

"Clancy, this is ridiculous," Shelley said, as she unlocked the front door.

"I agree. You shouldn't be afraid of your own husband, but I'm going in with you anyway."

Both women came to a sudden halt when they saw Neal standing in the foyer.

"Hi, Neal!" Clancy said, smiling. "Listen, just so you know, it was my idea to take your wife out tonight. I was sure you wouldn't mind, it being Valentines Day and all."

Neal glanced at Shelley, then said to Clancy, "Listen…thank you. I felt so guilty about leaving Shelley on Valentines Day, I decided to cut my trip short to be with her, but, it looks like she had a good evening anyway."

Shelley wasn't fooled by Neal's cordial reply. She knew that underneath his smile and good manners, he was seething.

"Well, she was safe with Joe and me. We had a nice dinner, then we met our coworkers at the club," she added, making the evening sound as uneventful as she could.

"Goodnight, Clancy. Thank you for a wonderful evening," Shelley said, holding the door open, anxious for her to leave. She wanted to have what was going to happen behind her.

Neal watched the car leave the driveway, then, he turned to look at Shelley, his face red with anger. "You lousy slut! Did you have a good time tonight?'

"Neal, don't start," Shelley said, walking towards their bedroom. He pulled her arm, forcing her back in front of him. Shelley knew what was coming by the look on his face.

"I want to know what you did tonight," he said, through clenched teeth.

"I went to dinner with Clancy and Joe, then, we went to the club. Clancy already told you that." She tried to pull her arm from his grip, but he held it tighter.

"Do you think I'm that stupid, that I would believe one of your hooker friends?"

"Neal, let go of my arm. I won't put up with you hurting me anymore!" Shelley screamed.

"You won't put up with what, me? You slut!" he shouted. He spat in her face.

"You're nuts!" Shelley yelled, struggling to get away from him. He used his other hand to pull her hair towards him, but she managed to get away from him long enough to run out of the front door, into the dark night.

Furious, Neal ran after her and pushed her to the cold ground. Shelley screamed, hoping Ralph would hear her, but Neal covered her mouth with one of his hands. She felt the sharpness of the stones beneath her as he hit her with his free hand.

Shelley thought of the children and began to cry, sure with each blow she would never see them again.

After several minutes, Neal stopped hitting her so he could drag her inside. Every bone in her battered body hurt as he let go of her arms and began kicking her as she lay on the living room floor.

"Neal, leave me alone," Shelley moaned, certain she was going to die.

"I should kill you for what you did tonight!" he yelled, walking away to sit on his favorite recliner chair.

All Shelley wanted to do at that moment was hold Jackie and Jason. Clutching the coffee table, she struggled to pull herself up, trying not to pass out as she tried to walk.

"Go ahead, get up you whore!" he yelled, still seething.

"I'm not a whore, Neal," she whispered, barely able to breathe.

"Who were you with at the dance, Shelley?" he shouted.

"Clancy and Joe," she answered, totally drained.

"What guys did you dance with?" he demanded.

"Nobody," she answered.

He jumped out of his chair and smacked her one more time across the face, causing her to fall to the floor again.

"Look at you! And why did you wear that dress, Shelley? I bought that dress for you to wear when you're out with me, not someone else, just me!"

He began pacing the room, then leaped at her again.

"Give me that dress!" he demanded, grabbing her.

"Neal, stop...leave me alone," Shelley pleaded.

"I said...give me that dress," he yelled, pulling her to her feet. The room began to spin as he ripped the back of her dress, pulling it off before he let her go. He watched as she fell onto the couch.

Dizzy, Shelley watched Neal go into the kitchen and return with a knife. She thought he was going to stab her, but he slashed the dress instead, until it was nothing more than rags. Shelley could not believe the hate she saw on her husband's face as he threw the remains of the dress at her.

He grabbed his car keys and Shelley thanked God when she heard his car leaving the driveway, and hoped that wherever he was going, he would die before he returned home.

Staggering to the bedroom, she realized her slip was covered with blood. She locked the door knowing that if Neal wanted to get in, there wasn't a lock in the world that would keep him out. Then, she picked up the phone and called the Police.

"Please, help me…I live on Homeland Drive and I need an officer here immediately." She tried to remain steady when an officer answered.

"Why?" the man on the other end asked in a monotone voice.

"My husband just beat me and I need help," she answered, desperately.

"Do you need an ambulance?" the officer asked with a gruff, indifferent voice.

"No, I don't want an ambulance. I have children," Shelley said. "I want you to come to my house and take him away from here!"

"And how do you think we should do that, Ma'am?" he asked, almost laughing.

"Just take him out of here…please!" she begged weakly.

"Ma'am, we don't just go into a man's home and carry him out of his house because he had a fight with the misses," he responded, acting as though Shelley was being unreasonable to expect such a thing.

"You don't understand. He's going to kill me, I know he is," Shelley pleaded.

"Ma'am, where is he now?" the officer asked.

"I don't know, he left in his car."

"There, you see? How can he kill you when he isn't even there?" The officer laughed at her.

"But, he will be here!" Shelley yelled into the phone, with the little bit of strength she had left.

"I'm sorry, Ma'am. I suggest you talk it over with him in the morning. Things always look a lot better in the morning."

Shelley hung up the phone, and started to cry. Feeling very much alone, she heard Neal's car idling in the driveway and as quickly as she could, unlocked the door. If the Police refused to help her, she did not want Neal to become even more angry than he already was. She limped back to her bed and crawled under the bed covers, wet from her tears and pretended to sleep.

Neal walked in and slammed his wallet on top of his dresser. Keeping her eyes closed, Shelley prayed he would leave her alone. He undressed for bed, and when she heard him brushing his teeth, she knew within minutes he would be in bed next to her.

The following morning, Shelley stayed in bed until she was sure Neal had left the house. The children were sleeping later than usual, and she was thankful for that when she looked at herself in the bathroom mirror.

My, God, this is awful! she thought, tears stinging her blackened eyes. She composed a variety of excuses in her mixed up mind that she would give the children when they asked what happened to her, hoping one of them would sound reasonable even to their tiny level of understanding.

As she limped into the kitchen, she heard the front doorbell and panicked. Through the curtains, she saw Clancy.

She'll never go away…I have to let her in, Shelley said to herself, as she opened the door.

"My, God!" Clancy gasped when she saw her friend. "Shelley, look at you!" Tears filled her eyes. "How could a man do this to his wife?"

Shelley's right eye was practically swollen shut, and her mouth actually pulled to the left side of her face. Enormous bruises had already surfaced on her arms and legs and that was only what was visible. The robe Shelley wore hid the rest of her injuries.

"Clancy, I'm okay," Shelley said, as she hobbled into the kitchen, craving a cup of coffee.

"You're not okay! God, I hate him!" Clancy said, following her. She took the pot out of Shelley's hand and began to make the coffee. "You sit down. God, that man needs to be dead! After you have some coffee, we're going to get you to a doctor," Clancy said, becoming more enraged as she filled the glass pot with water.

"Clancy, I'll make the coffee," Shelley argued, reaching for the pot.

"You're not making anything. Just go and sit down! It's time to call the Police, Shelley."

"I've already done that. They don't care. For some reason, they see Neal as the victim...this poor man, that some crazy woman wants dragged out of his house without good cause."

"That's sick. Something has to be done, now. You can't ignore Neal's treatment anymore, and what about your work? How are you going to show homes looking like you were run over by a Mack truck?"

"I guess I'll have to take some time off. I've done it before and no one has ever guessed the truth about my miserable life."

Clancy reminded Shelley. "No, that's only what you thought. I told you, Mitch has his suspicions."

"Clancy, I don't know what to do. I can't count on the Police," Shelley said as Clancy poured each of them coffee. "I don't think I can physically take much more."

"Honey, let me take you and the kids to the shelter," she begged. "You'll be safe there."

"But, I'm not ready to leave. I've got to prepare. I can't just leave with two children and no money. Neal controls all the accounts and somehow, I've got to gather enough money without his finding out about it."

"You might not live long enough to prepare!" Clancy shouted. She hesitated for a few moments, then mellowed. "Okay, fine, but get prepared, now. Don't wait!"

"Drink your coffee, Clancy," Shelley said, trying to smile. She winced as the hot liquid touched her swollen mouth.

"I'm serious, Shelley. You know it can happen."

"Yes, it's possible," she agreed, sadly. The truth being, she never thought she would see that morning.

After they'd finished a second cup of coffee, the doorbell rang. Shelley was too embarrassed to answer it, so Clancy offered to. When she opened the door, a delivery boy was standing there holding a huge arrangement of roses.

"This was supposed to arrive yesterday, Ma'am," he said. "I'm sorry, we're late."

Clancy took the heavy vase from him, thanking him before she kicked the door closed. "Here, belated 'Happy Valentines Day'," she said with a disgusted tone, handing Shelley the vase.

She read the card pinned to a large red bow arranged in front of the vase and read it to Clancy.

Dear Shelley,
Happy Valentines Day,
I love you, Neal.

"I could barf," Clancy said. "You don't damn near kill someone you love."

"How bad do I look?" Shelley asked as she threw the roses in the trash.

"I would hide out for a while," she answered. "Incidentally, I know this is certainly not the time, but what about the Real Estate Convention in Macon next month? If you went through this much hell for a dance, what will Neal do about a four day convention?"

"If I discuss it with him now, it'll be okay. When this happens, he's very remorseful for a week or two afterwards," Shelley said, knowing the routine.

"God! What a dirt bag!" Clancy exclaimed.

Shelley said with sadness, "I'll bring it up when he gets home tonight. By that time, he'll be willing to give me his mother, dead in a suitcase if I ask for it."

"That doesn't sound like a bad idea from what you've said about her," Clancy said, laughing.

"It sure doesn't," she agreed, feeling the pain as she laughed.

"Mommy...what happened to you?" Jackie was standing in the doorway of the kitchen, wiping the sleepiness from her eyes.

"I'm fine, Honey...what's the matter?"

"I heard Daddy yelling at you last night. Is he gone, Mommy?" she asked, her little voice sounding pitiful.

"He's at work, Honey. Come here and give Mommy a kiss."

Shelley held out her arms to her daughter. Jackie ran and jumped up on her mother's lap, causing agonizing pain in her legs and ribs, as her daughter snuggled close to her.

Shelley knew her new injuries would take longer to heal than usual, and she asked Clancy to take her scheduled appointments before she left, of course she said she would.

Jason woke up and joined his mother and sister in the kitchen. Shelley closed her eyes, hugging her children, knowing she would endure anything if it meant their comfort and security.

Chapter 33

Shelley couldn't predict what Neal's mood would be when he returned home that evening, so she thought it wise to be ready for anything. She had the children fed and bathed by six, knowing Neal would arrive around seven thirty. Even though it was early, she wanted them in a deep sleep beforehand, just in case.

Butterflies formed in Shelley's stomach when she heard Neal's car stop at the top of the driveway. He walked in and moved quickly towards Shelley, holding a gift box.

"Honey, I'm so sorry," he said, beginning to cry. Shelley remained indifferent as he handed her the box and watched her place it, unopened, and unimpressed, on the coffee table he'd thrown her on the night before. She knew nothing inside that box would resolve the problems in their marriage.

"We have to talk," Shelley said.

"Please, don't tell me you're leaving me. I couldn't stand it! I want to fix our marriage, Shelley," he said, sounding frightened.

"Then, you have to do something now. If you don't go for some form of counseling, I'll have to leave you to protect me and the children. Look at me, Neal!"

"Oh, Honey, I know. Baby, I'm so sorry. I'll do it. I'll do whatever it takes to save my family. I'll find a doctor who deals with my kind of problem," he promised, once again begging for another chance.

Shelley remained silent for a moment. That was new. Neal never suggested getting help before. In spite of everything, Shelley wanted her husband back and would do anything to make that happen, but she also had to be sure he was not pacifying her.

They talked for a long time, and Shelley went to bed with renewed hope for her marriage. Neal promised her things would be different, and she believed him because amazingly, she still remembered what it was like to love him.

Shelley saw her husband as two people, the good man, the one she'd fallen in love with, and married. The man that fathered her children and had brought her happiness like she'd never known before. Then, there was the hateful man, evil, and violent, the one raised by an unbalanced mother and nurtured by a dysfunctional family. Shelley believed the good man would triumph over the latter. She agreed to give Neal another chance, but with certain stipulations. The most important being that he had to actively search for a program, or a doctor that would help him with his violent behavior.

That evening, Shelley brought up the convention and got the results she'd expected. Neal agreed to change his travel schedule so he would be home to care for the children the four days she would be gone. She compliantly accepted his peace offering.

When Clancy came to Shelley's house to make sure her friend was still in one piece, Shelley handed her Neal's check, covering her cost of the convention, since Clancy was the one handling the convention arrangements for their office. Clancy told Shelley she was being totally naive putting any trust into Neal's promises, while Shelley rationalized in her mind that Clancy's apprehension was due to the fact she'd never known the wonderful Neal. What he'd become, Shelley easily blamed on his mother. After all, things were perfect in their marriage until she found her way back into Neal's life.

The next few weeks remained calm, however, history guaranteed it was a matter of time before that would change.

It came on a Friday night when Neal returned home from a business trip to Brunswick, Georgia. He was excited about an antique car he'd seen for sale there. It was a red, thirty five Ford, with a chopped top, loaded with chrome and sporting a Corvette engine. Naturally, it was everything Neal had always dreamed of owning.

"I have to buy it, Shelley!" he said, pacing the room.

"Neal, we can't afford it. You had to borrow eight thousand dollars from your parents to close on this house," Shelley reminded him.

"But, this is truly a once in a lifetime deal. Once the owner advertises it, the car will be gone, believe me," he insisted. "What if I use part of my Spring bonus?"

"How much is this thing?" she asked, loathing his infatuation with cars.

"Ten thousand dollars." He looked away. "Ten thousand dollars for that car is a steal, Shelley."

"Ten thousand dollars! Neal, we can't!" she cried out, shaking her head.

"Shelley, it's worth forty!" he replied, in defense.

"I don't care if it's worth eighty, we still can't afford it," she said, firmly.

"I don't understand why my salesmen who make a hell of a lot less than I do are able to buy more than I can," Neal argued. "Larry just bought himself a brand new yacht. George and Carrie just got back last week from a ten day cruise to Hawaii, and Stu, just put an in-ground pool in his backyard. Why can't I buy this car? I work hard, earn good money, yet, I never get an opportunity to enjoy my life!"

We just finished putting sixty thousand dollars down on this house, eight of which, to my horror, you had to borrow from your parents. Also, the truth of the matter is, Larry married the daughter of a millionaire. George and Carrie's trip to Hawaii was their honeymoon, and Stu used money he received as compensation for the leg injury he received from his car accident last year to pay for his pool."

She paused, catching her breath. "If your bonus can pay back your parents, then, you should take care of that before you buy an antique car."

"What if my bonus covers both? Would it still bother you if I bought the car?"

Shelley thought for a moment. "No, I guess not," she answered, with reluctance.

Neal kissed the top of her head. "I love you!" he said.

"Neal, promise me...you'll pay back your parents before you do anything else," she begged.

"Okay, I will. I promise," he said, excited.

"By the way, just how much is the bonus you're getting?"

"About twenty thousand," he answered, proudly.

The following Saturday, Neal arranged to pick up the antique car in Brunswick.

"Did you get your bonus, Neal?" Shelley asked. She wanted to make sure he had before they followed through with any plans he might have made with the owner of the car.

"Yes. Corporate sent the checks to the office. I'm going to distribute them on Monday," he answered.

"Then, how can you buy the car today?" Shelley asked, puzzled.

"I made arrangements with the owner not to deposit my check until Tuesday."

Anxious to have the Jordons once again out of their lives, she asked, "Did you send your parents their check?"

"Yes, I did," he answered, sarcastically. "And I'm sick of hearing you nag about the money I owe my parents. It's none of your damn business. It's my money and my parents."

Shelley kept silent. Unless she wanted to start another argument, there was nothing left to discuss.

Neal arranged to meet Bill Wade, the seller of the car at the car dealership he owned. When they arrived, the man led them to the service area in the back of the building to show Shelley the car before completing the sale. The man apparently thought her opinion actually mattered. What she truly felt was disgust for Neal's extravagance. She couldn't stop thinking about the money, knowing she would never spend that kind of money on herself. Back in Bill's office, he pulled several papers out of a folder.

"If you're ready for the business part of our transaction, we'll be done," the man said, smiling, handling the papers to Neal.

Neal signed the papers and placed them on the desk in front of the owner. He pressed his pockets, looking for his checkbook. "Excuse me a minute, I must have left my checkbook in the car," Neal said, as he left Shelley alone with the car owner.

"You're not happy about this, are you?" Bill asked.

"I don't know anything about cars, only that Neal wants this one really bad. It seems like a lot of money to me…no offense."

He laugh quietly. "No, I understand. Actually, I'm selling this car in order to finish some work on another car I own. My wife will kill me if I don't sell this one first…because of the money."

Just then, Neal returned to the office without his checkbook. "Honey, can I speak to you for a minute?" He sounded embarrassed.

Shelley stood and excused herself as she followed Neal outside. "What's wrong?" she asked him.

"I was so excited about picking up the car, I left my checkbook on top of my dresser," Neal said.

"Oh, no, Neal! What are you going to do?" They'd made the long drive for nothing.

"Well, would you mind writing a check from your account, and I'll deposit the money for you on Monday?"

She knew how much Neal wanted to go home with that car, so she agreed to do what he asked, as long as he promised to deposit the funds back into her account. The money in her account was from closings she had during the month, and she intended to save it.

"Neal, please, don't let me down this time. We need to build our savings again."

"Shelley, I promise, Honey…I won't. I love you so much. Thank you," Neal whispered in her ear as he held her.

As soon as they drove into their driveway with the new car, one by one, the men in the neighborhood joined Neal to examine every inch of it. Shelley watched as Neal glorified himself as the proud owner of that totally, amazing automobile.

Neal was still outside when Shelley finished putting the children to bed. Just as she grabbed the book she was in the process of reading, ready to relax on the couch, the phone rang.

"Hello, Beautiful!" Jerry Skinner greeted her.

Shelley went cold. "Jerry, I told you to stop calling me. I don't want to talk to you, not now, not ever! Why don't you stop?"

She slammed the phone back into its cradle. He had taken her phone number off one of her Real Estate signs in somebody's yard, and continued to call her since the Valentines Day dance. Clancy was right. He definitely was persistent.

Shelley put Jerry Skinner aside, and decided to concentrate on the Real Estate convention. Since Clancy's car had been acting up, Shelley agreed to drive and added a car wash onto her list of things to do for her trip.

Chapter 34

During the drive to Macon, Shelley told Clancy about the calls from Jerry.

"He is such a lowlife, Shelley. If he keeps it up, you should call Glenda," Clancy advised.

"I couldn't do that to Glenda. She's got it bad enough being married to him."

Clancy nodded. "Poor, Glenda. She has no idea what kind of louse Jerry is."

"Sure she does, Clancy, just like I know what kind of louse Neal is, but it's easier to stick your head in the sand, than to deal with it. Besides, you always think you can change things. That things will get better."

Clancy gave Shelley an understanding look. "Well, let's just concentrate on having fun at this convention, okay?"

"That's fine with me, believe me, although, I'm not sure I remember how to have fun anymore."

"You'll do just fine," Clancy said, patting Shelley's hand.

I hope so, Shelley thought. She knew her situation at home would end one of three ways. Either she would leave Neal, or she would end up permanently disabled, or dead.

They arrived at the Macon, Hilton before most of the other agents. While the two women were unpacking, Jane, the secretary from Regal's office, called to tell Shelley that Neal's parents had been trying to reach her all morning.

Shelley had no idea why they would be calling her, especially while she was out of town, but she was thoroughly annoyed with their audacity. They had no business calling her. She'd assumed Neal made her feelings known to them.

"Why don't you just call them so you won't think about it anymore?" Clancy asked.

"Because, I can't stand those people. They're so evil."

She shook her shoulders as if by doing so, she would shrug off the wicked demons that she felt clinging to her life. She almost wished they really were dead. Her life was so much better when she believed they were.

Well, call and put your mind at ease," Clancy suggested, putting some blouses on hangers.

Shelley finally gave in and decided she would call. When her mother-in-law answered and heard Shelley's voice, the woman's tone immediately turned vicious.

"Why are you calling me, Mrs. Jordon?" Shelley asked, unable to mask her anger.

"You still haven't returned our eight thousand dollars!" The woman screeched into the phone with fury.

Startled, Shelley gasped. "What do you mean? Neal said he took care of that."

"Well, we never received the money, and we need it."

The woman's arrogance stole Shelley's breath. "Look, I'm away from home right now, so I strongly suggest you take this up with your son," Shelley answered, sick of the woman creating turmoil in her life.

"We don't want to bother him with this, the poor man. He works so hard to give you everything you want. And what kind of mother goes on a trip without her children?"

"First of all," Shelley screamed. "The children are with their father. Secondly, your son borrowed that money from you, not me, and as far as what kind of mother I am? On my worst day, I'm a better mother than you have ever been! Now, I suggest you call your son about your lousy money and do not…I repeat…do not…contact me again!" She slammed down the phone and turned away.

Clancy clapped, "Way to go!" she yelled, wearing the half jolly smile she took on when it wasn't entirely appropriate to laugh, while Shelley grew sick to her stomach. She knew, once again, Neal had lied.

That evening, after Shelley and Clancy had registered for the conference, the Regal Company attended a formal dinner. Once dinner was over and the band began to play, it took less than five minutes before some people at their table suggested they go elsewhere, rather than listen to the forties band, which didn't appear to be a good forties band.

When they reached the door, they ran into Vinnie Sitts, a broker from another Regal office in the same area as Mitch's. Vinnie, was a notorious womanizer, but everyone liked him anyway. He was a huge man, nice looking, and well dressed with a beard and moustache, and it was obvious he'd been instantly taken with Shelley.

Everyone decided to go to 'Macon East', a small country western club not too far from the Hilton. Shelley began to relax and honestly enjoyed the evening.

Vinnie sat between Shelley and Clancy, and because of his wonderful personality, and sense of humor, the evening was more fun. When Vinnie asked Shelley to dance, she gladly accepted.

"Welcome back among the living," Clancy whispered when Shelley and Vinnie returned to the table.

"Thank you," Shelley smiled. She was having a great time. She felt free away from Neal. Free to smile, free to speak to other people without being called dirty names, free to have fun and free to actually relax. She even felt free to feel safe.

The rest of the convention went well, and when it came to an end, Vinnie had sweet talked Shelley and Clancy into transferring their licenses to his Regal office.

"We might be ready for that, Shelley," Clancy said, while they packed their bags to leave. "Our business has been good, and I think in a busier office, we could do even better."

"I agree," Shelley said. She thought it might be good to make the change if for nothing else, than to strengthen her financial position in preparation for the day she might leave Neal.

As much as she needed the break, she was more than ready to be with the children. She'd missed them terribly. However, going home to Neal was not as easy, especially after spending four days with normal people.

When Shelley arrived home, the kids were excited to see her. She picked them up one at a time and swung them into the air. They meant everything to her. They were her reason for living.

"Did your parents call you?" Shelley asked Neal, once she'd become settled.

"Yes. My mother told me she called you in Macon and that you were rude to her," he said, brusquely.

"Well, the way I see it, she was rude for calling me to begin with. You borrowed the money from them, not me. She should have taken it up with you. To call me at the convention took a lot of nerve."

"Well, I handled it," he told her.

"Neal, you said you paid them. When we discussed buying the car, you promised to pay them first. Why didn't you? Was that just another lie to get your way?"

"Look, I took care of my parents. Beside that, I think there is a much bigger issue that you and I have to discuss."

"Which is?" Shelley asked.

"While you were away, the phone kept ringing and the person on the other end, kept hanging up when I picked it up. Who was it, Shelley?"

Oh, my, God, it must have been Jerry Skinner! Glenda didn't go to the convention. He probably knew nothing about it. There is no way I can tell Neal about the way he's been bothering me. He'll be sure to blame me!

"Neal, I just got home and I'm not going to fight with you. How should I know who was on the phone...and as far as settling the debt with your parents goes? I really don't care if they get paid, or not."

"Oh, that's a nice attitude, Shelley. Just great."

Shelley sighed, knowing he was deliberately trying to start an argument.

"Neal, why are you attacking me? I'm the one who should be mad," she said.

"You have no reason to be mad! You've just had a four day vacation, remember?" Neal shouted.

"Oh, here it goes. You're away all the time. I go for four days, which, by the way, is the first time since we were married that I've gone anywhere by myself, and I get harassed by your crazy mother!" Shelley yelled back.

Neal glared at her, his face turning red with anger. "My mother was right about you, Shelley, You're nothing but trash. You probably slept with every guy at that convention!" he yelled.

Shelley knew the scenario by heart. She also knew she was through with them, and wondering where she got the courage to say the words, she finally said them, "Neal, I want a divorce!"

He stopped and looked at her. She had never actually said that to him, so he knew he had reason to beware. "You don't mean that, Shelley," he responded in a chilling tone.

"Oh, yes, I do, Neal! I'm tired of living in fear of my husband, and I'm tired of your emotions always coming before mine. I have issues in my life that are equally important and I can't deal with them and keep you calm at the same time!" she shouted.

Stunned, Neal walked into the bedroom.

She was surprised he'd walked away without physically hurting her somehow, until a moment later, when he returned to the living room with a gun in his hand.

"You're not going to leave me, Shelley," he said, pointing the gun at her.

"Where did you get that?" she asked, beginning to tremble.

"I've had it for a while now," he said, maliciously.

Another secret, Shelley thought.

The children saw the gun in their father's hand and ran to the couch where they sat huddled together in fear. They were two, innocent toddlers, afraid of their own father.

"Neal, you're scaring the children…please…put the gun away," Shelley said, trying to remain calm.

Neal's voice shook. "I don't care if I'm scaring them. I'll shoot them, too, if I have to. I'm sick of you loving those kids more than me anyway. You're just like my grandmother, the way she loved my brother more than me, and how easy it was for her to move away from me. I loved her so much, but it was always about the new house and my brother!"

Shelley did not know the stranger standing in front of her. A surge of quaking chills ran throughout her body and she prayed she could control her shaking.

Is it possible? Could he have killed his grandmother? For a brief moment, she pictured Neal hanging the poor, old woman, but pushed her crazy thoughts aside to deal with the present.

"Neal, stop!" Shelley shouted, aware that Jason and Jackie were relying on her to keep them safe from the madman they called, 'Daddy'.

"Sit down, Shelley," he demanded, pointing the gun at her again.

Trying to remain calm, she did as he told her to do, and sat down. For the following two hours, Neal carried on his own delusional conversation. He rambled about Shelley being unfaithful, and about his grandmother who'd betrayed him. He also whined about the little girl so many years ago who tried to persecute him after she'd been pushed into the fire that eventually led to her death. He babbled about how she'd made fun of him as he walked past her and the little boy that day as they were grilling marshmallows. He gloated about the girl's death.

For the first time, Shelley sensed an explanation. One of truth about both startling events. Horrified, she understood that Neal was informing her that he was capable of killing. She had to think of a quick plan of escape, and her opportunity came when the children said they were thirsty.

"I have to go to the kitchen to get them water," she said. "You can watch me, Neal."

He thought for a moment, then, nodded. "Well, go ahead, but hurry. I want you to sit here until you come to your senses about leaving me," he said.

Frantic, Shelley walked to the kitchen, aware that Neal was watching. She knew if she promised not to leave him at that moment, it would anger him more, because he would know she was lying. She was trying to think of what to do. She could run out the kitchen door, but that would leave the children alone with Neal, so that was not an option. The phone rang, and Shelley seized the moment by quickly grabbing the receiver. It was Meg. Before she had a chance to speak, Shelley shouted into the phone. "Mother, Neal has a gun, call the Police!"

She hung up and looked directly into Neal's piercing eyes, so he could absorb the hatred she felt for him at that moment. He had crossed the line by involving the children, and that was unforgivable to her. There would be no promises, no sweet talk, or affection, that would allow her to excuse Neal's horrifying behavior.

"Thanks a lot, Shelley," Neal said as he ran to the bedroom. Just as she heard him lock the door, the phone rang again.

"This is the Peach Haven Police Department," a male voice said. "We have a car on the way to your house. Where is your husband now?"

The officer stayed on the phone with Shelley, until two Police officers were inside the house. One officer stayed with Shelley and the children in the living room, while the other went to the bedroom to deal with Neal.

Confident that their nightmare was over, Shelley began to cry. She had tolerated so much tyranny from Neal, yet the love between them, somehow had always been there to stop her from leaving him. It saddened her to acknowledge that love obviously was not enough to survive violence in a marriage.

"Where will you take him?" Shelley asked the officer who'd stayed with her. In spite of everything, she was concerned with Neal's welfare.

"Take him? What do you mean?" the officer asked.

"Where will you take him when you take him out of here?"

"We're not taking him anywhere, Mrs. Jordon. This is his home, too," the officer answered.

Shelley stared at him, suddenly, feeling panicked. "You're kidding, right?"

He's kidding...he must be! Neal threatened our lives...he can't be serious!

The second officer came out of the bedroom and said to his partner, "Everything's fine now. He'll be okay. He's been under a lot of pressure lately and he realizes that he handled it badly. We can go." The officers started towards the door to leave.

"Okay? Who is okay? The man held a gun on us and that's not okay with me!" Shelley cried.

"Mrs. Jordon, your husband assured me that he never had any intention of shooting you, or the children. He's under control now."

Shelley couldn't believe her ears. "But, you can't leave him here! Please help us! He'll kill us if you leave him here!"

"No, Mrs. Jordon, he won't. I confiscated the gun. He can pick it up at the Police station here in town sometime this afternoon, after he has simmered down from this."

Near hysteria, Shelley tried to stop them. "No! You can't leave him here, gun, or no gun. Can't you commit him?" she asked, desperately.

"Not without two signatures from family members," he answered.

Shelley stood astonished. Neal actually had more rights than his victims. As weary as she was, she had to ask, "Officers, just out of curiosity, what would happen if my husband went next door, and held a gun on my neighbor's wife?"

"Then, he would be taken to jail on an assault with a deadly weapon charge, but this is his home, Ma'am, and that makes this incident a domestic dispute," the officers told her. "If your marriage is bad, you need an attorney, not the Police. We can only become involved if there is an actual shooting. We go through this all the time."

She wondered if the officer knew how ludicrous he sounded. "You can't be serious. My marriage license is not a license for abuse. I want him out of here!"

"Well, I'm sorry, Mrs. Jordon. We can't do that. Hire a divorce attorney, you women always want us to arrest your husbands just so you can drop the charges later."

Within a moment, they were gone, along with any hope she had for help. She knew, then, it was time for her to leave.

She decided the next morning, after Neal left for the office, would be the best time to go. So, for the rest of that awful Sunday, she did whatever it took to keep peace. That was the safest way to handle the situation, so she ran into his arms when he finally came out of the bedroom.

"I'm so sorry, Neal. I love you and I don't want our marriage to end either, but what can I do to make you happy?"

"I have been nothing but good to you and the children. I need more understanding and respect from you, and I don't want to hear you say you're leaving me again. I love you, and I'm sure you can see how the law protects good family men like me from crazy, hysterical wives like you!"

Shelley felt that if she had access to the gun at that moment, she would shoot him.

Whatever happened to the 'justice for all' system I was raised to believe in? she wondered. *Why am I expected to endure abuse just because I'm someone's wife?*

Shelley could not believe what had just taken place in her home. She'd never felt so alone in the world as she did right then. Somehow, she had to leave Neal to stay alive and to keep her children from harm. Jason and Jackie would never forget the day their father held a gun in his hand and threatened their safety. A man was supposed to make his wife and children feel safe, as if the world could not possibly harm them as long as he was around, and suddenly, he was the danger. Shelley knew there would be no coming back from that day, that trust would be a rare commodity in their lives. She had to leave, without help from any so called law officers who had 'to protect and to serve' painted in gold on the back of their cars.

Chapter 35

Shelley made it through Monday morning, staying in bed until Neal's car left the driveway. As soon as he was gone, she jumped out of bed to make breakfast for Jackie and Jason. She felt it would be best to leave as quickly as possible.

There was a note from Neal on the Kitchen table. "I took your car in for service, you will have to use my car today." The keys were waiting next to the note.

Damn him! He did this on purpose so I couldn't leave. Now what will I do? The phone rang and Shelley jumped. *It must be him. I'd better answer it and sound happy.* She picked up the receiver as if a bomb would go off when she held it to her ear. It was Clancy.

"That's it, Shelley," Clancy said, after Shelley filled her in about Neal's latest outlandish behavior. "Get the kids and come stay with Joe and me."

"No, because that will be the first place he'll look. I don't want your life disrupted because of my problems. My parents left for their vacation this morning and won't be back for two weeks. I have a key to their house, so I think I'll go there."

"That will be the second place he'll look," Clancy said. "I can't believe your parents still went away, knowing what you're going through," she added.

"You have to understand my parents. When I became of age and left home, I was no longer their concern. There is no such thing as burdening my mother with problems. Which brings me to another one. Neal took my car in for service today, so I have to leave in his company car."

"Oh, Shelley, I don't know if you should do that. Why don't you let me take you to the shelter where you and the kids will be safe? I just don't trust Neal."

"I don't know, Clancy. Let's see what happens at my parents house first. He can always trade my car for his company car, and if he tries anything, we won't be in "his own home" and the Police will have to remove him."

"Listen, Honey, you had better call me if you need me for anything, you hear?" Clancy insisted.

"I will. I'll call you anyway, no matter what. How's that?"

"Good. I'll talk to you later."

Shelley hung up the phone and woke the children. She could not be positive that Neal went to his office at all. He could have decided to have her car serviced, then come home for his. He could show up just as she was leaving with the children. She knew if that happened, he would go to any lengths to stop her from leaving, and she had to avoid another violent scene.

She fed the children and once again, filled overnight bags with the same amount of clothing and the same amount of resentment that she had the first time Neal hit her, and they were forced to leave home in the middle of the night. She looked forward to the day when she would not have to leave home anymore, when Neal could no longer terrorize her. She looked around the house at all the things she'd found in different places, stores and shops, to make the house the warm and cozy place it was, and felt determined to find a lawyer who could convince a judge somewhere, that Neal should move out of the house, not her and the children.

Chapter 36

Shelley felt safe within the refuge of her parent's home without understanding why. When her mother called the night before to tell Shelley they would be leaving the following morning for their vacation, she wasn't stunned by how unaffected her mother was about her horrifying experience that morning. She was, however, disappointed when her mother told her to work things out with Neal. Her reasoning was, "So your father and I won't have to worry. We want to enjoy our vacation."

Feeling very much alone, she assured her mother she would try, then waited until nine o'clock that morning to go to the house, knowing they would be gone. She did not want to hear her mother's words of wisdom about her daughter's failed marriage.

Somehow, it would all be Shelley's fault. She was hurting, and instead of a misguided lecture, she needed a hug and someone to tell her that no matter what Neal tried to do, she would be okay.

Shelley no sooner got the children situated in the house when she realized there was no milk in the refrigerator, or bread in the pantry. Her parents, of course, had not planned on anyone being there. She had to put the children back in the car for a trip to the store. It was only noon, and already she was physically exhausted and emotionally weary.

When Shelley returned with the groceries, she lifted the first bag out of the trunk, and noticed a large manila envelope with 'bank books' written across the front in Neal's handwriting with a red marker.

Now what? she wondered.

She slowly set the bags down. The envelope was sealed, but she opened it anyway, finding five, savings account books. One was for their joint savings account, and the other four were in Neal's name only, all from different banks, in different states.

What the hell is this? Shelley thought. *Why would Neal have secret bank accounts in different states?*

The first one she opened belonged to an account in New Jersey. Shelley thought perhaps it was from an old account Neal might have had when he lived there, but she noticed the dates of the deposits and withdrawals were current. Adding more confusion, the balance of the account was twenty two thousand dollars.

She put the savings book back in the large envelope, and shoved it in one of the grocery bags. She'd sit and look at the other books after the groceries were packed away. Suddenly, she wasn't tired anymore.

After putting the children down for a nap and pouring herself a cup of coffee, Shelley couldn't wait to go to the family room to look at the savings books. She felt mentally exhausted as she pulled them out of the envelope again, setting aside the one for their joint account, and the one she had already seen from New Jersey. The next book she picked up was from a bank in Pennsylvania. The balance of that account was eighteen thousand dollars. Like the New Jersey account, the dates of deposits and withdrawals were current. *This is unbelievable. What is Neal doing with all this money?* she wondered.

The next book was from a bank in Florida. It had a balance of thirty three thousand dollars. Not only were the dates of deposits and withdrawals current. But the account had not been open as long as the other accounts. The first transaction was dated in April, three months earlier.

Why would Neal open a secret bank account in Florida? she asked herself, as if by doing so, the answer would follow.

The last book was from a bank in Tennessee, also showing current deposits and withdrawal dates, and a balance of five thousand dollars. Bewildered, she sat back in her chair and sighed. *What are these books about? Why would Neal borrow eight thousand dollars from his parents if he had all this money? Neal, why is everything in your life such a mystery? I don't know who I'm married to anymore, and why does it still hurt so much?*

She put the books back in the envelope and did her best to reseal it, hoping Neal would not know she'd opened it. Obviously, his intentions were to keep the books hidden from her. Until she had a clearer idea about what they meant, she did not want him to know they were discovered, so she returned them to the trunk.

At eight o'clock that night, the bell on the door leading to the driveway rang loudly against the silence of the house. She looked out the window to see Neal and Ralph standing there. Neal looked furious. She felt safe with Ralph being there and believed Neal would not try anything violent in front of his friend, so she opened the door.

Neal walked in first with Ralph following behind him. He grabbed her arm, pulling her into the family room, while Ralph, once again, followed his friend.

Shelley pulled her arm away as he pushed her onto the couch.

"Get the kids and let's go now!" Neal demanded, his face red with anger.

"No, Neal, not this time. I can't live with you anymore!" Shelley responded.

Neal pulled her off the couch and threw her onto the floor. Immediately, Ralph jumped in front of Neal, clearly stunned by his friend's behavior.

"Look, buddy, let's just get your car keys and leave," Ralph said firmly, as he helped Shelley up.

"Shelley, this is your last chance," Neal said, the veins in his forehead bulging with rage. "Leave with me now, or pay the consequences!"

"Go to hell, Neal! The only way the kids and I will return home is after the court has ordered you to leave!" Shelley informed him.

"Well, then you have a long wait, because I don't intend to go anywhere."

Somehow, he moved his arm before Ralph could get a firm grip on it, and slapped her face.

Shelley heard Ralph shouting at Neal in the background, demanding that he stop, but Neal obviously did not hear anything but the pulsing of his own anger. Finally, Ralph was able to grab Neal from behind. "Get your keys and let's go!" he yelled. "This was not necessary, Neal!"

Shelley stumbled into the kitchen and sat on a chair by the table.

"No matter where you go, Shelley, I'll find you, and one way, or another, you will come home! By the way, the bank books you found in my trunk, except for ours, belong to my father."

Shelley stared at him for a second. *I don't believe it, he must have looked in the trunk before he rang the doorbell!*

"Did you really think you could hide the fact that you opened a sealed envelope?" Neal asked with a smirk.

Ralph made sure Neal walked outside, then, he put his arms around Shelley. "I'm sorry, kid. I didn't know it would turn into this. He's so upset about your leaving, he's acting irrationally. Are you okay?"

"Please, Ralph, get him out of here. I never want to see him again," Shelley whispered.

She watched as Neal and Ralph drove away in their separate cars. It was then, that she saw the two Police cars as they pulled away from the curb and followed. She had no idea Neal actually brought the Police with him to her parent's house. He must have told them she had stolen his company car. Since the car was safe, their job was done. She locked the door again, realizing that Neal had not bothered to bring her car. Apparently, it was okay with the law that Neal had kept hers.

Feeling weak, she collapsed on the couch and began to cry. Her entire body shook with each aching sob. In complete despair, she thought, *What will I do? I'm basically alone in the world with two children who will count on me to take care of them. Lord, I don't know if I can. I'm such a mess, and I have nowhere to go to be safe from Neal and his vengeance. I feel finished, God, I can't take anymore. Why can't I die? Other people do. And if I have to live, why can't I have a normal life, like other women do? Why is this happening to me?* Shelley cried, in her loneliness.

She remembered that during the drive to her parents' house, she'd stopped at a traffic light. In the car next to her was a man and woman with two children in the back seat, much like Jackie and Jason. She looked at them, and thought, *I wish we were them! I want to be anybody, who isn't me.* Not knowing what their problems were, she only knew she wanted their lives, instead of her own.

Clancy called at ten o'clock, and Shelley fought to appear calm.

"Shelley, what's wrong?" her friend asked, at once.

"Neal was here," Shelley answered, bursting into tears. She described the awful scene and listened to Clancy gasp with disgust. Shelley knew it was hard for anybody to understand a world filled with abuse, unless you lived in one.

"That's it, Shelley. Tomorrow morning, I'm going to make arrangements for you and the children to enter the shelter!" Clancy insisted.

"Clancy, no...I can't. I'm not ready for that yet," Shelley argued, not sure exactly what it was that she was ready for.

"In what way are you not ready for this? Where are you going to hide...your mother's house? Eventually, Neal will pull his next stunt. Besides, listen to you. You're not emotionally strong enough right now to deal with you, much less the children."

She paused for a moment, catching her breath. "Shelley, you have got to get help to keep safe. Please don't argue," Clancy pleaded, in a much softer and controlled voice.

Shelley thought for a moment. As much as she did not want to go, she agreed with Clancy. Neal would try to torment her if she stayed in a place he had access to her and the kids.

"Okay, Clancy...okay," Shelley finally agreed, beginning to cry again. "Please, when you talk to them, warn them that I'm a basket case, because I think I'm really losing it. I can't stop crying, or shaking, and I'm so scared."

"It's okay, Honey. You've been through a lot, but, the good thing is you're still alive and in one piece. You could be dead."

Clancy called first thing the next morning. Shelley was too frightened to let the children play outside in case Neal was somewhere out there, so she kept them indoors. Without toys, it was hard to keep them amused, but paper and crayons kept them busy drawing until Clancy called.

"Are you ready, Shelley?" she asked. Clancy sounded anxious, but determined to bring her friend to a safe place.

"I guess so," Shelley answered, tears already covering her face. "Clancy, I just can't stop crying. I feel completely useless."

"It's okay. The woman I spoke to at the shelter said tears are normal, so stop thinking you're nuts."

"Okay...I'll try, but it's really hard. What time will you be here?"

"An hour perhaps, okay?" Clancy asked, trying to sound cheerful.

"I'll be ready," Shelley said, softly. "Thank you."

Shelley felt a sense of relief when they were in the safety of Clancy's car. She'd had an awful night of no sleep, swearing every creak in her parents' house was Neal trying to break in.

"Where do we have to go?" Shelley asked.

"I don't know, but Margo, the Director of the shelter, said to meet her at a gas station on Old Highway 85. We're supposed to circle the street a few times to make sure no one is following us, and then, she'll lead us to the shelter. Not even our Government Officials know where the shelter is...it's protected by immunity."

"I never thought of Neal following us," Shelley said, immediately looking at the surrounding cars. She knew he was capable of anything.

"Margo said you'll be fine, just trust her."

"Do I have a choice?"

"No, not really, but you do believe this is the best solution, don't you?"

"It's just the fear of the unknown," Shelley said. "It would be different if it were just me, but my whole life is coming with me." She looked at Jackie and Jason.

Clancy pulled the car into the service station and looked around. A few minutes later, a young, red haired woman, also pulled in. She was driving the old, beat up, gray station wagon, she'd told Clancy she would be driving.

"Margo?" Clancy called out to the woman.

"Clancy?"

"That's me!"

"Okay, follow me," the woman said as she pulled out of the station.

Clancy had a hard time keeping up with the woman as she made the ride around the same streets, four times. Finally, she pulled into a parking lot in front of a large, white building resembling an old plantation house with four large columns standing on its big porch.

Margo jumped out of her car, and seriously looked around again for anyone who might have been following them.

Meanwhile, Clancy got out of the car while Shelley took the children out of their seat belts. She was a wreck, and the children sensed she was frightened as they clung to their mother.

Margo cheerfully introduced herself to the two women as she bent down to greet the children.

Shelley began to feel more at ease when the woman managed to make her children laugh within minutes. Margo told them about all the fun things waiting for them inside the house, and they quickly, took her hands as she led everyone up the stairs on the side of the house.

Margo stopped to explain the function of the built in buttons next to the metal door.

"This is our code box for the residents to get in using this door. Each week the code is changed to keep safety at a maximum. This week the code is one, three, five, six. You will need to remember that if you go out anywhere," she said, opening the door.

Shelley began to sob as Margo led them up a flight of stairs to another door that she opened with a key. "This is usually unlocked by this time of the morning, but my assistant is out on vacation. She'll be back in a few days."

It's like a prison here with this door and that door. I want to leave! I want to take my children and run!

Clancy put her arm around Shelley's shoulders and said, gently, "Honey, it's going to be okay. Give it a chance. I know you're scared, but this is the only safe place for you to be right now. Besides, you know you can leave whenever you want. It just wouldn't be a good thing to do right now."

After Margo opened the door, she pointed towards a room and asked Clancy to take the children there so she could talk to Shelley alone.

"There is a freezer full of ice cream right in that room. Help yourselves," Margo told Jackie and Jason, giving them a warm smile.

"Great! We could use some ice cream, right guys?" Clancy asked, as she took their hands and led them to the other room.

"Now. Let's have a seat so we can talk a little bit, okay?" Margo asked, after the children were out of sight.

Shelley did not want to be away from her children, not even for a few minutes, and Margo seemed to sense this.

"I'm sorry. I'm behaving like such a baby, but I can't help it. I feel so depressed and I don't know what will make this feeling stop," Shelley said.

"You're not expected to feel happy. You have a lot of healing to do. For a long time now, you've been abused. You've been so busy caring about the emotions of your husband, doing anything you could to keep him calm, it has become a full time job for you whether you realize it, or not. Keeping your husband calm has taken priority over caring for your children, or yourself. Now, for the first time in a very long time, you're able to respond to what you're feeling, instead of worrying about his reactions. As it would be with anybody in that situation, you're feeling apprehensive, and scared. It's like breaking an addiction."

"But, why do I feel so unsure about leaving him? He's a dangerous man, and there's no way I can continue to live with him and expect to survive. And yet, I'm petrified about leaving him. I don't know if I can do this," Shelley whispered.

"Women stay with abusive husbands for various reasons. Lack of money, the children, a religion. The fear of failure, or the commitment they made for better, or worse. I could go on and on, but the reality of an abusive situation is, none of those reasons, justifies you staying in a marriage that hurts you, or quite possibly might cause your death. Shelley, no one has the right to hit you under any circumstances, and your husband has you convinced that you can't function without him, and that if you try to, you will be punished, or fail."

Shelley completely broke down. She knew Margo was right, that she was the injured party, not Neal, contrary to what he'd taught her to believe. Yet, all she could think about was what he would do. As if he had the legal right to torment her and take away her feeling of safety, because she was his wife.

"Now, you have a job to do. You need to get healthy again, and not just physically, but emotionally and mentally. You have to recover the strength you lost during your marriage. You need to remember your identity, and your ability to see situations through your own eyes again, instead of Neal's. Shelley, he had control of all those things for such a long time, that is what you're afraid of. He has convinced you that you can't make it in life without him, or at least that you don't have the right to. You have to begin feeling safe, which is why you're here."

"Then, why do I feel so weak?" Shelley asked. "As if I don't know how to bring myself in out of the rain?"

"Of course you feel that way. You haven't had to make any decisions for yourself, because your husband did that for you. You haven't had to plan your time, because he did that for you. You probably haven't been able to have an opinion, because only his mattered. Shelley, that's control, and now, it's time for you to put these functions back into your daily routine."

"I'm afraid of what Neal will do next. He won't let go easily. He'll try to force us to come home any way he can," Shelley told her.

"Yes, he probably will. Most of them do. Whenever there is a break in the control, the abuser freaks, because he has become addicted to that control, and when it's taken away from him, he has to think of ways to get it back. Don't be frightened by it, Shelley. We'll stand up against the problems he gives you one at a time, and we will help you get through them. In the end, I promise, you'll be okay."

"I don't even know what my next step should be," Shelley said, wiping her tears from her face with the tissue Margo handed her.

"The first step is to get settled, then we'll arrange for you to speak with an attorney. We have a women who helps our residents pro bono. I'll call her and arrange an appointment for you. You'll have to file for divorce, that's one of the rules of the shelter. We can't help you, if you're not going to help yourself. You will be expected to file a warrant against your husband for abuse, and you can't drop the charges while you're a resident here. Again, we can't help you unless you are willing to help yourself. Besides that, it's for your protection. Irate husbands are a lot less gutsy when they know the law has an eye on them," Margo explained.

Shelley was frightened. Somehow, Neal would find a way to stop her from doing anything.

"Margo, I can't take a warrant out on him. Believe me, He'll kill me!"

"It's okay, you're safe here. That won't happen if you listen to what we say. Now, let me give you the grand tour of our facility and introduce you to the other women. There are only two staying here right now, a mother and her two children, and another woman alone. Follow me," Margo said with a smile, as she opened a different door leading to the living quarters of the shelter.

Shelley was surprised when they walked into what looked like an ordinary living room. There were two flowered couches, and two fluffy chairs, a coffee table, along with a huge television and a phone. Warm lamps and pictures on the wall created a cozy room. It felt peaceful.

"Obviously, this is our living room. As you can see, it's like any other living room, except both of these couches turn in to sleepers. The only rule for this room, is no television during the daytime hours.

This applies to the children as well. The YWCA is downstairs and they offer a structured and happy daycare facility. I'll take you down there when we're finished, so you can see what I mean. You name it, and they have it, for the kids. Daytime hours are spent getting your life back together, and we don't want soap operas to interfere with that," Margo joked.

She led Shelley into the hall where she almost bumped into a black woman. "Oh, I'm sorry. You must be the maid," Shelley said, not thinking.

Margo looked at her strangely. "No, this is Molly. She's one of the residents here."

Oh, my, God! How stupid can I be? Shelley asked herself.

"Look, Shelley. We have worked hard to make this a nice place to visit, but it certainly isn't the Ritz. There's no maid service here," Margo said, as Molly gave Shelley a look of disdain walking into the kitchen. Shelley was totally embarrassed.

Margo led Shelley into the kitchen area. It was large with a freezer along one wall, and two long tables joined together in the middle of the room. There was a refrigerator, sink, and a row of cabinets filled with dishes. It even accommodated a washer and dryer. Another door led to a full bath. Shelley was amazed at the facility's cleanliness.

Jackie and Jason were sitting at one of the tables eating ice cream cones.

"Mommy, look what we have!" Jackie yelled, elatedly. Clancy was holding Jason, and Shelley experienced a rush of contentment when she realized they were all smiling. It felt nice.

Molly was busy ignoring them. She was cooking something for a little girl who was sitting in a high chair at the end of second table. The child looked about two years old.

"That's Rebecca," Margo said, introducing Shelley to everyone. Rebecca gave everyone a smile. "We really enjoy this kitchen," Margo added. "The cooking is shared, along with washing the dishes and the cleaning. All chores are rotated among the residents, so no one gets stuck doing the same chores everyday."

They went back into the hall where Margo quietly opened one of the bedroom doors. "This is Molly's room right now. We have to be quiet because her baby is sleeping," Margo whispered. Shelley saw what looked like a newborn asleep in a crib.

There was also a double bed and a set of twin bunk beds. Although a little cramped, the room was full of sunlight and femininity.

When Margo opened the other door in the hall, Shelley saw two twin beds next to a double one. "This is where Dina sleeps. You can put the children in here on the spare twin beds, or you can all stay together by using the sleepers in the living room."

"I would like us to stay together, otherwise I'll worry about the children," Shelley responded

"That's fine, I understand. This is our second full bath," Margo said, showing her the last room in the hall. It also was very bright and feminine. "Now, let me take you downstairs."

As they left the apartment, she called Jackie and Jason who were more than pleased to join their mother.

When they entered the massive double doors downstairs, a cheerful woman greeted them. Jackie and Jason saw the other children and released their mother's hand to join them. Shelley tried calling them back, but Margo assured her it was fine and that Elaine, one of the counselors for YWCA, would take very good care of them.

After touring the Y, Shelley felt comfortable leaving the children behind to play with the other children. They needed some fun time, and Margo suggested Shelley and she return upstairs. Once outside, Clancy hugged her friend and got the phone numbers from Margo to the resident's phone so she could check on her when she got home.

Meanwhile, Margo tried to call the attorney she knew, while Shelley waited alone on one of the living room couches. She desperately wanted to be in her own home. She wanted her children to sleep in their own beds with all their wonderful things surrounding them. She wanted Neal to die, and began to cry over her gloomy situation.

How could I let this happen? Neal threatened to kill me and I'm the one in a shelter! And, they don't understand how clever he is. He will outsmart everybody and hurt us. I just know it. He always wins...always. Shelley thought in despair. She sat for hours unaware that it had grown dark outside, unaware that her children were brought upstairs, and that Molly had fed Jackie and Jason, along with her own children. They were bathed and dressed in their pajamas, and made ready for bed, while Shelley remained dead to the world around her, so much so, that no positive words could bring her out of it.

"Mommy, why are we sleeping here?" Jason asked, twirling a piece of his mother's hair between his fingers, as he often did when she held him.

"We just have to right now, Baby. Don't worry, everything will be okay. We'll be home real soon, Sweetie, you'll see."

Chapter 37

The next day brought more of the same. Shelley remained resentful thinking about her circumstances. Fortunately, Margo was able to arrange a meeting between Shelley and her attorney friend, Shawna Harris, seven o'clock that evening.

Molly cooked again, and Dina, the other resident, washed the dishes, even though Molly let it be known it was Shelley's turn. Dina offered to do them because of Shelley's state of mind, and her appointment with Shawna.

Molly was wonderful with Jackie and Jason, but cool with Shelley. It was apparent Dina got along well with Molly by the sound of their laughter and easy conversations. Shelley, on the other hand, decided it wise to stay out of Molly's way after that stupid remark she'd made the day before. On top of everything else Shelley had on her mind, she could not forgive herself for what she'd said, It connected with her many other reasons for a sleepless night, leaving her staring at the ceiling most of the night, worrying about what Neal was going to try next. She looked at the children sleeping next to her, and wished life were better for them. Her feelings of guilt overwhelmed her, and she felt so responsible for where they were.

Margo and Shawna were thrilled to see each other. It obviously had been a while since Shawna visited the shelter.

"How are things going with the new firm?" Margo asked.

"It's okay, except they keep me busy. I'm hoping the Senior Partners will let me take this case for you," she answered, with a concerned look on her face.

"Shawna, I know I don't have to ask you this, but please do the best you can for this girl. She really needs your help."

"You know I will," Shawna answered.

"Yes, I do, and I thank you a thousand times," Margo replied with her usual smile.

"Where is she?" Shawna asked.

"In the living room."

"Okay, I'll see you before I leave."

"Hi, Shelley, I'm Shawna Harris," the attorney said, standing in front of Shelley, who was still sitting on the couch.

Molly and Dina once again took care of Jackie and Jason. Shelley told them she would like to get them ready for bed herself, but Dina insisted, and Molly basically told her to take care of her lawyer business and leave them to take care of the children.

Facing the lawyer, Shelley hoped she would stop crying. She felt so weak.

Shawna was close to Shelley's age, perhaps a few years older, and seemed very together, leaving Shelley more embarrassed about the lack of control she had over her own life.

"So, Shelley, tell me what has happened, what brought you here?" Shawna asked gently. She took a legal pad out of her briefcase. Looking at Shelley's bruises, she made notes as Shelley went into all the sordid details about Neal's parents, the Valentine's Day Dance, Neal's constant lying, and the gun incident.

"He sounds really sick, Shelley. We'll have to take a warrant out for the abuse. I'm sure Margo explained those rules to you. At the same time, we'll serve him the divorce papers." Shawna made notes on her pad as she spoke. "Usually, in abuse cases, whoever serves first has the advantage, and since he doesn't have a clue where you are, we'll probably beat him to the punch."

"I'm frightened," Shelley said. "Neal is not a predictable person."

"Stop worrying. I know it's hard to feel secure right now, but you are safe here," Shawna assured her with a smile.

"I can't stop worrying. Nobody understands how clever Neal is! You can't underestimate him. He'll reach me when I least expect it."

"Shelley, Neal can't get you here, I promise," Shawna responded.

"It doesn't have to be here. No one can comprehend what I'm trying to say. I put myself in danger the moment I left him," Shelley said solemnly.

Shawna looked at Shelley as she stood to leave. "I'll get back to you. Try to relax."

The next morning, Shawna called Shelley from her office. She sounded upset.

"The owner of my law firm told me I can't take on any new cases from the shelter at this time. He feels it would impact the busy caseload I've been assigned to that actually brings money to the firm."

"What if I could pay you?" Shelley asked. She never expected Shawna to help her without being paid.

"That would be great. Do you have your own money you can use? Because you can't use any joint funds right now."

"I have a little over ten thousand dollars in my own account," Shelley told her.

"Honey, that's wonderful! At least your not destitute like most of the women who come to the shelter. Usually their abusive husbands have controlled all the money, leaving them virtually penniless until we get to court."

"Well, Neal does handle all our finances, except for my personal account."

"What a guy!" Shawna said, joking. "Okay, a regular divorce retainer is two thousand dollars, and hopefully, before that's gone, the court will order Neal to pay your attorney fees. I'll get your papers ready, and you bring me cash or a check so we can get started. And Shelley?"

"Yes?"

"I'm glad that I'll be able to take your case after all."

Shelley ended her conversation with Shawna and called Clancy. "Can you take me to the bank this morning? I'm still without my car."

"Sure, but why don't you just give Shawna a check?" Clancy asked.

"Because I need some money anyway. I think I have twelve dollars with me," Shelley replied.

"Well, why didn't you tell me? I could have given you some money," Clancy scolded.

"I didn't need any. It's not like I've been anywhere the past two days."

"That's true. Okay, Is eleven okay?"

"That will be fine," Shelley said as they ended their phone conversation. The children were excited about Clancy coming, and seemed more than ready to get out for a while.

Shelley would have been afraid to drive through Peach Haven alone, even if she had her car. By now, she was sure Neal would be actively looking for her whereabouts. Her fear was confirmed when Clancy picked her up, and told her that Joe saw Neal and Ralph driving past their house several times. Shelley knew Neal's anger would soar when he realized she was not coming home. Although a shelter would be the last place he would look, it made her nervous knowing he was searching for her.

Inside the bank, Shelley handed the teller a check for twenty two, hundred dollars. Several minutes later, the woman returned with the check.

"Mrs. Jordon, I'm sorry, but at this time your account doesn't have enough funds to cover this check," she said, politely.

Shelley's heart began to pound in response to the woman's words until she swore it would pop out of her chest. "What do you mean there's not enough funds?" she asked. "There should be a little over ten thousand dollars in this account."

"You had a balance of ten thousand, two hundred dollars, but a check for ten thousand dollars cleared your account this morning," the woman informed her.

"But, wasn't a deposit of ten thousand dollars made in this account last week?" Shelley asked.

"No, Ma'am, there wasn't."

Tears formed in Shelley's eyes. *Why am I surprised? Again, Neal lied to me. He never replaced the money he'd used for the antique car as he promised he had.*

"How much is in my account?" Shelley asked.

"Two hundred dollars, Mrs. Jordon. I also think you should know that your husband asked the bank to notify him immediately if you came here."

Shelley knew Neal had developed a special relationship with the manager of the bank, but totally resented the lack of privacy allotted her now because of it.

"This is my account, not my husband's, and no one in this bank has a right to discuss my business with anybody, including him!" Shelley yelled, angrily. She wrote a new check for two hundred dollars to close her account. That would end the problem.

Thinking of her children, she felt completely helpless. She had no idea how she would care for them without that money. It would be months before her next scheduled closing. She was then, at the mercy of the court's ability to force Neal to pay child support.

Back in the car, Shelley told Clancy what Neal had done with her account as she wept during the drive back to the shelter. Clancy helped Shelley bring the children upstairs, then told Margo about the money, while Shelley continued to sob.

"What will I do about getting an attorney with no money?" Shelley asked Margo.

She thought for a moment. "Let me make some phone calls to some other attorneys who have helped us in the past. Maybe we can get help elsewhere."

"Do you think so? I just don't know what else to do."

Shelley walked Clancy to her car. Through her tears, she thanked her friend for the ride to the bank.

"Shelley, look. I know you don't believe this now, but every day is going to get better. You'll make it through this," Clancy said, trying to console her friend.

"Well, please, don't take this the wrong way, Clancy, but that's an easy statement coming from someone who is on her way home."

Clancy frowned and shook her head. "You're absolutely right. How could I possibly pretend to know what you're feeling right now? But, what I can do is take one step at a time with you, and help meet any obstacle that comes your way. How's that?"

Trying to smile, Shelley nodded. "That's all I can do, too, and I appreciate having you by my side, Clancy. You're a great friend, and I'm sorry for the way I've been acting, but I'm so scared."

"I know," Clancy responded. She paused before she spoke again. "Shelley, there is something else I want to discuss with you."

"Oh, no. What? Not another problem, I hope. My, God, I sound like my mother."

Clancy laughed. "Vinnie keeps calling me to ask if we've made a decision about transferring to his office."

"Under the circumstances, I haven't given it much thought, but what do you think?"

"Well, I think now is a great time for you to think about it. Neal has been calling Mitch. He refused to give him any information, but how long can you avoid working? Especially with your recent financial development."

Shelley thought for a moment. "I'm sure you're right, but how do you think Mitch would take it?"

"I've already discussed it with him, and he honestly understands, and he'll just keep telling Neal that you're not in, so he won't know you moved to another office," Clancy answered. "And we can put my signs on any listings we get, since you can't be reached at the phone number on your signs anyway."

"So, what do you want to do?" Shelley asked.

"I want to make the change. I think it would be better financially, and you'll have peace for at least a little while, knowing Neal doesn't know where your working."

"Does Vinnie know my situation?"

"I told him what I had to, no more. Actually, no offense, but I think hearing that you left your husband was good news to him," Clancy laughed.

"Well, if he doesn't mind my circumstances, then let's do it," Shelley agreed, sure it was the right move.

"Great! I'll call Vinnie when I get back to the office. By the way, everyone there is asking about you. What do you want me to tell them?"

"Tell them what you think they should know. I just can't talk to anyone now."

"Look, Shelley, you have been through a lot, you don't owe anybody an explanation, and none of the things that have happened are your fault. Do you believe that?"

"No, but I'm working on it," Shelley answered, trying to smile.

"Good! By the way, Joe hit Jerry Skinner with a club on the golf course the other day. Then, he tried to run him over with our golf cart. It was quite grand, I must say," Clancy said, laughing again.

"Oh, no! Tell Joe to stop. I don't want Joe to get hurt," Shelley said.

"I wouldn't worry about anything Joe does to Jerry. That clown still won't get it," Clancy replied. "Now, give me a hug," she said, before she got in her car.

Margo met Shelley at the top of the stairs when she came back in, and gave her the bad news. She had no luck with the other attorneys she had called for help. Shelley was back to square one.

For the sake of the children, Shelley tried to hold onto the small amount of sanity she had left. It was quite a battle. Leaning against the living room wall, she slid down to the floor, once again, sobbing.

Margo took Jackie and Jason downstairs to give Shelley some time to think and hopefully gather some composure. All the emotions, the fear, the pain, that she had been stockpiling were coming to the surface and it was hard for her to deal with all at once.

"Shelley?"

She looked up an saw an attractive, smartly dressed woman standing in front of her. She had no idea how long the woman had been standing there.

"Hi. I'm Mary. We haven't met before because I was away on vacation when you arrived. I'm another one of the counselors here. How are you?" her voice was kind.

Shelley began to sob uncontrollably. "I'm sorry," she said, feeling drugged with grief.

"I'd like to talk with you, if that's okay," Mary said, gently.

"I really don't feel like talking now," Shelley responded.

Mary nodded with understanding.

"I just feel like I want to die. Do you know what that feels like? I don't want to talk, I want to die!" Shelley said, devastated.

Mary sat next to Shelley on the floor and took her hand. "I know you're feeling pretty messed up right now, but let us help you. We can get you through this, but you have to try to get yourself together."

"I don't understand how, in this so called human society of ours, this could be happening to me and my children? I hate Neal! I hate myself for letting all this go on for as long as I did, and I hate the Policemen who gave Neal permission to abuse his family, all in the name of marriage!"

Shelley cried, unaware that the room had turned dark. It was evening and once again, she didn't know who had been kind enough to feed and bath her children, or who had put them to bed. She barely remembered kissing them goodnight.

Mary sat by her side and listened as Shelley told her about Neal's mother treating her so badly while Neal watched. How she marveled that her face was not deformed from all the swelling it had endured at the hands of her husband, and how grateful she was that she never had to spend time in a hospital, as many other women in her situation had to. She also wondered if there were other women who might have called the Police, only to be told to forget it, it was nothing, just a domestic dispute, something to be forgotten in the morning. How many nights did she pray to be alive the next day, if only for the sake of her children? She thought of the friends she'd avoided because Neal insisted those friends would eventually break up their marriage. He was probably blaming Clancy for her leaving, never looking at himself as the cause. She thought of all the places she would have gone if only Neal wouldn't have become angry if she had. The clothes she'd returned to stores because Neal said they were inappropriate, and the times Neal told her not to talk to people so they would not find her too friendly. Anger and grief poured out of her, and when she was finished draining her cup of drama, she felt a small bond of friendship with this woman named Mary.

"Shelley," she said, gently. "Tomorrow is group. It starts at seven and everybody meets downstairs. You're going to find that you're not alone with what you've been through and experienced in your marriage," Mary said.

"Oh, no, I can't. I don't want to go," Shelley objected.

"You have to, Shelley. It's required as part of your stay here. Besides that, trust me when I tell you that you will feel a lot better," she insisted.

"Please…I can't go. I don't want to talk to anyone."

"You just did, Shelley," Mary responded. She hesitated for a moment. "I promise, after the group meeting, you'll feel much better, and it will help you begin your healing process. I have to leave now, but, I'll see you tomorrow night at seven."

Shelley watched Mary leave. Afterward, she went into the kitchen, feeling hungry from not eating all day. Molly was just sitting down to eat something herself. Shelley soon learned that Molly was the one who had cared so well for her children.

Molly had put them to bed before she fed herself, so Shelley and Mary could talk without being interrupted.

With tears still running down her face, Shelley took a plate off the counter and filled it with mashed potatoes.

"Is that all you're going to eat?" Molly asked, sounding irritated.

"I'm not very hungry," Shelley answered through her tears.

"Look, Miss Toothpick, I spent all afternoon cooking dinner for you all, and I expect the people I cook for, to eat it."

"Can't you see I'm upset?" Shelley asked, getting irritated herself.

"I see a skinny girl who's gonna get a whole lot skinnier, if she doesn't eat. What's got you so upset anyway?" Molly asked.

"Gee, well, let's see. I have a stinking two hundred dollars to my name, I have no attorney, and not much hope of getting one with my new found poverty. I've been forced to leave my home with my children, and it doesn't look like we'll be going back there anytime soon. What else do you want to know? And, by the way, my weight is fine for my height, which hardly makes me a toothpick!"

Shelley stormed out of the kitchen to take her place on the couch with her mashed potatoes, leaving Molly in the kitchen to eat alone.

"Skinny thing. Ain't much taller than a minute either, so I guess she is the perfect weight for her little old self," Molly muttered to herself, amused.

Dina came in just as Molly got ready to do the dishes.

"Good, you're home. Eat something, then if you would, start the dishes, I have to go talk to Miss Thing out there. I think I might have offended the child," Molly said.

"Sure, go ahead," Dina said. "I think you made her cry. Actually, I feel sorry for her. Every minute something new happens to make her world fall apart all over again."

"Yeah...and here's the latest. Poor baby only has two hundred dollars to her name!" Molly smirked, mocking her. "I ain't seen two hundred dollars at one time for ten years!" she added.

"Well, go see if you can make her feel better," Dina said, as she started to fix her dinner. "We're all in this together."

"Yeah, you're right," Molly agreed.

She sat quietly across from Shelley, like a queen fidgeting on her throne. "Look, child, I'm sorry if I made you feel bad. I do that sometimes. I guess I just felt mad cause you thought I was some black maid."

Shelley stared at the woman, stunned by Molly's sincerity. She knew she had to match her remorse to be fair, and was ready to make peace herself. "Well, I'm sorry too. That was really stupid of me," Shelley said, wiping her tears.

"Yeah, you're right," Molly said, laughing. Then, she became more serious. "I know right now you think your life is over, and that there's no hope for a better day, but you will begin to feel better, and stronger each day. I promise," she advised.

"She's telling the truth, Shelley," Dina said, joining them in the living room.

"Now, why don't you get yourself a cup of that great coffee I just made and we'll sit and pour our hearts out to each other? Maybe, you'll find we're not all that different from each other," Molly suggested, grinning.

Shelley took her advice and returned from the kitchen a few minutes later, sipping a cup of Molly's wonderful brew. That night, the three women stayed up past three o'clock in the morning talking and sharing the events that had led each of them to the shelter.

Molly had left her husband, James, a month earlier, fleeing with her two year old daughter and newborn son. After years of physical and mental abuse, her moment of enlightenment came during the drive home from the hospital, after she'd given birth to Quinton. She told her husband they would have to stop at the store to buy diapers and formula for the baby since she was sure he had not prepared for their homecoming. James pulled out seventeen dollars from the huge wad of money he always kept in the pocket of his pants. This was the amount he gave Molly each week to buy groceries for their family of three, while he hoarded thousands of dollars in an account he had opened in his name only.

When Molly told him that seventeen dollars would not even cover the cost of the formula and diapers, much less their regular groceries, he smacked her across the face as he drove. He was unconcerned that she was holding their newborn son, or that his daughter was in the back seat. He told his wife to stop being greedy, and to somehow make it work.

It was at that moment, Molly knew she was done. After James had dropped his family off at the dilapidated trailer the called home, Molly put the children in her car and brought them to the shelter.

Dina ran to safety when her husband accused her of being attracted to their family dentist. He had beaten her senseless when she refused to go with him to shoot the unsuspecting soul. Fortunately, her husband couldn't find the dentist, but threatened to kill his wife instead. She reported his intentions of killing the dentist to the Police, and he went to jail. She fled to the shelter, knowing it would not be long before he would be out on bail.

After their talk, Shelley definitely felt better, and a lot less lonely in her grief than she had earlier. They were all experiencing the same nightmares, and the same fears about the future.

"You want a laugh, Shelley?" Dina asked, at the end of the evening.

"Yeah, I could use one," she answered.

Dina imitated the way Molly had made fun of Shelley earlier. "When Molly and I were in the kitchen washing dishes, she said to me, "Poor, baby, only has two hundred dollars to her name!""

Molly looked mortified when Dina told her new friend what she had said in jest, but when Shelley began to laugh, she did too. They both realized they had unidentified prejudices, and by the end of the long evening, Molly and Shelley bonded with each other, sure they would be friends for life.

Unfortunately, the next morning, Shelley's mother called from New Hampshire. Meg had managed to get the shelter's number from a reluctant Clancy at the office, who at first had refused to give Meg any details until it was absolutely impossible not to.

Shelley knew things would never be the same between Meg and her again once she discovered her daughter was in a women's shelter. It would be more than Meg could bear.

"Why in the world are you in a place like that, Shelley?" Meg asked, horrified.

"Because I can't live with Neal's abuse any longer," Shelley explained.

"Oh, Shelley, your father and I have had plenty of bad times, but we always worked through them. Why can't you do the same with Neal? I thought you had more stamina than that. That's the problem with young people today, they quit at the drop of a hat!" Meg exclaimed, annoyed with her daughter.

"Mother, we don't have normal problems. Neal is dangerous. You should understand that since you know what we went through with the gun incident. Don't tell me you think that was normal, or that you went through that kind of drama with Dad."

"Well, no, but Shelley, you have a beautiful house, a brand new car, and all the clothes and money you need. Can't you ignore a little strange behavior for all that?" Meg asked.

Shelley could not believe what her mother was asking her to do. Her question was so ignorant and offensive, that for the first time, Shelley truly became aware of just how out of touch her mother was with any life besides her own.

"Well, anyway, there's another problem," Meg continued.

"Now what?" Shelley asked, sensing something terrible.

"Linda next door called your father and I at our hotel here in New Hampshire, and it seems the Sheriff's Department knocked on her door the other day, looking for information about you. She said they had a warrant for your arrest!"

Shelley grew silent. There it was, the beginning of Neal's revenge. That definitely sounded like something Neal would generate against her.

"Why did the Sheriff's Department go to Linda's house looking for me?" Shelley finally asked.

"Because our address, was the one Neal's parents gave them and we were away on vacation. Shelley, we have lived in our house for yeas and never had the Police come to..."

Shelley instantly interrupted her mother. "Hold it, Mother! Neal's parents took a warrant out on me? For what, leaving their son?" Shelley yelled.

"I don't know, Shelley. Fortunately, I had given Linda the phone number where we would be staying in case something happened to the house while we were gone."

Shelley was still on the warrant and Neal's parents. "What in Heaven's name did Neal's parents take a warrant out on me for?" she asked.

"I don't know. I called the Sheriff's Department, hoping to get some information and the officer said it was for theft, or something. She said if you would call them, they would explain the situation to you."

"Oh, I'm sure they would. This is ridiculous!" Shelley shouted, not sure how much more she could take.

"Now, don't get crazy, Shelley. The officer said this could all be worked out."

"Fine, Mother. I'll have my attorney take care of it this morning," Shelley said, without knowing where, or when, she would find a lawyer that would help a desperate mother with no money.

Shelley phoned Shawna as soon as she got off the phone with Meg, hoping she could at least tell her what to do.

"What are they doing, do you know?" Shawna asked, when Shelley told her that Neal's parents were behind the warrant.

"I have no idea. I only know they are even more evil than Neal. Who knows what they're capable of doing?" Shelley answered.

"Well, you're not exactly on the ten most wanted list. I'll call and see what's going on. Meanwhile, you just relax. They probably just wanted to help their son. Obviously, they were informed that if a person has a warrant out against them, they're not permitted by law to take a warrant out on someone else, and they saw an abuse warrant coming against their son. Can you find an attorney as soon as possible?" Shawna asked.

"I don't know how. Margo called a few people, but she couldn't come up with anything. I'm scared, Shawna. I have the children to worry about," Shelley said.

"I'm so sorry, Shelley. I wish I could take your case, but I'm new to this firm and I have to do what they tell me."

"I understand, I'm just upset. I need an attorney immediately, and I can't afford one."

"Well, make some calls yourself to different attorneys this morning while I call the Sheriff's Department for you. Maybe one of the attorneys you'll call will have a soft heart," she suggested. "You know the court could always appoint you an attorney."

"I'm afraid of that, especially since Neal can afford a good one."

"I know. It would be much better if you could find an attorney on your own."

"Well, I guess justice only prevails if you have enough money to pay for it," Shelley said.

"I'm afraid so. But keep your chin up and I'll call you after I find out something, okay?" Shawna asked.

"Okay, and I appreciate your help, Shawna," Shelley said, feeling miserable.

Chapter 38

Shelley went into Margo's office to tell her the latest ordeal.

"This is one of the many problems our women face, they have no money because their husband's control it all, so the husbands can get whatever attorney they want, while they do awful things like this warrant mess to their victims," Margo said.

"I can't imagine why his parents would do this to me," Shelley said, honestly appalled by their cold hearts. "Have they given any thought about what they're doing to their grandchildren?"

"Of course not. They just knew they had to do something first. That way Neal remains safe, and that's all they cared about," Margo responded.

"Because I could press charges against Neal for the gun incident?" Shelley asked.

"Sure, and the beatings," Margo said.

"But the Police didn't do anything about those anyway, so why would his parents bother doing this?" Shelley asked.

"This is common strategy used by abusers. Even more outrageous is the fact that it's usually done with the guidance of some lowlife attorney," she answered.

"And the law permits this to go on, but refused to help me, when the man held a gun on his family for two hours?"

"I'm afraid so," Margo answered, weary with the failure of the southern justice system regarding women and children.

Shelley phoned Clancy to vent about Neal's parents.

"You mean, all the times he beat you to a pulp, and the Police wouldn't do a damn thing, they're going to help him and his crazy family do something like this?" Clancy shouted.

"I just don't know what to do," Shelley sighed. "This is so unfair. I had the money for an attorney, but Neal cheated me out of that, too."

"I know, I know. Look, let we talk to a pair of attorneys that I know, they're old friends," Clancy offered.

"I appreciate it, but everybody wants money up front," Shelley responded.

"Well, these guys are great, so let's see what they say. Their office is in Fairville. They're really good, too," she said, cheerfully, almost encouraging. "One of them is a Magistrate Judge."

"Do you really think they'll help?" Shelley asked, beginning to feel a little hopeful.

"We can try. I'll check and get back to you as soon as I find out. How's that?"

"Oh, Clancy, that would be wonderful! I love you!"

Clancy laughed. "I love you, too. Now, just try not to worry."

"Okay, I'll wait to hear from you before I hang myself."

"Oh, and before I forget, we are now with Regal Sales of Clayton. I brought your license along with mine, to Vinnie's office yesterday. Is that okay?"

"That's great," Shelley said. "I just don't know when I can get to work again."

"I've already explained that to Vinnie and he said he'll give you as much time as you need. He's got this huge crush on you, remember?"

By two o'clock, John Black, one of the attorneys Clancy spoke about phoned Shelley. He asked to meet with her for a free consultation, knowing the woman had no money. They made arrangements to meet in the lobby of the YWCA at four o'clock. Shelley was excited about the meeting. The fact that he was willing to talk to her without a retainer made him very special in her eyes.

When Shelley opened the huge door downstairs, she saw John Black sitting on a bench in front of the doorway. He stood when he saw her, greeting her with the sweetest smile she had ever seen on any man. He was quite overweight, and perfectly round. His height gave him the appearance of Santa Claus, all warm and trustworthy, as he offered Shelley his hand and introduced himself.

"Hello, Mrs. Jordon. I don't think you remember me, but you closed on your home in my office a few months ago. I didn't realize you were the woman Clancy was talking about until I saw you just now."

Shelley thought for a moment, then, it came to her. "My, goodness, you have a good memory, I was only in your office for ten minutes," she said, amazed he'd remembered her.

"Shelley, Clancy explained your circumstances to me on the phone, and before I came here I stopped by the Sheriff's Department to find out what that warrant is about. It seems your in-laws have taken a warrant against you for 'theft by conversion'," John explained.

"What is that?" Shelley said.

"They claim you borrowed money to buy a specific piece of property and then used it to buy something else," he answered.

"What money, and what something else?" Shelley asked, irritated.

"They claim you borrowed eight thousand dollars from them to buy your home, then used the funds to buy an antique car," John explained, reading the information off his yellow notepad.

"First of all, Mr. Black, I didn't borrow any money from Neal's parents, Neal did. And it was my understanding that this money was paid back. I had nothing to do with any loan arrangements Neal made with his parents."

"Well, unfortunately, that's what they have said, and now we have to prove they're lying," he told her. "And, please, call me, John. You make me feel like an old man," he chuckled.

Shelley smiled back. "Okay, John. So now what? Can you help me?"

"I spoke to the judge who issued the warrant, and he has scheduled a small hearing tomorrow night at the Sheriff's Department. He smells a rat also, and this will help him determine whether or not he's going to send the case to the Grand Jury."

Shelley gave him all the details leading up to her leaving home. "I'm supposed to take a warrant out against Neal. Can I still do that?"

"Right now we have to handle this situation, then we can go forward." He smiled again, comforting Shelley with the warmth of it.

"So, once again, Neal gets away with hurting me and the children?" she asked.

The look on his face assured her, she would be okay.

"Just for now, Shelley. Some people, like the Jordons, have no morals and they're not afraid to do bad things. Throughout this case, it may seem at times that Neal is winning, but in the long term of events, he won't," John assured her. "By the way, I'm going to stop by the Peach Haven Police Department to pick up a copy of the Police report involving the gun incident. And, I hate to ask you this, but do you still have any bruises anywhere?"

"Yes, why?" the question made her feel uncomfortable.

"I would like Clancy, or someone else to take pictures of them. Is that okay with you?" he asked, gently.

"I'm willing to do whatever it takes to get Neal out of our lives, and out of the house forever," she answered, disgusted that she had to experience such awful things.

"Okay then, tomorrow night at six o'clock, you'll go to my office and meet with Jack Pope, my partner. He's a criminal attorney and he's going to take you to the judge to determine if he'll dismiss the warrant, or not. There's nothing for you to be afraid of. Jack will take good care of you, all right?"

Shelley said, tearfully, "I'm truly grateful for your help. Please, don't think I'm not, but I'm nervous. I know Neal is capable of anything and quite frankly, I'm petrified of him."

"I know, but we're going to stop him from ever hurting you again, no matter what circumstances he throws our way, we'll eliminate them one by one, I promise."

Chapter 39

That evening, with Molly's help, Shelley finished washing dishes by seven o'clock so the chores would be done in time for group meeting. Shelley and Molly joined the other twenty women already assembled in a circle of chairs with Margo presiding.

Shelley looked around the room as Margo introduced her to the group. She felt sick to her stomach. One of the women, Pat Ward, had a broken nose covered in bandages, courtesy of her husband. She also sported a broken arm set in a cast, and two of her ribs were also broken, yet somehow, Pat managed to smile.

Another woman, Barbara Hogan, also had one of her arms in a cast. The others basically wore black eyes, or stitched faces. Some were between stages, or had left home sometime ago, and were already beginning to heal.

This is a world, no one could possibly understand until it happens to them, Shelley thought, studying the assembly of broken women.

Margo began the session, and Shelley listened as some of the women gave the group updates on their drawn out court cases, or the results of different job searches. Every step was important to their survival, and that was all most of them had left.

Eventually, Margo looked at Shelley and said, "We haven't heard from you yet, Shelley."

Shelley stiffened, as twenty heads turned towards her, waiting for her response. She wanted to pour her heart out after listening to the many different stories told there, but had no idea where to start. For so long, she'd thought she was alone in her private, violent world, ashamed, and embarrassed by the lack of dignity Neal had cast upon her.

But, listening to the other women that night took away all her feelings of isolation. She realized she had plenty of company, not just those women, but every fourth woman in the United States that statistics confirmed were victims of spousal abuse.

One night, Pat Ward, cooked dinner when she returned home from her job with the telephone company. Throughout the meal, her husband complained about the way she'd cooked the meat and that the potatoes were too lumpy. Then, he wanted to know why the house was such a mess. When she refused to respond to his mad desire for an argument, he threw his first punch, breaking her nose. Pat managed to run out her front door and into her car. She always kept a set of car keys in her pants pockets in case she had to leave in a hurry, as she had that night.

Her husband grabbed his own car keys and followed her. Blood was pouring from Pat's nose, so she was forced to pull into the parking lot of a convenience store where she saw a Police car parked. She ran towards the car, screaming for help, but they drove off. Her husband then, jumped out of his car, and broke two of her ribs and her arm before a man and his wife leaving the store, interfered and called 911 for an ambulance. Her husband left, leaving Pat unconscious.

Barbara Hogan was a young newlywed who had received two oil hurricane lamps as a wedding gift. Her husband hated the smell of scented oils and forbid Barbara to light them. Apparently, the group already knew about the lamps and how much Barbara wanted to light them. It had become a weekly joke. One of the other women asked her if she had lit them yet.

That night, she came to the meeting with a broken arm, accompanied with a black eye. The rest of the group remained silent as Margo asked her what happened?

"The other night, it became real important to me to light those lamps!" Barbara answered. "I finally left. I'm living with my mother until I can get on my feet."

After seconds of silence, Barbara began to laugh with tears in her eyes, and the group joined her, clapping. They were proud of her for finally lighting the lamps, but sad at what it cost her.

Juanita Green was a music teacher. One night, a pea rolled off her dinner plate. Her husband called her a pig, and beat her so badly, there was permanent brain damage. Juanita's slightly bizarre behavior, due to her head injuries, made her husband the victor in the end of their divorce proceedings as he was given custody of their two children. Juanita was devastated. Her children meant everything to her, and two years later, she was still fighting to get her life, and children back.

Those were just a few of the stories Shelley heard that night. They left her full of major concerns about her own future. *Where will I be in two years?* she had to ask herself. *As unfair as it is, and no matter how abusive these men are, they seem to get away with it. They seem to win. There are no guarantees any of these men will see justice...ever!*

Chapter 40

Shelley slipped into her bathrobe so Clancy could take Polaroid pictures of her leftover bruises.

Clancy let out a gasp when she saw Shelley's side and stomach. "Damn, Shelley…how did these bruises look a week ago?"

"They're a month old," Shelley informed her. "Can we just get this over with? I feel completely humiliated."

"I understand. I'll hurry." Clancy snapped the photos as fast as the camera would move. The pictures came out clear. There would be no mistaking the bruises for anything other than what they were. Margo was sure they would help in court when she saw how clear the bruises photographed.

Margo loaned Shelley the shelter's station wagon the next day so she could keep her appointment with John's office at six o'clock. Because it was after hours, the receptionist was gone for the day. As she walked towards the back, she heard a man's voice echoing from one of the large rooms in the old converted house.

Shelley saw the back of a man's head over the top of his high backed, leather chair. He was holding a telephone to his ear, so she quietly sat on one of the chairs in front of his desk, not knowing whether to leave, or stay, trying not to be rude.

Immediately, sensing her presence, the man turned around and appeared motionless as he stared into Shelley's eyes.

"Okay, that's good, I'll talk to you, then," he said, hanging up the phone. He stood and offered Shelley his hand. "Hi, I'm Jack Pope, and you must be Shelley."

"Yes, I am," she answered quickly, blushing as he continued to stare at her.

He gave her a warm, empathetic smile. "Well, John was right. You are certainly beautiful. Hopefully, that will help us," he said, before he took his seat again, and began to write on a yellow, legal pad.

The smile and comment embarrassed her. "Excuse me, Sir?" she asked, confused.

"Look, we will be working closely together, so please, don't call me sir. It's Jack…okay?"

"Okay," she answered, nervously.

The man had taken her by surprise. There was something incredibly sensuous about him, and she wondered if she was the only woman who ever thought that. A rugged looking man, Shelley thought he had the largest brown eyes she had ever seen, almost doe like. She guessed he was about forty five, and as much as he made her blush, she liked him instantly.

Good. Now, there's another problem," he said, hesitantly, looking at Shelley as if he was sure she would be upset after he explained what the new problem was.

"What new problem?" she asked. "Things can't get much worse."

"Three people phoned the Sheriff's Department and said you're a cocaine user."

"That does it!" Shelley shouted, jumping to her feet. "I don't know anyone who would do such a thing, but I guarantee my husband does!"

"I'm sure he does," Jack answered. "However, we have been asked to talk to a detective from Narcotics before we go into the judge's chambers for our meeting, okay?"

Shelley was getting sick to her stomach. "This constant harassment. How can this keep happening?" she asked, tears forming in her eyes.

"Your husband is a lowlife, and has hired a lowlife for an attorney," Jack said, not taking his eyes off Shelley.

"I didn't know Neal had an attorney," she said.

"Oh, yes, he does, and both your husband and his attorney, know you have a solid case. They're going to do all they can to stop you from going to court," he explained.

"We're going to lose! He's going to win as usual, I can feel it," Shelley cried.

"Shelley, we're not going to lose anything. We'll just keep blowing up every barricade they want to throw in front of us," he assured her.

Shelley noticed his dimples were as large as his eyes, and became embarrassed when he caught her staring at him.

"So, now what?" she asked, blushing.

"Looking at you, it will be obvious to the detective that you've been set up and he'll get angry. But...we'll leave the results of that to the detective. When we go into the judge's chambers with your in-laws, don't say anything. Even if you want to scream. Don't even look at them," he said. "Do you understand? This is very important. If you don't know where to look, look at me. I won't mind," he said, warmly smiling again.

Don't I have to say something?" she asked.

"No, we have that option and we're going to use it," he answered, clearly trying to comfort her.

"So, why do I have to go at all?" she asked.

"Because, unfortunately, it's the law," Jack answered, grabbing his suit jacket off the back of another chair. He looked at Shelley. "Are you ready?"

She shrugged. "I guess so. Will Neal be there?"

"He's not required to be there, since this is his parents' deal, but I'm sure he'll come anyway, if for nothing else than to see you."

Jack led Shelley to his car, an old, black Lincoln. It had red leather seats, cracked with age. The car was huge and Shelley felt small inside its roomy interior.

The narcotics detective, Andy Bryant, was waiting for them when they arrived at the Sheriff's Department. Jack briefed the detective on the situation, and after he spoke to Shelley for a few minutes, the detective knew his department had been used. Anger colored the detective's words as he asked Shelley to wait outside of his office while he tended to some business with Jack.

Several minutes later, both Andy and Jack came out of the office and asked Shelley to join them. While she'd been waiting, they contacted the people who made the false reports and asked them where they'd received their information about Shelley using drugs. All three confirmed that the information had come from Neal, who also encouraged them to call the Police Department to file a report in order to help him save his children.

"Andy, this is a blatant plan of conspiracy. What are you going to do about it?" Jack asked. "Arrest him, I hope."

"I will take care of Neal Jordon, and in the meantime, he'd better not so much as spit on the streets of Fairfield County," he responded.

Angry, Shelley took Jack aside. "So, let me get this right. Unless Neal spits on a street in Fairfield County, he's free? I'm going through this garbage with his crazy parents, and he's free?"

"Hold on, and remember what I said. One step at a time," Jack replied softly. "Thank you, Andy," he said, extending his hand to the detective.

Jack led Shelley to the judge's chambers, which were located in the same building. There were ten chairs placed in a semi circle, all facing the judge's desk.

Neal's parents sat in two of them, while Neal and his attorney, Lyle Maggitt, occupied another two. Jack and Shelley took the last two seats on the opposite side.

Shelley's body began to shake when she saw Neal. He sat, giving Shelley that arrogant stare he always used when he was getting ready to physically attack. Jack noticed the way he was trying to intimidate her, and patted her hand.

"Don't look at them," he whispered, reminding her.

Neal's parents were also giving her a burning stare. Shelley could feel the impact of Neal's eyes on her throughout the entire inquiry, which took a total of five minutes. After both attorneys stated their cases, the judge decided that even though he thought the charges were ridiculous, he had to refer the case to the Grand Jury.

The judge knew both Neal and his parents had used the system, but because of the Jordon's civil rights, he had to refer it. Shelley wondered when her civil rights, and the rights of her children, would become important.

Jack whispered in Shelley's ear. "Don't get upset. This is what we wanted. We'll be ready for them, trust me. They won't like the results of this."

Shelley had no idea what had just happened, she only knew she had to remain confident in her attorneys.

"Your Honor, Mrs. Jordon, is staying in the Shelter for Battered Women," he explained. "For her safety, and to maintain the shelter's anonymity, I'm asking that she not be required to notify the court where she is currently residing. I'm also asking that you please shortly detain Mr. Jordon and his parents', to assure that Mrs. Jordon won't be followed, as we're positive that is Mr. Jordon's intention."

When Shelley and Jack returned to the law office, they sat outside on two wrought iron benches that she thought were as old as Jack's car. They talked for hours, and not once during their conversation did Shelley think of Neal, or feel afraid. She felt drawn to him, yet sure her weakened emotional state was the source for those feelings.

"John is already in the process of petitioning the court to have Neal removed from the house, along with a request for temporary child support," Jack said. He gave Shelley a reassuring pat on the shoulder, sending a strange sensation through her body. "We're also going to request a restraining order. If he comes within fifty feet of you, he'll be arrested. And after the Grand Jury throws out the charges the Jordons have brought against you, we'll be ready to sue them for false arrest. That's why I wanted the judge to send it to the Grand Jury."

Shelley drove back to the shelter, certain that it would not be long before she would be able to return home with her children, without facing Neal, guns, or beatings. She felt safe for the first time in a long time. Her new attorneys had given her a new sense of hope.

Chapter 41

The following day, John called. "We have a court date set for two weeks from today," he told her.

"John, that's fantastic. Do you think the judge will make Neal leave the house immediately after court?"

John hesitated. "It's not going to be that easy. We first have to prove that Neal abused you, and that was the reason you left your home."

Shelley was beside herself, excited with the thoughts of going home. "Well, that should be easy. Especially when we present the court with the Police report about the gun incident," she said. The silence on the other end alerted her that something was wrong.

"John, what is it? No, wait a minute. Do I want hear your answer?"

John finally broke his silence. "The Police officers who were called to your house that day didn't file a Police report."

Tears formed in Shelley's eyes. "Why, John?" she asked, her voice quivering. "Why didn't they file a report?"

"They said it was a domestic dispute and didn't in their minds, require one," John answered, clearly embarrassed by the obvious prejudice of the men working for the local Police Department.

"I don't believe this!" Shelley cried.

"Shelley, Honey, I understand your pain, and I'm so sorry. If it's any comfort, one of the officers who came to your house that day, followed Jack outside and told him that he remembered the incident and would be glad to testify in court for you. But, I'm afraid his testimony won't hold water without a Police report to back it up."

"Why not for God's sake?" Shelley asked.

"Because it gives the impression that the Police officers saw no immediate danger. Don't you see? They certainly would have to say that to save face," John answered.

Shelley felt plagued. John must have sensed that because he agreed to give her what she wanted.

"Okay, we'll try getting the officer to testify without a Police report. I certainly understand your anger, I just don't know how the officer's testimony is going to work."

"John," Shelley pleaded. "I'm in a battered women's shelter. We have no clothes, no money, and nowhere to live. Neal is sitting in our beautiful house with all his things and a bed to sleep in, while his children sleep in sleeping bags on the floor. Where is the justice in that? Yes, I'm angry. I'm very angry. We have to try everything."

"Jack and I have every intention of proving to the court what a criminal Neal is. I've already filed your divorce papers, and Neal will soon be served. I promise, this will be over soon, okay?"

John calmed her. "I'll hold you to that Mr. Attorney," she said, satisfied. She trusted both him, and Jack, and their ability to win, even against Neal.

Shelley's next issue of the day, was to retrieve her car from the shop that had serviced her car the day she left Neal. She asked Clancy for a ride, and as usual, her best friend was glad to help.

Clancy suggested she have her daughter to drop her off at the service shop, where she would retrieve the car, then, she would drive it to the shelter. Shelley would then, drive Clancy to work, where Joe would pick her up when she was ready to leave.

Several hours had passed and Clancy still had not arrived at the shelter. Shelley had an uneasy feeling in the pit of her stomach. She knew the car was ready, because earlier she'd phoned the garage. Since Neal had paid for the work when he'd brought the car in, the mechanic, one of Neal's friends, said it would be sitting out in the lot with the keys in the ignition, ready to go. All she had to was drive it away.

Shelley decided to phone Clancy at home, then, at Regal, but Marie, the secretary there, said she'd not been in. There was no answer at the garage either.

Another hour went by, while Shelley sat in front of the living room window waiting when she saw an old, black Lincoln pull into the empty parking lot of the YWCA.

That looks like Jack's car, Shelley thought. *It is Jack!* she whispered to herself, watching him get out of the car. His grim expression startled her. Her body went numb for the long second it took for her to run down the stairs leading outside.

Something is wrong with Clancy, my God, something is wrong! Shelley agonized as she flung the big, metal door open.

Margo ran after her when she saw the panic on Shelley's face.

Jack stopped at the bottom of the stairs and looked up. "Shelley, Honey, you need to come with me," he said, softly.

She felt sick. "What's wrong?"

Jack hesitated, but finally, told her. "Clancy has been shot," he said, opening his arms.

"No!" Shelley screamed, falling into Jack's embrace. He cradled her there as she cried.

"They think she's going to be okay, but the Police want to ask you a few questions. They're waiting at the hospital. I told them I would come for you, rather than let them call you. I didn't want you to find out that way."

Margo told her, running upstairs "I'll take the children downstairs, Shelley. You go with Jack."

"How bad is it?" Shelley asked, as they got into Jack's car. She could not get to Clancy fast enough.

"I don't know, yet. Somehow, the Police knew to call me, and I rushed to get you without asking for all the details."

"Jack, this doesn't make sense, who would want to hurt Clancy?"

Jack stopped at a red light, and looked at her. "You don't get it, Shelley, do you?"

She looked puzzled. "Get what?"

"The person who shot Clancy, thought she was you."

Of course. Jack is right! Shelley thought. *Clancy was picking up my car. My God...that bullet was meant for me!*

Once more, she thought of the little girl in the fire, and Neal's grandmother swinging from her basement rafters. "Dear, God! Neal shot her, didn't he, Jack?"

Jack shook his head. "No, I don't think so. He would have known it was not you. My guess is, that he hired someone to shoot you, and that person didn't know he'd shot the wrong target. But, listen, let's get some more facts before we start speculating."

He looked at Shelley with a serious look. A look filled with affection. "I'm going to make sure you're safe."

Joe was sitting in the waiting room with two Police officers along with a plain clothes detective. He stood and put his arm around Shelley.

"Joe, I'm sorry. Can you ever forgive me?" she asked, beginning to sob.

"Honey, it's not your fault. I've already spoken to Clancy and she wants me to make sure you understand that!" he said, adamantly.

"What did the doctors say?" Jack asked.

"They said it looks like Clancy was a very lucky lady. She dropped her car keys and bent down to get them just as the shot was fired. The bullet caught her shoulder, instead of her chest. The surgeon is removing the bullet now," Joe answered.

"Will she be all right? Will there be any permanent damage?" Shelley asked.

"They're not sure. The bullet is in tissue instead of bone, so she'll probably be as mean as ever before we know it," Joe responded, trying to smile.

"Mrs. Jordon, we would like to ask you a few questions, if you don't mind. Dr. Gannon has been kind enough to offer me his office," Detective Morgan interrupted.

"Sure," Shelley answered, looking at Jack for some kind of reassurance.

"That's fine. We'll be there in just a moment," Jack said.

The man gave him a curious look. "Jack, we're not accusing Mrs. Jordon of anything. We just need some information."

"And Mrs. Jordon, wants me to be with her while you get it," Jack shot back.

Detective Morgan threw up his arms. "Let's get to it, then," he said.

Jack walked with his arm around Shelley, and once again, she felt safe.

Detective Morgan took the seat behind Dr. Gannon's desk, while Shelley and Jack sat in two leather chairs.

"Mrs. Jordon, who besides Clancy and yourself, knew that the car was going to be picked up today?"

"The owner of the shop, Jim O'Brien, Clancy's daughter, Jill, and I believe Joe, her husband."

"How did O'Brien know?"

"Because I called him and told him I would be coming. Of course, that was before Clancy suggested that she pick up the car," Shelley answered.

Detective Morgan wrote some notes on a small notepad. "Is there anything else you know that you think might help us?"

She shook her head. "No, I can't think of anything. Did Jim O'Brien know anything?" Shelley was sure he'd played a part in what happened.

"No. He was out to lunch, which has already been verified, but we'll keep you posted if we find out anything to the contrary. No one saw the person who did this," Detective Morgan said. "But, who knows? We might get lucky."

"I know in my heart that somehow my husband is behind this," Shelley said, angered by the detective's lack of enthusiasm.

"Well, that will be difficult to prove when your husband is out of town on business. We checked him out first, along with the owner of the shop, and came up empty. It could be that it had nothing to do with you. Maybe it was just some nut with a gun."

"You know, Morgan, it's highly possible that Shelley's husband hired someone to do this. She just filed for divorce, and the man has a history of abuse," Jack said.

"We'll look into it, Jack, and I'll keep you informed," the detective assured him.

Jack stood. "Thanks, I appreciate it." He shook hands with the detective before he escorted Shelley out of the office.

While Shelley waited to see Clancy, Jack phoned John to inform him of Clancy's condition. "I'm going to stay with Shelley for a while, John. She's pretty upset."

"Do you want me to come? Is there anything I can do?" John asked.

"No, we're fine, but thanks anyway. I'll see you later."

"Okay. Tell Clancy I was asking about her, and tell Shelley, I'm here if she needs me."

"I'll do it," Jack said, ending the conversation.

Two transport nurses brought Clancy to the room they had ready for her.

Joe came out of Clancy's room, smiling, once they had her situated. "She's bossy as ever. The doctor said she's going to be fine and should be up and running in about a week."

"Thank God," Shelley whispered, closing her eyes.

"She wants to see you, Shelley," Joe said.

Shelley walked quietly into Clancy's room, passing by a Police officer posted outside her door. She was told that was standard procedure for a gunshot victim.

"Why are you tip toeing in here?" Clancy asked, with her eyes half closed.

"I wasn't sure you were awake," Shelley answered, tears forming in her eyes.

"I'm awake, and fine…come in," she said, still drowsy.

Standing beside her bed, Shelley said, "Clancy, I'm so sorry. I can't believe this happened. You could have been killed!"

"Well, as usual, I was clumsy enough to drop my car keys." She paused, then, said what she really wanted to say. "Shelley, someone tried to kill you. You have got to be careful. I would bet my life Neal is behind this. I want to talk to Jack. Joe told me he's here. I have to tell him, he's got to watch you like a hawk from now on."

"Clancy, he's a lawyer, not a bodyguard, but I'll get him anyway. I don't want you getting upset," Shelley said turning towards the door.

"Shelley, he used to be a detective, so he'll know how to keep you safe," Clancy said.

"Okay. If talking to Jack will make you feel better, then I'll go get him."

"No, wait! Give me a hug and promise me you'll be careful," she said.

"I promise," Shelley said, trying to hug her friend without hurting her. "Now, let me tell Jack to come in, so you can get some rest." At the door, Shelley paused. "Just get well, Clancy," she said through fresh tears. "I'm so sorry this happened."

"Let's just concentrate on nailing whoever did this, instead of burdening ourselves with crazy regret and unjustified guilt," Clancy said, trying to smile.

"I'll try, Clancy. I just want you to be all right," Shelley responded.

"And I will be. I promise. Besides, you all need me to keep you in line. Now go out there and get my good friend, Jack," Clancy said, her eyes still half closed.

Chapter 42

As expected, there was no closure regarding Clancy's shooting, but both Jack and John stayed in close contact with Shelley and the children to assure their safety.

When her court date arrived, everybody argued with Shelley about driving herself to court, but she felt it was time to make things as normal as possible under the circumstances, and normal did not include bodyguards.

During the five mile ride from the shelter to the courthouse, Shelley swore Neal was waiting, gun in hand, behind every tree and building she passed on the highway. She doubted she would ever feel safe again.

Jack, and John were waiting for her in front of the courthouse, along with Clancy, wearing a shoulder sling, and Mary, who were both there to testify on Shelley's behalf. Neal stood a few yards away, looking smart in one of his impeccable suits, his attorney by his side.

Shelley's stomach rumbled at the sight of him. *What deceitful ideas do you have ready for today?* Shelley wondered. *I'm sure you're going to try something,* she thought, knowing he would have something evil planned. Neal would never allow himself to be seen as a bad guy.

At nine o'clock, they entered the courtroom. Shelley's team took their seats to the right, and Neal's team took their seats on the left. The witnesses were led to a special room guarded by a deputy, there to make sure the witnesses didn't talk to one another.

Jack handed Shelley one of his yellow, legal pads and whispered, "I'm going to be right here next to you during the entire session. Anything you want to say, write it on this pad."

Shelley could feel Neal's piercing gaze. She refused to look at him, remembering what Jack told her about looking at Neal.

"Shelley, under no circumstances are you to get upset, or make a scene in here over anything Neal might say, okay?" Jack asked her. "Neal will try to intimidate you."

"Okay," Shelley responded in a whisper.

The attorneys spoke first, stating their case and their intent. John stood first making an immediate request for the court to order Neal to vacate the house, and grant his client some form of temporary child support. He further informed the judge that Shelley and the children were living in a shelter for battered women, and that the children were sleeping in sleeping bags on the floor because there weren't enough beds there. He explained how the children did not even have their clothes or personal things since they had to flee for safety.

Neal sat in his seat shaking his head at all of John's comments, as if false accusations were being made about him. Once John finished, Lyle Maggitt, stood up and began his plea for Neal, claiming that Shelley left him for no apparent reason, taking his children with her, whom he had not seen in weeks, and how much Neal missed them and was truly concerned about their welfare.

Shelley felt sick listening to the lies pouring out of Lyle Maggitt's surly mouth. Those who knew Lyle Maggitt, said they were surprised that he showed up in court sober, since he was well known through the county as an alcoholic, with no ethics.

Shelley was called to the stand first, and Jack patted her hand. "You'll be fine."

But, she was not fine. She was petrified. She was sworn in and almost fainted when Lyle Maggitt stood in front of her.

"Please, state your name and address for the court," Judge Pierson said.

John stood immediately, and objected. "Your Honor, Mrs. Jordon and the children currently reside in the Shelter for Battered Women, and her husband and his family are present. Amnesty applies with regard to her answering that question."

"That's fine. You don't have to answer my question, Mrs. Jordon. Your address will be documented using the address of your attorney's office."

Shelley just sat in the stand, hoping John would object to every question Lyle Maggitt threw at her so she wouldn't have to answer any of them.

Lyle Maggitt asked Shelley a lot of questions about the household expenses for the house and the children. She had no idea what point he was trying to establish until he progressed further in his questioning. "So, then, Mrs. Jordon, since both you and your husband administered the upkeep of the household, you are fully aware of the costs involved, is that correct?"

"Yes, pretty much, as far as the costs are concerned," Shelley responded.

"Then, you are aware that after the mortgage is paid, the utilities, car payments, etcetera, there isn't too much money left over?" he asked.

Shelley was confused. *Why is this man lying? He's supposed to be an attorney. Why is he lying? Neal has a good income,* Shelley thought.

"No, that's not true. We were fine financially, except when Neal pulled one his extravagant spending tricks."

"Mrs. Jordon, did you recently attend a Real Estate convention in Macon for four days?"

"Yes, I did," she answered.

Maggitt paced in front of the stand several times before he continued, a quizzical expression on his face. "Why, if your husband is as dangerous as you claim he is, would you leave your children in his care?"

"At that time, Neal had not involved the children with his abuse, and I asked our next door neighbor if she would keep an eye on them for me, just to make sure everything was going well. She said she would."

"So, you felt your husband would never hurt his children, isn't that so, Mrs. Jordon?" he asked, then quickly said, "I withdraw the question. The answer is obvious if she left the children in his care."

Shelley wanted the court to know her children were not safe with Neal. Not any more. Not since the gun incident. She wanted to tell the judge how he had threatened to shoot the children because he was jealous of them. She also wondered why she had to defend herself, when she was the victim.

After forty minutes of John objecting to Lyle Maggitt's unethical line of questioning, the lawyer finally said, "I have no more questions at this time, your Honor."

Once Maggitt returned to his seat, John stood before Shelley. Relieved to see him instead of Lyle Maggitt, she hoped the exhausting ordeal would soon be over.

John began. "Mrs. Jordon, how often did your husband hurt you in your home?"

Maggitt jumped out of his seat, shouting, "I object, your Honor! It has not been established that Mrs. Jordon has ever been hurt by her husband!"

Before John could respond, the judge overruled the objection. "And it won't be if we don't allow the testimony that would establish that. Please answer the question, Mrs. Jordon."

Finally, I get to tell the truth! Shelley thought. "Towards the end, every night," Shelley answered, embarrassed that all her personal business was being thrown out to a courtroom full of strangers.

"Do you consider your husband a danger to his children?" John asked.

"Yes, I do."

Maggitt once again objected. "Your Honor, Mrs. Jordon is not an expert witness to make that determination!" he shouted.

"Objection overruled," Judge Pierson ordered, clearly annoyed with the entire proceeding.

"Mrs. Jordon, what happened to your husband's gun?" John asked, after Shelley presented the court with the horrific details of that decisive Sunday morning.

"The Police took it, and told Neal he could pick it up at the station after he calmed down," Shelley answered. She heard gasps from several women sitting in the courtroom.

By five o'clock, their first day in court was coming to a dramatic close, but not before John asked for temporary child support. The entire courtroom appeared to be disgusted when Judge Pierson denied his request.

"I don't feel as though I can make a proper decision on child support at this time. However, I think Mr. Jordon does have the right to see his children, so I'll grant him immediate visitation rights, beginning this Friday at five o'clock, ending six o'clock, Sunday evening. Since Mrs. Jordon is staying at the shelter, you will need to determine a meeting place for him to receive his children. Also, I feel in order for the children to remain in the custody of their mother, she will have to obtain a bond in the amount of fifteen hundred dollars to guarantee she will not leave the State of Georgia with the children. I consider this necessary because of the accusations of abuse she has made against Mr. Jordon. I want this done by nine o'clock Friday morning. If Mrs. Jordon does not obtain the bond, and Mr. Jordon does, custody of the children will go to him. If neither parent obtains the bond, the children will be placed in Foster Care, since the custody issue of this divorce cannot be determined at this time."

Shelley screamed. "No! Please...no!"

Jack grabbed her arm to stop her from saying anything else.

"Jack, what is he saying? Please tell me the children don't have to go with him anywhere. Please...tell me that. And what does that bond thing mean?"

"Take her out the back door, Jack," John said, clearly furious with the judge's decision. "I'll meet you both at the office. I'm going to speak with Judge Pierson. This is crazy."

Outside, Clancy and Mary joined them. They'd been in the witness room all day, unaware of what had taken place at the end of the session. Jack put his arm around Shelley.

"Honey, this is going to be all right. Give John a chance to talk with Judge Pierson," he said, softly.

He gave Clancy and Mary the details of Judge Pierson's orders, while he continued to hold Shelley.

"Jack, what can happen? I need to know the truth," Shelley pleaded, desperate to know her children would be safe.

"If you dont get a bond for fifteen hundred dollars by Friday, and Neal does, he will get custody of the children. If neither of you gets the bond, they will be placed in Foster Care until the judge comes to some kind of decision about custody," he explained, angrily. "The request is completely inhumane and totally absurd. Never have I seen a judge make such an unreasonable decision. The children's well being and peace of mind were never considered."

Near hysteria, Shelley cried. "What can I do? I can't let them take my children. I don't have fifteen hundred dollars! Neal won't get the bond because he doesn't really care if his kids go to Foster Care, or not." *My, God, I just want to die!*

"Shelley, leave your car here and ride with me to the office. You will have to sign some papers for the Judge," Jack suggested. "I'll bring you back later. Neal might try to follow you back to the shelter, if you go there now, and John won't be back for a few hours, because there were still several cases Judge Pierson had to hear."

"All right," Shelley said. Although she wanted to go back to the shelter to be with Jackie and Jason, she knew she had to talk to John first to find out the results of his discussion with Judge Pierson. "Jack, I'm scared," Shelley said, as she got into his car.

"Knowing John, he's probably going to ask Judge Pierson to accept a property bond instead of a cash bond, so someone can put up their property for you, since it can't be your own property," Jack added.

"Oh? And who might that be?" Shelley snapped. "No one I know," she said, frantically.

"What about your parents?"

Shelley laughed. "You don't know my parents. I guarantee you they would never go along with that. They don't have a clue about what we're going through. My mother wanted me to stay with Neal so I could keep my nice house and brand new car. Does that explain them?"

"Well, let's see what John has to say when he gets back to the office. We're going to do all we can."

He patted her hand before pulling onto the highway. Eventually Jack turned the Lincoln down a gravel road. Shelley could see that the road led to an old abandoned, fishing lake.

"Where are we going, Jack?"

"I want to talk to you alone for a few minutes, and no one ever comes down here. Clancy and Mary will be at the office when we get there, but John won't be back at the office for almost two hours anyway. I thought we would be able to talk more privately away from the office."

"It's so beautiful here, Jack," Shelley said, as the car approached a lake.

He parked in a patch of grass and they both got out.

Jack removed his jacket and tie, and threw them on the back seat of the car before he joined Shelley as she walked closer to the lake, partially hidden behind a line of trees.

Shelley caught Jack watching her. He was so valiant all the time. She hoped he couldn't sense what she felt just standing next to him. He was married, and so was she, for the time being anyway. She knew her strong attraction to him was unhealthy.

She'd heard Jack's marriage was over from Clancy, but didn't know any of the details surrounding it, and avoided asking him, in case those circumstances were painful.

"I can't let them take Jackie and Jason away from you," he said, softly.

"I don't know how you can stop it. If John can't reason with Judge Pierson, it will kill both me and the kids," she answered, sadly.

"I could give you the money. I brought you here because I didn't want anyone to hear me discuss this with you, since it's really not something we're supposed to do."

"That's out of the question, Jack. You could be disbarred. I have to figure something else out."

Shelley looked at Jack's face and saw that he truly shared her pain.

"Jack, I appreciate everything you and John are doing for me. My, God, I can't even pay you! And you're both working so hard for me, I would never let you, or John, put yourselves in jeopardy for me like that."

"Well, if all else fails, somehow John and I will see that the bond is taken care of," he assured her.

"No. Neither of you can do that. If Neal, or that slimy attorney of his had the chance to prove something like that in court, they would run to the judge, and the Bar Association to win their case. No...I have to believe that this is all going to turn out okay for us."

Jack walked over and put his arms around her as if he wanted to consume her. She looked into Jack's eyes.

"Is that the only reason you brought me out here?" she asked.

He was silent for a moment, as if he had to gather his strength to say the right thing, instead of what he obviously wanted to say.

"No, but the other reason would definitely get me disbarred," he said, smiling.

They walked back to the car, hand in hand. Neither of them had to say anything.

Chapter 43

As anticipated, Clancy and Mary were waiting when Jack and Shelley arrived at the office.

"Where have you been?" Clancy asked, looking suspiciously at Shelley, adjusting the sling holding her arm, so its weight would not pull her healing shoulder. Fortunately, she'd had a quick recovery, and had already returned to work. Shelley was too frightened to do that. After the shooting, she knew Neal was capable of anything.

"We had some things to discuss," Jack answered quickly.

Shelley went to the phone and called Molly, partly to escape Clancy's scrutiny, but also to make sure the children were all right. She'd decided to wait until she returned to the shelter before telling Molly the dreadful details about what happened in court.

"It didn't go very well, Molly, but I'll explain it to you when I get back," she said.

"Child, that's fine. The kids are okay. You do what you have to do and I'll take care of your babies for you."

"Thank you, Molly, and please…say a prayer for me and my kids. Believe me, we really need it."

"I sure will, and don't you worry, it will all turn out fine."

"I'll try not to," Shelley answered. *If you only knew,* she thought, ending the conversation.

A few minutes later, John returned to the office. The look on his face said it all.

"He wouldn't do away with the court order, would he?" Shelley asked, beginning to cry again.

"Come into my office for a minute, will you?" John asked, closing the door behind them. He placed his briefcase down and turned around to face her. "The judge agreed to accept a property bond. That's all he would do."

Shelley sat down, feeling the hopelessness that Judge Pierson cast upon her. "It might as well be a cash bond, John. Both are impossible for me to get!"

Jack entered John's office and listened to the details of John's unreasonable discussion with Judge Pierson. "This is crazy! I have never seen a judge order something so ludicrous. Judge Pierson's incompetence is beyond belief!" Jack said.

"I want to pay for the bond. Jack, I know we can find a way to do it without raising suspicion."

"I agree," Jack said. "But Shelley won't let us do that. I've already spoken to her about it."

Shelley stood up with tears in her eyes. "I love you both for wanting to do this for me, but I need to find another way, one that won't cost you two your practice."

"What about your parents, Shelley?" Jack asked. "Could I at least try? Maybe if I talk to them, if I explain that there is no danger of them losing their home," he suggested.

"You can try, Jack, but they won't do it. They don't understand any of this. Quite frankly, I'm not sure I do anymore. I thought the court system was supposed to be just."

"Give me their phone number," Jack said, handing her a piece of paper and a pen. After she'd written down her parent's phone number, taking the piece of paper, he went into his office and closed the door, as if by keeping Shelley out of earshot, the pain would be less if they refused.

After he'd made the call, Jack rejoined the hopeful group in the waiting room. He looked at Shelley.

"I'm sorry, Kid. I don't think your mother understood the intensity of the situation. She was afraid to sign a property bond."

Silence filled the room until Shelley stood up with tears in her eyes.

"I really need to be with my children right now," she said, running outside.

Jack ran after her, catching up to her by the wrought iron benches, where they'd sat and talked for hours the night they'd met. "I'll drive you back to your car," he said, pulling his car keys out of his pocket.

"I can take her, Jack," Clancy said, right behind them. "I haven't had a chance to talk to Shelley since I got out of the hospital."

Shelley and Jack looked at each other, their need to be together unmistakably marked on their faces. "That will be fine, I'd like that," Shelley answered, tears flowing down her face.

"I'll call you later at the shelter," Jack whispered, grabbing her hand.

"Okay, thanks. Look, I appreciate you trying anyway. I don't know why it hurts so much. I've dealt with my mother's indifference for a long time," Shelley said, looking at the ground.

"Somehow, Honey, we'll make this turn out right," Jack assured her. "Please trust me."

"I do, but unfortunately, this is something not even you and John can fix, and I'm scared."

"I know you are. But, we'll find a way," Jack squeezed her hand, then, let it go when he saw Clancy watching him.

"Goodbye," she said, climbing into Clancy's car.

Jack looked at her through the open window on the passenger side. "Goodbye," he whispered.

Clancy pulled out of the parking lot. "What are you doing, Shelley?"

"I don't know. I have to think about everything and discuss it with Margo. Maybe she'll think of something I can do. Are you supposed to be driving?"

"Stop trying to change the subject, that's not what I'm talking about."

"Then, what are you talking about?" Shelley asked.

"I mean, you and Jack. Do you think I haven't seen the way he looks at you?"

"You're wrong," Shelley replied.

"Shelley, he's your attorney. And as done as his marriage is, he's still a married man," Clancy reminded her. "You're a young, beautiful woman, and Jack has been married a long time. You don't need the drama. I know you're going through hell right now, but you've got to be careful. You're both good, decent people and what I say, I say out of love. Do you understand?"

Shelley tried to smile. "Yes, Clancy, I understand, but you're wrong. Nothing is happening between Jack and me," Shelley assured her.

"Yeah, well…the only reason that's so is because of what I said. You're both good, decent people."

"Everything is under control. Besides, all I can think about right now is keeping my kids."

Clancy gave a laugh that broke the tension. "You know, I knew we were in trouble when I saw that puny judge! Just how tall do you think he is? Four feet maybe?" she asked.

They were both laughing as they approached Shelley's car. Clancy grabbed Shelley's arm as she moved to get out of the car. "Listen, this will all be okay. Please believe that."

"Clancy, I'm just numb right now. I want my kids to be safe, and even if a miracle occurs, and I do get the bond, they'll still be forced to visit Neal this weekend. They'll be petrified!"

Shelley got out of Clancy's car, and unlocked the door to her own, while Clancy waited. She'd insisted on making sure Shelley wasn't being followed.

When Shelley pulled her car onto the highway, and saw that no one was behind her, perhaps it was the impact of being alone for the first time since Judge Pierson handed down his insane court order, or the total feeling of hopelessness, but the effect of both those things, compelled her to scream at the top of her lungs.

All she could think of was the awful possibility of her children being dragged off by social workers to a strange place where she would not be allowed to talk to them, or kiss their faces, or hold them as they fell asleep. Her pain was gut wrenching, and the drive to the shelter was not long enough to ease any of it.

Chapter 44

Slowly, without feeling, Shelley climbed the stairs to the shelter. Mary had already informed Margo about what took place in court, and she was waiting for her on the landing.

"Margo, wants to talk to you, and I think she might have an answer to your problem," Mary said, excitedly.

Shelley entered Margo's office, and saw a strange, friendly looking woman sitting there. Margo made the introductions.

"Shelley, this is Brice, you might remember her from downstairs. She handles a lot of the business for the Y and us. She's here to help you," Margo said. "Brice, this is Shelley."

Shelley took a seat in the only empty chair, waiting to hear the solution the woman had to offer her, willing to try anything.

"I'm part of an underground organization that keeps women and children safe from domestic violence," Brice informed her.

"I don't understand," Shelley responded.

Brice and Margo looked at each other. "We are prepared to send you and the children to a safe place until your attorney can work things out legally for you regarding the bond requested by the judge handling your case," Brice said.

"You mean leave Georgia?" Shelley asked.

"Yes. You wouldn't know where you're going until you get there. We've helped a lot of women successfully relocate to escape bad court decisions, Shelley," Brice assured her.

"Is this legal? Can I get in trouble with the court?" Shelley asked. She'd heard horror stories about women who ran away with their children. Women who were willing to risk jail to save their children, and she knew she would do it too, if that was all there was.

"You would be guilty of kidnapping, according to the court system, if you were located," Margo answered.

"What are the chances of that happening? And what about you two? How safe are you from the court system?"

"We have both gone to jail before to protect some of the women and children we have helped. Unfortunately, it goes with the job. Also, I must tell you that we have only had two women located, and that was because they both did something to cause that," Brice answered.

"Such as?" Shelley asked.

"Such as contacting someone before their attorney had fixed their legal problems."

"You mean, I would never be able to talk to anyone I know, ever?"

"Not until your attorney gets your court decision reversed," Brice replied.

"Shelley…look, this is a last resort. Let's use the time you have to make things work, and you can think about it during that time. One of the biggest reasons we do this, is to stop children from being forced to spend time with abusive fathers who are granted visitation by negligent judges," Margo said.

"I'm worried about Neal's visitation, Margo. I'll do whatever I have to do to keep my kids safe, but I don't want them to be forced into living half a life, either."

"What Brice is proposing, is an 'if all else fails' option," Margo said. "We can see what happens with the bond. You never know, miracles can happen."

"We just don't want you hysterical, or worrying about losing your kids over a stinking fifteen hundred dollar bond. You also shouldn't have to bite your nails off every other weekend because Jackie and Jason are being forced to visit their abusive father, by an incompetent judge," Margo added.

"I'll definitely think about it. Thank you," Shelley replied, knowing she would take them up on their offer before she would lose Jackie and Jason. She would do whatever she had to do to keep her children, and to keep them safe.

"This conversation has to be kept confidential. You understand that, don't you?"

"Yes, certainly," Shelley said, standing to leave. She desperately wanted to see her children.

"Margo can contact me if you decide to do this," Brice said.

"Thank you...both of you. I know you're putting yourselves in jeopardy helping mothers like me, and I appreciate it. I'm also very scared and confused about a system that forces children to endure this kind of heartache, because of a lack of money and the 'good ole boy' network running our lousy court system. I'll do whatever I have to for my kids, and if that makes me a criminal, then, that's what I'll be. I owe my kids that," Shelley said, tears flowing once again.

"Okay, then," Brice said, with tears in her eyes also. "I'll get things lined up in case we have to act quickly, and if you decide not to go, that's okay too. At least we'll be ready for the worst."

Shelley found Molly sitting in the living room.

"Hi, Molly, are the kids asleep?" she asked, feeling emotionally drained.

"Yes, Child, I didn't think you'd mind. They had such a busy day, and they were surely tired," she answered.

"I understand," Shelley replied, sadly. "Maybe I'll just peek at them."

She wanted to hold her children. As if every moment together was crucial.

"When you're done, have some coffee with me, and tell me what's going on. From what I've been told, you had a busy day, too," Molly said.

"Yes, I did, and coffee sounds great." Shelley went to Molly's room and quietly sat on the edge of her double bed, looking at her children. Molly had put them in her bed so they could talk when she returned. They looked so precious. Jackie squinted her eyes to see her mother better.

"Hi, Mommy," she said, half asleep.

"Hey, Baby. Why are you still awake?" Shelley whispered, in order not to wake Jason.

"I missed you, Mommy. Where were you so long?"

"I had to take care of something, Angel. But, I'm here now, can I have a hug?"

Jackie smiled and wrapped her arms around her mother. Shelley kissed her several times, making her giggle, then, covered her with her blanket. She waited until she fell asleep again, then kissed Jason on his forehead, lightly, in order not to wake him.

"I love you, Mommy," Jason whispered, half asleep.

Shelley turned around by the door.

"I love you too, Baby," she said, and closed the door. Tears ran down her face.

This just isn't fair! Shelley thought, traumatized. *They're only three and four years old! How could that judge take them away from me to protect the rights of their abusive father? I won't let him do it. If I don't get this bond, I'm leaving with my children!*

Shelley sat down and accepted the cup of coffee Molly handed her.

"Mary told me most of what happened," Molly said. "She also told me what Margo has set up for you, even though she wasn't supposed to. But, that's all right because I sure wouldn't say anything to anybody. I'm sure you know that."

"Yes, I do," Shelley replied, sipping her coffee.

"Girl, you do whatever you have to do to save your children, no matter what that means," Molly said, looking directly into Shelley's eyes.

Shelley smiled at her friend. Molly understood the strong love of a mother. That love gives a woman the strength to endure anything necessary to keep them safe.

"I know. I intend to do just that," Shelley responded softly.

Chapter 45

Shelley could not sleep at all that night worrying about her inability to obtain the bond. Molly stayed awake with her, brainstorming, trying to come up with an idea, but no solutions came to either one of them.

None of Neal's beatings hurt as much as the threat of losing her children. Shelley thought of the people she would have to leave behind if she fled with her children. Clancy, her parents, such as they were. *Elkie? Surely I would not have to give up Elkie. I couldn't do that. She's like family. But, then, she's in Cuba right now. She doesn't know about any of this. Leah...what about Leah? I could call Leah in West Virginia and at least say goodbye to her. She doesn't know about this either. Maybe by the time they both find out, Jack and John could have this all resolved. Jack...oh, my God. I can't imagine never seeing Jack again. That's ridiculous. There can never be anything between us, ever, so I need to get rid of these crazy feelings. Leaving might be the best thing for me to do.*

The next morning, Jack called, pleading once again with Shelley to let him pay for her bond. Still, she refused. He told her that John was on his way to the court house to make one last, final plea with the judge, and that he would call her with the results, the moment he returned. She felt blessed having Jack and John on her side. They fought hard for her, and she had no idea where she would be without them.

Meanwhile, Shelley finally called Leah and told her what was happening. Like the good friend she was, Leah cried with Shelley, and let her repugnance be known over the way the court system was victimizing Shelley and her children even worse than what Neal had.

Two hours after they ended their emotional phone conversation, Margo came into the living room and sat down on the couch in front of Shelley.

"You won't believe this!" she said, tears forming in her eyes.

"What?" Shelley asked, sadly. Time was running out and more bad news would kill her.

"Your friend, Leah, called after she spoke with you on the phone to get routing instructions to the shelter's bank. I didn't say anything to you until I was sure she could do it in time."

"Do what?" Shelley asked, still confused.

"She just wired seventeen hundred dollars into our account. Fifteen hundred dollars for the bond, and two hundred for you and the children!"

"No!" Shelley shouted, stunned. Mary and Molly came rushing in and began screaming with excitement.

"Wait, I'm not done yet! Margo shouted. "The news of your situation spread throughout the community, apparently, from people who were in the courtroom during your session. It seems, the general public was outraged with Judge Pierson's court order, and the Association for Battered Women has received hundreds of calls from people offering to donate wedding rings, car titles, property deeds, savings bonds, cash, anything that would get you the bond you need for your children."

Shelley burst into tears, so touched by the compassion of strangers who were trying to help a poor mother keep her children. "They don't even know me, Margo. My, God, my own parents refused to help."

The phone rang again. It was Jack. Clancy and Joe were in his office with the deed to their home.

"Oh, my goodness. Are they standing there with you, Jack?" Shelley asked.

"They're right in front of me."

"Tell them my friend, Leah, in West Virginia, wired the money a few minutes ago!" She heard a thump. "Jack, are you there? Jack? Where are you?"

Clancy picked up the phone. "He's on the way to the shelter!" she shouted. "Oh, Honey, Joe and I are so happy! This has been a horrible strain on everybody."

Shelley wiped her tears. "Clancy, listen. I appreciate what you and Joe tried to do. Please give Joe a big kiss for me," Shelley said.

"Hell, no! Then, I'll have to finish what you started," she laughed. "I'll visit you later, okay?"

"No, I have a better idea. I'll come to the office for a while this afternoon," Shelley said. "I feel ready to start living!"

"Well, hallelujah!" Clancy said. "I'll see you later. I sure have missed you!"

From the living room, Shelley saw Jack's car pull into the parking lot. She ran outside to meet him, clutching the check made out to the Fairville Court System that Margo had given her. They ran to each other and Jack instinctively, picked her up, laughing.

"It's over!" Shelley shouted, when he put her down.

"Not until you sign the papers I have in the car," Jack said. "I prepared the papers yesterday, knowing I wouldn't let the State of Georgia take those kids. With, or without your permission, John and I decided we were going to get that bond. I was on my way to the bank when Clancy and Joe arrived. They delayed me long enough for your friend to save the day." He gave Shelley another hug. "Let's celebrate. Let me take you out to lunch!"

"Do you think we should, Jack? I don't want to cause anymore problems for you."

"Hey! Attorneys have lunch with their clients all the time. As a matter of fact, I have an even better idea. Let's pick up some food and go back to the lake."

"That sounds great!" Shelley answered. She asked Molly if she would be there for a little while in case Jackie and Jason decided to come upstairs early from their fun day at the Y, which they never did, and as usual, she was willing to help anyway she could. She thought lunch with Jack would do Shelley a lot of good after what she'd been through.

Chapter 46

After they obtained the bond, and had presented it to the court, Jack stopped at a delicatessen he liked, and picked up some sandwiches and bottles of water. He drove to a secluded place by the lake, where they sat on a blanket near a huge shade tree. Shelley felt at peace with the world, and it was obvious that Jack felt the same with Shelley.

"I feel so much better," Shelley said., watching the water ripple along the lakes edge. "I've even decided to go to the office later."

"That's great. You are feeling better," Jack teased.

Shelley noticed that he wouldn't take his eyes off her. Even the terrible heat didn't faze him. He looked like a man that was exactly where he wanted to be.

"Am I entitled to confidentiality between a client and her attorney?" Shelley asked, smiling, lightly scraping the dirt with a stick she'd found.

"Absolutely. You can tell me anything," Jack said, grinning.

"Last night, I made arrangements to go into hiding with the kids," she said.

"What? Why? You weren't going to talk to me, or John first?"

"No. I was told I couldn't. Margo was going to discuss my legal matters with you after we were safely tucked away somewhere."

The hurt look on his face bothered her. "Jack, I was not going to lose my kids."

"And you didn't trust me, or John, enough to know we wouldn't let that happen?"

"No, I didn't want you to do something that would hurt you, or John for the rest of your lives. Besides, Counselor. It almost did happen, so don't look so offended. Based on what I have just been through, I don't think anyone is safe from our court system, not even you and John," Shelley said, in defense.

"Well, it's over and you don't have to go anywhere," Jack said, gently brushing the wind blown hair from her face, as if he wanted to see every part of it.

"Not really. I still have Neal's visitation this weekend to worry about."

"Oh, before I forget. John and I discussed the visitation issue, and we thought it would be better for all concerned if you brought the kids to my house and I'll deliver them to Neal."

"That's way too much of an imposition, Jack. I can't ask you to do that. What about your family?" she asked.

"Believe me, no one will know or care what I'm doing. I promise," he answered, seriously.

Shelley looked into his eyes. "Is that what attorneys do for their clients?"

Brushing his hand softly across her cheek, feeling the softness of her skin, he replied. "No, that's what this attorney wants to do for this client," he whispered.

"Why?" she asked, softly.

"Because…the second I turned around in my chair that night that you came to my office, and I saw you sitting there, I wanted you," he said.

She stared into his eyes, inviting him to the inevitable. He gently pulled her close, guiding her down on the blanket he'd spread out on the grass, kissing her tenderly, the way she'd dreamed he would so many times.

Shelley had never known such pleasure as he unbuttoned her blouse. She could feel Jack trembling with his want for her, as he removed the blouse, then his shirt.

When he pressed his body against hers, they both became vanished in their pleasure. One piece at a time, they removed their clothing, basking in the heat of the moment. They cast aside all apprehension about giving into their feelings, and were completely immersed in the passion of their lovemaking.

Jack made love to Shelley beautifully, long and softly. Their patient desire captured both of them, bringing them to another place.

Away from the courtroom and Neal. Away from all the reality that suggested it was wrong. It was not just urgent lust, or satisfaction for the incredible longing they kept restrained for each other. It was generated by nothing less than the love that had developed between them.

In the blaze of their desire and powerful enchantment, they were deaf to the click of the camera behind them.

Chapter 47

Three hours later, Jack dropped Shelley off at the shelter. She felt deliriously happy, but at the same time, ashamed about what she had done. Jack was wonderful, and she was submerged in her thoughts of him making love to her. She could still feel the warmth of his body, and soft skin, and as guilty as she felt, she couldn't help but long for the time when they would be together again, as she knew they would.

Shelley checked on Jackie and Jason who were still happily at play downstairs. After she'd showered, brushed her hair, and refreshed her make up, she left for the office.

"Where have you been?" Clancy asked when Shelley walked into their private office.

"Taking care of the court business. Why? Is everything okay?"

"I called the shelter to see if you wanted to have lunch, and they said you were with Jack."

"I had to sign the papers for the bond," Shelley answered, looking away.

"For four hours?"

"Yes, why?" Shelley asked.

"I don't know, Shelley. I just hope you're okay, that's all."

"I'm okay," Shelley assured her.

Clancy looked at her friend. "I hope so."

At that moment, Vinnie came in, interrupting the uncomfortable conversation.

"I don't believe it. You've finally arrived. Welcome!" He gave Shelley a kiss on her cheek. Shelley looked at Clancy, and smiled.

"How are you?" Vinnie asked her.

"I'm better. I feel good," Shelley answered, honestly.

"Great! We're glad to have you on board. Listen, Clancy has been taking some agent duty at a sub-division I have listed. I thought, to give you girls a good beginning, I would assign the models to you two exclusively."

Clancy gasped. "Oh, Vinnie, that's wonderful!"

"I've already gone over the builder's specs with Clancy, so Shelley, meet me here tomorrow, let's say, eleven thirty? I'll not only treat you to lunch, but I'll personally give you a tour of the models and go over the options and so forth."

"Oh...okay...that's fine, eleven thirty," Shelley responded, looking at Clancy, who was resisting the urge to laugh in Vinnie's face.

"Specs my ass!" Clancy laughed, once he'd left the office. "I didn't get lunch. I just got the keys to the models and a bunch of house plans thrown in my hand, and lousy ones at that."

"Oh, no, are they lousy?" Shelley asked.

"They are more than lousy. We won't sell any of those ugly houses, but we'll pick up a lot of good prospects. I've already made quite a few contacts from them."

"What the heck? It's a free lunch, and what can Vinnie do in a public place?" Shelley asked, joking.

"I don't know, I hear he's pretty slick," Clancy teased.

Chapter 48

With a heavy heart, when Friday arrived, Shelley gathered together the little bit of clothing the children had with them at the shelter. It was almost time for their visitation with Neal.

Jason had not been able to sleep the night before, because of the frightening nightmares he had of his father shooting him. Jackie was withdrawn, and clearly nervous.

All of John's efforts to get Judge Pierson to rescind the visitation order were denied. Therefore, Shelley took the children to Jack's house at five thirty as planned, so he could meet Neal in front of the Police Department by six.

The court order clearly stated that if the children were not turned over to Neal by six o'clock sharp, Shelley would be in contempt of court, and since everything had a way of working out to Neal's benefit, she was not taking any chances.

It broke her heart to see the children leave in the back seat of Jack's car to visit their abusive father. She would worry the entire weekend about their safety. Was he hurting them? Was he feeding them at all, much less right? Were they scared? She would have given anything if Neal had vanished from the face of the earth, never to be heard from again, out of their lives forever.

When Jack returned, he insisted on following Shelley back to the shelter, claiming Neal was furious that Shelley did not bring the children herself. Obviously, he thought he would have a chance to see her, or talk to her. Jack said he didn't trust Neal at all where Shelley was concerned, and he certainly was not giving him any opportunity to hurt her, or the children again.

When Shelley told Jack that she'd accepted agent duty in Vinnie's sub-division for the weekend, he was upset. He didn't want her sitting alone in an empty house.

"I'm going to be fine, Jack. There's a phone there and I can see anyone coming in the house though the windows," she assured him. "I have to keep busy and work."

"I could keep you busy," he responded, with a smile, softly rubbing his finger along her face.

After a moment, he said, "I understand. I really do, but I would like us to sit down and discuss the future of our relationship. I know things are complicated right now but soon they won't be. I have relived those hours at the lake in my mind a thousand times, and a thousand times, it was the best experience of my life," Jack said, kissing her.

As much as she wanted to stay with Jack, she left him to go to the model, but knowing he was falling in love with her.

As Clancy predicted, she didn't sell any of the houses, but gathered some much needed prospects by the time she closed the model on Sunday. She wanted to arrive at Jack's house by five thirty. He had called her several times in the model over the weekend to make sure she was all right while her thoughts were focused mostly on holding her children again. Jackie and Jason remained on her mind every moment. She knew how much they meant to her, and how little they meant to Neal.

She also could not stop thinking about that afternoon by the lake, reliving it over and over again, as Jack had. Each time she did, she found the same pleasure that consumed her that afternoon, understanding what Jack meant, and she was sure she too, was falling in love.

Shelley saw the children in the back of Jack's car and felt relieved, glad it was over. She hoped that before another two weeks passed, John would convince the judge to end Neal's visitation rights, or at least make it restricted so someone would have to be with him when he visited the children. Shelley knew if that happened, he wouldn't show up because the embarrassment would be too much for him.

Molly had a wonderful dinner waiting for them, and watching her children enjoy their meal, Shelley was thankful they were home.

She began to wash the dishes before Molly stopped her.

"Child, you go spend some time with your kids, I can do this," she said, taking the dishrag out of Shelley's hand. "They looks pretty tired, and I don't think they can last too much longer."

"Oh, Molly, would you mind?" Shelley asked. She hated taking advantage of her friend's loving nature. Molly had cooked a great dinner, and Shelley knew she too, had to be tired.

"Go...please, enjoy your babies," Molly answered, with a smile.

Shelley joyfully ran the water for the children's bath. She wanted to get them bathed so she could read them a bedtime story and talk for while before they grew too sleepy. As she pulled their clean pajamas from the overnight bag they had taken with them, she commented, "Well, at least your father washed your clothes," she said.

"Daddy didn't do that, Mommy, Nana did," Jason said.

"Nana was at our house, Honey?" Shelley asked, angry that her mother-in-law was in her house, while she and the children were living in a shelter.

"Yup. Pop too," he said, his large blue eyes growing bigger.

"Why were they there, Sweetheart, do you know?"

"So, Daddy wouldn't have to work hard with us," he answered. That information made Shelley even more resentful.

She tried to calm down. *Nothing is going to ruin what's left of this evening with my children,* she thought. *Not even Neal, and his evil mother!* As she pulled the clothes off her daughter to put her in the bathtub, she stopped when she turned Jackie around to lift her. For a full minute, she couldn't move. She was frozen, then, she quickly undressed Jason.

"Molly!" Shelley screamed.

Molly came running into the bathroom, holding her chest. "What's the matter with you, Girl? You gonna give someone a heart attack yelling like that!"

"Look at this," Shelley said, pointing to the bruises on her children's bodies, tears running down her cheeks. "Damn him!" she yelled.

"Daddy said we were bad, Mommy," Jackie said, her little face scrunched up.

"Honey, you weren't bad, you're wonderful," she said, giving her daughter a hug.

"What you gonna do?" Molly asked, seeing the fury in Shelley's eyes.

"I'm going to fight that lousy judge that allowed this to happen to my children."

Shelley ran to the phone. "Molly, can you please put some clean clothes on them for me while I call Jack?'

"Sure, you go on," she said.

Shelley saw the tears in Molly's eyes. Molly loved her children, the same way Shelley loved hers.

Within a few minutes, Shelley had the children in the car, racing towards Jack's office. Jack said he would be waiting there with deputies from the Sheriff's Department. The moment they arrived, a female deputy took Jackie into one office to examine her and a male deputy took Jason into another, while Jack silently held Shelley. Under those circumstances, there were no adequate words he could have spoken to comfort her.

"Honey, this will be taken care of, I promise," Jack said, finally.

Shelley wept. "What kind of man does this to his children? And what kind of men are ruling our courts that would force children to go with an abusive father?"

"I don't understand any of this either," John agreed, walking into the office. Jack had called him, asking him to meet them at the office. "I've never seen a judge make such irrational decisions."

"Why can't we request another judge?" Shelley asked.

"Because it would take six months to do that. We're better off waiting to see what happens here," John answered.

"I won't allow the children to go with Neal again," Shelley said. "I mean it, John. Even if it means my going to jail."

"I understand, but let's hope it doesn't come to that," John replied.

After they witnessed the bruises, the officers followed procedure, by calling Judge Pierson at home.

"Ma'am, I'm sorry, but Judge Pierson refused to issue a warrant tonight. There are still some facts he wants cleared up," the officer said, when he hung up the phone.

"What other facts does that idiot need cleared up?" Shelley shouted, furious with Judge Pierson.

"Shelley, calm down, we will handle this," Jack said. "I know this hurts."

"I will not calm down! These are my children! Does that legal moron care about their welfare at all? Do they have any rights?"

"The judge has ordered a special hearing in the morning," the deputy said.

June, the female deputy, interrupted. "Jack, can I see you and John a moment alone?"

"Sure. Come into my office," Jack replied, leading the way. A few minutes later, they returned to Shelley and the other deputies in the conference room. Jack took Shelley's hands into his own.

"Shelley, listen…Jackie told one of the deputies something that has them concerned. The judge has ordered a raid on your house seven o'clock tomorrow morning. That's why he didn't issue the warrant yet, there might be other charges."

"What is it? What did she tell them?" Shelley asked. Her heart sank into despair.

Jack frowned. "This is the hard part. You can't know. If I tell you, and it comes out during the testimony that it was discussed, any possible charges against Neal will be dismissed. Please trust me. For the benefit of the children and our case, okay? Do you trust me?" he asked, looking straight into her eyes.

"Of course I do, but I want Neal to be dealt with once and for all, and if he hurt Jackie, I need to help my daughter."

"If you don't believe another single word I tell you, believe this, someone like Neal, always messes up eventually," he said. "This could be his time. Hopefully, you know that I would never jeopardize Jackie's well being."

Shelley conceded. "I know, but, Jack, Neal is a genius. He keeps winning. Look what's already happened."

Jack squeezed her hands. "Trust me, he will mess up. Let's hope this is that time."

Shelley learned later that the next morning the Sheriff's Department woke Neal at seven thirty sharp, storming the house like a swat team, without his permission. His approval, or disapproval, was of no concern to the deputies. Unfortunately, whatever it was that the officers searched for that day was not there. Once again, Neal managed to escape any kind of justice, and still, Shelley was kept in the dark, in case they could outwit him at a later time.

With the search completed, wearing an obnoxious smirk, Neal made the special criminal hearing by nine, totally unaffected by the morning's events.

Jack took over the courtroom, while John sat next to Shelley, yellow pad in hand. During his argument, Jack told the court what had taken place during Neal's first visitation, and then asked the judge to rescind his decision regarding visitation.

Judge Pierson listened, and at the end of the hour, casually announced his decision.

"Since none of the evidence believed to be in Mr. Jordon's home could be substantiated, I feel Mr. Jordon should still be allowed to visit with his children. However, on those weekends, the children must be taken to the Sheriff's Department and examined by deputies before they leave their mother on Friday night, then, re-examined on Sunday evening before they are returned to her."

The judge looked directly at Neal and warned him. "If it is established, Mr. Jordon, that you have abused your children in any way during one of those visits, you will be restricted to supervised visitation."

Jack remained adamant that Shelley was not to say a single word in the courtroom, no matter what took place, because he didn't want Judge Pierson doing anything reactionary, as he had with the bond issue. Outraged, and confused about what the judge meant by 'examined'. She asked John to explain on the yellow pad, why Neal wasn't being prosecuted for abusing his children.

John whispered, "The children will have to be inspected for bruises, before and after they visit Neal by a deputy. Shelley, I'm sorry, but at least he will know someone is watching him."

Shelley stood, looking at Judge Pierson with total contempt. In her mind, he was just as guilty as Neal of abusing her children. Overwhelmed and sickened, she ran out of the courtroom. At the shelter, she barely made it upstairs.

Jack had already phoned the shelter twice by the time Shelley finally arrived. Margo was waiting for her in the hall.

"Are you okay?" Margo asked. "I heard the results of the hearing from Jack."

"No, I'm not, okay. I don't know how much more I can take, Margo. The children and I have been through so much, and I'm tired of Neal's rights costing us ours. My kids are still sleeping on the floor, we have no money, and the kids are being legally abused!"

Margo smiled bitterly. "Well, outside of that, Mrs. Lincoln, how did you like the play?"

Shelley paused, her devastation consuming her. Wearily, she said, "I know I have become a habitual complainer, but Margo, what can I do? When does Jackie and Jason's rights not to be abused mean something?"

Margo shook her head. "They probably won't. Not in this lifetime, I'm sorry to say." She studied the floor for a moment. "Look, if you want, the offer to disappear still stands."

Shelley thought, *Neal has won every battle so far. Maybe Jack was right.*

I can't help my children if I'm in jail. That could happen the way things have been going for her. I can't let my children get hurt anymore. With the inspections, Neal might be more careful about what he does. But, what an awful thing to endure, having to get undressed every other weekend in front of strangers. What is wrong with that crazy judge?

"Okay, if my kids get hurt again, we will definitely go. I'm not going to sit around every other weekend wondering if my children are being hurt by their father."

"You just say the word," Margo said. "I think it's crazy that women and children have to run like criminals from jerks like your husband and Judge Pierson."

"Well, maybe someday this won't be allowed to happen," Shelley responded.

Sometime later, Jack and John called Shelley on their speaker phone, knowing that if Shelley and the children went through too much more, she would make plans to go into hiding.

"We have another court date," John said. "Hopefully, we'll finally get that bastard out of the house and force him to pay child support, since apparently, he needs a court order to do that. Anyway, give Mary and Clancy the new court date because their testimony is going to be important. Jack will give you the details."

"Okay, John," Shelley answered.

"I think Jack has some things to go over with you, so I'll leave you two alone, I have another call to take anyway. Keep your chin up, Honey. We're going to win this."

"I'll try, John. It hasn't been easy," she answered.

"I know. I'll talk to you later, bye," John said, as he walked out of Jack's office. Jack immediately took the phone off its speaker. "Shelley, meet me at the lake. Please."

"I guess I can do that. I'll check on the kids downstairs. If they're okay, I'll be there within an hour."

Chapter 49

An hour later, Shelley turned her car onto the gravel road leading to the abandoned lake. Jack was waiting for her there with sandwiches and a bottle of 'Asti Spumante', her favorite.

"Well, you certainly came prepared," Shelley greeted him as she stepped out of her car.

"I thought we both could use something after this morning's fiasco."

For a moment, her smile faltered. "I can't talk about it, Jack. I'm so damn mad."

"I know, and I certainly understand. But we have to talk about it," he said, handing her a glass of the wine.

"Are you trying to get me drunk?" Shelley asked, sprawling out on the blanket he'd spread on the ground.

He gave her a wicked smile. "Absolutely!" he said, jokingly, stroking her throat with his finger.

Shelley eyed him seriously. "Jack, we can't. We shouldn't let that happen again."

"Look, Shelley, I want you more than I have ever wanted another woman."

"What exactly do you want me for?" she asked quietly.

He collapsed next to her on the blanket. "I'm so sorry, Shelley. The important issue here is, what do you want from me? This isn't just sex to me, and I don't want to add more pressure to your life right now. You're going through enough without me giving you more to think about," Jack said.

"Well, this isn't just sex to me either, Jack, but let's face it. You have a lot to lose," Shelley said, looking into his handsome face.

"I don't care about losing anything except what I feel for you. What do you want to hear? Do you want to know all the crazy thoughts that run through my mind on an hourly basis? Such as how I wish I were free to marry you tomorrow, or that I wish I met you before Neal had the opportunity to hurt you, or that I wish I was the father of your children instead of him? How about this one, that every night I crawl into bed, wishing you were next to me, permanently. It's better to ask me what I don't want, and that's anything that doesn't involve you!"

Tears pooled in Shelley's eyes. In a choked voice, she said, "I'm sorry, Jack, I didn't want this to happen. I don't even know when, or how it did."

"No, I'm sorry because it's too late for me to go back. I'm in love with you and even if I could go back, I wouldn't."

Shelley wiped away her tears. "Make love to me," she said, softly.

"Why? What would it mean to you, Shelley?" he asked.

"Make love to me because it's too late for me to go back, too. I love you and I can't change that either," she whispered.

Jack hesitated…but only for a moment.

Chapter 50

Shelley's next court date arrived, and Jack sat next to her once again, holding the important yellow pad. He was ready to assist John, and both lawyers were prepared to do battle.

John called Neal to the stand first. During the questioning, he led Neal to the place where he could prove him the liar that he was.

Lyle Maggitt sat at the defense table full of his usual venom, as Shelley studied him. Maggitt had to know he had a compulsive liar for a client. She was certain the attorney cared little about the reasons behind Neal's penchant for tormenting his family.

"Mr. Jordon," John began. "If you were granted custody of your children, who would care for them while you travel? Isn't travel a major condition of your employment?"

"Yes, it is. However, my parents would be more than happy to care for my children," he replied, flashing a smile at his mother, falling into John's trap.

"Oh? Your parents are still living?" John asked, trying to sound surprised.

"Of course they are. They're sitting right over there." Neal pointed to the Jordons sitting on his side of the courtroom, as if they had taken their place on the groom's side at a wedding. They were not there as witnesses, and probably hoped to intimidate Shelley by sitting right there, in the front row.

"Well, then, Mr. Jordon, why did you tell your wife and the rest of the world they were deceased?"

The Jordons gasped when they heard John's question.

"I never told her that!" Neal protested. "If she said that, she's even more disturbed than I thought she was. That's just one more of her insane stories!"

"If that's true, Mr. Jordon, then, why did you sign a Federal Oath declaring that your parents were deceased? Here is a copy of your application for a marriage license, where you clearly stated in your own handwriting, that your parents were killed in a car accident."

The observers in the courtroom began to whisper. John handed Neal a copy of the application, and another copy to Judge Pierson.

Neal looked at the application fully aware that he'd been caught. "Well, I guess I did say that," he answered, looking at Shelley with anger. It was the look she had seen many times during their marriage, the look that told her she was going to be hurt.

Jack realized Shelley was trembling, and quickly wrote on the yellow pad. Don't look at him! He can't hurt you anymore!"

Before she looked away, she read the message in his eyes, loud and clear. Neal was so sure Shelley would follow his rules, even during their divorce. It infuriated him to watch her step outside his tight control. How dare she allow these two men to enter his place in her life, and actually help them to betray him and their marriage? Shelley could see that he wanted to punish her for that kind of infidelity. She was aware of Neal's message through his angry glare, and it was enough to send chills throughout Shelley's body.

John began to question Neal about the abuse he'd inflicted on Shelley.

"I never laid a hand on my wife. I have done nothing but love her, and give her everything she wants. Maybe I shouldn't have done that, but I love her so much, I found it hard to say no to her about anything."

He took a breath, generating the tears he so easily generated upon demand.

"Mr. Jordon, look at these pictures," John said, handing him the pictures Clancy had taken of Shelley's bruises. Neal briefly glanced at them, a look of disgust twisting his face.

John declared, "Your Honor, these are pictures that were taken when Mrs. Jordon entered the shelter, pictures of the bruises Mr. Jordon left on his wife!" John snatched the pictures back from Neal and handed them to Judge Pierson.

Lyle Maggitt shot to his feet. "I object your Honor! There is no evidence that Mr. Jordon caused these bruises!"

"Objection overruled," Judge Pierson said.

"Okay, Mr. Jordon, I'm curious," John said. "How would you explain the bruises we see in these pictures?"

"My wife was in a car accident," Neal answered.

"A car accident?"

"Yes, a car accident," Neal repeated. "I can't believe she would try to blame me for those injuries, I could never hurt her in any way."

"And when did this car accident take place, Mr. Jordon?"

"Well, let's see. I believe it was in March," Neal said, rubbing his chin as if he in truth, wanted to get the facts right.

"These pictures were taken on July tenth, Mr. Jordon."

Neal hesitated. Plainly, by the look on his face, he knew his explanation was absurd, but he insisted on playing it out. "Well, it was a pretty bad accident," he answered.

The onlookers in the courtroom began to laugh.

In a voice that shook the courtroom, John asked, "Mr. Jordon, isn't the truth, the real truth, that you caused the bruises to your wife shown in those pictures? As a matter of fact, those bruises had not healed from the severe beating you inflicted on your wife weeks before she had to flee to the shelter with your children because you held them at gunpoint!"

"Absolutely not!" Neal shouted, indignantly.

Nauseated, Shelley wanted to run from the courtroom again, away from the wrath Neal promised her with the look in his eyes. All the feelings of fear she'd hoped were buried, once again consumed her. She knew Neal would never accept what had just taken place. That somehow, he would retaliate. She'd broken the vow of silence in their marriage by making public what Neal considered, 'private business'.

John directed his questioning toward the night of the Valentines Day Dance. The night Neal had almost killed Shelley, using false accusations as an excuse to beat her.

Lyle Maggitt, spent the next thirty minutes, unsuccessfully trying to make his client look like a saint by objecting to all of John's questions, then, John called Clancy to the stand.

"Mrs. Greer, how long have you known Mrs. Jordon?'

"About a year," Clancy answered.

"What is your relationship with her?"

"We're very close. She's my good friend," Clancy said, directing a warm smile towards Shelley.

"You work with Mrs. Jordon also, is that right?"

"Yes, we work as a team."

"So, in general, you spend a lot of time with Mrs. Jordon?"

"Yes, I do."

"While Mrs. Jordon was residing with her husband in their home, how often did you visit her, and find her bruised?"

"In the beginning, maybe every other week. But towards the end, almost every day."

"Did you discuss your concern with your friend?"

"Yes. The bruises kept getting worse, and I was worried," Clancy answered.

"Did anyone else discuss Mrs. Jordon's bruises with you?"

"I object, your Honor, that would be hearsay!" Maggitt shouted.

"Objection overruled. Strictly for my benefit, answer the question, Mrs. Greer," Judge Pierson said.

"Yes, our broker at the office asked me about Shelley. He was concerned too. He asked me because he knew how close I am to Shelley."

"Did you and your husband escort Mrs. Jordon to a Valentines Day Dance at the club in Peach Haven?" John asked.

"Yes. We invited Shelley to go with us because we knew her husband was going to be out of town. We didn't want her to sit home alone on Valentines Day."

"So, on February fourteenth, you and your husband took Shelley Jordon to the dance with you, then dropped her off at her home?" John asked.

"Yes," Clancy answered.

"Had her husband arrived home when you dropped her off at the end of the evening?"

"Yes. He had come home unexpectedly."

"And, when you dropped Mrs. Jordon off at her home that evening, was she bruised from what you could see?"

"No."

"And how soon after you dropped Mrs. Jordon off at her home that evening, did you see her again?" John asked.

"The next morning at nine thirty. I went to her house because I was worried about her."

"Did she invite you in?"

"Yes."

"What was Mrs. Jordon wearing when she answered the door?" John asked.

"She was wearing a white nightgown beneath a white bathrobe."

"So, it was apparent to you that she not left the house that morning?"

"Definitely. As a matter of fact, she was just making coffee."

"And in what condition did you find Mrs. Jordon at nine thirty, the morning after the dance?'

Clancy looked at her friend as tears formed in her eyes. Shelley already had tears running down her face. Jack held her hand under the table. Clancy's testimony was going to hurt.

She answered, her voice quivering. "Her mouth was split open. Both sides of her face were swollen, and were already beginning to turn black and blue. She had finger marks around her throat and chin, and her arms and legs were completely bruised and cut up."

"Mrs. Greer, what else did you see in the Jordon home that made you believe your friend had endured a horrendous beating between the time you dropped her off that evening, until you saw her the next morning?"

"I saw the dress Shelley had worn to the dance, torn to shreds on the floor."

The courtroom became silent as Clancy cried from the stand. "I didn't want to leave her there. I wanted her to come home with me and Joe!"

"No further questions your Honor," John said, solemnly.

"Mr. Maggitt?" the judge asked.

"No questions, your Honor, not at this time," the attorney answered.

Judge Pierson addressed the courtroom. "I suggest we break for today and schedule the next session within two weeks."

John spoke up. "Your Honor, I request that the court order temporary child support for the Jordon children, and ask that Mr. Jordon be ordered to vacate the Jordon home, so his wife can return there safely with her children."

Lyle Maggitt objected. "Your Honor, awarding child support at this time would be a great injustice to Mr. Jordon. May I remind the court that Mrs. Jordon left of her own free will, deserting her husband and home?"

John immediately responded to Maggitt's ridiculous argument. "Your Honor, what kind of injustice is being inflicted on the Jordon children? And may I remind the court that Mrs. Jordon and the children left their home to flee for safety from Mr. Jordon's abuse? May I also remind the court that the children are still sleeping on the floor in sleeping bags, and that they still don't have their clothes with them? All this, while Mr. Jordon continues to live in total comfort?"

Judge Pierson remained silent for a moment before he responded to John's rebuttal.

"I don't feel I have enough information at this time to grant proper temporary child support. However, if Mrs. Jordon wants to get the clothes that were left in the home, I will allow a one time visit to the home, escorted by the Sheriff's Department, so she can get their things...say, Wednesday morning, eleven o'clock?"

"I give up!" Shelley said, enraged. "Now we have another two weeks before we go back to court?" she asked John as they left the courtroom.

John looked disgusted. "There is always an order for temporary child support issued. I don't understand why Judge Pierson is refusing to do that."

Jack and John looked at each other.

"I'm just as bewildered about Judge Pierson's unusual decision as you are. Shelley, your case is growing more bizarre with each court appearance. Something isn't right here, that's for sure." John said.

Chapter 51

Shelley continued to work through all her adversity, realizing the only way she could live at that point, was from one court date to the next. Besides the children, Jack was her only shining star in her life. She met him as often as she could without raising suspicion. She wasn't ready for the answers she would need if the relationship was questioned.

The YWCA provided free day care for the children staying at the shelter, which enabled her to work without worrying about the cost. Jackie and Jason loved the Y's program, and every morning they rushed through breakfast so they could run downstairs to join their new friends. She found peace in that when she had to leave them to go to the office. The bottom line was, she had become a single mom, and like the rest of the fifty percent of single moms in the United States, she was not receiving any form of child support, or government assistance.

Tuesday morning, Flo Martin, another sales agent for Regal Realty, stuck her head in Shelley's office. "Hey! Do you want to rent a condominium for a few months?" she asked. "It's in the complex behind the office."

"Are you serious? That would be great, but is it free?" Shelley asked, joking.

"No, but it is half price," Flo responded, smiling. "It can only be rented for a few months because the owner is going through a divorce and the condo is part of their marital assets. No one is supposed to do anything with it."

Clancy walked in as the two women were leaving and quickly joined them. It was perfect and Shelley agreed to take it if the owner agreed to work out the deposit and first month's rent. Flo felt that could be arranged since Shelley had a closing coming up that would more than cover those costs.

Back at the office, Clancy did not waste time. "Listen...why don't I go to the house with you tomorrow morning?" she asked.

"Oh, Clancy...would you mind? I'm so nervous about going. Jack wants to go with me, but I don't think it's a good idea."

"Yeah...I guess it isn't a good idea," Clancy said, looking down at her desk.

"Clancy, you're doing it again. Please, don't do that," Shelley pleaded.

"Don't do what?" she asked.

"Don't make me feel as if I have something to be ashamed of."

"Shelley, I know you and I know Jack. I know things are not just attorney and client between the two of you. I'm not asking for details, I just want to talk about what this is all doing to you. How are you handling it with everything else you have going on right now?"

Shelley felt awful. *Maybe I am ashamed. Why shouldn't I be? I'm having an affair with a married man. What does that make me?*

"I don't know what is the right thing to do about anything. But, I do feel confused. I have no business feeling the way I do about Jack, he's a married man, but I'm nuts right now."

Clancy hesitated before responding to Shelley's vague confession. "Actually there's nothing wrong with you, anymore than there is something wrong with Jack. Besides, it's not all that sinful under the circumstances."

"Under what circumstances? My divorce is no reason to bust up a good marriage."

"Lacey will be gone very soon and she wants Jack to be happy. He hasn't been happy for two years. His whole life fell apart when Lacey developed Cancer," Clancy said.

Shelley could not move. All the questions that ran through her mind since the first time Jack made love to her were answered with one short statement. *Jack's wife is dying. That's why he allowed himself to fall in love with me. He's a good decent man. Not one to run around, or deceive anyone. And I go to his home and call him there as if his wife doesn't exist. And now Clancy has made her very real.* "Cancer?"

"He didn't tell you?" Clancy asked.

"Clancy, I have to know. I've had enough secrets dealing with Neal. I can't believe Jack didn't tell me this."

"I don't want to tell you," Clancy said, until she saw the tears in Shelley's eyes.

"Lacey was diagnosed with Breast Cancer two years ago. She had surgery, but the doctors recently discovered she's not in remission anymore, and the cancer has spread into her lymph nodes. There isn't anything they can do to save her."

"I can't see Jack anymore. I can't believe I have fallen in love with a dying woman's husband!" Shelley said, mad at her stupidity, as she began to pace back and forth.

"You're making the whole situation sound so terrible. It's not like that. There are things you don't know" Clancy responded quickly.

"Lacey wants Jack to begin a life without her. He didn't mean to fall in love with you, Shelley, but he did. Jack is a good, decent person," Clancy went on. "Listen, there is so much you don't know. At one point in their marriage, Lacey had a serious drinking problem. Jack not only stuck it out with her through dozens of rehab visits, but he also worked to establish his law career and raised his son by himself. He would have to pick Lacey up here, or there, in the middle of the night, usually after she'd been with some man just as drunk as she was. Now she feels she owes him this. He has given up a lot for her, and she doesn't want him to give you up," Clancy hesitated. "I know this, because Lacey and I have discussed the situation."

Shelley was astounded. "She knows about Jack and me?"

"Jack told her. He would never deceive her, or anyone else," Clancy replied.

"No, I guess that's just something he saved for me," Shelley said, feeling betrayed.

Shelley, that's not so! He'll tell you when the time is right. Do you truly care for Jack?" Clancy asked, concerned.

Shelley had asked herself that question, many times. Was Jack the fictional knight in shining armor to her, or was he something that would endure after she'd healed from her bad marriage? She already knew the answer, even in her weakened state.

"Clancy, loving Jack is the easiest thing I have ever done in my life. My feelings for him are so different than what I ever felt for any man, including Neal. God, I thought I loved Neal, until I fell in love with Jack."

"Well, I would go with those feelings. Both of you have endured a lot of hardship in your lives. If this is love, you both deserve it. and I don't want Jack to know I told you," Clancy said.

At that moment, Joan buzzed Shelley and told her Jack was on the phone.

"Do you want me to leave?" Clancy whispered.

Shelley shook her head. She knew she would forget the agony of what Clancy had just told her, the minute she heard Jack's voice. She loved him too much not to, and she knew he would discuss everything with her eventually. It was not another situation like Neal had subjected her to.

"Hey! I've been trying to get you all morning. You okay?" Jack asked.

"Yes, as a matter of fact, I just took a real giant step and signed a month to month lease on a condominium. Hopefully, my court business will get done so I can pay for it."

Jack hesitated. "Honestly? I wish you could stay at the shelter until we get Neal out of the house."

"I know, but I have to make some kind of move and I can't live in fear forever. Margo has already given me more time than what is usually allowed. Money, or no money, I have to do something."

"Honey, I told you not to worry about money," Jack said. "Why do you keep refusing my help? I don't want you to worry about supporting the children."

"I think Neal should take care of his own children financially," Shelley stated.

"I agree, but he doesn't seem to want to do that, so until the court makes him do it...please, let me help."

"I can't," she answered adamantly, desperately wanting to make it on her own.

Shelley changed the subject. "Now, about the condominium. What do you think?"

"If you're happy, I'm happy. I just want you and the children to be safe. Where is it? Is it nice?" he asked.

"It's okay. It's in 'Golf Club West', the complex behind the office."

"It sounds like a good deal. It's nice there. John and I had to take care of some business for a client who owns a condominium there, another crazy husband."

Jack paused. "Now, I have some good news, and I have some bad news. Which do you want first?'

"Great! Give me the good news first," Shelley said.

"The Grand Jury threw out that ridiculous case Neal's parents tried to charge you with."

"And the bad news?" Shelley asked, cringing.

"The bad news is, John had papers prepared to serve on the Jordons, suing them for trying to press false charges against you, but literally, seconds after the Grand Jury dismissed the case, your in-laws hightailed it out of Georgia. They must have had their car packed and ready to go."

"I really don't care about suing them anyway," she said. "I just want them out of my life. I truly loathe them!"

"And, speaking of people we loathe, I will pick you up tomorrow morning about ten o'clock to go to the house for your things," Jack said.

Shelley hesitated. "Jack, listen. I asked Clancy to go with me. I don't think it's a good idea for you to show up there with me."

"Why? No one knows about us, and Neal can think what he wants. I really don't care who knows anymore, especially Neal!" Jack said.

"I don't think you mean that. What about your family?"

"I don't want to hurt anyone, but indifference can hurt too. We need to talk about my situation at home. Every time I try to, you change the subject. There are things you need to know, Shelley. I haven't figured out how to handle it yet, but it has to be dealt with soon."

"We agreed to do nothing right now," Shelley reminded him, glad that Jack wanted to tell her everything, as she knew he would.

"I think we do have to do something about it. We're not the kind of people to have a back street affair."

"Well, right now, I can't deal with anything more," Shelley said, thinking about Lacey.

"I know, but after this is all over, we will have to talk about it, Shelley."

"I know, and we will, but at a much more appropriate time," she answered.

A deafening silence fell before Jack spoke again. "After you've finished at the house, I want you to call me to tell me how it went," he said.

Shelley whispered into the phone. "Is this my attorney talking, or someone else?"

"Both," Jack answered. "I don't like you being within a hundred yards of Neal!"

Clancy arrived at the shelter by ten o'clock. Shelley was nervous about going to the house while Neal was there, but it was arranged that he would wait at the end of the driveway with the deputies from the Sheriff's Department, while she and Clancy entered the house with another deputy.

As Shelley walked into the living room, she realized how much she'd missed her home. She gazed at the work she'd completed in the house. It was her efforts that made it a home.

Piled in the middle of the floor in the family room were three large bags Neal had apparently taken upon himself to fill with Shelley's and the children's clothes. The deputy instructed Shelley that she was not allowed to take anything out of the house, except clothes.

She stood her ground. "Well, I'm going to check the house and make sure none of our things were conveniently left out of those bags."

She walked toward the master bedroom and bath. When she took Jackie's blow dryer from under the cabinet in the bathroom, the deputy objected.

"Ma'am, just clothes," he told her.

"But, this is my daughter's blow dryer."

"Sorry. it's not clothes and unless there's another blow dryer left for your husband, you can't take this one from the house."

"So, what you're telling me," Shelley said, her anger rising, "Is that if there is only one blow dryer, my husband is supposed to get it? Even though it's not his, and he doesn't use one, he gets it anyway?"

"Yes, Ma'am, because you didn't take it with you when you left." The deputy gave her an impatient look. "You're actually pretty lucky the judge let you back in the house to get anything," he told her.

Angrily, Shelley said, "We were forced to leave our home because of my husband's violence. Does that mean anything to anybody?"

"It doesn't matter, Ma'am. We still have to follow the order from Judge Pierson. The rest will have to be battled out in court."

Clancy spoke up. "Let's just take the bags and leave Shelley. You're not going to accomplish anything here, not today anyway." Clancy gave the deputy a disgusted look.

"I guess you're right. Everything has to be dealt with in our wonderful court system. It just hurts to be forbidden from my own home. Everyone forgets this is my house, too! Mine and the children's!"

"I know, Honey, and I'm sure it will be all right, but unfortunately, it has to be done a certain way, and getting upset inside this house today isn't going to change that."

Shelley and Clancy brought the three bags back to the shelter. "How did it go?" Margo asked, as Shelley began to open one of the bags.

"I guess okay," Clancy answered. "Apparently, Neal had these bags ready so we wouldn't have to spend a lot of time there."

Shelley opened the first bag, and stared in shock. Suddenly, she ripped open the second bag, then the third. A look of horror, along with a flood of tears, captured her face.

"Shelley, what's wrong?" Clancy looked into the bags one by one. "Oh, my God!"

"What's going on?" Margo asked, and then, she saw what was in the bags. "You'd better call John, or Jack," Margo advised, as Shelley emptied all three bags onto the floor. When she was finished, there stood a big pile of old, dirty, torn up rags.

Too upset, Shelley asked Clancy to make the call to Jack. When he'd heard about Neal's latest stunt, he exploded.

"That bastard!" he shouted. "Clancy, can you bring Shelley to my office while I try to reach Judge Pierson?"

"Sure. We're on our way," Clancy said. "Margo, where are the kids?"

"They're fine. They're downstairs playing. Go do what you have to do. The Y has a picnic planned today for all the kids, so just go get this creep!" she said.

Shelley looked at Margo and whispered through her tears. "One day, Neal Jordon is going to get everything he deserves."

Chapter 52

"Jack, this is so unfair," Shelley insisted.

"I know it is. Judge Pierson is making some crazy decisions and I just don't get it, or why Neal Jordon is so damn cocky about doing the things he's been doing? He has gotten away with so much, I have to question Pierson's sanity on all of it," Jack answered, disgusted.

"My trip to the house was a total waste," Shelley said.

"We know this isn't fair, and that you feel as though you're always losing, but I promise, in the end, you will win. According to the judge, he ordered one trip to the house, and even though Neal did what he did, it has to be dealt with in court. He denied you a second trip," Jack said, clearly confident, in a system Shelley no longer believed in.

"That brings me to another issue we need to discuss," Jack said.

"What now?" she asked, afraid of what 'another issue' was.

"Let me start by explaining how the court system works. We can accuse Neal of anything we want to, as long as we can prove it," he said. "We are telling the court that Neal abused you, and that was the reason you left your home. Now, our job is to prove that to the court by presenting it with collaborating evidence that even Pierson can't ignore."

"We have the pictures, and Clancy and Mary's testimony. We need more?"

"We need an expert witness," Jack said.

"Isn't that what Mary is?" Shelley asked.

"No, that's what Dr. Peg Michaels is," Jack said. "John and I have done a lot of research trying to find a Psychiatrist that specializes in women that have been abused. Specifically, 'Battered Wives Syndrome'."

Shelley frowned. "What does that mean?"

"It means, we have to prove to the court that you are suffering as a result of Neal's abuse," he answered, hesitantly.

"And when do I see her?" Shelley asked, knowing they must have already arranged for a meeting.

"Tomorrow afternoon at four o'clock. She insisted on having four, two hour sessions before she will agree to come to court and testify for anyone, so you'll have to go to sessions every two days until our next court date."

Shelley didn't know what to expect from a Psychiatrist, and felt awkward sitting in the waiting room. *Thank God, Clancy is with me,* Shelley thought, smiling at her friend, as she flipped through a magazine.

"Mrs. Jordon, Dr. Michaels is ready to see you now," the receptionist said, leading Shelley to the gaily decorated room the doctor used for private sessions. Two soft, cushioned chairs welcomed her, one on each side of a round table facing a huge wall of glass overlooking Atlanta. The doctor apparently loved flowers. Arrangements embellished nearly every available surface.

Several minutes passed before a woman with a rugged face and slouched body entered the room. Shelley guessed she was about fifty years old. As an attempt to look feminine, the doctor was wearing a slinky, silk pants suit, which contradicted the rest of her appearance.

The woman introduced herself. "Hello, Shelley. I'm Dr. Michaels."

"Hello. It's nice to meet you," Shelley said, accepting the doctor's hands.

"Please, sit down," Dr, Michaels. "I'd like to start by getting to know a little about what you're feeling right now, what you're feeling is probably a hard issue for you to deal with. Then, we'll talk about your marriage and see where that leads us," Dr. Michaels said, trying to put Shelley at ease.

Shelley hesitated. She was being asked to talk about things she wasn't sure she was ready, or willing, to share. "Well, let's see. My life really was very uneventful until Neal came along."

"Okay, tell me what your life was like before Neal," the doctor suggested.

Shelley didn't know how to answer. She had so many thoughts about that.

"I thought it was missing something. During my marriage, everything was so crazy and insane, there were times I would have given anything to have that life back again," Shelley said. She felt that depressed feeling creep within her, the one that would consume her after one of Neal's beatings.

"How did your husband change your life?" Dr. Michaels asked.

"I can't think of anything he didn't change. He promised to love me, not just as his wife, but as the person I wanted to be," Shelley answered.

"And who was that person? The one you wanted to be?" she asked.

"Someone standing on stable ground. My mother made me feel so awful about myself after I told her that I didn't want to get married. It seemed like the easiest and best thing to do at the time. Now I feel stupid for buying into that."

"Why? Why did it seem like the best thing to do at the time? What was going on with you then?" the doctor asked.

"I don't know. I needed something, but in retrospect, I'm not sure what it was. Neal made me feel ready for change. He convinced me that new something I needed, was him."

"What did you think that something meant?"

"I think I was ready to trust someone beside myself," Shelley answered. "He meant peace to me."

"So, Neal was the person you decided to trust?"

"Yes, he was."

"How did you feel when it didn't turn out the way you thought it would?"

Shelley smiled. "Actually, it did turn out that way, for a few years anyway. I was so happy. When Neal became someone I could no longer trust, someone I was constantly afraid of, I felt devastated. Again I felt like I lost this other life. I was in love with Neal in the beginning."

"How did you love him?" she asked.

"My, God," Shelley answered. "He was my whole life, Neal and the kids. When he started to act so crazy, all I wanted was the man I married to come back, so I could be happy again."

"How do you feel about Neal today?" Dr. Michaels asked.

She stiffened. "I hate him. I'm petrified of him. I honestly believe he is capable of killing me."

"Do you really think he wants to do that? Don't you think he would have done that when he had a better opportunity if he was, in fact, planning to kill you?"

"No. Neal is far more clever than that. I'm sure he is going to try to kill me. I don't think anyone fully understands how ingenious he is. He can outsmart anyone," Shelley said.

She wanted to tell the doctor about the little girl in the fire and about Neal's grandmother, but she knew if he ever found out, he would be furious, he would find a way to punish her. Possibly, by using her children. No, she could never risk that.

By the end of their first session, Dr. Michaels assured Shelley she was definitely suffering the effects from what was legally classified as 'Battered Wives Syndrome'. Although Shelley would still have to complete her four sessions in order to make the testimony valid, Dr. Michaels assured her she would testify in court regarding her findings.

Chapter 53

Shelley's next court date arrived, and not a day too soon as far as she was concerned. She wanted the horrible experience over with. Her entire life, she'd tried to do the right thing, and had no understanding of how such awful treatment of women and children could take place in the civilized society she'd thought existed. Neal had taken her to a new, all time low.

She watched as the court clerk handed John something. After he looked at what appeared to be a little book, he approached Jack, sitting next to Shelley. "Jack, can I see you for a moment?" John asked.

Jack looked at Shelley and whispered, "I'll be right back."

After five minutes, Jack asked Shelley to join him in one of the back rooms.

"Shelley, do you know anything about a savings account holding thirty thousand dollars?" Jack asked.

"Does Neal have thirty thousand dollars?" Shelley asked, surprised.

"He's claiming he did, and that you took it all when you left him," John said.

"What? I don't know anything about an account holding thirty thousand dollars," she said. "What is this about?"

"Neal has some manipulative trick up his sleeve," Jack said to John.

"I agree. We just don't know what it is…yet anyway," John said.

"What's going on here?" Shelley asked, sensing the book meant some kind of trouble.

"Neal has produced a savings book, documenting a balance of thirty thousand dollars," Jack answered. "He claims he took it to the bank and the manager told him it was empty."

"Does Neal have the funds?" Shelley asked, she figured if he did, she should be entitled to half of it, more than enough to replace the ten thousand dollars Neal took from her.

"No, but worse than that, it isn't a real savings book," John explained. "Judge Pierson called the bank and spoke to the manager, who claims it was not a real account."

"I don't understand. You're saying there is a bankbook, but there isn't a bankbook? I'm confused."

"Yes, it's a bankbook that has been put together to look like an authentic bankbook from the Peach Haven Savings and Loan. But, in fact, it's a bogus book," Jack said.

"Where did Neal get it? And why, is this important, if there's no money?"

"He claims he got it from you," John exclaimed.

"What?" Shelley exclaimed with horror. "He's insane!"

"Apparently so. However, Judge Pierson is furious about it. He's threatening to call the G.B.I., and the F.B.I., and whatever other United States militant group he can use to find out who created this phony bankbook," Jack said. "And he wants you called to the stand first so he can question you personally about it."

Shelley said in a frightened voice, "I don't know anything about this book, and the way things have been going, I'm sure Judge Pierson won't believe that! What does he care anyway if Neal has a phony bankbook, it's not like it's worth anything?" she asked.

"Neal is trying to imply that you took thirty thousand dollars from him. The judge doesn't know if Neal is lying. He also feels whoever created this book could have done it with the intent of defrauding the bank," Jack explained.

"Jack, this is ridiculous. I can't take much more of Neal's lies!"

"Honey, just go on the stand and tell the truth. That's what always works and will never hurt you," Jack advised, trying to reassure her.

The court clerk entered the room to inform them that Judge Pierson wanted to begin. Judge Pierson called Shelley to the stand first. She felt sick. Everything was so bizarre in the court system, she knew she was playing Russian roulette by telling the truth. Truth had nothing to do with who would win. It was a question of who held the most cards. Neal had the morals of an alley cat, and the guts of a Mafia, Godfather. He would risk everything to destroy her. In his mind, she was his wife, and had to be punished for leaving him. If it worked, he would use the system to do that.

"Mrs. Jordon, I want you to take a good look at this bankbook and tell me if you have ever seen it before," Judge Pierson said, handing the book to Shelley.

She anxiously took it in her hands, desperate to see it. It had the same blue leather cover on it as their joint account had. The transactions in the book were handwritten. She couldn't remember if their joint account was documented by hand, or machine. "I don't think I have ever seen this book before," she answered.

"What do you mean, you don't think you have seen it, Mrs. Jordon? You have either seen it, or you have not seen it, which is it?" Judge Pierson sternly, demanded an answer.

Flustered and angry, Shelley answered, "I mean, we had a joint savings account with this bank, but Neal held the book to it, so I don't know if this is the book, or not!"

"That's all, Mrs. Jordon," Judge Pierson said, dismissing Shelley from the stand. "Mr. Jordon, take the stand please," he ordered next.

Neal had a smirk on his face. Clearly, he was happy with the way things were going. Shelley wanted to push him off a cliff.

"Mr. Jordon, look at this bankbook and tell me if you have ever seen it before today."

"Yes, Sir. This is the bankbook my wife gave me when I asked her for our joint savings account book," Neal said, giving Shelley an icy stare.

Jack grabbed Shelley's arm when she began to jump out of her seat.

"That's all, Mr. Jordon, thank you," Judge Pierson said to Neal.

Once Neal was seated beside his attorney, Judge Pierson made his statement.

"Since neither Mr. or Mrs. Jordon has taken responsibility for this bogus savings book, I will have to use my own method of getting to the truth. Both Mr. and Mrs. Jordon are to take a polygraph test as a court order, to be administered through the Fairville Sheriff's Department. Mr. Jordon will take his first. If he fails, it won't be necessary for Mrs. Jordon to take hers. The court will take action from there. Now, by all means, let's continue this session."

Lyle Maggitt called Shelley to the stand and asked her a lot of ridiculous questions about the household finances, and the cost of running the house. The questions served no purpose. Maggitt was obviously trying to stall any order for temporary child support.

Then, he hit Shelley with a line of questions that felt like a knife being driven into her heart.

"Mrs. Jordon, do you consider yourself a good mother?" he asked her.

"Yes, I do," she answered, wondering what he was up to.

"Mrs. Jordon, is this the picture of a good mother?" the attorney asked, handing Shelley a picture Neal had taken of her on his birthday, the first year of their marriage. Shelley had given him a new Polaroid camera. Walking out of the shower that night, he'd tried to snap her picture. She'd run into their family room and jumped on one of the chairs in their family room. When her towel fell off, Neal playfully, snapped the picture.

Shelley was absolutely mortified. She could not believe Neal had saved the photograph for so many years, and had actually shown it to a total stranger. Never had she felt so violated as she did at that moment.

Maggitt snatched the picture out of Shelley's hand, and turned it over to John and Jack. A moment later, he took it back again, so the judge could have his turn. Shelley wanted to die.

"I don't have any more questions your Honor," Lyle Maggitt said.

John approached Shelley. His heart seemed to ache for her when he saw the tears forming in her eyes. "Mrs. Jordon, where was that picture taken?" John asked.

"In the family room of our first home. It was Neal's birthday. I had bought him the Polaroid camera he wanted," Shelley answered, softly.

"Did you know your husband had that picture, Mrs. Jordon?"

"No. He promised me, he would destroy it. I didn't want a picture like that in the house, or anywhere else," Shelley answered, her voice trembling. "I thought he took the picture as a joke."

"I have no more questions, your Honor," John said, winking at Shelley to assure her everything was all right.

Lyle Maggitt called Neal back to the stand. "Mr. Jordon, did you take this picture of your wife?" he asked, handing Neal the photograph.

"No, I did not," he answered.

Agonized, Shelley buried her head in her arms. *How can he lie like this and get away with it? I can't take this anymore!*

"Mr. Jordon, do you recognize the location where this picture was taken?" Maggit asked.

"No, I've never seen the place before," he answered, looking smugly at Shelley.

"My, God," Shelley whispered. "Who is going to stop this man?"

At the end of the session, once again, Judge Pierson refused to set temporary child support. The people that kept returning to the courtroom during the Jordon's sessions to see how it all would end, began to whisper over the negligence of Judge Pierson regarding support for the children.

Outside the courtroom, both Jack and John tried to console Shelley. It had been an awful session.

Jack pulled Shelley aside and whispered in her ear. "Stop thinking about the picture. Believe me, you have nothing to be ashamed of," Jack said, half smiling.

Jack always knew how to make things better.

"I'm sure Judge Pierson has never seen anything that good, and I know Maggitt hasn't," Jack added, grinning.

Several minutes later, John and Clancy joined them. Clancy had been tucked away in the witness room with Mary, who'd left to return to the shelter.

"Hey, what's going on? Mary and I heard some people talking about a picture. What was that about?" she asked.

Shelley flinched. "What were they saying?"

"Well, some guy said he would sell his soul to see that picture, and the woman he was with, punched him in his stomach," Clancy answered.

Jack, John and Shelley, looked at each other, and all three began to laugh.

"Well, he didn't miss anything," Shelley stated, suddenly feeling better.

"Oh, yes he did!" Jack and John said at the same time, smiling.

Shelley took Clancy's arm. "Walk me to my car. I'll explain. Then, I have to meet Jack and John at their office."

A minute later, Clancy shouted, "That dirty bastard!"

Shelley thought she summed it up nicely.

At the law office, Jack scheduled a time for Shelley's polygraph test with the Sheriff's Department, and made the absurd arrangements for Neal's visitation the next day with the Police Department.

Shelley feared for her children. Once again, they were being forced to go with their father for the weekend, and if that wasn't bad enough, they would have to strip and suffer an examination by a stranger in the Police Department before they left with him.

Was Judge Pierson so ignorant, he didn't know the children would be humiliated by the examinations? There was still another two week wait before the next court session, that Shelley believed would end as unproductively as the previous session. But, at least Dr. Michaels would be testifying at that time.

"We will win the war, I promise," Jack told her, reading her thoughts.

"It's been seven months! Neal is still living in the house and hasn't made one child support payment. He hasn't paid one dollar towards his children's needs in seven months. I can't create miracles anymore, Jack. I need some kind of child support now. Not another month from now."

"Shelley, we're almost there. Don't quit on us now! Can't you hold on just a little while longer?" John asked.

Shelley looked at the kind man. He only wanted the very best for her and the children. Both Jack and John had fought so hard for them. How could she quit on either of them, ever?

"Sure...no problem," Shelley said, as she walked out of the office.

Chapter 54

Shelley brought the children to Jack's house as planned, and he took them to the Police Department to meet their father. He did not want Shelley around Neal under any circumstances. He knew Neal intimidated her too much, and she needed to stay strong.

A police officer walked outside to Jack's car and began removing Jackie's clothing. She began to cry, knowing even at her young age that the situation was wrong.

"Hold it! Why isn't there a female officer here to do this? And, did it ever occur to you to do this in a more private place, rather than the back seat of someone's car?" Jack asked, furious when he saw Jackie crying.

Neal just stood there with his familiar evil smirk, looking as though he had actually won something by putting his children through such an awful ordeal.

When the officers took the children inside the station to conduct the examinations, Jack and Neal were left alone on the sidewalk, staring at each other. After the examinations were completed and the children were brought outside again, Neal took their hands and led them to the car. The children turned and shouted, "Goodbye, Jack!"

Neal shot Jack a look of warning that clearly stated he did not like his children's attachment to him.

"I'll see you Sunday night," Jack said to the children, and the officer, giving Neal the same message, with his defiant stare.

Sunday, after spending a wonderful afternoon with Shelley, Jack went to retrieve Jackie and Jason from their father. The children seemed happy to see him.

Shelley knew they had grown fond of Jack. He had a son attending UCLA, but she could see her children had managed a special place in his heart.

Neal appeared to linger when he returned the children. Jack realized why when he saw Jackie's hair. Neal had cut her long, beautiful, blonde hair to her shoulders. He put the children in his car, and did not look back.

When Shelley saw her daughter's hair, she began to cry. "I want him arrested!"

"Honey, I'm sorry. There's not a thing you can do about it. The court would say he had as much right to cut his daughter's hair as you did not to," Jack told her.

Shelley drove the children back to the shelter feeling tremendous despair.

Following that, when Shelley arrived at the office the next morning, Joan told her to call Jack immediately.

"What's up?" Shelley asked him, at least feeling good that visitation was behind them for another two weeks.

"Can you come to the office for a few minutes?" Jack asked her.

"Is something wrong?" Shelley asked, frightened.

"Honey, please…just come in for a few minutes. Do you want me to pick you up?" Jack asked.

"Is it that bad that I won't be able to drive myself back to the office?"

Clancy walked in and heard Shelley on the phone. "Tell him I'll drive you," she said, throwing her briefcase on her desk, shaking her car keys to suggest they leave right away.

Jack and John were both waiting in the lobby when Shelley and Clancy arrived, certifying that something awful was about to take place.

"Come into my office," John said.

Jack put his arm around her. She looked up at him for some kind of comfort, but he had none to offer.

"Do you want me to wait out here?" Clancy asked.

"No, I think I need you with me," she said, looking at the two solemn men. They went into the conference room and took seats at the large, wooden table, meant to accommodate ten people. Suddenly, Shelley felt very far away from the real world.

"Neal failed his polygraph test," John said, once everyone was seated.

"That's wonderful, John! So why do you both look so down in the mouth?" Shelley asked, knowing there was more to the drama.

"Judge Pierson withdrew from your case this morning. He claims he's prejudice, and didn't think it would be fair to you if he continued hearing this case," John told her.

"What does that mean?" Shelley asked, hoping her first thoughts were wrong.

"That means...we have to begin again with a new judge," Jack answered for his partner.

"How long? How long is this fiasco going to take?" she asked, shaking, beginning to cry. *You did it Neal! At last you have beaten me down. I feel no hope.*

"It will take close to ninety days before we get a court date with a new judge," Jack told her sadly.

"No! Damn it, Jack, I can't wait ninety days to get back in my house. I'll have to move out of the condominium before then, and I need child support for my children! What kind of trick is this?" Shelley asked.

"Shelley, look. I know you don't see it this way, but we really have to be thankful Pierson stepped down. He was prejudiced, even though he knows that Neal is a liar. He already planned to side with him no matter what we proved in court. It's been the only right thing he's done throughout the entire case," Jack said.

"Can I sue him, Jack?" Shelley asked, consumed with anger. "If he was prejudiced at the end of the hearing, he sure as hell was prejudiced at the beginning."

"No, you can't sue a judge. We'll have to wait the ninety days. With a new judge, I'm sure you will get the house and the child support you deserve," John said.

"Why do we have to wait ninety days?" she asked, frightened about how she would be able to make it financially without the help of child support.

"Because the new judge will have to read the transcript and yours is a long one. Plus, the other documents involved with this unusual case," Jack answered.

"Why are you so sure I'll get the house and child support?"

"Because this entire case has been so nuts. John and I have even wondered if Judge Pierson wasn't paid off by Neal, which is still a possibility, as far as I'm concerned."

"It does seem kind of odd, that as soon as Neal fails his polygraph, the judge conveniently decides to step down from the case before he would have to respond to that. Doesn't it seem odd, John?" Clancy asked.

"Yes, it does. But my main goal is to get Shelley and the kids back in their house and for Shelley to start receiving the child support she is entitled to."

Shelley was disgusted. "What choice do I have, John? I guess I have to wait. Whether I like it or not, doesn't matter," she added.

Jack took her hand. "Are you all right?"

Shelley laughed. "How all right could I be? Once again, Neal comes out the winner, doesn't he?"

At that moment, contempt for Neal, the court system, her uncaring parents, Jack's dying wife, and life in general, filled her.

"No, because he hasn't got the one thing he wants, and that's you!" Jack said.

He was right. Heart and soul, she belonged to Jack, just as much as he belonged to her. Not even Neal Jordon could destroy the strong love they shared for each other.

Chapter 55

For two days, with Molly by her side, Shelley mourned. The two women had been through so much together, it was as if when one was broken, the other helped put them together again. Molly had taught Shelley that life goes on, no matter what one has to endure, so on the third day, she moved into her condominium, furnished with odds and ends from other people. For Shelley, the move was a total step of faith.

Jack pleaded with her to accept his help, but she didn't want money to enter into their relationship. She loved him, and wanted what they had together to be about them. When she was with Jack, she felt as if she could conquer anything life threw her way. When they made love, the world became theirs, peaceful, free from the ugly elements that continuously worked against a thing of substance, the love that consumed them.

The following Sunday, Shelley decided to take her shift in the model home, allowing Clancy a much needed day off. The children would return that evening from visitation with their father, and as usual, Jack would be picking them up, and would care for them until she closed the model.

Shelley decided she would have to be strong to get through the next ninety days. Financially, she was broke. Without child support, she had no idea how she would make ends meet. There was also the problem with the condominium. The owner would be going to court in the near future, and the condominium would become mutual property, and she would have to move out. The delay in her court case put her in a precarious situation.

A few times, Jack gave Molly money to give to Shelley, asking her to say it was from a friend of hers, so neither of them would be lying.

He couldn't do it often, because Shelley always wanted a detailed explanation where Molly got the money. She knew her friend, too, was without means.

Right after Shelley's move into the condominium, Clancy brought over several bags of groceries to add to the supplies Margo and Mary had given her to fill her bare cupboards and refrigerator.

Shelley hated feeling so destitute. It disgusted her that other people worried about the children eating, while their father felt like a warrior, legally avoiding paying child support for so many months.

So many people contributed different things to help her set up the condominium. Even Vinnie delivered two cushioned chairs from his office so she and the kids would have something to sit on.

Shelley opened the model home at eleven o'clock after spending the morning with Jack. They ate breakfast at the local pancake house, then, drove to the lake to be away from people. Shelley was beginning to feel rejuvenated. They began to talk about their future together, and even went as far as to make plans. She was too in love to let her hate for Neal inflict itself on her joy.

She put her briefcase down on top of the desk in the living room, then, went from room to room, turning on all the lights. Shelley knew lights always made a house appear warmer, more elegant, and that particular house needed all the help it could get to sell.

While Shelley was upstairs, she heard a door close. She walked to the top of the stairs to see if someone had actually stopped to see the house, but no one was there. As she finished turning on the lights, she heard another door close. Once again, she went to the top of the stairs to see who was in the house.

Suddenly, she heard footsteps from the lower level and could tell whoever it was, wanted to move slowly and quietly. Her heart began to pound. The only phone in the house was sitting on top of the desk in the living room. Whoever was in the house was coming from the lower level into the living room.

Trying to maintain her fear, she shook her head. *Stupid me. It's probably just Vinnie, or Clancy.* She quickly looked out one of the windows for either of their cars. *I must be hearing things. My nerves are completely shot!* She didn't see any cars parked in the driveway, or anywhere in front of the model. Walking downstairs, she felt rather foolish, until she stepped down from the last stair and found herself thrown against the living room wall.

"Hello, Shelley," the familiar voice said.

Shelley started to scream, but before any sound escaped, a strong hand clamped over her mouth and she saw Neal's angry face next to hers. Only a few hours ago she had stopped being frightened, but she realized at that moment, she never really was safe. The reality was, Neal could get to her whenever he wanted to. He'd just proven that.

"It would be real bad for you if someone came in here right now, Shelley," Neal growled through those all too familiar clenched teeth. She struggled to get away from his grip. "You'd better be still and listen to what I have to say."

He took his hand off her mouth and stepped back while Shelley remained pressed against the wall, her body quivering, sure he'd come to kill her. He'd certainly chosen the perfect time and place. Recognizing the look of fear in her eyes, Neal smiled, clearly pleased to find he was still in control.

"I'm not here to hurt you," he said. "I love you. I'm here to save our marriage."

"That's not going to happen," Shelley snapped back. "You don't know how badly I want this divorce!"

"Oh, but I do. However, my dear, you are never going to have Jack Pope."

"I don't know what you're talking about," Shelley responded, searching the room for a way out.

"You don't? Well, then, look at these." Neal pulled several photographs from his jacket pocket and shoved them into Shelley's shaky hands.

Horrified, Shelley leafed through several snapshots of Jack and her at the lake. Her heart sank. That beautiful day, while Jack made love to her for the first time Neal, or someone just as vulgar, had watched, and taken pictures.

"You always did like photographs, Neal," Shelley whispered, disgusted. "And what will these cost me?"

"Jack Pope," Neal answered, grinning like a Cheshire cat.

"Forget it. You don't control me anymore," she stated flatly.

"But legally I do. You're still my wife," he insisted. His smile chilled her.

"What do you want from me?" Shelley asked, her voice quivering, willing to do anything to make him leave. All she wanted to do at that moment, was fall into Jack's arms, and hold her children.

"I want you to come home and stop this divorce," he answered.

"That won't happen, so if you came to kill me, you should do it now." The boldness of her words surprising her.

"I don't think you're considering all the consequences," he purred, as he waved the photographs in front of her face.

"What do you mean?" she asked, sure Neal had something hideous in mind.

"Such as poor, Mrs. pope, dying while her husband stays busy screwing my wife. Oh, then, there's the court, to say nothing of the Bar Association," Neal said, "Do I pique your interest?"

Shelley stiffened. "What about the Bar Association?"

"Don't you know? It's a breach of ethics for Jack Pope to have an affair with one of his clients, something about trust. What judge would look at him with respect ever again? The scandal would kill his career, being a married man and all. He would never win a case, anywhere. All those years spent getting through law school, then, building the practice, all down the tubes. What about his wife and their prodigal son? What will he think of his father after he finds out the man cheated on his mother while she was dying of Cancer?"

Neal stepped further away, then, turned to look at her. "Then, there's John Black to think of. He'll go down with Pope. Neither one of them will ever be worth anything in this county, ever again. Obviously, I did my homework, and Shelley, you know I never make false threats."

Shelley looked at him trying to think. He knew she would never allow anything to hurt Jack, or John. She would never let them lose their careers. And, Shelley knew that given the choice, Jack would say to hell with his career. So, she could never tell him about Neal's threats.

He softened his tone, fully aware he had his wife's attention, and had already won.

"I want you to come home and fall in love with me again. I want things the way they were before my parents became involved in our marriage. Look, Shelley, I know I put you through hell in court, but it was only because I love you, and the thought of losing you made me crazy. I want you to come home."

"You don't love me, Neal. You wouldn't have done such awful things to me if you did. You don't even care about your children's welfare."

"Do you love him, Shelley?" Neal asked, clearly struggling to reserve his anger.

"Yes, I do," she answered, emphatically.

"I know I'm a total dog for using blackmail to make you come home, but I'll do whatever it takes to get my family back together again."

"I won't go back to a life of violence ever again."

"There is a new program called 'Men Stopping Violence'. I'll sign up for it. It's an eight month program, designed to control domestic violence. I'll do whatever you want. Just come home. I don't want this divorce."

Shelley began to cry. "And if I don't?"

"I'll do what I have to do," he answered.

"Which is what? Ruining Jack, who is a good, decent man? Hurting a dying woman, and her innocent son? And John? You'd actually be that ruthless?"

"Shelley, you loved me once. Can't you try to love me again?"

"Neal, Jack is different. I don't have to be afraid of him, and neither do the children."

"I'll make sure you will never be afraid of me again," he promised.

"Don't do this to me. I love him. I want to be with him," Shelley said, hoping he might have a morsel of common decency inside his perverse mind.

"You can't have him, Shelley," Neal snapped. "I love you. Either you come home, or I'll take copies of these pictures to the Bar Association and Jack's wife. And that's just for starters. You decide."

Shelley needed time to collect her thoughts. "Can I have a day or two before I give you my decision without you doing something horrible?"

She knew she could never let Neal ruin Jack's life.

Neal smiled. "Sure. I've waited eight months, I can wait a few more days. I'll come here Tuesday, the same time. Be here. And Shelley, think long and hard about your answer."

As arranged, Shelley phoned Jack at his home after he'd picked up the children. The plans were for her to pick them up after she closed the model at the end of the day.

"How did it go picking up Jackie and Jason?" she asked.

"Fine. Neal didn't even get out of the car. Listen...let's take the kids for pizza. They're so tired, I'm sure they're going to fall asleep before you cook anything."

Just the sound of his voice made Shelley happy. Right then, she needed to be with him. "You're on," she answered.

She drove to the condominium, and Jack arrived with the children shortly after that. He knew something was wrong as soon as he saw her face.

"What's wrong, Honey? Are you all right?" he asked, kissing her forehead.

"Yes. I just needed to see you, that's all," she replied, avoiding his scrutiny.

Jack smiled. "I like that. I'm anxious to be with you, too."

That evening, after the trip for pizza, and after the children were asleep, Shelley thrilled to Jack's every touch. They made love throughout the night, thrilling her as it had the first time. She knew the memory of that night, would have to last her the rest of her life.

Chapter 56

Shelley didn't tell Jack that night about going home. Not just to her house, but to Neal. She didn't want anything to take away from the magic of their last night together, and decided it would be easier to tell Jack and John, together.

She called John and told him she wanted to meet with Jack and him at ten o'clock. When she walked into the law office, Jack was on his way down the hall. He met Shelley and grabbed her hand, whispering into her ear, "I love you."

She wanted to die. Smiling, she avoided looking at him, sure he would know something was wrong. Leaving Jack would be the hardest thing she ever had to do. Already, she felt as though her heart had been torn out.

They walked into John's office. "Hey, Sweetie! Sit down," John said, smiling, always glad to see her.

"I think I should stand, John. This will only take a minute," she said, tears already forming in her eyes.

Jack stood more alert and asked, instantly concerned, "Shelley, what's wrong?"

"I've decided to go home," she blurted out. Silence followed.

"Honey, you can't go home until the court orders Neal out of there. You know that," John responded.

"I don't think you understand. I'm going home…with Neal still there."

Jack glared long and hard into Shelley eyes, disbelief clouding his face.

"You can't do that, Shelley," John told her. "He can have you physically removed from the premises."

Jack stood more alert, instantly concerned. His face turned pale and his body stiffened.

"I think what Shelley is trying to tell us, John, is that she is reconciling with Neal. Is that right, Shelley?" he asked, slowly.

Shelley looked into Jack's eyes, and whispered, "Yes…that's right."

As John looked at both of them, Shelley knew that he realized from the expression on both their faces, that they were in love. "Shelley, Honey, you can't mean this," John said, softly.

"I'm sorry, John, but I have to do this. I can't go on another ninety days without financial help, and after all, he is still my husband, and the house is still my house," she said, making no sense, unable to watch Jack, as he tried to handle the pain.

"Excuse us for a moment, John. We'll be right back," Jack said, grabbing Shelley's hand, leading her into his office. He slammed the door behind them, causing Shelley to step back.

"What is this about, Shelley?" Jack demanded to know.

"I think I explained that. I'm going back to Neal."

"This is nuts! What happened between last night and now? And don't hand me any nonsense about money. I'll give you whatever you need to take care of the children. I want an honest answer, and then, I would like to know when you had any conversation with Neal Jordon!" Jack shouted.

"Jack, please, don't do this. I'm sorry," she sobbed, running out of the law office.

Jack ran after her, catching up to her as she attempted to get into her car.

"Shelley, wait!"

"I can't, Jack. I have to go," Shelley shouted, still trying to get in her car.

Jack wouldn't let her go. *I can't weaken, I love him too much. How long would he love me after he'd lost it all?* She knew what she had to do.

Jack slowly pulled her away from the car and towards him.

"Something is wrong, Shelley. Why won't you tell me the truth? There is no way you would go back to Neal willingly. Has Neal threatened you in some way? I have to know, Shelley, is that it?"

"Look, Jack," she said, stepping away from him, unable to do what she had to do, while she was in his arms. "You can't promise me that I'll get my house back, and you certainly can't promise me any kind of future right now, can you?" she asked, contemptuously, hoping he would believe her act.

"Yes, I can. I've been trying to do that for months, but you won't let me. Every time I start any kind of discussion about our future, you cut me off. I know this is a bad situation for you, but I promise, there are circumstances I have not discussed with you, yet. Shelley, I love you. I want to marry you and help you raise Jackie and Jason. Please, don't do something you really don't want to do. Don't throw away what we have together. There is nothing that will convince me that you don't love me, too. I want the truth, Shelley!"

"This is what's best for everyone concerned," Shelley answered, feeling overcome.

"He's threatened you with something. What is it, Shelley? I'm going to find out, believe me!"

"It's me, Jack. I just feel like I have to try to work out my marriage."

"When did you speak to him?" Jack demanded. He slowly backed away from her.

"When was it, Shelley? Yesterday? Before, or after we were together, Shelley?" he asked, looking overcome with pain, as if his entire world had crashed.

"Before," Shelley whispered, as she got in her car. She didn't look up, because she knew she wouldn't be able to live the rest of her life, remembering the pain she'd inflicted on Jack.

Quickly, she pulled her car towards the edge of the parking lot, as the tears that she had held for two days, flowed down her cheeks.

Goodbye, Jack. I will love you forever.

She caught a glimpse of him in the rear view mirror, standing against the tree they sat under the night they'd met, totally destroyed. She pulled out as soon as traffic allowed her to, before her tears turned to heavy sobs. She was in complete agony. An agony worse than she'd ever felt after any beating from Neal. This was an agony that would never go away. It imprisoned her soul, and would follow her to her grave. For the rest of her days, she would love Jack Pope.

She made all the right turns leading to the model. She had called Neal and told him to meet her on Monday, instead of Tuesday, since there was no use prolonging the inevitable. Neal would be waiting there for her decision. That night, she and the children would be back in their home, but what a high price she had to pay.

Chapter 57

Shelley set the terms before she would bring the children home. She kept no secrets from Neal regarding the contempt she felt for him, and he was fully aware of her feelings for Jack. He accepted her feelings, and was prepared to help her get over him.

The most important stipulation was that Neal, send Jack and John, a check for ten thousand dollars.

"Just look at it as the money you stole from me for your antique car," she said.

The second term, was that Neal immediately sign up for the 'Men Stopping Violence', program. Shelley made it known she would not tolerate any violent behavior again towards her, or the children. She was also firm about attending her Wednesday night group meetings, sure that would be her only source of strength.

By nine, that evening, Shelley went home. Jackie and Jason ran to their rooms, seeking their favorite toys, while Shelley went into the kitchen, remembering the morning after they'd moved into the house, how she'd hoped the move would change things in her marriage. It sure had.

Walking into the master bedroom, she sat on the bed, thinking about the nights she'd cried herself to sleep, hoping Neal would not wake her up to hit her again.

What could possibly make him think I would forget the way he treated me? How could I just forgive everything? How could any woman forget that horrible life? And how could any woman forget Jack Pope?

Neal joined her in the bedroom, clearly exhilarated to have his family home again.

"Are you tired? Do you want to go to sleep?" he asked, smiling.

Shelley glared at him with disgust.

"I'm not sleeping with you, Neal. Not now, not ever," she finished, calmly. "So, don't even go there."

"Look, Shelley, Honey, you won't be sorry you came home to me, I promise. I'll make you forget everything I've done in the past, and whatever you feel for Jack Pope."

With that statement, Shelley stood and looked him in the eye, determined to let him know that he really did not win anything.

"Well, Neal, as much as you might hate to hear this, I don't want to get over him. If you really want me home as much as you say you do, you can be glad that I do love him this much, because, believe me, I would not be here if I didn't. He is a wonderful man, someone you would have a real hard time relating to, and he doesn't deserve the garbage you would bring into his life. That, Neal, is the only reason I'm within fifty feet of you. So, don't assume that I would want to share the same bed with you, because quite frankly, Jack would be too hard an act for you to follow!"

She turned to leave the room. "Oh, and Neal?"

Neal stood by the window, speechless.

"If you ever try to hurt me, or my children, lift one hand, say one rotten word, I will take that as a threat, and I will kill you. You see, I can do that, and get out of jail a lot faster than I can divorce you," she said, walking out of the bedroom.

The following day, Neal signed up for the Men Stopping Violence program after spending a hard night on the couch, sure that would be his bed until he'd completed the program. Neal would have to endure three private sessions with the Psychiatrist that originally designed the program. The doctor claimed it was beneficial to the group to eliminate participants who were not sincerely willing to fix their problem.

Some men tried to use the program as a way to get their families back. Shelley suspected Neal had agreed to the three weeks, looking at it as exactly that, a way to win back his family.

"I agree with Jack, something's up. I know as Shelley's best friend, that she is truly in love with Jack, and we all know how much she loathes Neal Jordon!" Clancy told John when he'd told her about Shelley going home.

"I was upset with Jack for falling in love with her to begin with. He was her lawyer for Christ's sake. But, he's a good man, and I know he thought Shelley was the one for him. I didn't force the issue because he deserved the happiness she'd brought into his life. I guess I shouldn't have ignored the situation. I knew his feelings for her were not what an attorney should have towards a client, as soon as he'd met her."

"What the hell are you doing, Shelley?" Clancy demanded.

"I knew you would be here bright and early. Who told you, Jack, or John?" Shelley asked, standing in her doorway in her bathrobe. Neal had already left the house, so she let Clancy in.

"John. Jack is too much of a basket case right now to talk about anything," she answered.

Shelley sat on the couch and began to cry.

"I knew it! Honey, why are you here? It's obvious you and Jack are very much in love. What made you do this?" Clancy persisted. "Shelley, this guy is going to kill you. You don't love him. Why are you throwing your life away? Surely, it's not the house."

"You know me better than that."

"Yes, I do, and I know there is some terrible reason you came back to this crazy man!" Clancy said.

"I can't talk about it."

"Well, I think you have to. Shelley, Jack spent the night on the floor of his office totally wasted from two bottles of scotch. He's devastated!"

"Has everyone forgotten Jack is a married man?" Shelley asked.

"Lacey Pope is dying, and she wants Jack to have you."

Startled, Shelley glared at Clancy for what seemed an eternity.

"I already told you that she knows about you and Jack, that he'd told her," Clancy said. "Jack has been a wonderful husband to her, but she will be gone soon. One of her last concerns while she is still on this earth, is that Jack will be happy after she is gone. Jack didn't plan it, you just showed up one day in his office, and he fell in love. Lacey saw the change in him and spoke to me about it. I assured her you were good for him because that's what I believe. Jack spent his entire married life taking care of a sick woman. He did it with a smile, and lots of love, and never once complained. Now, Lacey figures it's his turn."

Shelley couldn't believe her ears. "Does Jack know this?" she asked.

"No." Clancy shook her head.

"Are you going to tell him?" Shelley asked.

"No, I'm not. But, Shelley, if Neal has found out about you two and has threatened to tell Lacey, there is no reason for you to stay. She already knows!"

"That's not all of it," Shelley said. "You already told me Lacey knows."

"Well, then, what is it? I promise I'll keep your secret," Clancy insisted.

"If I tell you, you have to promise it can never leave this room."

"I understand," Clancy said.

Tears formed in Shelley's eyes once again. "Neal has some pictures of Jack and I that are really incriminating. He promised to send copies, not only to Jack's wife, but also to his son at school. On top of that, he threatened to file a complaint with the Bar Association to get Jack disbarred, and ruin his and John's practice."

"Oh, Shelley. He's such a lowlife," Clancy said, furious.

"I can't let that happen to Jack. He's worked hard to make a good life for his family, and I'm not going to let Neal destroy that."

"Do you think Neal would really do that?" Clancy asked.

Shelley gave her a look. "What do you think? Did you forget the infamous court photograph?"

"You're right. Oh, Honey, I don't know what's worse, to let Jack think you never loved him, or for him to face the threat of getting disbarred."

"He'll get over me, but neither one of us would ever get over him losing everything he's worked for. Every time he looked at me, I would be wondering if he was thinking about what I cost him? I don't want that for Jack, or me. He deserves to live in peace, and as long as Neal is alive, I won't, and neither would Jack. Can you understand?" she asked.

Tears welled in Clancy's eyes, too. "Yeah, I understand. You really love him, don't you?"

"Yes, I do. I'm so miserable, someone could kill me and I would consider it a mercy killing."

Clancy picked up her purse, preparing to leave. She turned around and looked at her friend. "I was right, Shelley."

"About what?"

"You are good for Jack," Clancy walked out and closed the door.

Shelley cried bitterly over her broken heart. She knew it would take time to get over the pain Neal had created in her life, and she knew her marriage would never be one of any quality. Who would forget Neal's history, and what he was capable of doing? However, she'd made the decision, after hours of crying, that she would do the best she could to make the marriage appear normal for the sake of the children. They had endured abnormal suffering during their short little lives, and she refused to intentionally inflict that kind of horrible lifestyle on them again.

Chapter 58

"Matt, I just think Atlanta is doing fine now, and I need a new challenge. I carried Atlanta from the bottom line to the number one district in the United States within six months. Although I agree it needs an eye kept on it, I feel I can do that from another region," Neal told his boss at corporate on the phone one morning.

He listened as his boss explained that the Regional Manager in Florida wanted to retire. Neal's mind went to work. A Florida assignment would work out perfectly if he wanted out of Atlanta. It would also mean a promotion.

"Can we look at a time frame of nine months?" Neal asked. "Great! And in the meantime, I'll add Florida to my list of travels. Sir, thank you. I'll be looking forward to our meeting with each other, so we can nail this down."

Neal hung up the phone and smiled, obviously seeing an end to the threat of Jack Pope ruining his reconciliation with Shelley.

"I love tropical weather and sunshine," Neal whispered to himself. "What better place could I move Shelley to than Florida?"

Shelley endured one day at a time, each running into the next, none very significant. She spent most of her time at home, afraid of the possibility of running into Jack somewhere. She knew she could not see him and remain strong. So many times, she'd reach for the phone, only to put it down again. She knew she had to try harder to make the situation work. Jackie and Jason were thrilled to be home again. That alone made her decision right.

Neal was doing everything he could to win Shelley's love and respect back. He even worked at becoming a much better father to the children by helping with their care. He was successfully completing his 'Men Stopping Violence' program and had been behaving so well, Shelley found herself beginning to relax around him.

Neal called Shelley from the office one morning, and asked if she could get Carl to baby-sit that evening because he wanted to take her out for dinner.

"I really don't want to go out anywhere," she told him flatly.

"Please, Shelley, just give me a couple of hours, okay?"

Thinking it might be all right if it was not a local restaurant, she asked, "Where do you want to go?"

"We can go to Atlanta. How's that?" he asked.

Shelley broke down. "All right, I guess that would be okay."

"Great! I'll pick you up at six," Neal said, sounding excited.

Shelley asked Carl to come a little before six, knowing Neal would be prompt. She had no idea why, but she decided to dress for the occasion, and wore a gray, and black tweed knit dress that flattered her hourglass figure. It had been long time since she cared about what she wore.

Shelley wondered at what point, Neal had returned her clothes to her closet. She hadn't noticed. Everything she touched, and everything she saw, somehow, brought back a bad memory, so she avoided as much as possible, making each day nondescript.

"You look absolutely breathtaking, Shelley," Neal told her softly, when he walked in and saw her. The look in his eyes said he wanted to hold her, to kiss her, and make love to her, like a husband should.

She trembled. "Let's just go wherever we're going," she told him."

"I thought we could go Anthony's, I know how much you enjoy it," he said.

"I don't want to go there, Neal. My memories of Anthony's aren't very pleasant," she said, trying to hurt him.

"Where would you like to go, then?" he asked.

"How about 'Babydoes'?"

"Babydoes is fine," he answered, smiling at her.

They ordered dinner, and enjoyed a cocktail while they waited. Shelley hadn't said a word.

"Shelley, there's something I have to talk to you about," Neal began cautiously.

"Oh, what is it? Do you want a divorce?" she asked, grinning.

"Look, I have been going crazy trying to make things right between us, but I feel you don't really care about what's going on," Neal complained.

"You blackmailed me into coming back, Neal and that's the only reason I'm here," she responded.

"I understand, but the time has come to make things civil, if for nothing else, for Jackie and Jason's sake," Neal said.

"Oh? All of a sudden we care about what's good for the children? Where were you when they needed food, and shelter? Were you thinking about them when you refused to pay child support?"

Irritated, Neal said, "Shelley, I'm sorry, I'm trying to be a good husband and father. Maybe I got my second chance with you in an unethical way, but you and the children are my life, and I did what I had to do to save what was most important to me. So, if you want to hate me for loving you, then hate me. But, please, stop the lousy indifference."

Shelley stared at him. He was trying to make a home for them, but instead of trying to remember what life was like when she'd first married Neal, she was thinking of Jack. She had to accept the fact that he was no longer a part of her life, it was over, but she didn't know how to do that. The pain, the constant craving to be with him, his eyes, his smile. Thinking of all those things, hurt so badly. She couldn't put Jack's memory behind her.

"Neal, why did you bring me here? To lecture me?" she asked.

"No, actually, I have been offered a promotion with Skiff as Regional Manager for the entire Southeast."

"Well, that's great. I'm sure you stabbed enough people in the back to earn it."

Neal continued, ignoring her remark. "There is one little hitch."

"Oh? What's that? Do you have to kill somebody?" Shelley took a sip of her Black Russian, and looked around the room.

"We have to move to Florida."

Shelley nearly dropped her glass.

"Maybe a move would help put everything behind us," Neal said, quickly.

Shelley glared at him. "What you're really saying, Neal, is that a move would be a good way to get Jack Pope out of our lives permanently. Isn't that what this is all about?"

Neal looked at her for a second, not able to deny it. "Yes, it is," he answered, softly.

"Well, what do you know? Something new in our relationship... honesty."

"Shelley, I told you, I'm trying."

Shelley thought for a moment. *This probably would be the best thing for me. Maybe I could get on with my life. I wouldn't have to worry every time I went to the store about running into Jack. I wouldn't feel tortured about knowing he's only five minutes away, or when I pass his office, and see his car in the parking lot.*

"Maybe you're right. Moving to Florida might be a good way for us to get on with our lives," Shelley said, holding back her tears.

She would never see Jack again. She had to begin trying to make her days more tolerable. Perhaps that would come easier in another state, away from Peach Haven.

Shelley asked Clancy to list the house, and as unhappy as it made her, she agreed to take the listing. She also promised not to tell Jack that she was moving, and where to. Shelley believed that would be the only way to get any kind of closure on her feelings.

Neal would be finished with his program by the time they moved, and was making a very successful attempt at being a good husband and father. Excited about the move to Florida, during one of his trips there, he'd gathered several home brochures to show Shelley.

One of the homes that Shelley liked was a resale, and Neal made arrangements with the Realtor handling the property to see it the following week. He took pictures of the house, inside and out, and Shelley liked it so much when she saw them, sight unseen, they'd made an offer on the home.

Skiff provided Shelley with a trip to Florida so she could see the area. It didn't matter to Shelley where she was going, as long as she was going somewhere, far away from Peach Haven and the State of Georgia.

She spent her last night in Peach Haven with Clancy and Joe. Neal had left the day before, and she was not ready to stay with her parents, thinking of her mother's joyful reaction when she'd told her she was reconciling with Neal. Besides that, staying with them would add another hour to the already lengthy drive to Florida.

It saddened Shelley that her mother didn't have a clue about what she and the children had endured for eight months, and she never felt the same about her parents after her mother had refused to help with the bond. She never understood the woman's lack of love, or concern regarding the fate of her grandchildren during that awful time.

The next morning, Shelley said goodbye to Clancy and Joe, before securing Jackie and Jason into their car seats. Saying goodbye was really tough.

"You'll write, won't you? Maybe call once in a while?" Clancy asked, through a veil of tears.

"Of course," Shelley promised, hugging her wonderful friend. "Clancy I can't begin to tell you what you have meant to me, and my children," Shelley said.

"Oh, stop. You know I love you and would take bullets for you and those kids!" Clancy said, trying to laugh through her tears.

"I think you already did that, remember?" Shelley asked, trying to laugh.

"Every rainy day," she replied. "Stay safe, Shelley. Don't let him hurt you again, and if you need us, pick up the phone."

"I promise, Clancy. I will, and trust me, Neal will never hurt us again," Shelley assured her, giving her friend one last hug.

Joe waved from their living room window, then blew her a kiss. It was easier for him to say goodbye from the window.

She got in the car, and knew she had to pass the house one more time before she left Peach Haven for good. It was sold, and would soon be filled with other people. Strangers, that had no idea what kind of ugly things took place within the walls of that beautiful house. Doubts and questions probed her mind, and through them all, the only thing she knew for sure, was that she had to get to a place far away from Jack Pope. Doing that, maybe, she would discover who she'd become. But at that moment, she had never felt such overwhelming anguish.

Chapter 59

Shelley followed Neal's easy directions to Palm Harbor, Florida, finding the 'Howard Johnson's Motel' with no problem. They would be staying there for two nights until their furniture was delivered to the new house.

To Shelley's surprise, Neal had rented only one room.

"I'm not expecting anything," Neal told her. "I just think it's better for the children if they see us living as a normal family.

"I guess we should start trying to make things a little more natural," she answered.

"I won't ask anything from you," Neal assured her.

"Thank you. I'm just not ready for anything like that."

Two days later, Shelley and Neal moved into their new home, a three thousand square foot ranch with four bedrooms, and two full baths, complete with a screened in pool, centered in a huge lanai. The backyard was completely surrounded with privacy fencing, with a section of landlocked woods behind it. It was a beautiful home for Shelley to begin her new life in.

Neal became heavily involved with his traveling. Shelley believed the time away was helping with her recovery. He worked hard to make their marriage work, and at times his commitment actually made her feel guilty when she couldn't demonstrate the same amount of determination.

She spent most of her time fixing the house to her liking, and meeting their new neighbors. They made some friends, and in effect, began to have a social life together.

Since Neal had completed his program, she no longer worried about him becoming jealous, or argumentative. She was able to relax and enjoy herself, and for the first time, they'd developed mutual friends.

The following September, the children were enrolled in the same private school as their neighbor's children, having found the public school unsatisfactory the past school year. Shelley joined the carpool team, settling in as the perfect homemaker.

Neal and she had become active members in the local church, and soon most of their social life involved the congregation. For all purposes, they appeared to be living like every other couple they knew, and as time went by, they pretty much were, except for the relentless unrest churning inside of Shelley.

It was on a Sunday afternoon…Shelley left to go to the grocery store. When she'd returned, she found the Jordon's white Thunderbird, with Florida plates on it, parked in front of the house. Irate, she slammed her car door and stormed into the house.

From the foyer, she could hear Neal's mother laughing in the family room. With clenched fists, she went directly to the master bedroom, and slammed the door, letting it be known that she didn't want the Jordons in her house. Neal joined her immediately.

"What are you doing?" he asked, clearly embarrassed over her behavior.

"No, Neal. The question is, what the hell are you doing? How did those people get our new address?" she asked, enraged.

"I gave it to them. They're still my parents, Shelley. I became close with them again during our separation."

"Your parents, Neal? Why would you give the two people I hate the most in this world, our address? Why don't you just go back pretending they're dead? I absolutely will not tolerate those people coming to my home! Get rid of them now, or I swear, the kids and I will be on our way back to Georgia tonight!"

Neal went back to the family room to speak with his parents, leaving Shelley alone in the bedroom. A few minutes later, he joined her again.

"They heard you shouting and said they didn't want to stay where they're not welcome. They're gone."

"Good! Then, this won't happen again," Shelley said, walking into the kitchen. She shook with anger. Every time the Jordons got involved in her life, there was trouble. They were not going to take over her home again. If Neal was adamant about having them in his life, she would leave, blackmail, or no blackmail. They were like poison to her, and she refused to allow them to spin their evil on an already shaky marriage. Especially when things were barely settled down from the separation.

Neal had not been violent, or aggressive in any way since he'd completed his program, but Shelley still wondered if she had taken a chance, throwing a tantrum like that. All the previous trouble in their marriage had begun with the re-entry of the Jordons into Neal's life. She refused to take a chance with her safety, or the children's, and she certainly was not leaving another home due to fear.

Surprisingly, Neal seemed fine with her demands, leaving Shelley somewhat amazed. But, at that point, she also knew that Neal did not want to jeopardize the little bit of progress he'd made in winning his wife's affections back.

Several days later, Shelley was taking some clothes to the dry cleaners and decided it would be a nice gesture to take some of Neal's too. He usually took care of his own dry cleaning, but apparently, he hadn't the time that week.

In a hurry to get to the dry cleaners before she had to pick up the children, she emptied the pockets to three pairs of pants. From one pair, a folded piece of paper fell to the floor. She picked it up and placed it on Neal's dresser, but suddenly, it hit her as she turned away, that it was a bank deposit slip from that same bank in New Jersey. It was the same bank that she saw on one of the bankbooks she'd found in the trunk of Neal's car, the day she'd left him in Georgia. Oddly enough, the date on the deposit slip showed that he'd made the deposit two weeks earlier, in the amount of five thousand dollars.

What is this? Shelley wondered, staring at the crumpled piece of paper. *Why would Neal have a deposit slip for one of his father's bank accounts?* She shook her head. *This is ridiculous. I won't drive myself crazy with suspicion again. I'm sure Neal wouldn't risk losing his family again by hiding more secrets.*

But, just to be sure, she decided to visit Donna and Ernest in South Jersey, where Neal lived before they got married. She'd always wanted to see his house, and was never given the opportunity. Maybe she would find out about this bank deposit at the same time. It would be great to see Donna again, and she could use a vacation.

She went into Neal's office, converted from an unused fourth bedroom, and made a copy of the deposit slip before returning it to the pants, where she'd found it earlier.

I've changed my mind. Let him take his own clothes to the cleaners!

Chapter 60

Shelley called Donna, and arranged a visit. She seemed excited and eager to have them. Surprisingly, Neal thought the trip was an excellent idea, and that the time away would be good for her. He'd always liked her to spend time with Donna.

The children were fascinated with the airport, raring to go on their first flight. Jason was thrilled when the plane took off, but Jackie hung onto her mother.

An energized Donna met them at the gate with her children, hugging them all at once. "My, God, Shelley, look at the kids! They've gotten so big. And look at you pretty as ever."

"Look at yourself," Shelley said. "You look wonderful!"

Ernest was away on a business trip, which left the two women alone to catch up on everything that had been going on.

After all the kids were in bed for the night, Donna made coffee, ready to settle in for an all night talk.

"So, how are things?" she asked. "Tell me everything."

"We're making it work, I guess," Shelley answered.

"I can tell there's more to this story. I know you. Don't you want to talk about it? Exactly what does making it work mean?"

Shelley frowned. "Things will never be good again. I just can't get past the nightmare Neal inflicted on the children and me. It was so awful, you can't imagine a father would do such things to his family, then claim to love them."

Donna finally asked. "Why did you go back to him?'

Shelley became quiet for a moment, trying to decide if she should pour her heart out to her friend. After all, Donna was married to Ernest, one of Neal's best friends, but she trusted in her friendship with Donna. She decided to tell Donna the truth about falling in love with Jack, and Neal blackmailing her into coming home. When she was done, Donna made another pot of coffee, sure it would be a long night.

The next morning, Donna and Shelley mapped out their itinerary for the day, which included lunch at a diner. The one thing Shelley missed the most living in the South, was the absence of diners.

"Should we go to the bank first?" Donna asked. After listening to Shelley's story, Donna was clearly in awe of her friend's strength. The new Shelley was hardboiled, having survived circumstances that would have put many people in a mental hospital.

"I don't know if I would have survived all that misery," Donna told her. "I don't know if I would have been as unselfish as you, giving up the man I loved to spare him hardship. And coming as close as you did to taking your kids into hiding like that!"

Shelley really was a new woman, one to be watched. She was no longer the unsuspecting, young woman Neal had married so long ago. She was a woman of steel, and although it had taken a long time and much suffering, she was ready to invade Neal's secret life with a new vengeance. She was going to get to the bottom of his past at any cost, and Donna had agreed to become her partner.

"Actually, I would like to find Neal's old house first," Shelley said. The anxiety she felt about finally being given the opportunity to see the house that had caused her so much unrest over the years, besieged her.

"Is it nearby?" Donna asked.

"Yes, I think so. I found it on this map before I came here," Shelley answered, pulling the crumpled map out of her purse. "It shouldn't be more than a twenty minute ride, if that long."

"Well, let's go!" Donna said, excited. "By the way, why are we doing this? What will seeing Neal's old house do for you now?"

"I don't really know. It's just a feeling I have," Shelley answered, seriously.

"Do you have the map ready?" Donna asked, when they got back into the car after stopping first to have lunch.

"Yes, do you want to look at it?" she asked.

Donna took the map from Shelley, studying it before she turned on the motor. "My, goodness, Shelley. It's right here. Let's go."

Donna found Tessie Drive with no problems. Midway down the street, they'd found number six, nineteen. Donna slowed down, trying to take it all in as she drove. It was a two story, cameo-colored home, very well kept and pretty large.

"Should I pull in the driveway?" Donna asked.

"I don't think so, but turn around so we can see all of the house," Shelley said, her heart pounding heavily.

They both felt ridiculous, and began to laugh like two young schoolgirls until Shelley saw something that brought her laughter to a quick halt. Parked in the backyard was a little, black Renault that looked like the one she used to own. It was sitting in front of the three detached garages, obviously built after the house had been there for a while.

"Stop the car!" Shelley shouted, grabbing Donna's arm.

"Why? What is it?" she asked, startled.

"That's my Renault in the backyard!"

"Shelley, you're nuts. Why would your Renault be in New Jersey at a house Neal doesn't even own anymore? Besides, didn't Neal trade that car in for that weird truck?" Donna asked.

"I'm telling you, that's my Renault! Let me out. I'll go look at the side of it. I scraped the side of it in our garage when we lived in Norcross."

Donna pulled her van into the driveway of the house next door. There were no cars in sight, so she figured no one was home.

Shelley jumped out and like a thief, walked along the side of the house. Her chest was thumping the way it used to during some of her most fearful nights with Neal. She poked her head around the corner of the back to see if there was any way she would be seen from inside the house. There was a big picture window in what appeared to be the dining room, but, she realized if she went around the back of the garages, she could examine the side of the car without being seen.

Donna waited in the car. *This is pretty ridiculous, but I have to know,* Shelley thought, as she ran to the side of the garages. She bent down and crept to the side of the car. There it was. The scrape left by the support pole in the two car garage of the Norcross house. She remembered that she had tried to get the scratch out with a steel wool pad, and in the process had taken off a fine line of paint.

What is my car doing here? Neal traded in this car for that redneck truck he'd bought two years ago. She ran back to where she left Donna, then, suddenly stopped. Her body stiffened when she saw an elderly woman standing by the side of the van talking to Donna.

Oh, my God...I'm sure she's questioning Donna about who we are, and what I'm doing crawling through her neighbor's yard.

"Hello," Shelley said, nonchalantly slipping into the passenger side of the van. "I hope we didn't block your driveway," she added.

"Oh, no. Don't you worry, you're fine," the old woman answered cheerfully.

"Well, goodbye, Mrs. Hunter," Donna said, in her friendly voice. "It's been nice talking to you. Thank you for helping us."

"Oh, you're welcome, Sweetheart. I'm glad I could be a help to you," the woman replied.

Donna carefully backed out of the woman's driveway. "Shelley, this is unbelievable! I was so scared when that woman tapped on my window."

Shelley ignored her. "Donna, that's my car," she said.

"What? Are you sure?" Donna asked, shocked.

"I'm positive. The scrape I put on the side of it is still there."

"I don't get it. What does all this mean?"

"I have no idea, but I'm going to find out," Shelley exclaimed.

There was a pause, then, Donna said, "Shelley, there is something else you should know. It's kind of weird."

"Oh? What is it?"

"That woman told me that the woman who owned Neal's house was left alone a lot by her husband who traveled with his business all the time. She said the wife was recently found dead in her basement."

Cold dread gripped her. "Dead in the basement? How did she die?"

"Her husband found her hanging from the rafters. She hung herself!" Donna said.

Shelley sat motionless, too paralyzed to respond. She thought of Neal's grandmother. *Surely, my thoughts are wrong. It couldn't be true.* Finally, she asked, "Did the woman tell you her neighbor's name?"

"Not all of it. She couldn't remember the couple's last name, but the woman's first name was Marielle."

"What about the husband?" Her voice quivered from the fear of her thoughts.

"He still keeps up the house, but he travels most of the time with his business," Donna said.

"Imagine that," Shelley whispered. She decided not to discuss the strange death of Neal's grandmother with Donna in case she was thinking things that were not true. However, her car was there. She was positive about that, and somehow, in the pit of her being, she knew that the death of that woman was connected to Neal.

They stopped at the bank next. Shelley went inside, wondering how she would get information on the account without raising suspicion. Apprehensively, she approached one of the tellers.

"Excuse me, Miss, I would like to get a copy of all the transactions on this account, please."

Shelley handed her the copy of the deposit slip she'd made the day she'd found it. She looked away, as if by doing so, the teller would not ask questions.

"Is this your account?" the young girl asked.

"Yes, it is," Shelley lied.

"Can I see some identification?" the teller asked.

"Sure, of course," Shelley said, producing her driver's license. After all, the last names were the same, it might work.

"Ma'am, this is a Florida driver's license. The owner of this account has a New Jersey address," the girl informed her.

"No, Miss, you're wrong. The owner is my husband. We have accounts in several states, but we live in Florida," Shelley answered.

"Well, Ma'am, that might be, but the owner of this account definitely lives in New Jersey," the girl insisted.

Shelley thought about her answer. "Oh, you must mean the house on Tessie Drive. We rent that out, but we live in Florida. We're here to take care of some business," she answered.

The teller looked at the information on her computer. "Well, you have the address right, but our records indicate that Mr. Jordon still lives there. He receives his statements there, and still maintains a New Jersey driver's license. If you want information on this account, Mr. Jordon will have to either come in and get it himself, or give us written permission to give you that information, since his name is the only name on the account," the teller informed her.

"I understand...thank you," Shelley said, leaving.

She'd been given the most important piece of information anyway. Neal was using the address on Tessie Drive for that account. He still owned the house. The facts were too condemning. The whole situation was bizarre, and Shelley had to get her thoughts together to figure out her next move.

Chapter 61

Shelley managed to enjoy the rest of her visit with Donna, but returned home with a heavy mind. She knew it all meant something, but she had to be careful about the way she obtained information, and kept going over the strange details in her mind. The Renault was in New Jersey, she was sure that was her car. Then, there was the woman who'd hung herself in the basement of Neal's old house. *Just like Neal's grandmother,* Shelley thought. *How eerie!*

Shelley believed there was a connection. She also knew that if Neal found out she was researching anything involving his past life, he wouldn't care anymore about risking his reconciliation with her. Asking questions meant trouble, and even though their marriage was not made in Heaven, for the time being, it was safe.

Shelley was determined to find out if Neal really sold his house since all evidence suggested otherwise. She believed Neal still owned it, and decided in the interim, to act as though she'd conformed to their marriage. From the time she got off the plane, she led Neal to believe she was pleased to be home, and glad to see him. As far as Neal was concerned, she was a changed woman.

She hadn't discussed all her fears with Donna, wanting to analyze all the facts and gather more information before she discussed it with anybody, or made a game plan. The last thing she needed was for Donna to go to Ernest with her fear that Shelley was living with a serial killer.

Early Monday morning, Shelley and the children dropped Neal off at the airport. She was anxious to get home to make phone calls. Neal going out of town for the entire week would hopefully allow her enough time to find out what she wanted to know.

Shelley waved goodbye to her children when Dawn, one of their neighbors, picked up Jackie and Jason for school. She made a list of people she wanted to call who might have the information she wanted, starting with City Records in new Jersey to see if she could obtain the name of the present owner of the house.

When a pleasant woman answered, Shelley told her what information she needed, and the woman asked her to hold on while she tried to locate the records for the home on Tessie Drive. The information was considered public record, so there was no argument regarding confidentiality. Several minutes later, the woman returned to the phone.

"Ma'am, the present owner of that property is Neal Jordon. It was originally deeded to Neal, and Marielle Jordon," the woman told her.

"Marielle? Are you sure?" Shelley asked.

"Yes, the name on the tax records was Marielle. I also found a divorce action filed against Neal Jordon, never finalized due to Marielle's death. At that time, papers were filed giving full ownership of the home to Neal Jordon."

"Can I get a copy of all that information?" Shelley asked, baffled. *Who was Marielle? What was she to Neal? She must have been his wife, like that neighbor said she was. Then, there was the possibility that she might have been talking about Neal's father. After all, Neal did say the bankbooks in his trunk were his fathers. But, then, Neal is a liar.*

"Sure, I'll give you our address. You will have to send us a money order for four dollars in order for us to send both documents," the woman told Shelley.

"That's fine, thank you."

Shelley wrote down the address, then went to the post office. She bought the money order and two overnight mailing envelopes. One was to send her request for the information, along with the money order, and the other was to have the documents sent back to her through overnight mail. She didn't want to waste time waiting for regular mail.

Her mind flashed back to the day Donna helped her find Neal's house. She tried to break down parts of the conversation.

"Did that woman tell you her neighbor's name?"

"Not all of it, she couldn't remember, but the woman's first name was Marielle."

"What about the husband?"

"The woman who owned the house was left alone a lot by her traveling husband. She was found dead in her basement."

What does all this mean? Shelley kept asking herself. She knew she had to read those documents to figure out at least a part of it.

Her next call was to the bank. She called the phone number printed on the deposit slip, and was immediately transferred to a manager.

"Ma'am, we are unable to give you any information since your name is not on this account," the stuffy woman said, giving her the same answer she'd received in New Jersey.

"But, I'm Neal Jordon's wife!" Shelley protested.

"I'm sorry, but our records indicate Mrs. Jordon is deceased, and we don't have a new wife listed on this account." The woman abruptly ended the call.

Neal had an account with Marielle? They apparently owned the home together as man and wife. The woman from the bank called her Neal's wife. I don't understand any of this. He told me his ex-wife's name was Arlene.

The answers had to be in the documents she'd requested.

Thursday afternoons was Shelley's scheduled time to work as a teacher's aid in Jackie's classroom. If her calculations were correct, she would receive the documents sometime that day, and left for the children's school, feeling optimistic the documents would be there when she got home. She left a note taped to the door, instructing the deliverer to leave the envelope on the porch. Neal was not due back until the next day, at which point she would have to pick him up at the airport, so there was no fear of him coming home without her knowing.

As it was, Neal did come home a day early. Unable to reach Shelley, he used an airport service van to get home. He saw the overnight mailer on the porch and grabbed it, assuming it was something from his office. He put his bags down and opened the envelope without looking at the address label.

"My, God! She knows!" Neal said out loud, looking at the documents. "I don't believe that bitch!" He appeared panicked. He wasn't sure how much Shelley already knew. Taking the documents, he slipped them into his briefcase, making sure he locked it afterward.

Several hours later, Shelley arrived home with the children, clearly disappointed when the overnight envelope was not on the porch. She was inside the house before she realized that Neal had returned home a day sooner than he was expected. She felt him watching her closely and felt nervous as he greeted her.

"Hey, Honey," Neal said, stepping towards her. "Where were you?" he asked, as if nothing were wrong.

"Thursday is my teacher's aid day in Jackie's class. Did the mail come yet?" she asked.

"Yes, it did. I put it on the kitchen counter for you to go through," he said, nonchalantly.

"Did an express mailer come for me today?" she asked, boldly, when she didn't find it among the mail.

"No, are you expecting something?" Neal asked, innocently.

"Yes, I sent away for some reading material, and I really thought it would arrive today."

"Well, maybe tomorrow."

"Yeah, maybe so," she replied.

"Listen, I was thinking during my flight home, why don't we take a vacation?"

"A vacation? I just got back from the trip to Donna's, and you travel all the time, so I know you're not eager to fly away from home any time soon."

"I know, but I mean a real vacation. Somewhere exotic, like Hawaii."

"Hawaii? Neal, what is this about? I know you, there's always a hidden motive whenever you do anything spontaneous."

He ignored her spiteful remark. "I just think we could use one. We haven't gone anywhere together since you came home and I really would like to take you away, maybe show you that I can actually be fun," he said. "Maybe your parents would take the kids for us."

"I don't know Neal. Let me think about it for a while."

"We could even bring another couple with us if you want to. I have enough frequent flyer miles to fly four people, first class to Hawaii, plus fly the children to your parents house, if they agree to watch them, of course."

Shelley grew suspicious. "And, who would you want to take?'

"Oh, I don't know. How about Clarissa and Kenny?"

"Our minister and his wife?" Shelley laughed. "What made you think of them?"

Neal relaxed a little. Shelley knew he thought she was taking his bait.

"Because I had a conversation with Kenny last Sunday, and he was telling me how stressed out Clarissa has been lately. I just thought it would be a good opportunity for them to get away too. Why? Does that upset you? Aren't you and Clarissa friends?"

"Yes, but I don't want to take a trip to Hawaii, then be afraid to have fun because our minister and his wife are with us," Shelley answered.

"We always have fun with Clarissa and Kenny," Neal responded.

"Yes, that's true," she agreed.

He watched as she wrestled with such a wonderful temptation. She saw him almost holding his breath waiting for her response, and couldn't wait to find out the real reason taking the trip was so important to him.

"I do have a lot of fun with Clarissa. You're right. Let's go!" She finally agreed, smiling. *I've always wanted to go to Hawaii, I might as well take the trip, no matter what his real motives are.*

"Great! Why don't you call them and see if they're interested in going?" he suggested.

"When do you want to go?" she asked.

"In a couple of weeks. I can take my vacation whenever I want to. Skiff knows it's been a rough year, and that I need some time off."

"But, that's so soon. What about the children's schooling?"

"Don't they have Spring break in a couple of weeks?"

"Yes, you're right again, and Clarissa is a teacher there, so she'll be off too," Shelley said. "Okay, I'll call them."

The next day, Neal phoned from his office to tell Shelley he'd made their flight arrangements so she could give the dates, and flight information to Clarissa and her parents, who'd agreed to keep Jackie and Jason for them.

Neal's plans were successful. Their return flight itinerary included a lay over in Atlanta, which meant Meg and Tim could bring the children to the airport at that time, and they would all fly back to Florida together. He had managed to get everyone on the same flights.

It was apparent that Neal wanted to get Shelley out of Florida for a while, and the trip would do that. Even though it most assuredly, saddened him, it was obvious he had a plan to carry out, and that there was no other way out for him, and Shelley was so busy getting ready for their trip, she didn't look into anything else.

Finding out the truth about Neal, can wait for two weeks. I'm going to Hawaii, she thought.

Everything worked out as intended. Shelley and Neal took the children to the airport the morning before they would be leaving, and put them on a flight to Atlanta. The flight attendant assured Shelley they would be well taken care of and that she would be sitting with them during the entire flight, and when they arrived in Atlanta, she would personally escort them off the plane and would not turn the children over to her parents until they produced the proper identification.

When Shelley saw the plane take off, tears streamed down her face. Her two babies were on a flight to Atlanta. Neal looked at Shelley and smiled, as she wiped her tears to drive home with him. It was not until after her parents called, assuring her that the children had arrived safely and were excited about their visit, that she felt relieved. She started to get energized herself about going to Hawaii. The trip would help her sort out her thoughts about Neal, and what might be going on.

They landed in Maui, right on schedule. Neal rented a car and they drove along the magnificent cliffs to their hotel. The scenery was so incredibly beautiful, it actually looked like a painting, almost artificial. Shelley had never seen a more beautiful place.

Because Neal acted completely indifferent towards her the first week of their trip, Shelley began to suspect something was wrong. Nothing they saw, or did, delighted him the way it had everyone else. Even the elaborate Luau at the Maui Sheraton, with its amazing pageantry failed to please Neal. Hawaiian natives danced with fire, and beautiful island girls dressed in grass skirts, danced the hula using coconut shells and flowered leis for the top of their costumes. The show was incredible, and everyone had a great time, except Neal, who remained noticeably deep in thought.

Shelley grew leery of Neal's new mood. Since she'd returned home from their separation, he'd worked hard to make their marriage work, but suddenly, he started acting completely indifferent.

"Neal, what's wrong?" Shelley asked him, when they returned from the Luau. "You're acting weird. Even Clarissa and Kenny mentioned your behavior to me."

"I'm fine, really. Just have a good time. I love watching you have fun."

Neal smiled, but Shelley knew the signs. Something major was going on. She began to get that gnawing feeling that always warned her that Neal had a secret, guaranteed to be a problem.

During the two week trip, Neal also let his beard grow out. It was the first time Shelley had seen him with any kind of facial hair. He said he'd wanted to grow a beard and thought his vacation was the perfect time to do so.

Shelley knew Skiff would never permit an executive with their company to wear a beard. More odd was the strange personality Neal had acquired that seemed to progress with the growth of his beard. He was changing into a totally different person, like a man going through some kind of midlife crisis.

When it was time to turn in the keys to the hotel, they did so, with great sadness. Hawaii was spectacular, and although Shelley and Clarissa missed their children, they hated to leave. There was something magical about Maui that had won their hearts, and Shelley promised herself that one day she would return there with her children.

Honolulu airport was a mess. The bags had to go through some sort of inspection to make sure no one was smuggling plants, or fruit, to the mainland. The government officials that conducted the inspections tore through everyone's luggage, then left the weary travelers to repack their suitcases. Normally, that would have angered Neal, but he handled it without an angry scene.

Shelley studied Neal, as he calmly repacked their things. There was no doubt in her mind, that something was happening.

Chapter 62

It took Shelley several days to recuperate from jet lag. Their third day home, after she'd sent the kids off to school, she fixed herself a cup of coffee and sat down to read the newspaper. After a few moments the phone rang, and it was Neal.

"Can you pick me up at Tampa Airport in two hours?" he asked.

Confused, she asked, "Where are you? I thought you were going to the office this morning." Neal's office was a two hour drive from Palm Harbor.

"I'm in the office now."

"Well, then, why do I have to pick you up at Tampa Airport? Are you having trouble with your car?"

"I don't have a car," he responded.

"How did you get to the office then? You're not making any sense."

Totally composed, Neal explained. "I've just been fired. I had to turn in my car."

"What? Neal, I'm sorry, but why?" she asked, totally confused. Neal was the best man Skiff had.

"I don't know. I guess we'll talk about it after you pick me up, okay?"

"Sure, I understand. Are you all right?" She wasn't sure when she'd begun to care if he was all right, but she did care at that moment. Neal worked hard for Skiff, and he'd carried the company to new heights. None of it made any sense.

As usual, Neal was waiting outside the baggage claim. He climbed into the car on the passenger side, informing her that she would be driving home, something he usually tried to avoid.

"How are you?" Shelley asked, as she followed the signs leading out of the airport. Neal was deep in thought.

"I'm okay. I'll get another job," he said, calmly.

"You seem very unaffected for a man whose just been fired," Shelley said, "Did they give you a reason? Was it the beard?"

"No, it wasn't the beard. They didn't give me a reason. When I walked in the office this morning, Ed and Frank were there, waiting for me. It was a scene I've been a player in many times over the years. Ed took me to the back office, gave me the good news, handed me a ticket back to Tampa, then dropped me off at the Orlando Airport. I guess neither of them wanted to make the trip to Palm Harbor."

"Oh, Neal. What about Frank? He was supposed to be your friend," Shelley said, still shocked over Neal's news.

"Shelley, there are no friends in business. Offer a man a fancy title, a good raise, and he'll screw his mother."

"Why do you think they did this?"

"Because two months ago, Ed asked me to transfer to Alabama. I turned him down because we still hadn't recovered financially from the sale of our house in Peach Haven. I wasn't going to take a loss on this house too," Neal explained. "Turning down any transfer is the kiss of death in the corporate world."

"Why didn't you tell me about Alabama?"

"Because, like I said, I had no intention of taking the job."

"But, Neal, you didn't mention to me that Ed had even spoken to you about it."

"It wasn't necessary, because I had no intention of taking it," Neal repeated himself.

"But, I still should have been informed," Shelley insisted, pulling into their driveway.

"I didn't think two months ago you wanted to be informed of anything going on in my life. Besides, maybe I was afraid you would want to go since it's only a ninety minute drive to Peach Haven."

Shelley got out of the car. After Neal retrieved his things from the trunk, they walked in. Neal placed his briefcase on the kitchen counter, and followed Shelley into the family room.

Facing her, he said, "I'm sorry, Shelley, I shouldn't have said that."

"That was low, Neal. I am trying to make this marriage work, whether you believe it, or not."

He hesitated. "I know, and I appreciate it. Things are just a little unusual today. Please, forget I said such an awful thing."

During dinner the phone rang continuously. The calls were from other companies in the bearing industry trying to recruit Neal before someone else got him. Shelley answered the last call so Neal could finish eating.

"It's someone from G.A.F. Corporation," she whispered, covering the mouthpiece.

"I'll take it in my office," he said.

Once Shelley heard him pick up the receiver, she hung up the phone in the kitchen. She was still surprised about the whole situation, and was sure Neal hadn't told her everything. There had to be a more definite reason why he'd been dismissed from Skiff.

She'd decided in Hawaii, to make an urgent effort to solve the mystery about the house in New Jersey. She wanted to know why the documents she'd sent for never arrived. Possibly, the day Neal arrived home early, he'd found it and confiscated it before she had a chance to get it.

She dropped Neal off at the airport, wishing him luck on his interviews. He would be gone for two days, and hopefully employed when he returned. Shelley didn't know what their financial situation could endure without a paycheck coming in, but Neal didn't seem concerned about it.

Later that evening, Neal phoned her and told her he'd accepted the position with G.A.F. Bearings. Relieved that he was no longer without a job, she wrote down his return flight information so she could pick him at the airport the following afternoon.

By the time Shelley picked up Neal and returned home, the mailman had been there, and had left an express mail envelope on the porch. Shelley was nervous thinking it was the envelope she'd expected so long ago, until she read the return address. It was from G.A.F. Bearings.

"Here, it's something from G.A.F," Shelley said, handing Neal the envelope. "They didn't waste any time. They must have mailed it as soon as you left yesterday."

Inside was a signed, American Express charge slip, imprinted by a restaurant called, 'Donnatello's', one of the most exclusive restaurants in Tampa. The slip was signed by Douglas Reese, Neal's new boss. He read the note included with the charge slip aloud.

Dear Neal, please have dinner on me. Order your favorite wine to celebrate coming on board with G.A.F. Welcome to the family, Douglas.

"Oh, how nice," Neal said, handing Shelley the note along with the charge slip.

"That is nice," Shelley agreed.

"Didn't you say Elkie and her new husband are visiting us this month? We could take them there," Neal suggested.

"They're coming back to the United States this week, but they won't arrive in Florida for two weeks."

"Well, good...we'll take them to Donnatello's," Neal said.

The next day, Shelley returned from taking Neal to the airport. He was on his way to New York to meet the other executives from G.A.F. She'd just made a pot of coffee and kicked off her shoes when the doorbell rang. It was a young man, somewhat hidden behind a huge flower arrangement. The spray was meant to be a table arrangement, she was sure, but it was so large, it looked like a grave wreath, with an incredible mat of greens, and at least ten dozen roses scattered throughout.

Shelley placed the huge arrangement on the dining room table It was so long, the tips of it touched both ends of the table. She reached for the card pinned to the big, red ribbon at one end.

Dear Neal and Shelley, Welcome to G.A.F.!
From the Corporate Office of G.A.F.

They were definitely giving Neal the red carpet treatment. First the dinner, then the flower arrangement, which had to cost a minimum of three hundred dollars. The dinner was worth at least another two hundred. She was impressed, but remembered the old saying, "All that glitters is not gold."

Chapter 63

Neal came home from New York, excited about his new company. He said G.A.F. was much more laid back than Skiff. Everyone Neal met under the charge of Douglas Reese had great things to say about the man. Reese was known to be fair and understanding.

Neal's main office would be based out of Atlanta, and his phone service would run out of there also. When the phone in his office at home rang three times, the call would automatically be forwarded to the service in Atlanta. He also had a Post Office Box to receive mail from G.A.F.'s headquarters in Connecticut, and to use as the company address for the Florida region. He received his pay and expense checks at the Post Office box too. It was convenient, because Shelley was able to pick up his mail, and do his banking when he was out of town, which was most of the time.

When Neal was away, Shelley would either answer the phone, or call the service to retrieve Neal's messages. She also typed reports he didn't want to wait for the secretarial service in Atlanta to complete, and enjoyed driving the brand new Chevy Caprice the company provided Neal with while he was out of town.

The fourth of July was approaching. Neal and Shelley decided to hold a barbecue and pool party for their friends and neighbors. Two weeks before, everyone chipped in twenty dollars to buy fireworks for the children to enjoy.

Shelley spent the day of the barbecue, making the house sparkle, and putting together seventy patriotic party favors.

Meanwhile, Neal's behavior continued to change. He was acting like a teenager, constantly making a fool of himself, and embarrassing Shelley. She decided to speak to him about it after everyone went home from the barbecue. He was leaving for a three week trip the next day, so they had things to discuss anyway.

While Shelley was mixing the macaroni salad, the phone rang. It was Tom Baker, one of Neal's salesmen. Neal was supposed to be with him.

"Hi! What's going on?" Shelley asked, confused. Neal said he would be with Tom until five o'clock, and it was only two.

"Can you give Neal a message for me?" Tom asked.

"I guess so, Tom," Shelley said, slowly. Tom was acting as if he hadn't seen Neal.

What is Neal up to now? He lied. He hasn't been with Tom, and I can't ask Tom, if he'd seen Neal.

"Tell Neal I'm right behind him" Tom said, before he hung up the phone.

Once again, Neal was keeping secrets. He'd lied about being with Tom, and she got the distinct impression that Tom was threatening him in some way. Shelley was sure something peculiar was happening, but had no idea what. It certainly had something to do with Neal's new personality. It was as if he were changing into a different person, another side of Neal, she had not known before.

Shelley hung up the phone and thought for moment. She went into Neal's office to call the service to see if there were any messages that might shed some light on where Neal was spending his day, sensing deception.

"G.A.F. Bearings," the familiar voice said on the other end.

"Hi, Gail. Are there any messages?" Shelley had become phone friends with Gail since Neal joined G.A.F. The friendly voice grew silent. "Gail is something wrong?" she asked.

"Mrs. Jordon, I'm not allowed to give you Neal's messages anymore," Gail stated awkwardly.

"Excuse me? Why not?" Shelley asked, taken by surprise.

"I don't know. Those are just my new orders," Gail replied.

"I don't understand, Gail. Neal didn't say anything to me about this."

"I'm sorry, Mrs. Jordon, but that's what I've been told to do," she said, again.

Shelley felt her temper rising, but masked it with kindness. "I understand. I didn't mean to put you on the spot. I'll discuss it with Neal when he gets home." She hung up the phone.

At six o'clock, Neal arrived home and Shelley confronted him. "Neal, we have to talk!"

"What's the matter?" he asked.

"Where have you been all day?"

"I told you. I was with Tom," Neal answered, casually.

"Then, why did Tom call here at two o'clock?" Shelley asked.

"Shelley, I'm having problems with him. He must have called you right after he left me, because two o'clock is when we finished our business," Neal said. "He's crazy, believe me."

"Then, where have you been for four hours?" Shelley asked, knowing he was lying.

"Tom and I were fifteen minutes away from my parents' house, so I stopped in to see them."

"You stopped to see your parents'? Neal, I thought we agreed to keep them out of our lives. Plus, how could you stop anywhere, knowing we have a crowd of people coming here at seven?'

"My mother found out where I'm working and called there looking for me. They said they needed to talk to me, so since I was in the area, I figured it was better for me to stop and see them before they tried showing up here. As it turned out, they had nothing urgent to say."

Shelley had a strange feeling. She didn't have a clue what was happening. She just knew something was going on. Something very dreadful, and typical of Neal.

The barbecue went well, and when all the guests left, Shelley and Neal cleaned up together. It surprised her when Neal offered to stay up and help since he was leaving at the crack of dawn.

"You don't have to help me," she said. "You have to leave early in the morning."

"No, I want to. We have to talk over some things anyway since I'll be gone so long. I've never been away for three weeks before."

"Listen, I didn't have a chance to ask you about this earlier, but the weirdest thing happened today," Shelley said casually, while loading the dishwasher.

"Oh? What was it?" Neal asked, as he put away the last of the leftover food.

"Well, first of all, as you know Tom called before you got home, and he left a rather odd message."

"What was the message?" he asked.

"He told me to tell you that he is one step behind you," she answered. "Whatever that means." Shelley looked at his face for a reaction. The look was there. The one she'd come to know through their miserable history.

"I don't know what that means either. He drives me nuts. What else happened?"

"Well, I called in for your messages, because I thought maybe you'd left one explaining where you were, and Gail said I wasn't allowed to retrieve your messages anymore."

"Oh, I forgot to tell you. Good ole Tom had his wife, Susan, call my service and tell them she was you so he could get my messages. When I found out what was going on, G.A.F. gave the service strict orders not to give my messages to anyone but me. It has nothing to do with you. It's just the new policy," Neal explained.

"Why would Tom Baker do such a thing?" Shelley asked.

"I told you, I'm having a lot of problems with him. He'll probably end up getting fired."

"Well, if he's doing things like that, it's a miracle he hasn't been fired already."

Neal went to the table and pulled out a chair. "Sit down with me," he said, taking some money from his wallet. "I want to go over a few things with you."

Shelley sat with him, her curiosity rising. The things happening were too odd. Something had changed.

"Here is five hundred dollars," Neal said, handing her cash. "Use this before you start using money from our accounts. I transferred some funds for you, just in case, but they will take a few days to clear."

"Why? I've got plenty of money in my household account if I need it."

"I've never been out of town this long before, and I don't want to worry about you not having enough money. Please, do as I say. Use this money first, before you use any funds from the accounts."

"Okay," she agreed, but thought he was overreacting.

"I'm going to leave around five in the morning,, so I won't see you before I go," he said. "I have paid all the bills that came in so far. The ones that come in later, I'll pay when I get home. Don't pay anything," Neal said.

Shelley woke up before Neal. Feeling uneasy and unable to sleep, She decided to get up and make some coffee. Somehow, she knew this trip was different. She felt a sense of obscurity, without knowing why.

Shortly after the coffee was done brewing, Neal walked in the kitchen to say goodbye.

"I love you, Shelley," he said, solemnly.

"That's nice, Neal, but why so glum?" she asked, studying is face.

"Because I want you to know that. I will always love you," he said, picking up his briefcase.

She didn't quite know what to think. "Well, I guess you'd better hit the road," Shelley said, slowly.

He turned and held her for a moment. "Take care of the kids," he said.

"I will. When will I hear from you?" she asked, beginning to feel that anxious feeling that always accompanied one of Neal's surprises.

"Not for a few days."

Shelley walked him to his car. In the back seat she saw the metal car rack he'd purchased the week before. He'd bought one so he could pack sufficient clothes for his lengthy trip.

"That worked out well," she said, pointing to it.

"Yeah, it did. I always laughed at guys I saw with one of these in their cars. Now, I understand why they use them," he said, flinging his briefcase onto the back seat.

"Goodbye, Neal," Shelley said.

He kissed her gently on her forehead the way he used to before the Jordons entered their lives. The way he had before the violence and lies crept in to decay their happy marriage.

Before she'd fallen in love with another man.

Chapter 64

A week later, the air conditioning in the house stopped working. Shelley tried playing with the thermostat, but it refused to kick on. Finally, she went outside to look at the compressor, and to her horror, a long snake was wrapped around the jammed blades of the fan. She didn't know what to do. She had to call a service man to fix the unit, but she wasn't sure how Neal would want her to pay for it. He'd been so adamant about her not using any money in the bank until she'd used the cash he'd given her. The best thing to do was call him, but she didn't know where to reach him. Strangely, he hadn't called home since he'd left. She decided to call his service.

"Hi, Gail, this is Mrs. Jordon. I need the phone number where I can reach Neal."

Once again, there was a long silence on the other end. "Gail, did you hear me?"

"Yes, Mrs. Jordon, but, I'm sorry, I'm not permitted to give you that number."

"What? Are you crazy? I'm his wife. We have an emergency at home, I need to talk to my husband!"

"Ma'am, I'm sorry, but I can't give you that number!" Gail insisted, as if she were talking to a stranger.

"Fine, I'll just call his office and I'll be sure to tell my husband how cooperative you were!" Shelley said, slamming down the phone, furious.

The house was becoming more hot by the minute. Florida in July was not the time to be without air conditioning. The increasing heat made Shelley more ornery than she was from her ridiculous conversation with Gail. She decided to start with the Atlanta office. Surely, his secretary could tell her where to reach Neal.

"Hello, may I speak with Faith, please?" Shelley asked the switchboard operator, without identifying herself.

"I'm sorry, but Faith is no longer with G.A.F. Can someone else help you?" the voice asked.

"My, goodness, that's a surprise. What happened to Faith?" Shelley asked.

"She left us to get married," the woman answered, cheerfully.

"Oh...I didn't know she was engaged. That's nice. Actually I'm calling to reach my husband. I called the service and Gail refused to give me the phone number where I can reach him."

"Gosh, I'm sorry. Let me see if I can help you. Who is it you're trying to reach?" the kind woman asked.

"Neal Jordon," Shelley replied.

The woman gave no response.

"Did you hear me? I'm trying to reach Neal Jordon," Shelley repeated.

"Yes, I heard you, but I'm sorry, I can't give you that number. All I can do is ask him to return your call."

Livid, Shelley shouted into the receiver. "I'm his wife for God's sake! I need to talk to my husband now!"

A short silence followed, then, the woman responded, "I'm sorry. Why don't you call Mr. Reese in Connecticut? Perhaps he will be able to help you."

"This is ridiculous," Shelley cried. "When Neal calls in, tell him to call home immediately. This is an emergency."

Shelley waited for Neal's call, but it never came. Desperate, she called G.A.F. Corporate Headquarters with no results there either.

Several days later, Neal still had not called home. Shelley was beside herself with anger. She called G.A.F. a few more times, without success. Meanwhile, the heat in the house had become unbearable. She had to do something. If Neal wasn't going to contact her, she couldn't wait any longer. She had to get the air conditioning fixed.

The repair had taken all of the five hundred dollars Neal had given her, so she had to go to the bank to get more cash.

She wrote a check for one hundred dollars from their joint account, and handed it to the teller she had done business with for three years. After punching several keys on her computer, the girl said, "Mrs. Jordon, I'm sorry, but these funds are not available at this time."

"Oh? I wonder why? I guess my husband's transfer hasn't cleared yet," Shelley replied. "Oh, well, I'll just take the money from my personal account. There's always at least three thousand dollars in there."

Shelley took the other checkbook from her purse, and quickly wrote a new check. After a few minutes, again the girl returned to the window with her check.

"Mrs. Jordon, I'm sorry, but there aren't enough funds in this account either," the girl told her, awkwardly.

"There must be some mistake," Shelley insisted. "I keep a large balance in that account."

Clearly embarrassed, the girl said, "Mrs. Jordon, I think you should speak to our Manager, Mrs. Hartwell. Stay here a moment, please, and I'll page her."

Within moments, the Bank Manager approached the window and invited Shelley and the children to come inside the bank, so she could speak with her.

"Is something wrong?" Shelley asked, that sickening feeling attacking her again. The one she'd felt that day at the bank in Peach Haven when she was told she only had two hundred dollars in her account.

"It would be better if you could come inside the bank so we could discuss the situation more appropriately."

Shelley parked the car, then entered the bank with the children. Mrs. Hartwell was waiting for her in the lobby to lead them to her private office.

"Sit down, Mrs. Jordon, please," she said, politely.

Once Shelley and the kids were settled, she continued. "Mrs. Jordon, there is no easy way for me to tell you this."

"Tell me what?" Shelley asked, tremendously uncomfortable. She didn't like the sound of what the woman said, preparing her for tragedy.

"Last week, your husband came in here and cleaned out all your accounts. He failed to tell you that?"

Shelley sat speechless for a moment, without a response in mind. Wild thoughts ran through her head, all running in different directions.

"No...no, he didn't," she said, steadily. "What about my children's accounts?" she asked.

"All of them, Mrs. Jordon. He left nine dollars in your personal account, probably because we would have had to contact you before he closed it out entirely."

Shelley stiffened. "I can't believe this! Why would he do such a thing?" Shelley asked, knowing it was a ridiculous question to impose upon the Bank Manager. What did she know? What did she know about Neal's history, or his crazy parents? What did she know of his ability to blackmail his wife, or lie in court?

And what was she going to feed the children for dinner? They were out of everything.

Mustering all the dignity she could, Shelley left the bank. *Why the kid's money, Neal? They saved that money from birthdays and other holidays. Gifts* given *to them in cards. How dare you steal the little bit they saved!*

The moment Shelley walked in the house, she collapsed. How could Neal have done this? Again. Better yet, how could she have let it happen again? She'd been so self absorbed in her unhappiness, she ignored the major signs.

Jason crawled on the couch, and put his arm around her.

"Mom, are we broke?" he asked. He was nine years old.

"Honey, Mommy will take care of it," she said. "Why don't you go play with your friends outside? Mommy will be fine, I promise," she added, kissing the top of his head.

"Okay, but I'll be right outside if you need me," he said, causing her heart to melt, as her little boy looked up into his mother's grieving face, wanting to help her.

Later, after Jason left to go outside, she heard a knock on the door. It was Teri, a neighbor Shelley had become friendly with. They went to aerobics class together twice a week, and out to lunch occasionally.

"What's going on?" Teri asked when she saw Shelley had been crying. "I just saw Jason and Jackie outside. They're worried about you. I told them I'd come in and try to make you feel better."

"I don't know...I'm not sure what's going on, Teri," Shelley answered. She explained what happened at the bank.

"Shelley, Neal has left you!" Teri exclaimed, looking horrified.

"Left me? Oh, I don't think so, he worked too hard to get me back," Shelley blurted out, without thinking. Having said too much, she explained how she'd left him three years earlier.

"Wait a minute," Shelley said, in the middle of her story. "He couldn't have left, his clothes are still here."

Teri and Shelley both jumped up at the same time and ran towards the master bedroom. Shelley threw open the closet doors.

Stunned, she was unable to move. Neal had taken all of his clothes, replacing them with old clothes he had stored in the garage so she wouldn't notice an empty closet. She suddenly remembered how he deviously did the same thing when he'd left P.L.K.

"That bastard!" she screamed.

"Shelley, I'm so sorry...is there anything I can do?" Teri asked, clearly at a loss.

"This time...Neal is going to pay!" Shelley answered, viciously. "He has ruined too many years of my life. Now, I'm going to ruin a few of his!"

Chapter 65

Shelley continued to call G.A.F. trying to locate Neal, but this time for different reasons. Apparently, his company was fully prepared to help him disappear, because they still refused to give her any information regarding his whereabouts. She wanted to find him, but was wise enough to know she had to proceed with caution, that it was much more advantageous for her to keep him working.

Shelley knew Neal would be making at least one more trip to the house, since his antique car was still in the garage. She would be ready.

She called the local newspaper and placed a classified ad, advertising an estate sale the following Saturday. She was going home to Georgia, and the only way she could do that financially, was to sell everything of value in the house.

Shelley also put a call into her investment broker in Atlanta. Soon after her reconciliation with Neal, she'd bought some stocks with inheritance money her aunt had left her when she died shortly after she returned home. As much as she hated selling the stocks, they were worth seven thousand dollars, and she needed the money.

"Shelley, what can I do for you?" Norman, her broker asked when he returned her call.

"I want to sell all my stock, Norman, Something has come up, and I really need the money," Shelley explained.

She waited during what had become the all too familiar moment of silence.

"What's wrong?" she asked.

"Shelley, have you forgotten? You already sold your investments."

"Norman, I never sold my stocks."

"Yes, you did. I even called you to talk you out of it because that particular stock was expected to jump shortly after you sold it. Which, by the way, it did."

"Norman, I never sold my stock. I never received a phone call from you," Shelley insisted.

"I phoned your home, and my call was forwarded to some answering service. I left a message and your husband returned my call. The two of you were in Hawaii, and he said you were resting on the beach, but he assured me you still wanted to sell. I sent the check to your Post Office box, as he instructed me to do."

"Norman, if I sold, wouldn't I have had to sign something?" Shelley asked, figuring she had him.

"Yes, and you did. It's a standard permission form...and yes, you signed it."

She heard the shuffling of papers.

"I have it right here."

"No, I didn't, Norman. I believe Neal signed my name on that form. Can you send me a copy of it?" Shelley asked.

"Sure, but Shelley, understand that all signatures have to match what we have on file before we sell," Norman told her. "If someone forged your name on those papers, he or she, did an excellent job."

"Well, lately, my husband is an expert at many things," Shelley said, burning with anger. "Please send me that copy, Norman," Shelley said as she hung up.

That lowlife piece of scum! Once again, he had to take everything. This isn't going to happen to me a second time. If anyone is going to lose this time, it's going to be Neal!

As Shelley had predicted, Neal returned home to get his antique car out of the garage. She didn't know much about cars, but she'd been there the day Neal put the new gas pedal on the car, so she knew how to remove it.

Neal gave Shelley a brief glance, as he walked into the house, and then went directly to the garage. It was obvious he'd planned to get the car and be out of the house within minutes, avoiding having to give either Shelley, or the Police, an explanation.

After a few minutes, he came back into the kitchen where Shelley was waiting for him at the kitchen table.

"Ready to face me now?" Shelley asked, glaring at him.

"What do you want me to say?" he asked.

"Why don't you start by telling me what you're doing?" Shelley demanded.

"I've got to leave, Shelley. It's not my choice," Neal answered.

Void of emotion, she asked. "Oh, really? Why?"

"I can't answer that," he said. "But, I promise you, it has nothing to do about loving you. I will always love you."

Shelley stood slowly, wanting to scratch his eyes out.

"Actually, Neal, when I found out that you stole every dime from me and the children, I began to think...is Neal's love worth two hundred thousand dollars? Hell, no! As a matter of fact, your love isn't even worth the one hundred and seventy four dollars you stole from your son, or the one hundred and fifty nine dollars you stole from your daughter. And the stock you fraudulently sold was part of my inheritance from my aunt, who you never even met, but who I spent a lifetime loving. The mere sight of you sickens me!" Shelley said, controlling the overwhelming desire to hit him.

"Shelley, I need the money. You can have everything else," Neal offered, sounding desperate.

"Like what, Neal? A house I can't pay for? Furniture and some household objects? Why don't we trade, if its such a good deal? You stay here, while the kids and I leave with all the money?" Shelley shouted.

"I can't stay here and that's all there is to it!" Neal said.

She looked at Neal with absolute contempt. Did he think it was about him staying?

"Understand this, you bastard! I want one half of everything you stole, except for my inheritance, I want all of that. I also want you to sign a paper promising to pay fifteen hundred dollars a month for child support. If you don't give me that before you leave this house for good, I promise you, I will be wherever you are. I will follow you to the ends of the earth, and every time you look over your shoulder you will see me there. If the children go hungry, so will you. If they don't have shoes on their feet, neither will you. I will see to it that you are fired. You will never be rid of me, because this time, we will not suffer alone. You see, Neal? I thank you for being such an atrocity in my life, because you have created such a strong person in me that now, I can deal with you the way you should be dealt with."

She opened the oven door and pulled out the gas pedal. Neal ducked when she threw it at him. "Now, you can leave."

Jason watched as his father pulled out of the garage in the antique car his father had promised would, one day go to him. Shelley's heart broke for her son.

As Neal drove down the street, Jason ran next to the car on the sidewalk, screaming for his father to stop. "Daddy! Daddy! Please, stop!" he shouted.

Neal kept going. He never stopped to say goodbye to his son, or comfort him. He never kissed his daughter goodbye, or shed a tear. He left with the cold, calculating non-committal stare on his face that Shelley had learned to hate. How could this man not love his own children? How could he leave them with no money, or means to get any?

Jason came into the house, and sat next to his mother on the couch. He gave her a hug, and Shelley noticed his toes. They were cut, and bleeding from the rubber sandals he wore as he ran down the street, trying to stop his father from leaving them penniless.

"I love you, Jason," Shelley whispered into her son's ear as she held him.

"I love you, too, Mom, and don't you worry. I'll be the man of the house now."

"You always were," she said, as tears streamed down her face.

Chapter 66

Shelley made the much, dreaded call to her family. As expected, they turned their backs and refused to help, even after she'd poured her heart out, they wanted to know how it all would effect their own, personal lives.

Next, she called Molly, who excitedly searched through the newspaper for rentals. She had to work fast as the estate sale was going to take place in three days, and she would need a place to live in Georgia when it was over.

She wanted Molly to search for something on the north side of the airport, because it had more industry and she thought she would have more success in obtaining a job.

"Child, I have missed you so much, and I couldn't afford to call you very much in Florida," Molly exclaimed, while rummaging through the classified ads. "There are a couple of duplexes…is that okay?"

"Great. Where are they?" Shelley said.

"There's one in North Creek, and one in Millburn," Molly answered. "That's the area you wanted, right?"

Shelley wrote down the phone numbers, thanked her friend and hung up. Next, Shelley called Elkie, who now lived in New Jersey.

"My, God! Hank and I were just there," Elkie said. "Neal seemed so happy. Shelley, this is a shock! Is there anything we can do for you?"

"No, just listen to me when I whine," Shelley said, tears rolling down her face.

"Well that's easy to do," she answered. "Do you love him, Shelley?"

"No. I'm angry. I'm angry that he thinks he can father children and owe them nothing. I'm also scared to death. I look into my children's little faces and feel frightened that I'm the only person they have to rely on. It's so scary, Elkie, I don't know if I can do it!" Shelley admitted.

"You would be surprised what you can do when you have to," Elkie said. "You can do this."

"I don't know. I wasn't programmed to be head of household. You know how my mother thinks. In her eyes, marriage should be the ultimate goal for any woman. All my life, I was denied the opportunities my brothers received because I was a female. I was expected to get married and have babies, unlike the boys who would be providing for their families one day. So, here I am, forced to take care of my family without any of the preparation they'd received to do so. I can't begin to tell you how terrified I feel!"

"I think you're getting off to a good start by going home to Georgia. You're not just sitting there crying in your soup, you're making decisions," Elkie replied.

"Yeah, well, I just hope they're the right ones. Obviously, my parents won't be there to give me a big boost in morale," Shelley said.

"True, but when were they ever?" she asked.

"You're right," Shelley agreed, thinking of the time when she was twelve and had come home from a friend's house. She was excited because the girl's father was a Psychologist. He'd shown them his office and explained his work, and like every other child at one time, or another, Shelley knew right then and there, that was what she wanted to be when she grew up.

She'd told her mother who was outside raking leaves at the time. Leaning on her rake, Meg glared at her daughter.

"I'm not wasting money on an education for you. You'll just get married and have kids, and all that money would be wasted. No. Any money for education will go to your brothers."

Meg went back to her raking, and Shelley never recovered from that conversation. It disenchanted her to learn that her fate had already been decided for her the moment she was born a female.

"Well, I'll call you again after I have some solid plans," Shelley said.

"Call us if there's anything we can do," Elkie said.

During the next several days, with Molly's help, Shelley found a duplex and a lead on a good attorney in Florida. She also held the estate sale. Her goal was to make enough money for a good start in Georgia, and the retainer needed for the lawyer.

The sale went well, although Shelley wished she'd made a lot more money. She made enough to pay the owner of the duplex, and pay the attorney. Plus, she had enough left over to rent some furniture, pay deposits for the utilities, and live comfortably for a short while. A very short while.

Shelley and the children spent two days after the sale packing what they could in boxes to mail to her mother's house. She couldn't afford a moving van, so whatever could not be mailed within Shelley's budget, or couldn't fit in the car, would have to be left behind. It broke her heart to watch her children decide which things they would take and which things they would leave behind.

With the house packed up, and the car completely full, the last detail was finding an attorney. She made an appointment with Kathy Smith, a reputable Florida lawyer. She paid the retainer, and was assured they would be in court for temporary child support within fifteen days. Shelley hoped Florida would prove to be better than Georgia with regards to its treatment of women and children.

During the long drive to Georgia, Shelley noticed a strange noise coming from the back of her car. *I'd better have a mechanic check that out when I get to Georgia,* Shelley thought. They planned to stay three nights at her parents' house until the utilities were turned on in the duplex, and when they arrived at the Hemlos', Shelley was surprised that they were honestly excited to see them. It made Shelley feel a little better, and less alone.

The day after she arrived at her parents', Meg drove Shelley and the children to see their new house, while Tim took her car to his mechanic to find out what that noise was about. When they returned to the Hemlos', Tim was waiting for them.

He rolled his eyes towards the children, letting Shelley know he didn't want to talk in front of them. Fortunately, the problem resolved itself when some of the neighborhood children that knew Meg and Tim, knocked on the front door hoping some new kids had moved into the neighborhood. Jackie and Jason ran outside.

"Okay, what's up?" Shelley asked.

"My mechanic was a little upset with what he found in your car," Tim answered.

"Oh, no! What was it? How much?" she asked.

"It was your brakes," Tim answered.

"My brakes? I just had new brakes put in a month ago. Don't they usually last longer than that?"

"Well, it's not that the brakes were bad," Tim said, an uncomfortable tone to his voice.

"Then, what was it?"

"They were tampered with," Tim said. "Originally, they were fine. The mechanic said he found two points of wear on the brakes. The first, which was very slight, was from when they were first put in. The second, was from when they were tampered with," Tim said, softly. "Do you understand what I'm trying to tell you?"

"What do you mean, when they were tampered with?" Shelley asked.

"Apparently, someone went in and tampered with the installation of the brakes after they were put in, and he said it was done recently, judging from the color of the scrape marks on the brake shoes."

"So, what you're saying is that someone deliberately messed with my brakes?" Shelley asked.

"Bruce, the mechanic said it was amazing you weren't killed during the drive to Georgia," Tim told her. "Shelley, it's quite possible that someone tried to kill you."

The blood drained from her face. *Surely Neal wouldn't try to kill his own children. If he wanted me dead, that's one issue...but his children? That's another,* she thought.

Meg piped in. "This is just too dramatic. I'm sure Neal wouldn't do such a thing, he wouldn't hurt a fly."

Shelley just looked at her mother. *Where the hell have you been the past five years?* she wondered, looking at Meg, perplexed.

"Dad, we'll be okay. I'll handle it. I have to find Neal. That will solve a lot of things," Shelley said.

"Well," Tim said. "If it's any help, Bruce offered to testify in court about the brakes if ever you find out who did it. That's how sure he is someone deliberately tampered with them."

Three days later, Shelley and the kids went home to their new duplex shortly after dinner. Everyone was worn out from the day's events, and Shelley was looking forward to being alone with Jackie and Jason, their first night in their new home. They took turns taking showers, then, sat in the living room, discussing immediate plans. Shelley intended to job hunt the next day, while Jason was going to play baseball with some boys he'd already made friends with in the neighborhood. Jackie was invited to bring her Barbie dolls across the street to play with the set of twin girls that lived there.

Once Jackie and Jason were asleep, Shelley made herself a cup of coffee and sat on her rented couch to gather her thoughts. She made a list of the job interviews she'd scheduled for the next day. Unfortunately, employers wanted computer experience.

Times had definitely changed since Shelley was in the job market. Although she didn't have much to offer in the new marketplace, she still felt confident she would find something.

She wrote herself a note to call Kathy Smith to see if Neal had been served. She really needed the child support, and she knew he would have to be forced to pay it.

The fact that G.A.F. was not cooperating imposed a real problem. Shelley didn't want to jeopardize his job, but in order to serve him they needed an address. Kathy said she was going to put a plain clothes detective by his Post Office box with the hope of serving him there.

Shelley couldn't shake the uneasy feeling she had since her father told her someone had tampered with her brakes. She knew Neal was behind it. Either he did it himself, or he hired someone to do it. *Why would Neal try to kill me? I know in his sick little way, he loved me. But, then, he probably loved his grandmother too, and he did try it that last time we were separated when Clancy was shot. Something had changed, or happened. Maybe he thought I knew something he didn't want me to.*

Then, suddenly, it came to her. *My, God! The envelope from the Department of Vital Records. While I was working that day in Jackie's classroom, he must have come home and found the envelope on the porch. Something important must be in those papers. My investment broker said Neal had sold my stocks while we were in Hawaii, so he evidently planned that trip to get me out of town so I wouldn't find out what he was doing. I've got to get copies of those papers!* Shelley thought, immediately adding that to her list of things to do.

The pleasant woman Shelley spoke to at the Records Office, confirmed that the information had been sent overnight to her in Florida the day before Neal had come home early. That confirmed he'd taken the envelope. Whatever was in those papers, Shelley knew it had to be incriminating enough for him to leave her, and incriminating enough for him to try to kill her.

One more time, Shelley sent a four dollar money order by overnight mail, along with a prepaid return overnight mailer, to get the information back quickly.

Meanwhile, she made a call to Kathy Smith. It left Shelley frustrated. Kathy had not been able to locate Neal, or get any information out of G.A.F. The person Kathy spoke to there, said Neal had informed the company that Shelley was mentally ill, and left them instructions not to give out any information about him, no matter who called on her behalf.

"So, how are you going to serve him?" Shelley asked.

"I'm going to keep the plain clothes detective at Neal's Post Office box. If that doesn't work, I'm going to serve Neal at the corporate office of G.A.F. Neal will probably come out of hiding once that happens. He'll know we mean business and he won't want to be embarrassed that way. Trust me on this, okay?" Kathy asked.

"That's all I can do, Kathy. I need child support," Shelley said. "How you get it means nothing to me."

Meg arrived at the duplex to stay with the children while Shelley went on her search for employment. Shelley decided she would do her best to keep her parents out of her problems as much as possible because of their attitude on the phone before she'd left Florida. It hurt her tremendously at a time when she needed some good moral support, and love. She was, however, grateful when her mother offered to help with the children.

When Shelley returned home, she felt disheartened with the results of her interviews. She was worried that she had nothing to offer any of the employers she'd interviewed with that day. While she was home raising children, everything in life somehow, had become computerized. She needed a profession, and for that she would need an education and a grant.

The next day, while the children were playing outside, Shelley called the Department of Education in Washington, D.C. A very helpful man took his time with her, explaining every form of financial aid available to women in Shelley's situation. Then, he offered to send the information by overnight mail. Full of hope, Shelley hung up the phone deliriously happy for the first time in a long time. Finally, she would be given the opportunity to go to college.

Shelley called the Admissions Office of several schools in the area and decided to attend a nearby campus belonging to the University of Georgia. The next thing she had to do was choose a major. She wanted to major in English, but realistically knew that an English degree wouldn't provide an income for her children soon enough. So, she decided to enroll in the Medical Technology program.

A package arrived from the Department of Education the next morning. That afternoon, the man she spoke with the day before, gave Shelley a follow up call to make sure she'd received the information he sent her by overnight mail, and wished her the best of luck with her decision to go to college.

She couldn't believe she was finally going to be able to get an education. For so many years, she'd believed college was something that had passed her by in life. But, there she was, being given a chance to achieve the only thing she'd ever wanted as a young girl.

A few hours later, the doorbell rang again. It was the mailman with another overnight package. It was from the Department of Vital Records in New Jersey. Shelley's hands shook as she opened the big envelope and pulled out the large stack of papers. Apparently, the woman on the phone was touched with Shelley's story because she'd sent her every recorded paper she could find with Neal's name on it.

The first document was a copy of the deed to Neal's house in South Jersey. It appeared that Marielle, and Neal Jordon originally purchased the home. The house had then, become the sole property of Neal Jordon after his wife's death. *Wife?* Shelley wondered. *Neal said his wife's name was Arlene. Who the hell was Marielle?*

Then, she found the divorce papers the woman on the phone had discussed with her. The papers had been filed, but the divorce was never finalized due to the woman's unfortunate death. Again, the name on all the papers was Marielle.

Shelley was totally confused. First of all, according to the dates on the application for a divorce, Neal was married to Marielle Jordon the first five years of his marriage to Shelley. The grounds stated in the divorce action were desertion, abandonment, and adultery. *Adultery? With whom?* Shelley wondered. *Why would Neal tell me his wife's name was Arlene if it was really Marielle. The Jordons had spoken about Arlene. This is so confusing. Was I the woman he committed adultery with?*

Marielle Jordon, stated in her divorce action that Neal had flown to France during December of 1977, on a business trip, never to be heard from again. Marielle also stated that Neal had stolen all the assets accumulated during their marriage, leaving her with nothing except a mortgage payment and a lot of household bills. She also requested the return of her car that he'd stolen during the night, a 1978 Renault, Limited Edition.

France? My, God! His wife's name was Marielle, and the Renault Neal gave me, was stolen from Marielle. He had to convince me he'd traded it in on the truck so I wouldn't know what really happened to it. And according to the dates on these papers, Neal was a bigamist! He still is a bigamist! That's what he was afraid I would find out. My, God. He killed her to avoid prosecution for bigamy.

Scrutinizing the first five years of her marriage, Shelley tried to sort out any details that could have suggested Neal was married to someone else at the time. He traveled a lot, but he was home every weekend with her and the children.

Neal was living a double life! That's why he didn't want me to get these papers. He knew it was just a matter of time before I would find out. That's why he insisted that he had to leave!

On top of the filed divorce action was the name and address of the attorney Marielle Jordon had used. Shelley decided to give the attorney a call.

"Hello, Andrew Letterman speaking," the attorney answered after his secretary transferred the call.

"Mr. Letterman, my name is Shelley Jordon, and I think you have some information I need," she said.

"Do I know you? Are you a client of this firm?" he asked.

"No, but the person I'm calling about was a client of yours at one time."

"Why don't you tell me what this is in regards to, and I'll decide if I'm able to help you?"

"Several years ago, you represented a client named Marielle Jordon. Do you remember her?'

"Most definitely. That was an unusual case, one I would have loved to continue," he answered.

"Can you tell me about it?" she asked.

"Perhaps part of it, but you do understand, much of the information is protected by attorney, client privilege?" he asked.

"I understand, but with all due respect, Sir, Marielle Jordon is deceased. Nothing can hurt her anymore," Shelley reminded him.

"Yes, I know about Mrs. Jordon's death but I still prefer to be careful about the questions I answer."

"Mr. Letterman, were you aware Mr. Jordon was married to another woman when you filed Marielle's divorce papers?"

"Yes, I was."

"Then, why didn't you add bigamy to your list of grounds?" she asked.

"Because I didn't want any questions imposed about the legality of her marriage to Neal Jordon. It was much more advantageous to our case, to present Marielle as a woman legally married to Neal Jordon. Not that any of that would have been an issue. Doing so would have affected the legality of the second marriage, not Marielle's."

Shelley was stunned with the attorney's information. So, was her marriage to Neal legal? That was something she had to address. "What do you know about Marielle's death?" she asked.

"I know she supposedly hung herself in her basement," Mr. Letterman answered.

"Do you believe that's what happened?"

"I can't be certain. I do know Marielle was extremely overwrought at the time," he replied.

"Well, what is your opinion?" Shelley asked, holding her breath.

"My personal opinion doesn't really matter, but I have always suspected something different. However, the Police were satisfied with the idea that she had killed herself."

Shelley ended the conversation feeling uneasy about many things. Now she knew for certain that Neal was guilty of bigamy, and she had every intention of pressing charges against him.

Chapter 67

Shelley filled out the application packet and financial aid forms to bring to the college. She took the papers to the proper office in the school, then, dropped off her application in Admissions.

The smell of the halls excited her. It reminded Shelley of the awesome feeling she got every time she walked into a library as a child, knowing that all the information, about anything she wanted to learn in life, was at her fingertips. Registering for college truly was a remarkable privilege to her.

She kept calling Kathy Smith. The attorney had guessed right about Neal coming out of hiding once she'd contacted G.A.F. He hired an attorney out of Florida, who had called Kathy, requesting she serve Neal at his law office. Shelley was not entirely happy with Kathy's performance, but she couldn't afford to pay another retainer to a new attorney, besides, the papers were already filed. It was just a question of waiting for a court date.

Shelley decided to handle the bigamy matter herself since too many of her conversations with Kathy Smith were being discussed with Neal's attorney. She wanted to take Neal completely by surprise after child support had been ordered by the court.

She called the Police Department to ask how to proceed with pressing charges against Neal for bigamy and abandonment. They said she would have to fill out a Police report with an officer, then the report would be forwarded to the District Attorney's office where the case would be investigated. Neal would then be prosecuted if sufficient evidence was provided to confirm he was guilty, which the documents she received in the mail would do. Her child support would be ordered long before that would happen.

She planned to go ahead and fill out a Police report that afternoon against Neal for bigamy, since it would take several months to even start proceedings for Neal's prosecution.

The new school year was getting ready to start for both the kids, and Shelley. She was found eligible for one grant, and two scholarships. That gave her an income of four thousand dollars per quarter. After her school expenses were paid, she would be left with an income of nine hundred dollars per month, each quarter. If she could find a job around her school schedule, it would still be tough, but she could make it work. Of course, things would be much easier if Neal would pay child support.

Shelley received a call from Kathy Smith. Neal had been served through his attorney, and they were scheduled for court on November twenty second.

"November twenty second?" Shelley asked. "That's three months away!"

"I'm sorry, but that's the earliest we can get into court."

She desperately needed the money and she complained. "Kathy, that will mean that for six months Neal has gotten away with not paying child support."

"Support payments are retroactive, so stop worrying. Neal will pay."

"You don't know what a conniving bastard Neal is. Besides, I have two children to take care of. I can't stop worrying. They start school in a few days and I can't even buy them shoes!"

Clearly, Kathy had no clue what she and the children were going through and seemed to care even less. It made Shelley furious, stirring up the same anger she'd felt the last time she went through the court system with Neal. Only this time, she was alone.

In a flippant tone, Kathy said, "I never understood why parents think just because school is starting, they have to run out and buy new clothes and shoes for their kids."

Shelley slowly counted to ten. "Maybe, Kathy, because you were given those things, you never had to think about the importance of them. Also, they outgrow the clothes they wore the year before. And maybe their shoes have holes in them, like my children's shoes do. I want child support. Now…not three months from now!" Shelley demanded.

"And, you'll get it. Be patient for God's sake. I'll let you know when I receive a response from Neal's attorney."

"Will I have to go to Florida for this?" Shelley asked, wondering who would get stuck for that expense.

"Yes, definitely."

Disgusted, Shelley ended their conversation. Neal would be free and clear for another three months. She knew if she didn't support the children for three months, she would be found guilty of child neglect and sent to jail. Yet, a father was permitted to disappear for six months without paying a dime towards the needs of his children, with absolutely no consequences because the children were not in his home.

Meg stopped by the duplex before Shelley had to leave to register the kids for school.

"Your father and I went over our finances to figure out a way we could buy the kids shoes for school," she said "Why don't you put them on my J.C. Penney's charge?"

"Hey, that's not a bad idea. I should try to use mine," Shelley replied.

"Don't you think Neal closed those accounts?" Meg asked.

"Probably, but maybe he missed that one. They're my accounts too."

"Well, if he did close yours, I'd better come with you in case you need my card."

"Sounds good," Shelley said, pleased her mother was willing to help in some way, though the old wounds still hurt.

"Why don't you want us to help you?" Meg asked, offended.

"We're not your responsibility. My children have a father who earns over $200,000.00 a year. He needs to take care of his children," Shelley insisted.

Meg agreed. "Okay, let's go. We'll register them for school, then, we'll get their shoes…one way, or another."

"We have two other stops, too," Shelley told her mother.

"Oh? What are they?" Meg asked.

"First, I have to fill out a job application with Kelly Girls, and then I want to fill out a Police report against Neal."

"What kind of Police report?" Meg asked carefully, a frown clouding her face.

"It seems my husband is a bigamist," Shelley informed her mother flatly.

"What? How do you know that?"

Shelley handed her the papers she'd received in the mail. Her mother looked them over.

"My, God, Shelley...I can't believe this! All those years Neal had another wife?"

"Looks that way, Mother."

"This woman...Marielle...she killed herself?" Meg asked, stunned.

"I don't think so," Shelley responded, leading her mother and the kids towards the door.

"How do you think she died then?" Meg asked, when the kids were out of earshot.

"I think Neal killed her."

Chapter 68

When Shelley went to the Police Department to file her report, the officer in charge told her it would take two weeks before she would be contacted by the District Attorney's office. He also said she would have to file the abandonment charge in Magistrate Court. She decided to do that the next day while the children were in school.

Meg had to use her charge card to get the children's shoes after all. Neal had canceled all their credit cards, and when Shelley argued that it was her credit too, they said she would have to reapply. Without an income, she was sure they would not take her application seriously.

G.A.F. still enabled Neal to remain hidden, so Shelley decided to call the corporate office and talk to someone with authority who might be able to help her. She had no doubts that they knew where he was living. Whatever story Neal told them about his marriage, she had to convince them it was a lie. She placed a phone call to Human Resources and gave it her best shot, but once again, struck out. They refused to help.

She wouldn't have access to Neal's address until November when they went to court. Meanwhile, she would wait to hear from the District Attorney's office.

The next issue was telling her parents her plans to go to college. She felt sure they would be upset, and she was right.

"Shelley, you can't go to school!" her mother objected.

"And why not?" Shelley demanded.

"Because you have children," Meg argued.

"What does my having children have to do with my going to school?" Shelley asked.

"Who will take care of them? How much time will you be out of the house?"

"Mother, the cold hard facts are, that I'm totally unemployable. I have no skills and no education. Learning a skill is my only chance of ever taking care of my children properly."

"But college is something you do when you're young and have no responsibilities," Meg continued to argue.

"Well, unfortunately, that opportunity wasn't given to me when I was young and 'had no' responsibilities. According to you, I was born the wrong sex for an education, remember?"

Meg gave no response.

When three weeks had passed and Shelley had not heard from the District Attorney, she decided to call his office, and was transferred to Manny Parker, the Assistant District Attorney.

"Oh, yes, Mrs. Jordon. I remember reading your Police report. I decided not to prosecute that case," Manny Parker informed her.

"What do you mean, you decided not to prosecute? I'm pressing charges!"

"It's my prerogative to select what cases this office will prosecute, and I decided not to prosecute this one. That case is closed."

"Oh, I don't think so. I want to know why you made that decision."

"Because I have bank robbers, murderers, and rapists to spend the taxpayer's money on, and a bigamist, doesn't fit into the current budget."

Shelley's anger began to consume her.

"Mr. Parker, what the man has done to his family ranks right up there with all those crimes. As far as I'm concerned, Neal Jordon might as well have stabbed us and left us for dead for all he has put us through. He has stolen everything from us and if I'd known he was married when I met him I wouldn't have gone out to lunch with him, much less married him. He has ruined our lives."

A long silence followed. Manny Parker was obviously working on an appropriate response.

"Mrs. Jordon, if you're trying to do this because you're angry, and want to get even with your husband or make him suffer for leaving you, I can't waste my time, or the taxpayer's money by prosecuting him," he said.

"You're right, I'm angry. I'm very angry. Because as far as I'm concerned, men like you within the justice system, by doing nothing, have encouraged Neal to do the horrible things he's done. You think it's a waste of the taxpayer's money because it involves a woman and two children. And after all, men will be men, right Mr. Parker? I would have to wonder if things were reversed and I did this to him, then would you still consider it a waste of the taxpayer's money to prosecute me? Mr. Parker, if you don't respond to my charges, I plan to tear your office apart with discrimination charges."

"All right, Mrs. Jordon, all right. I'll order the investigation. But, I'm not going to promise you anything."

"Well, I'll just have to take things one step at a time, won't I?"

"A detective will be assigned to the case. He'll go over the evidence you have, and that will start the investigation. That's the procedure of the United States Judicial system, Mrs. Jordon, and we will have to follow it."

"And how long will the investigation take?" Shelley asked.

"About three months."

"Three months? That must be the magic time frame for the court system," she complained.

"That's what it takes for the investigator to gather all the facts and evidence for any felony case, and bigamy is a felony. Like I said, we have to follow procedures."

"But, what do you have to investigate? I have all the evidence you need," Shelley said.

"And we certainly will look at it," he replied. "But, we still have to perform the investigation."

"So, what happens after the investigation?" she asked.

"Once the investigation is completed, I decide if there's enough evidence to take the case before the Grand Jury for a indictment. If your husband is indicted, the judge will order a warrant for his arrest, and the case will go to trial," he explained.

"What is the punishment for bigamy?" she asked.

"For a first offense? A smack on the wrist, some fines. A second offense, you're talking jail time."

"What about an abandonment charge?" Shelley asked.

"If your husband left the state, abandoning you and the children, that also is considered a felony and is treated the same way. If he were to be arrested on an abandonment charge, in order to get out of jail, he would have to pay what the court thinks is reasonable back support to get out."

"I see."

"I will have the detective assigned to the case, call you to set up a time when the two of you can sit down and go over the details."

"Fine. I'll wait to hear from him," Shelley said.

Shortly after Shelley finished her phone call to Manny Parker, Kathy Smith called and said Neal's attorney had filed a motion asking for custody of the children.

"Here we go again," Shelley groaned, rolling her eyes. "We don't even know where he lives, do we? He walked out on his children almost four months ago, and has blatantly refused to support them, much less raise them, and he's asking for custody?"

"I wouldn't worry, Shelley," Kathy responded. "He's just being a bastard, and he doesn't stand a chance of winning. By the way, Neal's attorney said your husband was furious when he heard you filed for child support and a divorce."

"Oh, well. He's going to be upset a lot more before it's over, believe me," Shelley said. "Believe me."

Manny Parker called in Detective Bernie Gianni, his best detective. He knew he could trust him with just about anything.

"What's up, Manny?" Bernie asked, laying his black leather jacket across the empty chair next to him.

"I need a favor, and I know I can trust you," Manny said.

"What is it?"

"I have a woman who claims she just found out that her husband is a bigamist. I don't want to prosecute this one, but this women is a pain in my ass, so I had to give her something," he said.

"Like what?"

"I told her I would start the investigation process. But, I want this case to be history. If she knew about the other wife before she got married, the Statute of Limitations would do that for me. I want you to find some kind of proof that she knew."

"She claims she just found out now?"

"Yeah. Go talk to her. Find a way to get rid of this. Put a tap on her phone, see if she talks about this to anyone. Maybe she'll admit to one of her friends that she knew about the other wife earlier. Do whatever you have to do. I want this case thrown out."

"Why not just throw it out, then? You're the boss, why are you messing with this?" Bernie asked.

"Because she's one of those female warriors with the 'if I wasn't a woman' routine," he answered. "Election is around the corner I need the female vote."

"All right," Bernie said, getting up from his seat. He took the paperwork from Manny Parker, and grabbed his jacket. "I'll see what I can do."

Shelley kept her appointment with the Financial Aid Director of the college. Her advisor had good news. She had been approved for a Pell Grant, plus two scholarships, and the college just awarded her a small scholarship that a former student had lost due to grades. These would cover all the costs of her tuition, books, and some household expenses.

The only drawback was that the funds wouldn't be available for three months. She wanted to start that Fall term. The cost of classes would be deferred, but not the cost of her books. She had to come up with one hundred and fifty dollars to pay for her textbooks.

Since Jackie's birthday was coming up also, Shelley decided it was time to pawn her jewelry…the one thing Neal had left her. Hopefully, she would gather enough cash to pay for her books and to give Jackie a nice birthday.

When all was said and done, she walked out of the pawn shop with four hundred and fifty dollars, leaving behind, five thousand dollars worth of jewelry. Once again, Neal had brought her to another all time low.

When Shelley arrived home, she received a phone call from Kelly Services. They had a part time receptionist job at Mepolex, a computer chip corporation, for the hours from twelve to five. Perfect for the class schedule she chose, since the children had to get the school bus at six thirty, she could take two classes each day from seven to eleven, and still have enough time to get to work. Things were slowly working out for her new life.

Chapter 69

Shelley started school, and her job at Mepolex, and was enjoying both. In November, she made arrangements with her professors and new employer, regarding her court date.

That settled, she planned to arrive at the courthouse before nine o'clock that morning to meet Kathy Smith outside of the court house fifteen minutes before the court session began.

A nervous wreck, Shelley thought of all the things that could go wrong in court. Then, too, there was the nasty thought of seeing Neal again. She felt such contempt for him and actually wished him dead. *This time, Neal, things will be different. I'm not the same jellyfish you went to court with last time. I won't let you rest a minute of your life. If you win in court, I'll win somewhere else. I'll get you every chance I can. You'll spend your last day on earth, cursing the day you met me, just like I do every day with you!*

She pulled into the parking lot of the same hotel she stayed in with the children the day they'd left Florida. Bitterly, Shelley paid for her night's stay, thinking of what the money could have bought the children.

She carefully had to budget her money, living frugally until she received the balance of her scholarship money. The cost of the trip to Florida was costing her dearly. The money Shelley used to go to Florida should have paid the electric bill, but she figured she would pay the overdue bill with whatever child support she received in court. Kathy told her to expect about fifteen hundred dollars a month based on the amount of Neal's salary, and the new Federal Guidelines for Child Support. If that happened, all of Shelley's problems would be over, and the children could start living above poverty level. The government designing the guidelines, presented a welcome change since the last time she was in court with Neal.

The guidelines were intended to take the decision regarding the amount of child support orders, out of the hands of the judges. However, Kathy warned Shelley, even though the guidelines were Federal law, it was still difficult to make some judges adhere to them. There were judges determined to protect men and their money in the courtroom, forcing women and children to be the poorest people in the United States.

Shelley parked her car across the street from the courthouse. She was not going to take any chances in case Neal decided to have someone work on her brakes again.

Seeing Kathy, Shelley waved to her as she crossed the street. "Are you ready?" Kathy asked, as Shelley approached her.

"I'm more than ready," Shelley answered. They walked together into the courthouse. Kathy pushed the elevator button that would bring them to the second floor…and a child support order.

Shelley's stomach did flip flops when the elevator door opened. Within minutes, she would see Neal again, and knowing how much her fate was contingent on how the proceedings went that morning, certainly did not help. The contempt she felt for Neal was so overwhelming, she couldn't guarantee Kathy she would remain civil during the proceedings.

He sat on a chair outside the judge's chambers, holding a file. A thin small man, seated next to him, whispered something to him when the two women entered the room.

Shelley noticed Neal's hands were shaking. *He is really nervous,* Shelley thought, happily. *He must know I found out about the bigamy. Don't worry, Neal. I intend to use that information to its full advantage. Not now, and not here!*

In Florida, procedures differed from those in Georgia. There was no room full of strangers listening to people's personal business. Instead, they sat at a big conference table, the judge, sitting at the end, like the CEO of a big corporation. Shelley and Kathy, took seats on one side, while Neal and his attorney sat on the other.

A court clerk entered the room, asking everyone to raise their right hands as they swore to tell the truth, so help them God. That oath meant nothing to Shelley anymore. There was no truth if Neal was involved.

Kathy spoke first. "Your Honor, my client was abandoned by Mr. Jordon, four months ago, and is here today seeking temporary child support, and the return of fifty percent of all their assets, that he took with him when he left his family."

"I object, your Honor. My client did not abandon his family. He came home from a business trip and found his wife and children gone," Neal's attorney argued.

"These things have to be established in the divorce proceedings. We're here to establish temporary child support," the judge interrupted.

"Your Honor, my client is in the process of paying enormous bills created by his wife during their marriage. He is almost to the point of filing bankruptcy. He can't even afford a place to live, but stays in hotels as he travels on business," Neal's attorney continued.

"Lies! Lies! Lies! Do you know anything else, Neal?" Shelley stood, shouting at him. Kathy grabbed her arm, pulling her back into her seat. She whispered to Shelley, advising her to keep quiet.

"Do I have all the financial statements from both parties?" the judge asked, looking at Shelley.

"Yes, your Honor," Kathy answered.

The judge took a few minutes to look over both statements, then, made his decision. "Let's see, there are two children. I think five hundred dollars should be enough to feed them each month," he said.

"Your Honor, we ask that the temporary child support be payroll deducted since Mr. Jordon has a history of not paying his child support," Kathy commented.

"That will be fine. Send me the proper paperwork, and I'll sign it. This session is over" The judge stood, then, left the room.

Neal and his attorney walked out of the room. Both bearing huge smiles on their faces. Once again, Neal felt as if he'd won by being ordered to pay only five hundred dollars a month. Shelley looked at Kathy in shock.

"What just happened here?" Shelley asked.

"You were awarded five hundred dollars a month temporary child support," Kathy said, looking at her. "What's wrong?"

"You said, according to the Federal Guidelines, I'm entitled to fifteen hundred dollars a month. Where did that go?"

"This is only temporary," Kathy answered, gathering her papers.

"Kathy, you and I both know, this will never be changed. It's over! I'm done with this lousy court system," Shelley said, throwing up her arms in disgust. "I'll take care of Neal Jordon myself!"

Both women walked out of the judges chambers. Outside, Neal was still talking with his attorney. Shelley headed for the door, then, turned around and looked straight into Neal's eyes, something she'd always avoided before.

"I will see you put in jail," she said, as she walked out.

Kathy ran behind her, and when the elevator door opened, she pushed Shelley inside.

"Are you nuts? You can't threaten him like that. You'll be the one going to jail!"

"You just don't get it, do you Kathy? Neal and I have been around this corner before. I've listened to biased judges make ignorant decisions, and I won't tolerate it anymore. Think of this, Kathy. Don't you find it a bit odd that at no point in there did the word 'visitation' come up? Neal doesn't care if he ever sees his children again, much less if they eat, or have shoes on their feet. I'm finished! I won't be a victim of this lousy court system anymore, and neither will my children."

Kathy finally responded, as the elevator began to move, "Shelley, you have to wait for the court to deal with Neal. You can't just do it yourself."

"Watch me! Neal Jordon thinks he won in there because he beat the Federal Guidelines. Tell me, Kathy, was he concerned about how his children would have to live with that small amount of money? Believe me, I will take care of Neal Jordon."

Shelley stepped out of the elevator when it had reached the lobby, and walked out of the courthouse, without looking back.

Neal spent twenty minutes talking with his attorney. He could only half listen, obviously thinking of the look on Shelley's face when she'd threatened him. He could tell Shelley knew what he'd feared she might know. The roles had changed. He was sure she would not stop there. The woman he'd married was gone, and rightfully so, and he was afraid of the new one.

"I'm sorry. What did you ask me?" Neal asked.

"I asked you why your wife would say such a thing to you? Is there something I don't know?" his attorney asked him.

"No, of course not. I told you she's unbalanced. She's actually suicidal. I've told you everything. What else could there be?"

Chapter 70

Shelley decided to drive straight through to Georgia, without stopping at a hotel. Not only did she want to save money, but more than ever she wanted to be with her children. Her overwhelming frustration filled her full of energy for the long ride home.

She called her parents from a phone booth to tell them what happened in court. They'd kept the children for her, and she wanted to assure them, that she was fine and on her way home, knowing they would be anxious to hear the results of the hearing. Meg had been sure the court would make Neal do the right thing for his children. Shelley had to let it go, knowing Meg would learn soon enough.

"Five hundred dollars?" Meg screamed into the phone. "That's ridiculous!"

"Actually, Mother, I don't think it matters how much I've been awarded. I'm sure Neal won't pay anything. He told the judge he doesn't have a permanent address, which should tell everyone where that's going," Shelley said, shouting above the loud trucks and cars flying past her on the highway.

"Well, drive carefully. We'll wait dinner for you," Meg said.

Shelley's entire life, she'd had a hard time figuring out her mother. Sometimes, Meg seemed not to understand anything about her daughter. Then, at other times, like that one, she understood Shelley was hurting, and needed encouragement.

Shelley smiled. Her mother was meeting that need the only way she know how to...by waiting dinner.

A few days later, Bernie Gianno phoned Shelley at Mepolex, hoping to arrange a time he could get together with her to discuss the investigation. He asked her for the actual documents she'd received from the Department of Vital Records in New Jersey, and was quite upset when Shelley offered to give him copies of the originals instead.

"No, that won't do. I need the papers with the seals on them," Bernie said, trying to intimidate her into giving them to him.

"You expect me to give you my original documents?" Shelley asked.

"Definitely. If you insist on going ahead with these charges, we'll need them," he answered.

"I'm not going to do that. What if Manny Parker conveniently loses them? It could take me a long time to get new ones. Why don't I run copies of them for you and you can witness the original seals? I should think your word would be sufficient for Mr. Parker," Shelley insisted.

"Yes, I'm sure it would be. I'll come to your office tomorrow, say, around two o'clock? I'll check out the seals and make the copies myself, so I can say I did it. Then, I'll meet you again at your apartment, let's say, seven, to begin the actual investigation. Is that safe enough for you?" the detective asked, sarcastically.

"That sounds fine. I'll see you then," Shelley said.

Two o'clock sharp, Bernie Gianno walked into Mepolex, looking like a Harley commercial, wearing his black leather jacket, black pants, black sunglasses, boldly smoothing his black hair. Shelley thought he was ruggedly handsome, but made a comical figure in all that black.

"You Shelley Jordon?" the detective asked, looking around the office as though he expected a sniper to jump out from under a desk.

"Yes, and who are you? One of the Blues Brothers?" Shelley asked, laughing. "I'm sorry, I didn't mean that. It's just that you look like John Belushi, and with that outfit...," Shelley stopped, realizing he was not as amused with her humor as she was.

"You don't work undercover like that, do you? Cause...duh! No one would ever guess you're a cop!" she added, laughing again.

"Do you have those papers ready for me to copy?" Bernie Gianno asked, his manner abrupt.

"Oh, yes, here they are," she said, handing him the stack of papers. She led him to the copy room, and watched as the detective made the copies he needed. He avoided looking at her.

"See you tonight," the man said, then, quickly left.

What a weirdo, Shelley thought and she picked up her original copies off the tray of the copy machine and went back to her desk. Half the sales force of Mepolex was staring at her, but she ignored them.

Shelley asked Jackie and Jason to stay upstairs when Detective Gianno arrived that evening at seven. She didn't want them to understand what was going on with their father until it was absolutely necessary.

Meg came over to keep the kids company while the detective was there. Also, her curiosity overwhelmed her. She wanted to get a glimpse of what a real detective looked like.

Bernie arrived wearing a beige sweater with brown pants. "Hello, Mrs. Jordon. Where do you want to do this?" he asked, stepping inside the duplex.

"Where do I want to do what?" she asked, moving aside as he brushed past her.

"To go over the information we have," he answered, studying her closely, as a man does when he's looking at a woman that interests him.

"Why don't we sit in the kitchen? I'll even make you some coffee," she said. "Sorry, I don't have any doughnuts," she said, smiling.

The detective just looked at her. "When are you going to start liking me?"

"Oh, I don't know. When are you going to stop acting like 'Kojak'?"

The detective smiled, too. "Okay, I promise to stop, if you do. I think we'll get along a lot better that way," he said.

"Deal." She led him to the kitchen. "Sit down, and I'll put some coffee on."

Bernie began without waiting for the coffee.

"Mrs. Jordon, I went over the Police report you filed, along with the documents you gave me this afternoon, and I have just a few questions. It's procedure, you understand."

"Okay. Go ahead," she replied, returning the glass pot to its place on the coffee maker. She pushed the 'on' button, then, joined Bernie at the table.

"When you met your husband, did he tell you his marital status?"

"Not his real marital status. He told me he'd been divorced for six years," she answered.

"Where was he living at the time. Did he ever take you to his home?"

Shelley got up to get their coffee. "Cream and Sugar?" she asked.

"Black."

"My husband traveled a lot, and his home was a two hour drive from the office, where we worked together, and my apartment. He stayed in a hotel near the office during the week and went home on weekends to collect his mail, and to take care of his personal matters," Shelley answered.

"So, you never went with him? You never saw where he lived?" he asked.

"No, I didn't," she replied, knowing how ridiculous that sounded.

"Didn't you find it unusual that he never took you home?"

"Detective Gianno, I think it's important that you understand something. My whole life, I've surrounded myself with honest people. It never occurred to me that Neal would lie about the things he lied about. Not just to me, but everyone. Myself, and the people I knew, would no more have said their parents were dead, when they really were alive, the way my husband did, than they would have tossed their firstborn into a river. Telling a friend she looked nice in a dress, when she really looked like a fat cow, was as dangerous as my world got. Do you understand? I wouldn't expect anyone in their right mind to lie about the things Neal lied about."

"I see. What about his phone calls at work? Did any women call him at the office?"

"No. As a matter of fact, I called him at his house on the weekends while he was there. But, thinking about it, I figured he must have had two phone lines with different numbers working in the house."

An hour later, Detective Gianno, was finished asking Shelley questions, and was preparing to leave.

"Mr. Parker will give you a call after I've finished my investigation and turned in my report," Bernie told her. "Oh, by the way...do you mind if I use your phone?"

"No, of course not. It's in the living room. I'll leave you alone so you can have privacy."

Shelley caught a glimpse of him before she headed back to the kitchen to deal with the dirty coffee cups. Something about the way he was standing, shielding the receiver of the phone with his back towards her, looked peculiar. She stared for a brief second before he turned to see if he was being watched. Quickly, she returned to the kitchen.

What is he doing? Surely he didn't do something to my phone? How ridiculous. It's not like I'm a gangster, Shelley thought. *I'm going to check it after he leaves.*

"Mrs. Jordon, thank you. I'm going to leave now," Detective Gianno yelled from the living room. Shelley joined him before he reached the door.

"Thank you, and I'll wait to hear from Manny Parker," Shelley said.

"You're welcome. And thanks for the use of your phone. Goodbye," the detective said, walking out.

"Yeah, your welcome," Shelley whispered as she looked out her living room window to watch the brown, Caprice, pull out of her driveway.

"Where are the kids?" Shelley asked as her mother made her way downstairs, having heard Bernie's car leave the driveway.

"They fell asleep," Meg answered. "I heard the detective leave…"

Shelley put her fingers up to her lips, signaling her mother to be silent as she walked towards the phone.

"What's wrong?" Meg whispered.

"Shhh!" Shelley pushed the redial button on her phone. "I'm sorry the number you are trying to reach is not in service at this time," the computerized voice said on the other end.

That's what I thought. He didn't call anyone.

Shelley pushed the receiver button down and quietly unscrewed the mouthpiece of the receiver. Inside lay a small chip Shelley recognized as a microphone, thanks to her job at Mepolex. Slowly, she took the chip out, then, replaced the mouthpiece. She unscrewed the earpiece to remove the other part. Once she put the phone back together, she placed the receiver back in its cradle and carried the tiny pieces to the kitchen table.

She motioned to her mother with her finger to follow her outside. Meg joined her on the front porch, closing the door behind her.

"What's going on?" Meg asked, keeping her voice low.

"I don't know, but for some idiotic reason, Detective Gianno found it necessary to bug my phone," Shelley said, with anger.

"Oh, my, God. Why?" Meg asked.

"I think he's hoping to hear something that would prove I knew Neal was married when I met him. Probably, so our wonderful District Attorney won't have to prosecute my case."

"Why?" Meg asked, in disbelief.

"Because, if I knew about his being married from the beginning, the Statute of Limitations would be over," Shelley answered. "It would be too late for me to press charges against Neal for bigamy."

"What are you going to do?" Meg asked.

"Follow me. I'll show you what I'm going to do," Shelley said, leading her mother back inside the duplex, to the kitchen. She opened one of her kitchen drawers and pulled out a zip lock bag. She put the microphone pieces on the floor and stepped on them before she dropped the tiny pieces inside the bag.

Shelley addressed an eight by ten, manila, bubble packed envelope to the address on the detective's card he'd left on her table. After scribbling a message on a piece of paper, she taped it to the side of the bag, and put three dollars worth of stamps on the envelope. "Do you think this will be enough postage?" she asked, sealing the flap.

"Shelley, no! Don't do it! You're going to get in trouble!" Meg gasped.

"Will you stay with the kids while I drop this in the mailbox at the end of the street?" Shelley asked. "I don't want this in my house."

"Of course I will, but this is scary!"

"Scary for who? Not for me. It just tells me what kind of people I'm dealing with!" She replied, leaving the house with the envelope.

Two days later, Detective Bernie Gianno, walked into Manny Parker's office, carrying the manila envelope. Disgusted, he threw it on the District Attorney's desk.

"What's that?" Manny asked.

"Look inside," Bernie suggested.

Manny pulled out the zip lock bag and laughed. "And what is this supposed to be?"

"Read the note," Bernie said.

"Okay, let's see..."

Dear Detective Gianno, this is not the way to win friends.

"That's the bug you wanted placed on Shelley Jordon's phone," Bernie informed him.

"You're kidding! She found it?"

"Yes! Manny, you're not going to beat this one. She wants Neal Jordon prosecuted, and quite frankly, she has the evidence she needs to do it."

"There has to be a way to get rid of this case," Manny said. He looked at the detective for a moment. "Why are you dressed like that?" he asked, suddenly noticing Bernie's light gray pants and sweater. "Where's your black?"

"I don't know, I thought I'd try something different," Bernie answered, fumbling his words.

"Uh huh. So, what does Shelley Jordon look like?" Manny asked.

"Come on, Manny. You know me better than that," Bernie said, avoiding the District Attorney's eyes.

Manny grinned. "She said something about your clothes, didn't she, Gianno?"

"No! Well, maybe something. She might have made some kind of reference to the 'Blues Brothers', I'm not sure," he answered, looking around the room.

"The Blues Brothers!" Manny broke out in laughter. "Damn! She's right!"

"Manny, why don't you just go ahead and prosecute this one?" Bernie asked, more gently. "This woman and her kids, have been kicked around by the system for years."

Manny caught his breath. "Because, I don't want to spend the money on a simple bigamy case that possibly could make this office look ridiculous. We're still getting stung because of that moron who arrested that pregnant woman for not returning her library books."

"Well, man, I don't think this one's going away," Bernie said.

Manny's smile vanished. "I'll have to find another way. I don't want to waste my time on some asshole who wants more than one bitch in his life."

It was Bernie's turn to laugh. "Well, don't say I didn't warn you. A year from now, I want to hear what you have to say about this simple bigamy case. I have a gut feeling about Shelley Jordon, and my gut feelings are never wrong!"

He walked out of Manny Parker's office with a smile on his face.

Chapter 71

The first week in December, Shelley received an overnight express envelope containing a check from Neal, made out for one hundred and twenty five dollars. Shelley called Kathy Smith, and told her she wouldn't cash the check without the balance of the five hundred dollars he was ordered to pay. Kathy understood, and promised to contact his attorney.

The next day, a second overnight express envelope arrived with the rest of her child support payment. She couldn't believe she actually had one in her hands. She was sure Neal was furious about being forced to pay the rest of his payment, but this time, he couldn't do a thing about it.

Saturday morning, Shelley was sitting on the couch, studying for an American Government exam when there was a knock on the door. She put her book aside and answered it. A grubby man was standing on her porch with a clipboard in his hands.

"Mrs. Jordon?" he asked.

"Yes," Shelley answered, noticing the tow truck in her driveway.

"I'm here to pick up your car," the man told her.

"Excuse me?'

"I have an order to pick up your car."

"There must be some mistake. I didn't call for a tow truck," she replied.

"No, Ma'am, the car's being repossessed," he informed her.

"Now, I know your mistaken. My car is paid for. I don't have a loan on it," she answered.

"Do you have proof of that?" the man asked.

"Of course. Do you have some form of identification?"

"Yes, here. And here's the paperwork that was given to me to pick up your car," he said, handing her the clipboard.

Shelley looked at the papers, confused. She didn't understand what it all meant. She went into the hall closet and found the receipt for her car, stored in her important papers. The ownership papers were in Neal's name, so she didn't have the pink slip. But, she did have the last statement from the loan company proving it was paid off.

"Here it is," Shelley said, showing the stranger her paid receipt.

"Hmm," the man said, handing the receipt back to her. "I don't know. This is really weird. I guess as long as you have that paper, you'll be all right."

Shelley watched him drive away, feeling uneasy.

Five o'clock in the morning, Shelley was preparing to get out of bed. She wanted to briefly review the material she'd studied for her exam before leaving for school. Sitting on the side of her bed desperately trying to wake up, she heard a grinding noise coming from her driveway. She jumped up and ran to look out the bedroom window. The man who had been there the day before was back in her driveway with his tow truck.

He had her car hooked up to the back of his truck, and it took a moment before she realized he was stealing it.

Shelley ran downstairs and called 911 to get the Police involved. They assured her they would dispatch a patrol car, plus send a helicopter up to track the car thief.

Jason heard the commotion and ran downstairs. When he heard his mother telling the officer on the phone that her car was being stolen, he grabbed his baseball bat and ran outside to chase the thief.

"You better get out of there! My mom just called the Police on you!" Jason shouted. Shelley was right behind him.

"Get out of here! You can't come here and steal my car!" Shelley shouted.

"Hurry, she called the Police!" the man instructed the rough-looking woman helping him. They sped away with Shelley's car swinging from the large hook on the back of the truck. It wasn't even secured properly, causing Jason and Shelley to hear the screeching metal as the truck raced out of their neighborhood.

Shelley watched her whole life vanish on the back of that truck...school, her job, her church activities, and the little bit of social life she'd enjoyed. She ran inside to call the Police again, but Jason was already on the phone calling his grandparents.

"Grandma wants to talk to you," Jason said holding out the phone.

"Shelley, are you all right?" Meg asked, sounding upset.

Shelley shook with rage and despair. "Mother, some man stole my car! I just know Neal is behind this somehow! When is this going to stop? I can't take much more!"

"Your father and I are coming over there," Meg said. "Hang on, Shelley. We'll be right there."

To stay emotionally uninvolved, Meg and Tim had always put distance between themselves and the bad circumstances Shelley and her children had endured, but things had changed. They were seeing firsthand, with no chance of pretending that they didn't know what was going on, what Shelley suffered at Neal's hand. Now they understood the torment she lived through on a daily basis.

Thirty minutes later, Meg and Tim arrived at the duplex. "Did you hear anything from the Police yet?" Meg asked.

"No, I'm still waiting," she answered, softly. She was completely, emotionally drained.

"Do you have any idea what this is about?" Meg asked.

"No, but it's crazy. When I went over all the details in my mind, I realized the man knew my name. It was on the papers he showed me. I don't get any of this."

Suddenly, the phone rang, and Shelley ran to it. "Hello, Mrs. Jordon?" a man's voice asked.

"Yes, this is Mrs. Jordon," Shelley answered anxiously.

"Mrs. Jordon, this is Officer McBride. I'm calling about your car."

"Oh, thank, God! Did you find it?"

"Ma'am, we've spoken to the man who recovered the car and unfortunately, he did have the proper paperwork to pick up the car. It was definitely signed by a judge. It seems there was a loan for eighteen hundred dollars taken out against the car, then, the loan defaulted," Officer McBride continued. "I'm sorry, I wish I had better news."

"But, I don't have a loan on my car," Shelley objected.

"Well, unfortunately, Mrs. Jordon, your husband does," he responded, gently. "Probably what will happen now, is your husband will pay the eighteen hundred dollars and take possession of the car without a court battle. It's a lousy thing to do, but we see it all the time, I'm afraid. I suggest you get a lawyer and go after this jerk," he added.

"Yeah, I'll do that. Thank you," Shelley whispered, hanging up the phone.

"What did the Police say?" Tim asked.

She sat quietly on the couch for a few minutes at a loss of words. *How could Neal legally steal my car this way?* she wondered, once again, amazed by the cruelty of Neal and the court system.

"How could your attorney let this happen, Shelley?" Tim asked, after Shelley told them what the officer said.

"I think I have to agree with your father on this one, Shelley," Meg said. "Maybe you should give her a call, and yell at her."

Shelley looked at them. All the questions. Did it matter? Her car was gone. They didn't understand that everything was meant to be a battle. A deliberate act to hurt her and the children. Neal was a pro at it, and Meg and Tim couldn't relate to that kind of devious thinking. Answering questions, was just added pressure. She felt as if her parents were saying, "Fix this somehow." As if, there were a defense against this kind of thing happening. The officer said it himself, "We see it all the time."

"Mother, she probably doesn't know anything about this, but I'll call her anyway. I want my car back. Maybe there's something she can do," Shelley said, beginning to sob.

Meg and Tim, stood to hold their daughter which was the only help they could give her. Without a car, Shelley had some serious problems, and Meg and Tim were financially helpless.

Shelley dialed Kathy Smith's phone number and got her answer machine, but it was Sunday, what did she expect?

A few days later, Shelley discovered that Neal had already paid the eighteen hundred dollars and had picked up her car. Of all the things Neal had stolen from her, taking her car, hurt her the most.

Chapter 72

Wednesday night, Shelley asked the choir director, Barry and his wife, Anita, for a ride to church. Her parents helped with getting her and the children back and forth, but she knew it was a great imposition to everyone.

After choir practice, the following Wednesday, Barry and Anita, offered Shelley the use of their Toyota for the holiday season, since they were going to be in Michigan for Christmas. They said it would be parked in the garage, serving no purpose.

Christmas was wonderful under the circumstances. Shelley felt tremendously blessed through all the adversity, they had a beautiful tree with ornaments given to them from all their friends, which made it special, and Shelley was able to give the children several nice presents. Then. there was the incredible use of Barry and Anita's car. She felt they had a lot to be thankful for, regardless of their circumstances.

Shelley managed to earn the B average she needed to keep her scholarships for the following quarter, and fortunately, her school schedule for Spring quarter, would not conflict with her hours at Mepolex. That meant she could keep her job there for another quarter. Getting through college meant a commitment from both Shelley and the children, to do whatever they had to for that degree. It was not unusual for students to change jobs every quarter to manage class schedules.

When Barry and Anita came to pick up the Toyota, Anita grabbed Shelley's hand as she offered them the keys.

"Listen, Barry and I thought about your car situation while we were in Michigan, and we want you to keep the car."

"What? Anita, I can't keep your car!" Shelley said astonished.

"Yes, you can. We have another one Shelley, and I don't go anywhere, it would serve a much better purpose if you used it," Anita insisted.

"How about you keep it, and when the insurance payment becomes due, you pay half of it?" Barry asked.

"Barry, I just don't feel right about this, what if Anita has to go somewhere?" Shelley asked.

"My schedule is flexible…she can either use my car, or I can take her, believe me, we won't be inconvenienced," Barry insisted.

"Shelley, we are adamant about this. You need the car more than we do, this is what we want to do," Anita said.

"Anita, this isn't a cup of sugar, a car is such a big thing to give away, I don't want you to be sorry," Shelley replied.

"We won't be, trust me," Barry said, handing the keys back to Shelley.

All she could do was cry. Even though things had been so hard for her and the children, it was the little miracles like that one, that gave her strength and renewed hope.

A month later, Shelley received a call from Manny Parker.

"Mrs. Jordon, Detective Gianno has finished his investigation and I've received his report," he informed her.

"Good! When are you taking my case to the Grand Jury?" Shelley asked, with an attitude. She was still upset about the bug she'd found inside her phone.

"Unfortunately, the Grand Jury doesn't meet for another month."

"And…you'll present it during that session?" she asked, knowing he did not want to do that.

"I guess I have to, right?" he asked.

"I guess so, Mr. Parker."

"Well, then, I'll take care of it next month," he said, flippantly.

"And, what about the abandonment charges?"

"Haven't you received child support, Mrs. Jordon?"

"Not for six weeks."

"Well, it's customary to wait until payments are past due, or at least ninety days late," he responded.

His sarcasm annoyed her, and she felt her temper rising. "Why? I don't have ninety days to feed my children. Besides, he didn't pay anything for six months."

"Okay! Okay! I'll do it. but, I doubt if it will go anywhere."

Shelley knew Neal had no intention of supporting his children. The check she'd received, would be the last. That was just the way it was with Neal. However, if he wasn't going to pay his support, she was going to make his life as miserable as he had for his children. That was a promise she'd made him, and she intended to keep it.

Shelley waited until the twelfth of February before she called Manny Parker again to make sure he was going to follow through with his promise to her. The Grand Jury was meeting the next morning.

"I'm sorry, but Mr. Parker is in a meeting. Can I take a message?" his assistant asked.

Shelley knew he was avoiding her. "Yes...please do," she replied. "Tell him, I'll be waiting to hear from him tomorrow, after the Grand Jury adjourns."

"Okay, Mrs. Jordon, I'll give him your message."

Shelley received Manny Parker's phone call around four o'clock. He told her he wouldn't know if Neal was indicted until the following Monday, six days from then.

She prayed for the indictment at least on the abandonment charge, if nothing else, so she could get her back child support and her half of the money that Neal took when he left. Sixty days had passed since she'd received her first, and what she'd considered most likely her last, child support check.

Friday arrived, and Shelley received a call from her mother while she was working at Mepolex.

"What's up, Mother?" she asked. It was unusual for Meg to call her at work.

"Have you seen the newspaper today?"

"No, why?"

"There's an article in there about Neal's indictment!" Meg told her.

"That's impossible. Manny Parker said he wouldn't have an answer on that until Monday."

"Well, Honey, it's in there. Page two. He was indicted!"

"Have you actually seen the article?" Shelley asked Meg.

"Yes, I'm looking at it now. I'm at the hairdresser's. The woman who does my hair, just handed me the paper."

"Oh, Mother, I'm sorry. Were you embarrassed?" Shelley asked.

"Absolutely not! Neal deserves whatever he gets. I was glad to see something finally went the way it was supposed to!" Meg stated.

"I can't believe Manny Parker lied to me like that," Shelley said. "He must think we never read the paper."

"It doesn't really matter. Neal's been indicted and there's not a thing Manny Parker can do to stop that," Meg reminded her.

"We'll see," Shelley said, swamped with doubt. "He's definitely someone who needs to be harrassed."

After Shelley hung up the phone, she was crazy with impatience to see the article. She took a break and retrieved the paper from the employee's lunchroom.

"Man indicted for bigamy. First time in thirty years."

The article brimmed with all the sordid details. There was even a quote from Manny Parker, who made fun of the idea that any man would want more than one wife.

That bastard thinks it's a big joke! Shelley thought.

She returned to her desk and felt the eyes of her fellow employees following her.

Well, I guess they read the article, too, she thought.

She didn't feel uncomfortable, because she worked with good people, and she was sure they would do nothing to make her feel embarrassed. She also had to keep reminding herself, that none of what was happening, was her fault.

"Mr. Parker, please," Shelley said, when she called his office and got the same woman.

"Can I tell him who is calling?" she asked, as always.

"Yes, you can tell him Shelley Jordon is on the phone, and no, he can't call me back. I want to talk to him now!"

After a few minutes, Parker picked up the phone, his manner casual. "Yes, Mrs. Jordon, what can I do for you?"

"Why did you lie to me?" Shelley demanded.

"I really don't know what your talking about," Manny Parker said.

"Why did you tell me the Grand Jury would not be making a decision until Monday, knowing they'd already indicted Neal?"

"The actual paperwork won't be back from the judge before then," he answered, seemingly unaffected by her accusation. "That means he isn't legally indicted until the paperwork is completed."

"Mr. Parker, why do I believe you were going to tell me the Grand Jury didn't indict Neal?"

"You don't know that, Mrs. Jordon."

"You're right. I can only guess where you're concerned. So what happens now?"

"The judge will sign the indictment and order a warrant for your husband's arrest," he answered.

"When?"

"Like I said, Monday."

"Then what?"

"A pair of detectives will be assigned to the case. They'll contact you to ask you more questions...get a picture...etcetera," he answered.

"How long will that take?"

"Just a few days. Mrs. Jordon, please relax. We're doing what you want us to do," Parker told her.

"Yeah, sure you are," Shelley said.

A week later, Shelley received a phone call from one of the detectives assigned to her case.

"Mrs. Jordon?" the woman on the phone asked.

"Yes?" she replied.

"My name is Culley Marsh. I'm one of the detectives assigned to your bigamy case. My partner, Pete Kensey, and I would like to schedule a time that we can come to your home and meet with you."

"Tonight is fine...what time?" Shelley asked. The woman sounded very nice, but Shelley, naturally, was leery of anyone from the District Attorney's office.

"Is eight o'clock okay?" the detective asked.

"That's good. I can get my children to bed a little early, so they won't have to hear anything we talk about," Shelley suggested.

"We'll see you then," Detective Marsh said, ending their conversation.

Shelley had the usual pot of coffee ready when the detectives arrived.

"Hello, Mrs. Jordon, I'm Culley Marsh, and this is my partner, Pete Kensey," Culley said, extending her hand.

"Please call me Shelley." she said, already feeling comfortable with the pair of detectives.

"Where do you want to talk?" Shelley asked.

"The kitchen's fine with me, if that's okay with you," Culley replied.

"Good. I made coffee." Shelley led them to the kitchen.

"I can tell…it smells wonderful!" Culley said following her.

Shelley watched as Culley and Pete took legal pads from their briefcases. Neither one of them looked like detectives. Culley looked like many of the mothers she encountered at the P.T.A. meetings she'd attended, and Pete reminded her of a computer specialist, or a bookkeeper.

"Shelley let's start from the beginning," Culley said. "Tell us how you discovered that your husband was already married when he married you."

Shelley spent the next two hours explaining everything Neal had done to her and the children. It pained her to once again, relive all the horrendous details, but, by the time the detectives were ready to leave, they were in awe of Shelley's fortitude. The three of them, had become friends with the same goal in mind…to make Neal take responsibility for the harm he'd caused his family. They earnestly wanted to bring him in almost as much as Shelley wanted them to.

"We'll be in touch with you as soon as we find him," Pete told her. "By the way, do you have a recent picture of him that you can give us?"

Shelley thought for a moment. The only picture she had of Neal was taken of them together at a luau in Hawaii. She found it, then cut Neal's picture out of the photo, and handed it to Culley. It made Shelley sick to her stomach to see Neal's face, even if it was just in a photograph. She'd avoided looking at it, knowing it was in a box in her closet.

Once they were gone, she cleaned up the coffee cups left on the table, ready once again to wait.

Since Neal was long past ninety days in arrears with his child support, she'd decided to see if Kathy Smith could do something through Neal's attorney.

"Shelley! Good work, you really got him!" Kathy shouted over the phone.

"What are you talking about?" Shelley asked, confused.

"Getting Neal indicted for bigamy!" she answered.

"How on earth did you find out about that?" Shelley asked, taken by surprise.

"Neal's attorney called me. It seems your husband has enemies in Georgia who sent G.A.F. a copy of the newspaper clipping. He was ordered to show up this morning at G.A.F.'s corporate headquarters in Connecticut. His attorney here, dropped him. He said he won't represent a liar," Kathy told her.

"That's amazing! I wonder who sent G.A.F. the newspaper clipping?"

"Everyone thinks you sent it. Didn't you?" Kathy asked.

"No. If I did, I would take credit for it, but actually it's much more advantageous for me to keep him working. I wouldn't mess with his job," Shelley answered.

"Well, someone did," she said, cheerfully, clearly glad Neal was about to get his.

"The funny thing is that he called his attorney here, to see if he could make the courts stop you from harassing him," Kathy added.

"I've only just begun to effect his life," she replied. "This is just the beginning."

Shelley decided she would attempt once more to call G.A.F., curious to know how Neal smoothed things over with them, if he did at all. It was obvious that the man who'd answered the phone, resented taking her call.

"Mrs. Jordon, I'm not going to discuss Neal's position with G.A.F with you. It is our understanding that you have done nothing but harass Neal since the man divorced you," he said, sounding annoyed.

"Excuse me, Sir, but Neal has not divorced me, and when it concerns him taking care of his financial responsibility to his children, you are involved. Why hasn't your company honored the payroll deduction ordered by the court?" Shelley asked, angry at the man's attitude.

"Because, legally, we don't have to. That court order came from Florida," the man argued. "Florida is not an enforcing state, its laws pertain only to Florida."

"So, you think it's okay for Neal to ignore his financial responsibility to his children?" she asked.

"I think this matter has nothing to do with G.A.F., and this conversation is over."

The man slammed down the phone, causing Shelley to cringe with disbelief.

Shelley long accepted the fact that Neal could be very persuasive and decided to let the detectives handle Neal. After a year, she still didn't have an address for him, and he still refused to support his children. For some bizarre reason, G.A.F. decided they would continue protecting him.

Shelley decided for the time being, she would put her energy into maintaining her grades in school, and managing to defy the laws of the universe, regarding money. She was certainly proving to the world how far a small amount of money could be stretched. But, she felt sure she would hear from Culley and Pete soon, allowing her to feel some hope.

As it turned out, she didn't have to wait long. Culley called her, irate with Manny Parker.

"What happened?" Shelley asked her.

"Pete and I located your husband in Alabama on a business trip. He was at a dinner party at the Sheraton in Birmingham with some of G.A.F.'s clients," Culley explained. "I called G.A.F. to ask them what they wanted me to do with Neal's company car after we picked him up? They were shocked that all this was really happening, and asked us not to embarrass the company by arresting Neal in front of their clients."

"What did you say?" she asked.

"I told the guy, that wasn't a problem that belonged to the State of Georgia, and that there were two Sheriff cars already on their way to the hotel to arrest him."

"Then, what?" Shelley asked, anxious to find out what Manny Parker did to anger Culley.

"Well, it seems Neal's attorney, who is also an assistant district attorney by the way, which is illegal, immediately phoned Manny Parker to make special arrangements for Neal. Parker called back the cars, and gave Neal ten days to turn himself in at his convenience," Culley said, disgusted.

"Excuse me? I don't understand. Bigamy and abandonment are felony charges. Do all felons receive that kind of special treatment?" Shelley asked.

"Hell, no! Plus, the plot thickens. Your husband's attorney is an Assistant District Attorney in another county. It's against the law for a District Attorny of any capacity to have a private practice, and it's also against the law for a property bond to be posted using property located in another county, but Manny Parker agreed to do it for your husband."

"What property is Neal using?"

"I don't know. Someone's property in Peach Haven," Culley answered.

Shelley knew it had to be Mary and Ralph's house. *How could they help him? With everything he's done, how could they help him, knowing he's a bigamist too? Unless they don't know. He could have convinced them he was innocent, like he has everyone else.*

"I'm going to call Manny Parker to find out what's going on," Shelley said, furious.

"Well, Manny Parker, has more, or less booted us out," Culley said.

"What do you mean?" Shelley demanded.

"It seems I had too much to say when he squashed my orders for your husband's arrest. I've been demoted to a court clerk. I work out of the courthouse starting next week."

"What?" Shelley cried, incensed. "Do you think it's because of this case?"

"I know so!" Culley replied.

"Can he get away with that?"

"He already has, and poor Pete is back in a patrol car."

"How is Neal's attorney getting away with representing him, being an Assistant District Attorney?" Shelley asked.

"Because the District Attorney's office answers to no one. Seriously, they do not have a higher power except for the Governor, who is very difficult to get to, and the taxpayers. Neal can do whatever Manny Parker allows him to do."

Shelley hung up the phone, out of her mind with anger over Manny Parker and his constant interference with justice. She dialed his office, surprised when he took her call.

"Mrs. Jordon, what can I do for you?" Manny Parker asked with an obnoxious tone.

"For starters, you can explain why you called back the Sheriff's cars that were dispatched to arrest my husband in Alabama," Shelley demanded.

"Because…I can, Mrs. Jordon."

She could imagine the smirk on his face, even though she had never laid eyes on him. She had her own ideas of what she thought he must look like.

"Well, Mr. Parker, if Neal doesn't turn himself in within the ten days you have questionably, given 'his highness' to surrender himself, please know, that I will file a 'Writ of Mandamus' against you, demanding that you perform your duties as an Assistant District Attorney. Because, Mr. Parker…I can," Shelley said, grateful for her American Government class.

Shelley could almost picture the smile leaving Manny Parker's face after her powerful threat.

"I'm sure your husband will turn himself in Mrs. Jordon. I want you to understand my thinking on this. If I can save my taxpayers the cost of having to extradite your husband to Georgia, I'm going to do it, even if it means giving him a few extra days to get here. My, God, it's not like he's a murderer!"

"Well, don't be too sure of that one, Mr. Parker. And I hope you understand my thinking when I say one way, or another, you will arrest Neal Jordon," Shelley said, adamantly.

Saturday afternoon, Molly came to visit Shelley at the duplex. It had been a long time since they'd seen each other, mostly due to Shelley's busy schedule, and they were excited to be together again.

"How are you, child?" Molly cried when she saw Shelley.

"Oh, Molly, it's so good to see you!" Shelley shouted, hugging her friend. She had plenty of coffee and sandwiches ready, knowing Molly would be full of conversation. After spending the day catching up on the details of each other's lives, Molly asked the question Shelley knew she'd put off asking the entire day.

"Have you tried to see Jack since you came home to Georgia?" Molly asked.

Shelley didn't want to be reminded of Jack. "No," Shelley answered.

"Why not, child?" Molly said, patting the top of Shelley's hand. "You two were so in love. Why haven't you called him, or gone to see him?"

"Because, I already hurt him too much, Molly. Besides, I'm sure by now any feelings he had for me are gone. I think it's best if things stay the way they are," Shelley said. It saddened her to think about Jack, which she'd done much more than she wanted to.

"What about Clancy? She calls me all the time asking if I've heard from you. I really think Jack puts her up to it."

"I'm afraid if I tell Clancy I'm back in Georgia, she'll tell Jack. I want to keep it this way, Molly. The same circumstances that caused me to leave three years ago, still exist today. Probably more so, and I think it's safer to leave things as they are," she explained. "Look, I'm still in the middle of this Neal mess. He's never going to go away."

"I understand. I just wish Jack Pope knew how much you really did love him," Molly said, opening the door to leave. Shelley began to walk her friend to her car. They were standing in the driveway, saying goodbye, when it happened.

Ping…ping. Something hit the house. Instinctively, they looked at the bricks surrounding the doorway of the duplex, and saw that the brick frame on the left side of the doorway was completely shattered.

"What the heck was that? Look at those bricks!" Molly shouted.

Shelley ran over and moved her finger inside a hole left in the center of the shattered bricks. There was something in the middle of it. She managed to get hold of it, and carefully pulled it out. It looked like a dented bullet.

"Molly, look at this!" she said, stunned.

"My, goodness, girl, someone tried to shoot us!" Molly screamed, looking around, clearly frightened that whoever shot at them, might still be there waiting to try again.

"I'm calling the Police," Shelley said, running inside the duplex.

"Well, don't leave me out here!" Molly said, running after her.

The Police arrived thirty minutes later. Shelley showed them the bullet she'd pulled out of the bricks and suggested there might be another one, since they heard two shots. When the officers searched, they found one more.

"Did you see anyone in the street after you heard the shots?" one of the officers asked.

"No, we looked toward the house when we heard the noise because that's where the noise came from," Shelley said.

She was so grateful the children were at a function with the church that afternoon. Otherwise, they might have been playing in the front yard.

What if one of the kids had been shot? Shelley thought, quivering. There was no doubt in her mind that Neal was somehow, behind the shooting.

The officers questioned several of the neighbors. Two claimed they saw a large red, sports vehicle without license plates on it, speed through the cul-de-sac. However, none of the neighbors heard the shots.

"Ma'am, we really don't have anything to go, the same Police officer told Shelley.

This is just like when Clancy was shot, and they passed it off as some crazy kids playing with a gun.

"I know who did this. It was my husband, Neal Jordon," Shelley said, shaking with fear, realizing that she was that vulnerable to him.

"Where does your husband live?" the officer asked.

"I don't know, but he works for G.A.F. out of Connecticut," Shelley answered.

"Why do you think it was your husband?" a second officer asked.

"Because he kills people all the time, and no one ever thinks it's him," Shelley said, her voice almost failing her.

The second officer cleared his throat after he gave his partner a funny look.

"Mrs. Jordon, I don't know what you're talking about, but we have very little to go on, and I don't know if we'll find anything worthwhile."

Shelley looked at him. "Of course, you won't," she responded, dazedly.

"Well, Ma'am, you understand we don't have anything concrete. It probably was some crazy, fool kids trying to act stupid," the first officer said.'

My, God! This can't be happening again!

"I'm sure. Are you finished here?' Shelley asked, making it obvious she wanted them to leave.

"Yes, we are. We'll let you know if we find out anything. In the meantime be careful and keep your eyes open in case anyone sees those kids again," the second officer told her.

"Sure thing," Shelley said, ushering them out the door. "Go to hell!" she said, after she slammed the door behind them. "I don't recall anybody seeing 'kids' to begin with, much less hoping they see them again, do you Molly?"

"Shelley! Why did you act that way?" Molly asked.

"I can't believe you, of all people, have to ask me that," Shelley answered. "You know exactly why I acted that way. I have learned, Molly. God, have I learned, that unless you have a penis, it doesn't matter who shoots at you, or beats you to a pulp, or steals everything you own. All of that's okay. And, if you happen to have a penis and a big truck...my, God, you can rule the world!"

Shelley shook, consumed with an overwhelming anger.

"I'm sorry, child, that you been hurt so bad you can't see anything other than that in this world," Molly said, sadly, as she hugged her friend. "Goodbye, child. I've got to go. Be careful, and I love you."

"I will. I love you, too," Shelley said in a calmer state. She watched her friend drive away, then, went back inside. She filled the cup she'd left on the kitchen table with the coffee settled on the bottom of the pot, then took it into the living room, where she sat on the couch.

Neal has hurt so many people, and always manages to get away with it. Every time! He knows how to use the system and how to make things work so he can slip by. Someday...I'm going to use that same system against him, and there will be no way out for him. It'll happen. I'll see that it does. she thought, sipping her coffee.

Chapter 73

Culley Marsh called Shelley three days after the shooting incident to inform her that Neal would be turning himself in that afternoon, at two o'clock.

"How did you find out?" Shelley asked.

"Hey, I still have friends in the jail. Everyone knows I was dealt a dirty deal because of this case, and they can't wait to set their eyeballs on this guy," she told Shelley.

"Culley, listen…is there any way you can tell me when Neal is released? I believe he shot at me a few days ago, and I want to make sure the kids aren't playing outside while he's still in town."

"I heard about that, and sure, I understand. You know, Shelley, when I spoke to your husband's company, they honestly believed you were crazy. Even after reading Parker's quotes in the paper, your husband convinced them that the whole incident was a sick story you made up. This guy is really good. The man I spoke to at G.A.F., said Neal stood before a board of three corporate attorneys, and seven of their top executives and convinced them he was telling the truth."

"Well, I would say his career is over now," Shelley said. "What did you tell them?"

"I assured them that it was the truth, that Neal Jordon, was going to be arrested, and that I had every intention of impounding his company car when it happened."

"I guess that's when they decided to take you seriously," Shelley said.

"By the way, do you happen to know what kind of company car Neal has?"

"Yes, it's a red, Chevrolet, Suburban," Culley answered. "Why?"

"Because some of my neighbors said they saw a large, red, sports vehicle, circle the cul-de-sac at the time of the shooting. I just know it was Neal. The Police, of course, were positive it was just some teenagers acting wild."

"I think a red Suburban backs up your neighbor's statements," Culley said. "Well, I'd better go, I'll be cleaning the courthouse next week if I don't. I'll call you as soon as I find out he's left the jail," she added, ending their conversation.

Shelley had good reason to be nervous. It panicked her to know Neal was a mere fifteen minutes away from her duplex. She was grateful the children would be in school while he was in the county jail. She didn't know how long Neal would be there, but she assumed it would not be too long since bail arrangements had already been made for him.

An hour later, Culley called again to tell her Neal had been released. Shelley hung up the phone, feeling desperate. For hours, she looked out her windows, wondering if he was hiding somewhere out there, waiting to kill her.

She ran to her car, so she could pick the children up from school, afraid to let them ride the bus, and when they arrived home, she kept them indoors, after notifying the neighbors to let her know if they saw the red Suburban again.

It wasn't until the sun went down that Shelley began to feel somewhat safer. Culley told her that the man she'd spoken to at the jail, said Neal was a nervous wreck, that his hands were shaking, obviously unsure of how much the Police knew. There were so many secrets. Culley's friends thought that was odd since he already knew he would be getting out quickly. He was only there thirty minutes.

A week later, Shelley received a subpoena to appear in court regarding Neal's bigamy charges. She called Manny Parker's office to ask about the abandonment warrant. Parker told her she would receive a separate subpoena for that court date, sometime within a month, since that calendar was pretty full.

Shelley waited several weeks for the second subpoena, but two days before the court date for the bigamy hearing, she decided it was time to call Manny Parker again.

"Mrs. Jordon, you must be psychic! I was just going to call you," he said, pleasantly.

"Oh? Why?" she asked.

"We have to postpone the hearing for your husband's bigamy hearing."

"Why?" Shelley asked, upset. She couldn't wait to hear his excuse.

"When you and your husband filled out your application for a marriage license, your husband claimed he had never been married before. Of course he had been, so his lying on that application, makes him guilty of 'Falsifying a Federal Oath'. That means I have to go back to the Grand Jury for a second indictment."

"Mr. Parker, I gave you a copy of our marriage license application when I gave you copies of the other paperwork. Why did you wait until two days before the hearing to address that issue?" Shelley asked, angrily.

"It was just an oversight," Parker answered, suggesting she keep the small setback in perspective.

Shelley was furious, and he was not fooling her for a second…he was trying to delay Neal's prosecution.

"And, just how long will that take?" Shelley asked.

"The next Grand Jury meets next month," he answered.

Shelley clenched her fist. Neal was already four months behind on his child support and she still didn't have an address to have him served, one way, or the other.

The abandonment warrant served on him when he turned himself in for the bigamy charge, was her only hope for financial help with her children. Her scholarship money was being stretched further than any miracle worker could make it stretch, and her bitterness toward the situation, was beginning to consume her.

"When do we go to court for the abandonment charge?" Shelley asked.

"Oh, I'll have to check that date and get back to you," Manny Parker said, before hanging up.

I hate this man! Shelley thought. *I don't even know him, and I totally loathe him. He has wasted eight months with this nonsense!*

She decided to wait a few days before she called Manny Parker again. He told her the subpoena for the abandonment charge was already mailed to her.

She received the subpoena the next day, and felt she was finally getting somewhere with Neal's prosecution. She knew Neal, and although he was one of the most fearless people known to man, he always said he would rather be dead, than go to jail. She wondered if he still thought that way with his pending court dates growing closer.

How brave are you now, Neal? Shelley wondered.

She decided, in spite of everything else going on in her life, that she would have to concentrate on her studies to keep her scholarships. At least those funds were dependable, and her degree was her only hope of changing things financially in the future.

The new quarter brought new problems for Shelley. The classes she needed were only available in the afternoon, at a different campus, which meant she had to find another job. She applied at the local hospital after she'd heard that they loved to hire students and would work around her class schedules, and was hired as a Nursing Courier. The hours were what she needed, and she would be making a little more money than she had at Mepolex.

Her job was to bring body fluids, or tissue samples to the lab, or diseased organs to Pathology from the operating room, while surgeons waited, scalpel in hand, for the results. The work intrigued her, and it kept her busy. Once again, things were working out.

Manny Parker took the Federal Oath charge against Neal before the Grand Jury, and once more Neal was indicted. Shelley was told she would have to wait for another subpoena for the new hearing date on both the bigamy, and the new Federal Oath charge. But, two days before the hearing on the new charge, Manny Parker called Shelley to cancel.

"What now, Mr. Parker?" Shelley asked, completely annoyed.

"All three charges have to be heard at the same time," Manny Parker informed her.

"What? That's ridiculous!" Shelley argued.

"It saves the taxpayer's money," Parker replied.

"I'm getting a little sick of worrying about the taxpayer's money, Mr. Parker. Are you that worried about my money? No, of course you're not, you've already lost my vote."

Shelley knew he was lying, but didn't know what she could do about it. She decided to go to the courthouse and speak to a judge, hoping to get some honest answers. Unfortunately, the only time she could go was three days later, on her day off.

Meg decided to go with Shelley, suggesting they take Jackie and Jason for ice cream afterwards.

They picked up the children after school, and when Jason climbed into the car, Shelley was horrified over the hole she saw in his shoes.

"My, God, Jason, what happened to your shoes?" Shelley asked.

"Mom, they've been like this for a while. I hid them because I didn't want you to see them. I know we can't buy new ones now, and I didn't want you to worry about me."

Shelley burst into tears, knowing Jason had to be embarrassed in school by his shoes. She imagined him sitting in weird positions, or walking a certain way that would hide the condition of his shoes from his classmates.

He is such a remarkable boy, Lord, she thought as she cried. *Neal doesn't know what he's missing by not knowing him.*

"It's okay, Honey," she said. "Thank you. We'll see what we can do about getting you new shoes, okay?"

"Okay, Mom," Jason answered, the smile on his face calming her.

The four of them held hands as they crossed the busy traffic leading to the courthouse. They found the Magistrate Court and took a seat, while the court clerk went to inform the judge that someone needed to speak with him.

A few minutes later, Judge Lucas, entered the courtroom, and asked Shelley to come forward to state her reason for being there.

"Judge Lucas, I'm a little confused about what's been going on with some court dates I have that keep getting postponed," Shelley said.

"Oh? What is this in regards to?" he asked.

Shelley handed the judge her subpoenas, and explained the phone calls from Manny Parker.

"Your Honor, I really need a court date on the abandonment charge as soon as possible. My husband hasn't paid child support for eleven months, and I desperately need the money. I'm trying to take care of my kids, work, and go to school at the same time, and money is a constant problem. I've worked hard to stay off the system, but the system isn't helping me at all."

"Will you excuse me for a moment?" Judge Lucas asked, before he left the courtroom with her subpoenas in hand.

Shelley looked at Meg and shrugged her shoulders. Shelley had no idea what the judge was doing.

Fifteen minutes later, Judge Lucas returned to the bench looking quite upset.

"Mrs. Jordon, I have some rather bad news for you, and I don't know how to tell you this."

"What?" Shelley asked, bracing herself.

"It appears your husband was never served the abandonment warrant, nor the warrant on the Falsifying a Federal Oath charge. These are phony subpoenas. Subpoenas are never issued when there are no court dates. And there can't be court dates on charges that have not been served. These charges are not on the schedules for the dates specified on these subpoenas and never were."

Confused and upset, Shelley said, "I'm not sure I understand."

"Mrs. Jordon, there are no warrants for abandonment, or for Falsifying a Federal Oath. Warrants were never served on your husband, except for the one charge of bigamy," Judge Lucas explained.

"You mean Neal was never served the abandonment warrant when he turned himself in for the bigamy charge?" Shelley asked, horrified. "How could that be?"

"It's up to the District Attorney to decide what he's going to prosecute out of all the criminal cases that cross his desk in the county. He probably decided not to prosecute your husband. Personally, I think it stinks. I've always supported my children, and I don't understand men who think they can just walk out on their responsibility. What makes me most upset, is the phony subpoenas. I suggest you go upstairs to the District Attorney's office and ask Manny Parker, why he did this. If you don't like his answer, come back to me, and I'll be glad to issue you new warrants, as long as you understand that they might end up in Mr. Parker's dead file, along with the other ones.

"Thank you, your Honor," Shelley said, turning to leave. She felt as if she'd just been hit with a cannonball.

"Mrs. Jordon?" Judge Lucas called after her.

"Yes?" Shelley asked, turning to face the judge again, with tears streaming down her face.

"Don't judge the entire judicial system by what you have experienced here," Judge Lucas said. "If I had anything to do with it, your husband would be in jail."

"Judge Lucas, I have had a lot more experiences, just like this one, to judge the judicial system by. But, I thank you for being so kind, it was a nice change," Shelley responded.

She grabbed her children's hands and told her mother to follow her. Meg looked nervous. She saw the fury in her daughter's eyes.

Shelley had taken all she would from Manny Parker. Somehow, she was going to retaliate.

When they reached the District Attorney's office, Shelley studied the glass cubicle the receptionist sat in and watched her push a buzzer to admit people into the back offices.

"Sit in the first row of seats in front of the receptionist," Shelley instructed her mother and the children. "Give me your shoes, Baby," she told Jason.

"Why, Mom?" Jason asked.

"What are you going to do?" Meg asked, nervously.

"Mother, just sit here with the kids when I go in there," she whispered.

"Oh, my God. We're going to get arrested," Meg whispered, looking around.

"Mother, stop, please!" Shelley responded with clenched teeth.

A few minutes later the receptionist pushed the buzzer to let a man into the office, and Shelley was right behind him, carrying Jason's shoes in her hands.

"Hold it! Wait! Where are you going? You can't go in there," the receptionist shouted at Shelley.

"Watch me!" Shelley said, quickly searching for Manny Parker's office.

She threw open the door bearing his nameplate on its front, and found him sitting behind his desk. Four other men were seated in a semi-circle in front of him, and it was obvious the five men were having some sort of meeting.

"Excuse me, may I help you?" the man behind the desk asked. He obviously was the one in charge, and clearly embarrassed.

"Are you Manny Parker?" Shelley asked.

"Yes, and you are?" he asked, as if he were trying to seduce her.

"Shelley Jordon."

Manny Parker's charming expression, turned into one of fear. She could tell by the look on his face, that he knew she'd discovered the truth, and that he was about to be humiliated in front of the four men seated in front of him.

"Tell me, Mr. Parker, do your children wear shoes like these?" Shelley asked, throwing Jason's shoes at his head.

The District Attorney raised his arm to protect his face as the four other men hid their laughter, by either turning their heads, or covering their faces with their hands.

"Obviously, Mrs. Jordon, you're upset about something. Why don't you have a seat outside and when I'm finished here, we'll talk?"

"No, we'll discuss this right now, Mr. Parker. I'm tired of your lies. I'm tired of your phony subpoenas…oh, yes, I found out. I promise you, Manny Parker, you will curse the day you met me! Your career is over! And, Mr. Parker, if you cause me, or my family anymore heartache, I will be glad to show the world the bogus paperwork you've been mailing to me for the past year! By the way, isn't that Falsifying a Federal Oath?"

Shelley grabbed Jason's shoes that had fallen sideways on Manny Parker's desk.

"Give me those. My son may have to wear them for another five months, thanks to you!" Shelley said, walking out, slamming the door behind her.

Shelley handed Jason back what was left of his shoes, then proceeded to lead her family out of the courthouse, barely giving him a chance to put them back on.

"My, God, Shelley, everybody heard you in the waiting room. If we make it out of this building without the Police running after us, it will be a miracle," Meg said, her voice trembling.

"Oh, fear not, Mother. I have too much to say about the wonderful Manny Parker for him to do anything that stupid," Shelley said.

She'd done it. She finally stood up for herself and her children. She knew it would be up to her to get Neal punished, now that there would be no help coming from Manny Parker's office. But, she was sure she would come up with a plan. A plan that even Manny Parker couldn't penetrate.

Chapter 74

Shelley had two options. One was to keep filing charges against Neal until Manny Parker got tired of hiding the paperwork, and prosecuted him. Another, was to reach out to the only people Parker answered to...the taxpayers. She chose the latter, but decided to do it with some political support, and she made an appointment with Councilman, Don Sweeney, whose office was down the street from the District Attorney's office.

Shelley also spoke to Carrie Gardner, a reporter with the local newspaper. Gardner was excited to scoop the story. It seemed Manny Parker was not well liked among his peers, and had stepped on too many toes to advance his career. Several people who knew the real Manny Parker, would derive great pleasure in seeing him publicly humiliated.

Carrie Gardner seemed anxious to get started, and told Shelley she would get back with her after she'd spoken with Manny Parker.

Shelley walked into Councilman Sweeney's office expecting to go through a lot of security protocol to get in front of him. Instead, his office was a little ranch house, and when she walked in, Councilman Sweeney personally came out of his office to greet her.

"Hello! You must be Shelley Jordon," the Councilman said, extending his hand to her.

Shelley smiled. "Yes, and you must be Councilman Sweeney," she responded, accepting his hand.

"Follow me. We'll sit in my office, where we can talk."

Shelley liked him. He was a regular person. Instead of a suit, he wore a golf shirt, that made her think he had plans after their meeting. He also seemed far too young to be a Councilman.

"So, Shelley," he said. "From what my secretary told me, you've been given quite a run around. Do you want to fill me in with the details?"

Shelley spent two hours telling the councilman her history with Neal, and the way Manny Parker had handled her case. She also told him about the special treatment Neal received from the District Attorney's office. He asked her a few questions here and there, but mostly, he just listened. When she showed him the phony subpoenas, he seemed genuinely appalled.

"My suggestion, Mrs. Jordon, is for you to take your case to Civil Liberties. They have attorneys that handle this kind of thing, and they'll get the best results for you. It's obvious your civil rights have been violated, all the way back to the incident when your husband held you and your children at gunpoint. There are laws against that, and a marriage license doesn't make it legal. Every detail of your case has been improperly handled. Unfortunately, in the case of the District Attorney, the taxpayers are your only hope. They are the only people Manny Parker answers to."

"That doesn't leave me in a very good position, does it?" Shelley asked, beginning to feel hopeless again.

"Actually, it does, because the taxpayers are also Manny Parker's worst nightmare. I'm going to give you the name of an attorney who does work for the 'Civil Liberties Union.' I'll call him for you this afternoon and set the stage. Meanwhile, you make an appointment with him and see what he can do for you and your children."

Shelley called Michael Thomas, as Councilman Sweeney recommended. Mr. Thomas was prepared for Shelley's call, and made arrangements to meet with her the following Thursday, Shelley's next day off. Meanwhile, Michael said he would speak with Mr. Parker, perhaps shake him up a little, let him know that the Civil Liberties Union was involved.

When Shelley didn't hear from Carrie Gardner, she called her office. After being told several times that she wasn't in, she realized that Parker, somehow, changed Carrie's mind about doing the story. So, Shelley took the next step and phoned the Atlanta paper to see if one of it's staff reporters would do the story.

Bob Harris jumped at the chance to deal with Manny Parker. He told Shelley he had no use for the man, and welcomed any opportunity to set Parker up for public ridicule. His first stop would be to Carrie Gardner's office to see what method of intimidation Parker had used to scare her from doing the story.

Meanwhile, Shelley had no alternative, but to sign up with URESA, a national organization that tracked down 'deadbeat dads', and enforced court orders for child support when the father had run to another state. Things had gotten worse for her financially, and she desperately needed help.

Many times, Jackie or Jason, would phone her at work to tell her one of the utilities had been turned off. It had become a daily battle to survive. Shelley was sick of coming home to find Jackie and Jason doing homework by candlelight, and URESA didn't offer too much hope for a quick solution. The biggest problem was that no one could get an address for Neal's whereabouts. URESA didn't have a state to connect with in order to enforce Neal's child support payments. Shelley hoped eventually she would get a break and discover where he lived. G.A.F. was definitely, a dead end. They were left out of the battle entirely, because Neal's Social Security number came up empty. According to the government, he was not working anywhere.

Michael Thomas seemed well informed about Shelley's case by the time their appointment rolled around.

"Mrs. Jordon, I have some good news, and some bad news," Michael said.

How many times had she heard that?

"Well, give me the good news first. That will put me in a better mood for the bad news," Shelley said.

"You have enough grounds to sue the State of Georgia," Michael told her. "The bad news is, Manny Parker turned your case over to another county."

"What do you mean, he's turned my case over to another county? Why? On what grounds?"

"Apparently, you and your husband were married in a church located in a different county from his jurisdiction," Michael explained.

"He knew that from day one. Why is he doing this now?" She already knew the answer. That was Manny Parker's way out. His final solution.

"To get rid of you. You're too much of a hot issue right now, for his cool career," Michael said. "Now, for the really bad news. The new Prosecutor will have to conduct the same three month investigation before he brings the charges in front of the Grand Jury again, and unfortunately, by that time, the Statute of Limitations for your bigamy charge will be over."

"What?" Shelley stood her voice loud and angry. "Tell me you're kidding!"

"I'm sorry, Mrs. Jordon. I'm not kidding. It's a way to get rid of you permanently."

"Mr. Thomas, please do whatever you can for me and my children. I'll have to think about what I can do," Shelley said., tearfully getting ready to leave.

"Sure," Michael Thomas said. He hesitated, then said, "I know what you're feeling. I'm a black man trying to make it to a higher place in the heart of the South. I know everything there is to know about men like Manny Parker, how they can break an individual piece by piece, heartache after heartache. You have a strong case, but somehow Manny parker will always have a stronger one. That's just the way it is."

Shelley couldn't speak. She picked up her things and left.

Bob Harris called Shelley after he'd spoken with Carrie Gardner. "Well, I found out why Carrie bailed out," he told her.

"Why?" Shelley asked, having reached the point where nothing surprised her.

"Our friend told her that if she pursued the story, she would be cut off from any future information coming out of the District Attorney's office. In other words, she wouldn't be able to do her job. He said he would make sure her newspaper was aware of her poor standing with his office."

"That bastard! And what about you?" Shelley asked. Aren't you afraid of the same thing?"

"Hell, no! We thrive on dirty politicians doing dirty deeds. You know, Shelley, most women get exhausted trying to make the system perform the way it should and they quit," Bob said. "That's what Parker is hoping you'll do. He's trying to wear you down."

"Well, I'm not one of those women. I love my kids too much not to fight for them," Shelley said.

"Good for you. Meanwhile, I'll see what I can do with this story," he said.

"Thanks. I appreciate any help you can give me."

Shelley made an appointment with the District Attorney, since Manny Parker was only the Assistant District Attorney, second in command. She hoped to convince the man to bring the case back to his county, since the reason Parker transferred it was bogus.

Matt Keller, was an overweight, tall man with silver hair much too long for a public official. Shelley felt uneasy with the man, and as their conversation progressed, things got worse.

"Mrs. Jordon, there is no evidence that Manny Parker has performed unethically in any of his duties," Matt Keller said, sternly, trying to intimidate Shelley.

"He mailed me phony subpoenas. He lied to me. He's your Assistant District Attorney. Don't you care about his unethical practices, or is that standard procedure in this office?" she asked.

Keller ignored the question. "Why don't I check the status of your URESA claim for you? I could let you know its status by tomorrow. Will that make you happy?"

His patronizing tone infuriated her.

"Mr. Keller, why don't you go to hell? Do you think I'm so stupid that I wouldn't know the status of my URESA case?"

She stood, then moved toward the door. Halfway there, she turned and faced him.

"Oh, and Mr. Keller, don't run for district attorney again. If you do, I will parade up and down in front of this so-called Justice Center, along with five thousand other women to see that you don't win. Do you understand what I'm telling you?"

The man just looked at her, speechless. By the sight of his dropped jaw, she knew he was sure that she meant ever word. She wasn't threatening him, it was a promise.

As it was, Shelley received a lucky break in the mail. Somehow, one of Neal's Holiday Inn Priority Club Point statements, came to the duplex. It was addressed to Neal at her address, and in a million years, she would never understand how that happened. But, grateful it did, she tore open the envelope, hoping to get any information that would help locate Neal's whereabouts. Before Neal left, there was twenty five thousand points on his statement. There was one hundred and fifty points left on the new statement.

She picked up the phone and dialed the toll free phone number listed on the statement. When a young female answered, Shelley went into her act, not missing a beat.

"Yes, hello. I have a rather ridiculous question. I feel so stupid, but perhaps you can help me?"

"Sure, Ma'am, what can I do for you today?" the nice girl asked.

"I seem to have spent my points on my priority club statement, and we receive points from so many hotels, I can't for the life of me remember what I spent those points on. Can you help me with that?" Shelley asked.

"Sure. Give me your priority club member number, and I'll look that up for you."

Shelley gave her the number and crossed her fingers. *Please tell me something, anything, that will help me find Neal,* she thought.

Seconds later, the woman returned to the phone and gave her a list of items.

"Let's see, there was a table, clock radio, travel bag, vacuum, and a toaster."

"Oh! that's right. I'm so sorry for taking up your time. Thank you."

"You're welcome. Feel free to call any time we can help you," the girl said.

That bastard has set up housekeeping somewhere. I've got to find out where. She knew she would have to make a second call. One more time, she dialed the toll free number, this time she heard a different voice.

"Hello, Holiday Inn Priority Club, may I help you?" the woman's voice answered.

"Yes, listen, I have a ridiculous question that perhaps you can help me answer," Shelley said.

"I would love to, Ma'am, what can I do to help you?"

"I used my points to get a vacuum, a toaster, a clock radio and a few other things, but the problem is, my husband and I own six homes, and I can't remember what address we had our order delivered to. Can you help me with that?"

Sure, give me your Priority Club Member number," the woman requested.

Shelley obliged and again crossed her fingers. A few seconds later, the woman returned to the phone and said, "Let's see, Mrs. Jordon, oh, yes, here it is. They were delivered to forty nine, Northdale Circle, Germantown, Tennessee. Is there anything else I can do for you?" the woman asked, cheerfully.

"No, thank you. You have helped me tremendously, believe me," Shelley said, writing down the address before hanging up again.

"Yes! Yes! Yes!" Shelley shouted, dancing around her living room. "I can't believe I pulled this off! Tennessee! What do you know?"

She called information in Tennessee and asked the operator for Neal's home phone number. Of course, the number was unlisted, but that confirmed Neal had phone service at the address given to her.

She hung up and called Tennessee information again, only this time, she asked for the phone number for G.A.F. The operator rattled off the number and Shelley quickly scribbled it down on another piece of paper.

"Hello, G.A.F." a man said, obviously not used to answering the phone.

"Hello, I'm trying to reach the Manager there. What's his name? Is it Neal?"

"Oh! You must mean Neal Jordon, but he's not here. He just left with his wife and little boy," the man responded.

Shelley felt as though a knife had sliced through her head. *He just left with his wife and little boy?* The words vibrated through her entire body, over and over again.

"Yes, that's who I mean. I do business with him and I wanted to surprise him. I can't remember his wife's name though. What is it?"

"Faith," he answered. "Lady, are you sure you know him?" he asked, suspiciously.

"Yes, I really do. I won't take up anymore of your time since he's not there. Thank you," she said, quickly, hanging up the phone before the man asked anymore questions.

Faith? Shelley asked herself. *Faith, the young secretary Neal had in Atlanta? Neal married again? He can't be that stupid! I have to find out! That woman in Atlanta did say that Faith left G.A.F. to get married.*

The next morning, after the kids left for school, Shelley called G.A.F. in Atlanta.

"Hello, may I please speak to Faith?" Shelley asked.

"I'm sorry, but Faith is no longer wih G.A.F.," the woman answered pleasantly.

"Oh, that's right. She got married, didn't she?" Shelley asked.

"Yes, she did and moved away to Tennessee," the woman responded. "Are you a friend of hers?" she asked.

"Yes, I'm an old friend. Didn't she marry Neal Jordon?" Shelley asked.

"Yes, she did," the woman replied.

"I really would like to get in touch with her," Shelley said, hoping for a phone number, but not expecting to get that lucky.

"I'm sorry, but I can't give you her phone number, but since you're a friend of hers, why don't you call her mother?"

"That's a good idea. Does she still live in Georgia?"

"Yes she does, in Chamblee," the woman answered.

"Thank you. I think I'll do that."

Shelley hung up the phone and called G.A.F. in Tennessee.

"G.A.F.," the same man answered that she'd spoken with the day before.

"Hello, may I speak to Neal Jordon?" Shelley asked.

"I'm sorry, but Neal doesn't work here anymore," the man said.

"What do you mean? I just called there last night and you said he did. Why didn't you tell me then, that he didn't work for G.A.F. anymore?"

"Because when I told the new manager this morning that someone had called for Neal, he told me to begin telling people he doesn't work here anymore. I honestly, didn't know what to say to you last night, because we were told not to give out any information about him if someone asked," he explained.

"But, you told me he'd just been there with his wife and son," Shelley said.

"He had been, but he was just picking up the last of his things from his office."

"Oh, I see. Do you have any idea where Neal is working now? It's urgent that I get in touch with him."

"I don't know for sure, but someone told me he was selling cars somewhere in Memphis, if that's any help. I can transfer you to the manager," he suggested.

"No, thank you. It's rather personal. I'll get in touch with him another way," Shelley said, ending their conversation.

Selling cars? Neal always said, when you hit rock bottom, you become a car salesman. If he's selling cars, I can be sure of one thing...he's selling Fords!

She had to leave for school, then go to work after classes, but as soon as she finished her shift at the hospital, she was going to start calling Ford dealerships in Tennessee.

Chapter 75

Shelley phoned information and was given several numbers for different Ford dealerships in Memphis.

She'd thought all day about Neal getting married again while he was still legally married to her. The only way her marriage was legal, according to Bernie Gianno, was because they'd lived together over seven years. It was bad enough he married again without first getting a divorce, but to father more children when he didn't take care of the children he'd so easily abandoned, made Shelley livid.

Over and above all the anger she felt toward Neal, was the fury she felt towards Manny Parker. *He must have known about Neal's second count of bigamy! Either there never was an investigation, because surely Bernie Gianno would have discovered the new marriage, or there really was an investigation and Parker covered it up, knowing there would be no way out of prosecuting him. Then there would be the cost of the jail time,* she thought. Both possibilities were dishonest, and a grave injustice to Neal's victims.

"Memphis Star Ford," a man answered.

"Hello, may I please speak with Neal Jordon?" Shelley asked.

"We don't have anybody working here by that name."

"Thank you, I must have the wrong number."

"Newton Ford," a woman answered.

"Hello, may I please speak to Neal Jordon?"

"I'm sorry, we don't have a Neal Jordon working here."

"Southdale Ford."

"Hello, may I please speak to Neal Jordon?"

"Sure, hold on a minute."

Shelley went numb. She'd wanted to hear somebody say that, but once she had, it frightened her. She thought of Jackie and Jason and the money Neal stole from them and the money he owed, and quickly gathered strength.

"Neal Jordon, may I help you?" he asked with the phony, cheerful voice he always used whenever he was trying to impress someone, evidently thinking she was a customer.

"You can start by paying your child support," Shelley answered, her voice quivering, not from fear, but from anger.

"Oh, hello," he replied, still using his phony voice. He was trying to make her believe someone beside himself, was in his office, as if that would put an end to her call.

"No one is in your office, Neal, so quit acting. I want the money you owe your children in back support, and my half of the money you stole!" Shelley demanded.

"How dare you call me here! This is my job. I'm not paying you a cent because quite frankly, I don't have to. I haven't paid you a dime for almost two years, and that's how it's going to stay!" he shouted.

"Just hold that thought, Neal," Shelley said as she hung up, and quickly redialed the number of the dealership before Neal could make up some lie to the person answering the phone.

"May I speak with the manager, please?" she asked.

"Certainly, please hold," the girl said.

"Good evening, Gene Prentiss speaking," the manager answered.

"Good evening. My name is Shelley Jordon," she said, hoping the man wouldn't hang up.

"What can I do for you, Miss Jordon?" Mr. Prentiss asked.

"It's Mrs. Jordon. Neal Jordon, is my husband," she told him.

"You mean ex-husband, don't you? His wife's name is not Shelley," he said.

"No, I mean my husband now. Neal never divorced me."

"But he's married to someone else," Gene Prentiss said, confused.

"Yes, Mr. Prentiss, he is, and that makes him a criminal. As a matter of fact, he's already been indicted by the Grand Jury in the State of Georgia, and is about to get indicted again when I press charges for another count of bigamy against him."

"Mrs. Jordon, I don't know anything about this. I don't know what I should say."

"Oh, I'm sure Neal will come up with some good lies regarding this phone call, he always does, and you'll probably believe him, unless you're smart enough to call the State of Georgia to find out the truth. Also, Neal is almost two years in arrears with his child support, so, I'm going to have him arrested at your dealership. Is that okay with you?"

"Look, I believe you, I just don't want any trouble here. I already know Neal is a smooth talker. That's why I hired him. It helps him sell cars. But, I don't approve of men who don't take care of their families. I promise you, he'll be gone by the end of the day."

"Thank you. Tell me, is there any way you can hold his last check?"

"If you get the proper paperwork to me within two weeks, I can probably do that. Paychecks don't come out again until then," Mr. Prentiss answered. "Of course, I will have to verify what you have told me to protect the dealership."

"I understand, and I thank you for your help. Do you want the numbers you need to call?" Shelley asked.

"No, I'll take care of it, and I'm sorry. I wish you and your kids the best," he said.

Shelley called her caseworker at URESA and explained the circumstances. She asked if they could put through a payroll deduction as soon as possible.

"Why did you get him fired, Shelley?" her caseworker asked. "We could have forced him to pay every month, now that we know where he's working."

"Because, Neal will quit before he pays child support. Believe me, this check will be the only one I'll get from him," Shelley said. "But at least now we have a state to work with," she added. "It's a lot harder to move, than to leave a job."

She took the piece of paper with the numbers of the other dealerships she'd called written on it and tucked it away in a safe place, sure she would need it again.

Bob Harris ran a story in the Atlanta paper about Shelley's situation. It raised a lot of eyebrows, as he'd said it would. News reporters, along with women's organizations and attorneys, phoned the newspaper constantly, hoping to do something more to raise public awareness on the neglect of the system regarding abandoned women and children.

Shelley remained frustrated about Neal's new family. Bigamy was a felony, and yet nobody wanted to deal with it, it was found comical, ignoring its profound effects on the victims. Neal was over ten thousand dollars in arrears with his child support at that point, and again, nobody seemed to care.

The 'Deadbeat Dad' statistics were so astronomical, government caseworkers were overwhelmed with work. She was just one more woman living below poverty level with her children.

Shelley called four different dealerships in Memphis after Neal had continued to change jobs. At one point he had apparently made arrangements with two dealerships to go back and forth when his place of employment was discovered, avoiding URESA's intervention, until URESA kept serving him at work. A few times, Neal was fired for his refusal to pay his child support, but those actions still didn't produce child support from him, and he still avoided prosecution. The State of Georgia blamed Tennessee, while Tennessee, blamed Georgia.

Shelley felt any results would have to come from a higher source, so, she decided to work her way up. Starting with her Senator.

Sam Nunn's office in Atlanta was a busy place. The staff went out of their way to be friendly, and Shelley found it very impressive. A well dressed woman entered the very large and ornate waiting room.

"Mrs. Jordon?"

"Yes, I'm Shelley Jordon," she responded, as she stood to follow the woman's lead.

"The Senator can see you now," the woman said.

Shelley felt nervous about actually meeting with Sam Nunn. She'd seen him on television many times, but never dreamed she would be in his office discussing her personal problems.

"Good afternoon, Mrs. Jordon, please have a seat," Senator Nunn said, greeting her. The room was amazing. It was almost entirely surrounded by walls of glass and from every angle, there was an incredible view of Atlanta.

"So, tell me about the troubles you're having with our government," he said.

Shelley spent an hour telling the Senator the horrific details of her story.

"Mrs. Jordon, my best advice, would be for you to take this matter to the Governor's office, because he would be the person who could give you the most assistance with it, beside the taxpayers, of course. If you'd like, I could speak to the Governor's office on your behalf. How's that?" Senator Nunn asked.

"Thank you, Sir. I really appreciate your help. You've been very kind," Shelley said.

He gave her an endearing smile. "You're more than welcome."

"When do you think I would be able to see the Governor?" Shelley asked.

"Today. Lucky for you, we're all in town this week. Next week everyone will be in Washington. I'll call the Governor's office, and tell them to expect you."

"Oh, thank you, Sir," Shelley said, standing to leave.

"You just hang in there, eventually, the system will work. So many women give up too soon and live through tremendous financial hardship raising their children. All children are entitled to receive their child support, and I'm truly sorry that it hasn't been easier for you to resolve this matter."

"Thank you, Senator."

Governor Zell Miller's office was a complete contrast to the one she'd just left.

Instead of a smiling, sophisticated assistant to greet her, the woman that met Shelley in the cold, marble lobby, wore a drab gray suit, and a loathsome frown.

"Follow me, please," the woman said, without even introducing herself.

She led Shelley to a small room, barely large enough to accommodate the small desk and two chairs, meant to function as an office.

"Okay, Mrs. Jordon, what kind of problems are you having?" she asked.

One more time, Shelley shared her story.

"Okay, Mrs. Jordon. I'll give my report to the Governor, and he'll be in touch with you sometime within the next eight weeks.

"Eight weeks?" Shelley asked. "My, God! I can't wait eight weeks."

"That's what it takes for the Governor to review each report, investigate it, and get back with a written answer,' the woman replied.

Shelley stood to leave, once again feeling disheartened. Although she was assured something would be done, she didn't have eight weeks to wait for a solution.

And, if things weren't bad enough, the following week the hospital had a massive lay off, the first one in twenty years, and Shelley's position was eliminated. She went back to the duplex, totally despondent. In the mailbox was a late notice from the electric company. She had six days to pay her overdue balance of three hundred dollars. Her last pay check was for two hundred and ninety four dollars. There was no food in the house, meaning some of that check would have to buy groceries.

Shelley sat on the couch and cried relentlessly until Jackie and Jason arrived home from school. She had to do something drastic, and quickly. They were in a mess, and she had no answers. Her next scholarship check would not be in for another month.

"What's wrong, Mom?" Jason asked, noticing his mother's red eyes.

"Mom, did something happen?" Jackie asked.

"Sit down, please," Shelley said to her children. "We have something to discuss."

She had to tell them about losing her job. She had told them several weeks earlier that there were rumors of a cutback, but that the staff had been assured by Human Resources that it was nothing more than rumors. She explained their bad financial situation. Normally, she kept money matters to herself, even though they knew it was bad, she tried to spare them.

"What is it, Mom?" Jackie asked, concerned.

"I was laid off today. The hospital had to cut back on expenses and to do that, they eliminated some of the staff. Unfortunately, being one of the last people hired, I was one of those laid off."

"Oh, no, Mom! What are we going to do now?" Jackie asked.

"Well, I have an idea. We have two choices. One, we can take my last two hundred and ninety dollar check, and put it towards the late three hundred dollar electric bill, or we can...," Shelley hesitated. "We can use some of this check to drive to Tennessee to have your father arrested," Shelley continued quickly.

"What good will that do us?" Jackie asked.

"If we have him arrested, from what I've been told, he will have to pay a lot of his back support to get out of jail."

The children thought for a moment.

"Would I have to go? Could I stay with Willis?" Jason asked.

"Sure, if that's what you would rather do," Shelley answered. Willis was Jason's best friend and like a second son to Shelley. Willis' parents felt the same way about Jason, so she was sure they wouldn't mind having Jason stay at their house for a few days.

"I don't ever want to see my father again," Jason said.

"I understand, Honey. I really do, and it's okay. What about you, Jackie, do you feel the same way?" Shelley asked.

"I want to go with you," Jackie said, smiling at her mother. "Does that mean I get to miss a day of school?" she asked.

"Actually, you'll have to miss two days of school, but you haven't missed any time and you've kept up your grades, so I don't see a problem. I'm sure your teachers will let you make up the work you'll miss. We'll leave tomorrow."

Chapter 76

Shelley and Jackie, left at nine fifteen the next morning, right after Shelley cashed her last paycheck.

They sang along with the radio, and had several deep conversations during the long ride. Eight hours later, they couldn't go any further from exhaustion, so they stopped at a hotel for the night.

They planned to finish the drive the next morning, and do what they had to do before heading back to Georgia. Shelley hoped to get something done in one day for the sake of their meager finances.

She called Meg and Tim from the hotel to let them know where they were, and that they were safe for the night.

"Shelley, listen," Meg said. "I may not always agree with all the things you try to do, but if ever I was proud of you, this is it. I don't think I would have the courage to do what you're doing."

Meg rarely had a positive word for Shelley, and her encouragement made Shelley even more determined to make something happen in Memphis.

Early the next morning, Shelley and Jackie finished the drive to Germantown. Two miles from Neal's house, they stopped at a drug store to look at a street Atlas without buying it, hoping that Northdale Circle would be illustrated on a map.

The manager of the store noticed them trying to figure out where they were, and offered his help by outlining the shortest route to Neal's subdivision on the book, probably assuming she would buy it. Comfortable with man's directions, Shelley bought a disposable camera to take pictures of where Neal was living.

She hadn't realized how close they were to Northdale Circle when they'd left the drugstore, and when Jackie pointed out the street sign, they both felt somewhat nervous.

"What if he's outside cutting the grass, or something, Mother?" Jackie asked.

"Then, we'll get a picture of him cutting it," Shelley said, understanding what Jackie was feeling. He could shoot at them, or begin a high speed chase through his neighborhood. But by this time, Shelley was so sick of him getting away with everything, if he was outside, she thought she might just run him over with her car.

Shelley drove slowly down Northdale Circle. It appeared to be a really nice neighborhood, the homes were anything but small. While Shelley drove, Jackie searched for number forty nine.

"There it is!" Jackie shouted, pointing to the end of the street on the left side of the cul-de-sac. It was a large, red cape cod. Through the windows, they could see it was beautifully decorated. It was not quite as nice as the homes Neal had bought them, but it was still a home, much nicer than the low-rent duplex her children were living in.

Jackie diligently snapped pictures, getting all angles of the house. They saw a brand new, shiny Corvette on the side of the house, in front of the garage. Jackie kept clicking the camera.

"God knows what's parked inside the garage," she said, glaring at the expensive car.

"Probably the antique car," Shelley said, a wretched disgust overpowering her.

They both took one last look before driving away.

"How do you feel?" Shelley asked, concerned about how her daughter was taking the blatant smack in the face by seeing how her father was living.

"Mom, I'm furious! How could this happen? He's living this way, and we live like sewer rats!" Jackie said, tears running down her face.

Shelley's heart felt broken. "Honey, I know. I don't understand it either, but we're not alone, I assure you. I guess the thing we need to focus on is how tremendously blessed we are compared to him," Shelley suggested.

"Are you kidding, Mother, like how?" she asked.

"Like the way he's missed watching Jason play baseball, or how he's never seen how well you ride a horse. How he'll never know what wonderful people his children are."

"Do you honestly believe those things mean anything to him?" Jackie asked.

"Not now, but someday. When he's lost all those other things... yes, I do," Shelley answered. "I think someday, he'll probably get sick of looking over his shoulder for me, or the Police."

She picked up Jackie's hand, and kissed it. Suddenly, she realized how fortunate they were to be together through all their adversity. Neal would never have that.

The signs leading to Memphis were easy to follow, but Shelley felt relieved when she pulled in front of the Memphis Justice Center. She wondered why they named those buildings, 'Justice Centers', when nothing could be further from the truth.

They entered the usual marble lobby, and Shelley realized it looked exactly like the one in Georgia. She hoped 'justice' would prevail more abundantly in Memphis.

"Hello, may I see Pamela Mailer, please?" Shelley asked the receptionist.

"Do you have an appointment?" the woman asked.

"No, but I drove ten hours to see her," Shelley answered.

"From where?"

"Georgia," Shelley replied.

"Wait here a minute," the woman said, as she walked down the hall behind her desk. A few minutes later, the woman retuned to her desk and said, "Ma'am, if you're from Georgia, then you have to go back to your caseworker there for any progress involving your case."

"I was told by my caseworker in Georgia that Tennessee was the reason for the delay in my case being processed, I gave URESA my husband's new address over a year ago, and I still don't have any money from him. Now, please go back to Miss Mailer one more time and tell her I would like to see her, or her supervisor," Shelley insisted.

A few minutes later the woman returned and said, "Miss Mailer will see you in a moment."

Shelley and Jackie waited another thirty minutes before Pamela Mailer came out of her office.

"I can see you now, Mrs. Jordon."

Shelley followed her, while Jackie waited outside the woman's office. "So, what can I do for you, Mrs. Jordon?" Pamela Mailer asked.

"I need my child support. My husband is over twenty five thousand dollars in arrears," Shelley answered.

"And what makes you think it's so easy, that all you have to do is stroll in here and ask for it?" Miss Mailer asked, rolling her eyes.

"Miss Mailer, I have a roll of film with pictures of Neal's beautiful house and brand new Corvette that tells me it should be," Shelley snapped, annoyed with the woman's attitude. "Obviously, he's not hiding from you," she added.

"Well, I'm sorry. You can just head on back to Georgia, because we can't do anything to help you on this end. Georgia has to enforce your case," Miss Mailer said.

"Really? Well then, maybe I would have better luck if I took the pictures I have of Neal's residence and the fancy ride sitting in his driveway, to your newspaper. Perhaps the general public would be as curious as I am to know why you haven't been able to collect back child support for twelve months from a man who lives in what has to be a two hundred thousand dollar house, and drives a brand new thirty five thousand dollar car. Especially, when he's living in your own backyard! Oh, and by the way, did I mention that he's a three time bigamist too? Yes, I really think your local readers would be interested in learning how efficiently their tax dollars are being used. What do you think, Miss Mailer?" Shelley asked, furious.

"Wait here a minute, Mrs. Jordon," Pamela Mailer said.

A few minutes later, another woman came into Miss Mailer's office.

"Mrs. Jordon? Would you like to come into my office so we can talk? I'm Mrs. Costello, the Director of this office."

"Sure," Shelley said, following her. Clearly, Pamela Mailer was relieved to get Shelley out of her office.

"Please, have a seat, Mrs. Jordon," she said. "Now, first let me explain to you how URESA works. Georgia begins your claim, and handles all the activity regarding your case, and we act as Georgia's mediator."

"Yes, I know that," Shelley said.

"Good. Then, you already know you have to tell your caseworker if you're not receiving your payments, or if your husband turns up missing. Then, they'll file another complaint. We then serve your husband with another summons to go into court to explain why he has not been paying his child support. Without the complaint from your caseworker in Georgia, we have no way of knowing that your husband is behind in his payments," she explained.

"That's fine, Mrs. Costello, but my caseworker in Georgia has sent me copies of the complaints she has filed with your office at least three times, along with copies of Pamela Mailer's responses. In view of that, I'm going to place the blame on your office, which is why I have driven ten hours to get some results. I refuse to leave Memphis without some kind of action, or promise from you," Shelley said, taking a deep breath when she was done.

The woman thought for a moment.

"Okay, Mrs. Jordon, this is what I can do. I'm going to increase your husband's ordered payment each month by half a payment to make up his arrears, but I must warn you, he'll probably run. They all do," she said. "There are a lot of men out there who would rather live half a life than make their child support payments."

"That's okay. Please do it," Shelley said. "The more he owes, the more nervous he'll be," Shelley said.

"Okay. Good luck, Mrs. Jordon, and have a safe drive back to Georgia," Mrs. Costello said, offering Shelley her hand.

"One more thing, Mrs. Costello. Can you write the order now, while I'm here, and I'll take it myself wherever it has to go?"

Mrs. Costello looked at Shelley and burst out laughing. She took a form from her desk and filled in the necessary blanks. When she was done, she looked up at Shelley.

"You certainly are tenacious, Mrs. Jordon. Come with me. We'll deliver it together," she said.

"Thank you, Mrs. Costello," Shelley said.

A few weeks later, when she opened the second and last child support check she would receive from Neal in the amount of nine hundred dollars, she mentally thanked Mrs. Costello again.

Baseball season was ready to start, and Jason needed ninety dollars to register for the county baseball league. Shelley somehow managed to save the money.

She'd found a job in a doctor's office that worked out well with her last quarter of school before she graduated college. Although it was only part time, it helped enormously.

She also received a letter from Governor Zell Miller. He apparently had spoken to Manny Parker, who assured the Governor that Shelley was receiving child support checks on a regular basis. He said he knew nothing about the status of the bigamy case, since it was under the jurisdiction of another county.

Shelley answered the letter and included copies of Parker's false documents, along with a request that the Governor ask Manny

Parker to forward to her the child support payments that he claimed were paid, since she hadn't received any of them.

Around the same time, Shelley read an article in the paper announcing that Matt Keller, the District Attorney, had decided not to run in the next upcoming election.

"We'll, I'll be! Shelley said to herself, smiling, putting the paper down.

Chapter 77

Shelley was physically and mentally drained, and decided to call Ralph Strong. He was probably the only friend, Neal ever truly had, and she hoped to get some information from him, especially since he'd put his house up as a property bond to keep Neal out of jail. She'd wondered often how he felt, knowing he couldn't sell his house as long as Neal's bigamy case was in an indeterminate state.

"Hello," Mary answered.

"Mary? This is Shelley!" she said, not sure how Mary would receive her. It was expected that Neal would lie to them about everything that had taken place.

"Shelley! How are you?" Mary asked, obviously surprised to hear from her.

"I'm okay, I guess, but I have a bit of a problem that I think you can help me with."

"What is it?" Mary asked, hesitantly.

She could sense Mary's apprehension.

"Mary, Neal has gotten married again without divorcing me. Are you aware of that?"

"What do you mean?" she asked.

"He married his secretary from G.A.F. when he is still legally married to me. With the other count of bigamy, that means jail time for Neal," Shelley explained. "The reason I decided to call you is that Neal is thousands of dollars in arrears with his child support, and I'm trying to talk to anyone who might be able to help us. I know you and Ralph would never want to be a part of anything that would hurt Jackie and Jason, and you two are probably the closest people to him."

"No, of course, we would never want to see Jackie and Jason hurt," she replied. "Shelley, Neal visited us a few months ago with Faith, and he told us he was divorced. Was he lying?" Mary asked.

"Yes, he was. I also found out that he has a three-year-old son with Faith," Shelley told her.

"Oh, Shelley, I don't know what to say," Mary said. "Can I have Ralph call you? I know he's going to be upset. He'll want to talk to you. Apparently both Neal and Faith have been lying to him."

"Of course, he can call me, I would welcome that," Shelley said. "Mary, you just don't know what we have been through with Neal. He's done some pretty awful things."

Mary was upset, and Shelley knew that Neal had hurt both she and Ralph with his lies. They trusted him, the same way she had for years. She was sure Ralph would feel like he lost his best friend.

Later that afternoon, Ralph phoned, and she could hear the pain in his voice.

"Listen, Shelley, I've spoken with Faith, and she wants to talk with you. Do you have a problem with that?" he asked.

"God, no! I want to talk to her!" Shelley gasped, excited with the possibility.

"Here's her number, and then, I don't want to hear the name Neal Jordon again," Ralph said, before he hung up.

What must he think of us? Shelley thought, before she dialed the number Ralph had given her. A young woman answered.

"Hello, is this Faith Jordon?" Shelley asked, nervously.

"Yes, it is...are you Shelley?" Faith asked.

"Yes! We have some things to talk about," Shelley said.

"I know, but, first of all, Shelley, let me start out by saying that if I knew Neal was married, I certainly never would have married him!"

"I understand, Faith, because he did the same thing to me, and I would never have married him either, had I known. Who would? Coincidentally, his wife supposedly hung herself in the basement of their house."

"Well, you're going to love what I'm about to tell you," Faith said.

"Oh? What's that?" she asked.

"He's married again!" Faith told her.

"What? Neal has another wife? Are you sure? What about children? Surely he doesn't have anymore children!" Shelley felt sick.

"No, no more children. You know I have a son with him, right?" Faith asked.

"Yes. Are you still living with him?" Shelley asked.

"No. He left me."

"Does Neal support your son?" Shelley asked.

"No. His mother has sent me quite a bit of money though, but he refuses to pay anything," she answered.

"His mother sent you money?" Shelley gasped.

"Many times. I get along with her okay," Faith said. "What about you?'

"We hate each other," Shelley said. *That bitch knew her son was a bigamist! She slept in my home. Ate dinner with my children. And lied for Neal.* "She's as nuts as he is," Shelley added.

She recalled the conversation she'd overheard in the laundry room that morning Neal's parents visited them in Norcross. She remembered Neal's mother asking him, "What will I tell the others?" Shelley understood for the first time, what she'd meant. She was referring to his other wives.

"When did Neal leave you?" Shelley asked.

"He just picked up and left last February and I couldn't find him until I dug up someone he used to work with, who I'd never met, but Neal had talked about. He told me Neal was living with his new wife in Florida."

"He left in February?" Shelley asked.

"Yes, does that mean something to you?" Faith asked.

"My daughter and I drove to Tennessee last February to have Neal arrested for back child support. Faith, we took pictures of your house! Wait a minute!" Shelley said, hit with a thought. "Can you hold on for a minute?"

"Sure," Faith replied.

Shelley grabbed the envelope full of the pictures Jackie had taken that day, and went into Jason's room. She was thankful she'd raised such an organized son, and was able to pick up his magnifying glass without having to hunt for it. She held one of the pictures under the lamp on the nightstand next to his bed, and placed the magnifying glass over it. Slowly, raising it from the picture, she found what she was looking for. There he was, standing in the window of his living room, half hidden behind one of the curtains. His pose was one she remembered well from all the times he'd stood that way in front of their living room window.

Were you looking, waiting, for one of your other wives to pull up in front of our house, Neal, the way I did in Tennessee?

She returned to the phone. "Faith, Neal saw us from your living room window when my daughter and I took the pictures of your house."

"When was that?" she asked.

"The first week in February."

"He left the second week in February," Faith responded, amazed.

Shelley found Faith to be young and as naive as she had been at one time. Neal had stolen her youth, and in return, left behind an unimaginable wisdom.

Shelley spoke with Faith another two hours. She listened to Faith's horror stories about Neal's physical abuse. He'd broken her jaw, and when the judge, who was also Neal's friend, and the judge who had handled her child support enforcement, squashed the warrant she'd taken out against him, Neal retaliated.

When Faith returned home from the hospital, Neal was waiting for her outside her door. He began shouting at her about the way she'd embarrassed him in front of his judge friend. He didn't leave until he'd broken two of her ribs.

Once again Neal walked, and Faith said, out of all he'd done, the abuse that hurt more than any punch, or any broken bone, was the way he continuously called her stupid.

"For what it's worth, Shelley, I believe you were the only one he ever really loved," Faith had told her. As if that would mean something.

Shelley kept going over her conversation with Faith. She felt something was missing. Something Faith didn't know either. Then it hit her. *The bankbooks!*

She went back in time to the night she'd left Neal so many years ago. The night she'd stayed at her parents' house, before Clancy took her to the shelter. She thought of the envelope she'd found in the trunk of Neal's company car. There were five bankbooks, each from a different state.

Let's see, New Jersey was Marielle. Tennessee was Faith. The book from Georgia was from his marriage to me. The Florida book was for the wife Faith had discovered. What's missing? she asked herself. There was a fifth book. *Pennsylvania!* Shelley shouted in her mind. She ran to the phone and asked information for a listing under Neal's name in the State of Pennsylvania.

"I have a listing in Hatsboro, but I'm sorry, it's an unpublished number," the operator told her.

Neal's place of birth. Of course it's unlisted.

Experience taught Shelley who to call next. The Department of Vital Records for Hatsboro, Pennsylvania.

"Hello, I'm trying to get some information regarding a marriage license," Shelley said, when a woman answered.

"Okay, who is the groom?' she asked.

"Neal Jordon," Shelley answered.

"Do you have his date of birth?"

"Yes," Shelley replied, giving her the date.

A few minutes later she came back to the phone. "Yes, I found it. He married a girl with the name of Arlene Jacobs."

"Do you have any record of a divorce?" Shelley asked.

"No, it would have come up with this information," the woman said.

"I see. Do you have a date of the marriage?" Shelley asked.

"Yes, August fifth, nineteen seventy. Oh, wait a minute, there's also a letter from some judge. It was written to grant her permission to marry again."

"Why did she need permission to get married from a judge?" Shelley asked, already sure she knew the answer.

"Because, apparently, Neal Jordon disappeared. After advertising for twelve months in the legal section of the newspaper, she asked the court to consider her marriage to Neal Jordon null and void, so she could remarry."

"When was that?" Shelley asked.

"Nineteen, eighty six."

Shelley hung up the phone. *My, God, Neal had five wives! How did he afford all the homes and cars?*

Shelley called Faith again, and asked a few more questions.

"Faith, what kind of car did you have when you were with Neal?"

"My last car was a 'Lincoln', but Neal took out a loan on it, which he didn't pay. It was repossessed."

"What kind of car did you have when you first got married?" Shelley asked.

"A dark, blue, Spectrum. He had the car in storage for a while before we moved to Tennessee. He brought it to our house."

"Thank you, Faith. I'll keep in touch," Shelley said.

So, he gave Faith my car, Shelley thought, remembering that awful Sunday morning. *Just like Marielle got my Renault. Who knows who he took that from when he gave it to me! And who knows who got Faith's Lincoln!*

Shelley gave the past seventeen years some serious thought. All the incredible secrets and lies Neal used to ruin lives. Nothing would ever change unless she made it happen. She had to outsmart the system…to use it, the way Neal did relentlessly, or it would never be over for her.

Chapter 78

Shelley phoned Donna, who had since moved back to South Carolina by way of another promotion for Ernest.

"Shelley, you scoundrel, I haven't heard from you for so long!" Donna said, teasing her.

"I know, and I'm sorry. Now, I have a really nervy question," Shelley said.

"You know you can ask me anything. What is it?"

"How would you feel about me and the kids coming there to stay for a while?'

"What do you think? Wonderful! What's up? Knowing you, there has to be a good reason, since you hate it here. For you to think about moving here even for a little while, must involve something pretty serious."

"I'll try to explain everything to you when I see you," Shelley said.

"All right. When are you coming?" Donna asked.

"Is two days too soon?" Shelley responded.

"No, not at all. We'll see you when you get here. I can't wait."

The hardest part of Shelley's plan would be telling the children they were moving to South Carolina.

Meg and Tim would be furious, but she was finished doing what other people wanted her to do. She had spent years waiting for other people to change her life and suddenly realized that only she could do that.

When the children came home from school, she sat down and told them they were leaving Georgia, and was pleasantly surprised by how well they received the news.

"Mom, we want to do whatever we have to do to help you," Jason said. "We know it's been hard on you, and we've had one bad thing after the next happen to us. We just want you to be happy again."

The following night, was Shelley's graduation. Five years of hard work, taking odd jobs that would fit her schedule, living below poverty level, all were coming to an end.

Meg and Tim were too busy to make the ceremony. She was the first person in her family to graduate from college, and they were too busy.

Shelley hugged her children, who were so proud of their mother, and watched as family members of the other graduating students shared the excitement of the enormous accomplishment of their loved one.

I don't know why this hurts so much, Shelley thought. *When did they ever come to a school play? Or a parent, teacher day? Or share in anything that meant something wonderful to me? This degree is proof of our survival. Mine and the children's. They are all that matters in my life.*

After her graduation ceremony, it was easier for Shelley to tell Meg and Tim about her move. Meg was furious, and told Shelley that if she moved to Georgia, she never wanted to see her again. That she would never forgive Shelley for leaving with the children. For the first time, Shelley realized she had given forty years of her life trying to win Meg's approval, and it took her the same forty years to realize that she really didn't need it.

The most important relationship she had, was the one with herself, and she had fought to get that back after the years she'd lost it to Neal.

"That, Mother, is your decision," Shelley responded to her mother's threat. "I've made mine! Besides, you'll probably be 'too busy' to let our moving bother you for any length of time anyway. And if your threat turns out to be real, I want you to remember what I'm about to say, and know that my threat is real also. When you begin to wet your pants, and throw your oatmeal, call your sons. They got the best of you, they certainly should get the worst of you."

Those were her final words to Meg.

Chapter 79

Shelley felt a beautiful sense of freedom when they reached Interstate Highway, 85. They stopped for pizza on the way, and arrived at Donna's Gift Shop by five o'clock, excited as usual, to see each other again.

It had been a busy few days in Shelley's life, packing up the duplex and getting her affairs in order to leave. It was tedious, but she did it.

"Donna, is Ernest okay with this?" Shelley asked.

"Of course. You know me...we always have people in the house."

"Yeah, I know you," Shelley said, smiling.

Donna closed her shop early and they went home to Donna's house to make dinner. Shelley and the children were excited, making plans for the next day. The first thing they had to do was register the kids for school. The second issue was for Shelley to get a job, so she decided to call clinics and the local hospitals, hoping they had some openings, which they did.

After dinner, Donna secretly took the kids shopping while Shelley insisted on cleaning the kitchen. Several hours later, they came home with new shoes, dresses, pants and shirts. They actually felt like normal children for the first time in a long time.

Tears came to Shelley's eyes when she saw how anxious they were to show their mother their new things.

"Thank you," Shelley said to Donna, beginning to cry.

"It's okay, believe me. It was my pleasure. They're such great kids, Shelley. That bozo doesn't know what he's missing," Donna said.

"Thank you," Shelley whispered again. "They really needed some new clothes."

Donna gave her a wide smile. "Well, now they have some. New clothes for a new life."

Shelley made a series of phone calls to attorneys, and made an appointment with Nathan Cole that morning. She felt her legs shake as she walked up the stairs leading to his office. If she didn't carry out her plan perfectly, or act exactly as she needed to, the move to South Carolina would be in vain.

"Good morning, I'm Nathan." the attorney greeted her with an open hand.

"Good morning. Shelley Jordon," she answered, introducing herself.

'Come into my office and we'll discuss what we talked about on the phone."

Shelley thought the attorney a bit eccentric, but she liked him, and he'd agreed to handle her legal work without a hefty retainer. They spent two hours going over the details and facts so he could present the matter to the local judge the best way possible. He took all the notes he felt he needed to file the proper papers, and gave her quite a bit of assurance that what she wanted to do, would work.

He finally received the court date, and there they were. Shelley looked at her watch and swallowed the last of her coffee. She picked up her coat and purse to go back up stairs, more than ready.

For all the times Jackie and Jason wore shoes with holes in them. For all the times there were no presents under their Christmas tree, or birthday gifts. The class trips the children had missed because the three dollars they had cost was needed for dinner. All the nights Shelley ran out of gas in dangerous places, or the many times the children were deprived of a doctor's visit, and medicine when they were sick. For the movies they weren't able to see like the other kids on a Saturday afternoon. For the years of watching their utilities go on and off. For all the years of humiliation they'd endured. The times they were lied to, the times they cried. For the experience it took to learn that the world was not a fair and safe place. For all of those miserable things and those forgotten, that day made it right for Shelley and her children.

Nathan smiled at her as she rejoined him in the courtroom. "The judge is ready for us now," he told her.

They were called to the stand, and Shelley knew she would get through it just fine.

"I have read your petition, Mrs. Jordon, and I have decided that all the proper documentation has been presented. The necessary legal ads were placed in the newspaper, and therefore I have decided to grant your request. Since you have not been able to locate the whereabouts of your husband and he has not been heard from for seven years, I hereby declare him deceased. I will order a death certificate to be issued by the Health Department, and of course your children will be entitled to your husband's Social Security benefits within eight months. Court dismissed!"

The judge stood to leave the courtroom, and Shelley began to cry. She hugged Nathan. "Thank you. Oh, Nathan, thank you!" she shouted.

She was free from Neal for the first time in almost twenty years, and her children would receive reliable payments each month from social Security all the way through college.

Neal was legally dead.

Chapter 80

It was three o'clock in the morning when Neal Jordon was ready to leave 'Jokers', a bar situated in the middle of the less tasteful part of Clearwater Beach, Florida. He had been working nights there for two years, and had resented every moment of it.

"Good night, Larry," he shouted to the owner of the run down bar.

"See you tomorrow night, John," the owner yelled back as he continued to count the cash in the register.

Neal cringed whenever someone called him, John. He'd used the name John Martin for many years to avoid his legal problems and astronomical back child support payments. In the process he felt as though he'd lost all contact with civilization. He was living half a life. And for that, he blamed those he'd left wounded and crippled along the way.

He began his twenty-minute walk to the pier, as he did every night after work. It was humid, causing him to unbutton his shirt. The mist of the heavy fog gave him some relief from the sticky air. He stopped suddenly, sure he'd heard footsteps behind him. He was sure he'd heard the same noise for the past three nights when he left work and was annoyed with himself for acting so paranoid.

He reached the pier and jumped onto the houseboat he'd rented for the past three years. At first he'd resented having to live in the cabin of an old beat up houseboat, but after a while it was the only thing that offered him any peace at all. The smacking of the salt water slapping against the boat's sides cured many sleepless nights for him.

He went to the small kitchen area and grabbed the bag of chocolate chip cookies jammed into the small kitchen cabinet. He ate several before he climbed onto his platform bed. The cookies were stale and soggy from the heaviness of the air that night, and he threw the bag into the trash pail next to his bed. *These cookies suck. They're not anything like my mother used to make,* he thought.

He thought of her briefly, and the fact that he would never see her again. He'd certainly burned his bridges behind him, leaving him alone in the world. Not a single person cared about the well being of Neal Jordon…except Neal Jordon.

He quickly put aside his depressing thoughts, and slid into a deep sleep. He never felt the boat moving out to sea. It was almost daylight when he woke up and quickly realized he was no longer anchored to the pier.

"Shit!" he grumbled, jumping out of bed. "That damn chain broke again," he said, grabbing the jeans he'd tossed to the floor earlier. He threw his legs into them as fast as he could, hoping the boat had not drifted too far from the pier that time.

When he ran onto the deck, he stopped suddenly. Someone else was on the boat. Frightened, he tried to see through the thick fog.

"Whose there?" he asked, his voice quivering. Suddenly, the figure appeared clear to him.

"What are you doing here?" he asked, surprised, backing up to the railing of the boat. He saw the gun and started to laugh. "You can't be serious! I always said you were stupid! Do you honestly believe you can get away with killing me?"

He remained silent for a moment, trying to think of a way to escape, and realizing that there wasn't one, he said, "Within a few hours, they'll find my body and you'll be the first person they'll suspect." He half laughed until he heard the click of the metal gun barrel.

He put his hands up. "Hey, come on…don't do this. I promise, I'll never bother you again…just don't kill me!" He pleaded for his life. "They'll come looking for me!"

The shots sounded muffled against the sound of the pushing waves. Neal Jordon's body slid easily into the water, what with the bag of his belongings and the gun tied to his feet. The owner of the boat was sure to think Neal had skipped out on him as so many tenants before him had done.

Even though the fog was thick, it was not thick enough to hide the frenzied group of sharks that immediately found Neal's body.

The boat was cleaned and anchored to the pier before daylight showed its full face. It promised to be a beautiful day. Everything worked out the way it was supposed to. No one else would suffer, ever again. The fear of Neal Jordon being out there somewhere was over for everyone. Permanently.

Parked just a mile from the pier, a white Chevrolet, Caprice went unnoticed sitting among the many other out of state cars parked there. Driving towards home, Shelley whispered, "Fool...no one is going to look for a dead man."

Printed in the United States
32532LVS00004B/37-510

9 781413 789768